INTERREGNUM

By S. J. A. Turney

I would like to dedicate this book to my parents,
who are largely responsible for who I am today.

Also to Bren and Sue, one of whom was my first
reader and has been incredibly supportive, and the
other is in it.

I'll leave you to work out which is which…

2⁰⁰

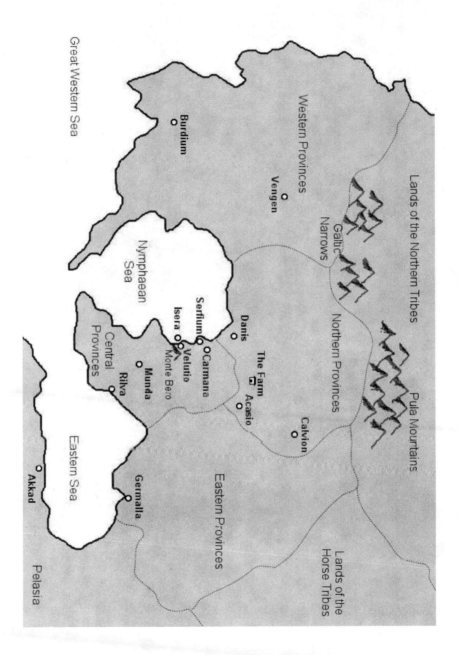

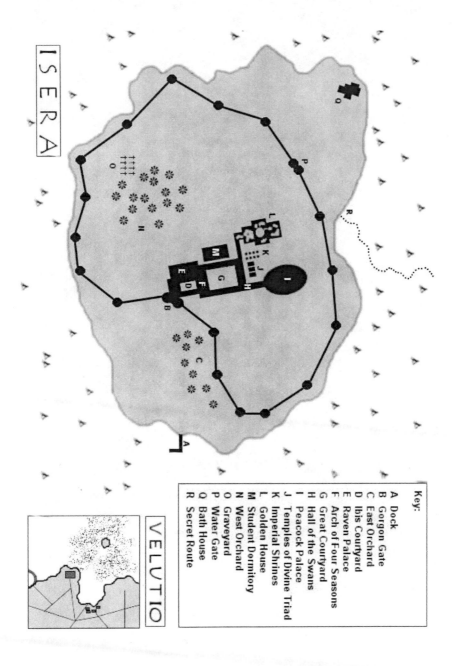

ISERA

VELUTIO

Key:

A Dock
B Gorgon Gate
C East Orchard
D Ibis Courtyard
E Raven Palace
F Arch of Four Seasons
G Great Courtyard
H Hall of the Swans
I Peacock Palace
J Temples of Divine Triad
K Imperial Shrines
L Golden House
M Student Dormitory
N West Orchard
O Graveyard
P Water Gate
Q Bath House
R Secret Route

Part One: Wolves and Sheep

Chapter I.

Kiva hadn't always looked like this; dusty, grey, scarred and hollow. Once, long ago, he'd been a fresh faced blond youth with piercing green eyes and a lithe build. In the days when he'd come out of the Northlands he'd had a budding, wispy beard and long, braided hair. He'd worn furs and leather and travelled out of the cold, swampy lands of his people into the heart of the Empire, golden and prosperous. It hadn't been unusual in those days, when the Empire was at its greatest extent; when the borders were being forced north and east by generals whose names even now carried the weight of history and valour. The tribes at the fringes of the Imperial world had sued for peace with the Emperors and were beginning to see the benefits. For the first time in the history of the north the tribes had running, clean water, with aqueducts and drainage systems constructed under the expert eyes of Imperial architects and engineers. The young men had begun to learn the Imperial language, and many of them had begun to travel south to find service in the Empire's bureaucracy or its military. All those years ago, the idea of a heated floor was unheard of in the north.

He sighed when he thought of that first day in the army. His braids had been cut away, his beard shaved and his favourite furs burned for fear of infestation. He'd stood with other young men of all colours both skin and hair, naked in a parade ground, while they were shorn and prepared for their training. Very little made Kiva smile these days; not properly, as though he actually meant it, but he'd laughed loud and often in those early days with his comrades. He shuffled under his blanket, trying to find a slightly more comfortable position against the rough wall. Pieces of plaster broke off and dust showered down his back causing him to shrug uncomfortably. He reached out and picked up one of the larger pieces. Painted plaster; an image of some sort of ornamental lake with a colonnade. This place must have been a rich house once.

He could remember just such decorative plaster work at the commanding officer's house in the Northern Army's headquarters fortress of Vengen, when he'd received his first military decoration. Over a mere three years, he'd made it through the lowest ranks and had become a non-commissioned officer. Then, little over a year later, as he received a golden torc for his defence of the Galtic Narrows against the barbarians, he'd also been made Captain, with his own unit. Barbarians?

1

Now that really *did* threaten to make him laugh. The force of northmen he'd held back with less than a hundred troops had been his own people, or people very much like them. It had been in that action he'd met a young soldier called Athas from the far south, his skin dark as night, who had grown throughout the following years to be Kiva's best friend and most trusted lieutenant. Others came to be trusted; his men had been a good crew even then, in the early days.

He glanced across the ruined building to Athas. The man slept little, but loud. Currently the big man crouched on a low and broken wall, watching the countryside in the night, alert and guarded. The charcoal-grey tunic, along with the colour of his skin, made him barely visible except for the eerie dancing light of the fire. The rest of the unit were asleep around the floor as Athas would be soon, once he'd woken the next watch. Then there would be snoring like the collapse of a marble quarry.

As he watched the fire flickering in the light breeze, his memory strayed once more to the age of glory in the Imperial army. In those days, the tunics had been emerald green and the arms and armour had been a standard issue. He remembered when he'd finally reached a position where he was not bound by the uniform code. He'd been made Prefect and given command over a thousand men, all new and eager for glory under the acclaimed commander. By that time he'd stopped wearing his military honours. They'd become numerous and bulky and had been taken to safety at the new estate that he was building at Serfium by the sea. Meteoric, people had called his ascent to command. No one in living memory had risen from the lowest ranks, without even Imperial citizenship, to become such a high officer. He'd made sure too that his trusted friends moved with him. Athas had been made Captain shortly before, and continued to hold a position as Kiva's right hand man. By then there had been others; men who had proved time and again that they could be trusted in and out of battle. In those days of fire and steel and the glory of Kiva's campaigns, with the ever-present Athas and a dozen men of skill and virtue, the Wolves had been born.

That was what they'd been called. Despite his command of a thousand, Kiva continued to travel chiefly with a party of a dozen men as his close companion unit. He'd made sure that they all achieved at least the rank of Captain; his influence in the Imperial bureaucracy was becoming powerful indeed. They'd taken to wearing wolf-pelts as a shoulder cloak. He'd also put in requisitions and had them agreed such that the regimental insignia was now a profile of a howling wolf, on both flag and standard. Their shields came to be painted with a wolf's head. And the analogy was good, too, for they became predatory. The army no longer held the borders against the Empire's enemies, guarding passes and constructing fortifications. Now, the Wolves forced campaigns into the wilderness, bringing the light of civilisation on the tip of a sword. They'd become hunters of barbarians and heroes of the Empire.

Once more Kiva's attention was drawn back to the camp. The firelight was beginning to burn low. He would have to get some wood before long or the light and heat would be gone altogether and the unit would have nothing to cook breakfast on in a few hours. Across the fire he could see the wiry Thalo, hunched asleep by the wall, his grey, oval shield propped next to him. No lupine symbols in evidence these days. The days of heroes were gone, and the Wolves had been consigned to legend.

Even when he'd been made Marshal, one of the four commanding Generals of the Imperial Army invested by the Emperor himself, he'd been wearing his distinctive shoulder cloak as he received his baton of office. Behind him, the Captains of the Wolves had stood straight and true, pride and discipline emanating from them. Those had been such great days. The glory and the vigour of constant battle, secure in the knowledge of a righteous cause and a goal: to bring culture and civilisation to the whole globe. He'd been proud; but then he'd been ignorant... they all had. To serve in the Imperial army was to serve blindly, and no yet man can stay voluntarily blind his entire life.

With a yawn and a stretch, Kiva straightened his legs, the blanket falling to the floor. For a brief second Athas's head snapped round at the noise. As he saw Kiva stirring, he nodded barely perceptibly and then turned his attention once more to the undergrowth. Stepping lithely between the slumbering forms of the unit, Kiva wandered out into the brush. His boots, old though they may be, were hardy and comfortable and he felt virtually none of the fractured pieces of crumbling masonry under his feet. At the fallen wall surrounding the once opulent room he picked up the hatchet Thalo had left there earlier and unfastened his belt, leaning the sheathed swords against the stonework.

The brush was prickly and painful, but Kiva's thick leather breeches and heavy tunic protected him well enough. His armour remained in the building where he'd slept, too bulky to rest comfortably in these days. For a moment he almost tripped, cursing himself for his clumsiness. He was still inside the boundary of the crumbling building and had failed to notice the raised threshold between two chambers. The

3

villa had been abandoned long enough that bushes grew within the rooms and much of the painted decoration had been eaten away by moisture or covered by lichens and thick green moss. Even a few small saplings tapered up from the walls, staking their claim to the light where one day the entire building would be lost in a forest floor. This place, Kiva thought, must have been one of the earliest casualties of the wars. He righted himself, considered turning to check if Athas had seen him trip, but changed his mind with a wry smile and continued on. Of course the hulking dark-skinned Sergeant had seen him; the man missed nothing. Beneath his feet as he followed a trail into the scrub he detected a flat, decorated area. Crouching, he hung the hatchet from a branch and peered at the ground. He was too far from the circle of firelight to get a clear view and yet still too close for his night vision to be fully attuned. He brushed the dirt floor with his fingertips. Mosaic. Despite a life of martial activity and an increasing despair with the world, he'd always maintained his fascination with mosaic, perhaps because they'd never had such a thing in the north when he was young. The need for firewood momentarily forgotten, Kiva reached into his pockets and withdrew his flint and tinder. After a few strikes, being very careful not to set the brushwood alight with a stray spark, the tinder took and a small beacon of orange light illuminated the floor. He moved the flame further away from the dry twigs; forest fires had their uses, but now was not the time. The dust was thick and with gravel, sticks and leaves and even small clumps of grass scattered among it. Leaving the light to one side, he began to brush away the dust and dirt with his hand, noting with interest a tooth and the broken tip of a dagger among the refuse, signs of the violent end the owners of such an opulent villa had met. Retrieving his water bottle, Kiva poured a small quantity onto the floor and watched as the colourful image came to life in the light cast by his small flame.

The God of wine sat in a gold and crimson chair, petting his goats, Tersiphory and Cilamna, while nymphs dropped grapes into his mouth with bright smiles and scant clothing. In the background were fruit trees and fields. Beautiful. Reaching out, he brushed more of the dust away from the edge and there was the first surprise of the night. A wolf.

Kiva had never been a deeply religious man; had never paid devotions as a boy to the Gods of the forest and, despite his oaths, had never truly taken on the Gods of the Empire. He wasn't sure that he liked the idea of Gods at all; Gods would imply a plan or some sense of purpose and the things he'd seen in his eventful life had made him

4

doubt the existence of anything but chaos and individual will. Besides, the Empire raised Gods from the mundane world, which was ridiculous in Kiva's opinion. One thing he did know was that, while the wolf was a revered creature among his own people, it was considered a barbarous symbol here and no respectable Imperial religious imagery would include such a thing. Frowning, Kiva began to brush further at the mosaic. Other images were revealed and he had to blow to move the dust, pouring yet more of his precious water onto the design. The images couldn't be right. If it were at all feasible, he'd have suspected a practical joke; an image designed specifically for him to see.

And yet there it was, the image of the sheep bearing a crown, the wolf running alongside - perhaps protecting it, perhaps hunting it. The image was deliberately ambiguous. Kiva sat back on his heels and stared at the mosaic. Unlikely imagery for the Empire. Not entirely dissimilar to a mosaic he'd paid ridiculous sums to have lain at his own estate so many years ago. Curious, the way coincidences...

A sudden rustling in the bushes drew his attention. He grasped automatically for his swords before remembering that he'd left them back at the wall. Reaching above him instead, he withdrew the small, chipped, but dangerously sharp hatchet from the branch where it hung. His had been the only unit on this side of the hill, guarding the flank of the largely mercenary army. After yesterday's skirmish there would be numerous corpses and wounded scattered over the battlefield, but they'd all be in the dip at the other side of the crest; unless perhaps one of the wounded had managed to creep all the way around the periphery of the field. Kiva drew a deep breath and challenged the intruder.

"This is Captain Tregaron of the Grey Company. Declare yourself" he intoned in a loud, clear voice. There was no answer. The rustling had stopped.

Without glancing around, he knew that Athas had joined him. He could smell the uncommon Basra oil that the sergeant used on his armour and moreover he recognised the eerie silence that was the only sign of Athas moving unobtrusively. He also knew Athas' modus operandi well.

"My Sergeant is here with a bow" he continued. "He's an exceptional shot. Declare yourself or prepare to meet the Gods in person."

There were several moments more of silence before the rustling began again and finally a pasty white hand appeared through the scrub. Kiva swung the hatchet back in a threatening fashion and growled "if you can't declare a unit, show yourself."

5

He waited, aware of a slight creak near his ear as Athas put a little more pressure on the bow. A moment later a second hand joined the first in a gesture of supplication and a pallid young face appeared among the leaves.

A light, well-spoken if nervous young voice called out "I don't belong to a unit. I'm a civilian. Please?"

Kiva raised an eyebrow in surprise and stepped back slightly, giving the young man room to manoeuvre.

"Come on out where we can see you" he said, his voice still clear, though less forceful.

With more rustling and the tearing sounds of cloth on bramble, the figure struggled out into the light. He was young, though not as young as Kiva had initially thought. Perhaps eighteen or nineteen years of age, he'd have been fighting battles for years had he been born among the northern tribes. This lad, on the other hand, had quite obviously never used a weapon in anger in his life. He was clean shaven with short, blond clipped and curly hair, the pale studious look of a scholar and a white tunic that had seen much better days. The material was torn in numerous places by thorns and here and there spattered with mud or blood. Indeed there was a spray of blood on the lad's neck and arm, though none of it appeared at closer inspection to be his own. Kiva pointed at the boy and gestured angrily out over the landscape.

"What the hell are you doing in the middle of a battlefield?"

The lad opened his mouth to speak, but Kiva cut him off sharply. "Nah, forget it. Don't really care. Just turn and head that way, downhill. Don't stop 'til you're well clear of this place. There's a town about five miles away where you'll be safe."

The young man looked frightened and raised his hands in supplication. His cracked voice warbled "I can't go on my own. Everyone else is dead."

Kiva became aware that Athas had his hand round the hatchet haft and was gently encouraging him to lower the weapon. He relaxed his stance and dropped the hatchet to ground level. He'd never even heard the second creak as his second in command had released the pressure on the bow.

The captain sighed. "Look, we're in the middle of a campaign here. I've a dozen men hungry for food and pay and I haven't got time to deal with your problems too. Fuck off and find someone else to bother, just stay out of the way of my camp."

He growled in irritation as he felt Athas' reassuring hand on his shoulder.

"I'll handle it sir," the hulking sergeant said in a reassuring voice.

With a shrug, Kiva stood and swung the hatchet in small circles around his wrist, glaring at his sergeant as he spoke.

"Don't be long. You're still on watch until three. And don't do anything stupid."

He walked back up the slight incline toward the ruined walls that sheltered the men of the Grey Company. With a sigh he took a seat on the wall and, while he began to strap his armour of interlocking plates back on he watched Athas and the boy in deep conversation among the scrub at the edge of the light. An irritating suspicion crept over him that the sergeant was busy consoling the lad rather than getting rid of him.

It never ceased to amaze him, with all the years gone by and the hard, rough, bloody life they'd lived that Athas could never let a problem go past without getting himself involved. Still, they'd all had pride and cared about these small things once, he supposed, in the days when they had been the Wolves and the Empire had celebrated their actions. So much time had passed since then. They'd been the Grey Company for around fifteen years, and Kiva'd been a mercenary Captain; money was the name of the game these days. There *was* no centralised army. Oh, some of the old guard were signed up more or less permanently with one Lord or another, but when the day came that that Lord fell, so would their military force and any renowned veteran among them became just another victim. Safer by far to be a mercenary, serving no longer than a season with a single Lord. Last season they'd been serving with Lord Jothus at Avarilum, and they'd wintered in the city before moving on to join another faction. During their season of rest they' been unlucky enough to see Lord Jothus' fall, from the storming of his palace right down to his breaking on the iron bed and disembowelling in the public square.

Kiva suddenly became aware of movement on the hill and returned his attention to his Sergeant. Athas and the boy were coming up the hill together. Damn it. Why'd he left the sergeant to deal with it? He fastened the last thong on his body armour of overlapping steel plates and stood.

"What the hell are you doing, Athas?" he asked, gesturing angrily with both hands.

The huge sergeant stopped a few feet away, lending some support to the obviously weary lad. "He's got a proposition" the man replied.

7

"I'll bet he has," Kiva growled. "Not interested." The captain turned his back, reaching toward his paired swords.

Athas grinned and, stepping in front of Kiva, held out his bunched fist. "I think you might be." He opened his hand.

The clink of coins was loud in the quiet night as the gold coronas hit the ground. Kiva looked down at the coins and then back up, surprise and irritation struggling for supremacy on his face.

"Gold?" he queried. "Where did a lad like you get gold currency?" He waved a hand dismissively. "I don't deal with thieves; we're honest men."

The young man took a step forward and fell to his knee in front of Kiva, his face downcast. "I'm no thief sir, and I know you're an honest man." He looked up into the captain's face and his voice took on the slight lilt of a youth trained in poetry and rhetoric. "I know who you are, General Caerdin." The voice had been low, but the intonation carried so much weight.

Athas blinked. Kiva growled and leaned forward in a menacing manner, his extended finger pressed against the young man's cheek.

"Don't be so damned stupid boy" he replied. "You know as well as I that Caerdin died when the Emperor fell. I'm Kiva Tregaron of the Grey Company, not some poncy 'hero' out of the days of old."

The boy shook his head and reached out, clutching the hem of Kiva's tunic.

"I'm not stupid! I've read the histories of Carolus and Phrygias, and all about your past. I've even seen your portraits. I know who you are, General, whether you care to admit it or not."

Athas leaned forward and whispered into the boy's ear. "Whether he *were* that man or no, it's not something you go around shouting. Be quiet for all our sakes."

Kiva nodded and, stretching his shoulders, drew on his gauntlet, fastening it round his wrist. He pointed an armoured finger at the boy, his face coldly neutral.

"Regardless, whatever you have to offer us, we're not interested. We're already commissioned by his lordship."

The boy shook his head as words tumbled from his mouth. "What I'm offering must be well over a year's pay for your company. You don't even know what I'm proposing, so you cannot tell me you're not interested."

Kiva turned his back on the boy again and reached down to the wall for his other gauntlet. "I said I'm not interested" he said coldly. "Now piss off and find someone else to bother."

8

The lad knelt for a long, quiet moment and then stood, nodding slowly and forlornly as he swept the worst of the dust and dirt from his white tunic and khaki breeches.

"Very well, Captain" the boy said in an emotionless tone. "If you won't help, you obviously *aren't* the General that I thought you were. I must be mistaken. *He* was a man of honour."

Kiva whipped round at the insult and opened his mouth to put the boy in his place but, as he caught sight of the pathetic figure, his words flitted away unspoken. He pointed angrily down the hill and the lad turned and stumbled painfully down the slope toward the brush once more. Athas wandered across to his commander and sat on the wall beside him, sighing.

"You do know that you've probably just condemned him to death, don't you?"

Kiva shrugged. "The whole world's gone to shit Athas," he sighed, "and we've not got time to help every stray you come across, no matter what he has to offer. We're contracted to Lord Bergama for at least the next two weeks and you know it."

Athas nodded and reached into his tunic, withdrawing a canteen of spirit. He unscrewed the lid with a thoughtful look on his face and took a quick swig.

"True," he replied, "but you know as well as I do the odds we're up against tomorrow. Only sunset saved us today. We're outnumbered about five to one. Bergama's gone; he just doesn't know it yet. Another tower fallen in the game."

Kiva stared off into the distance, his eyes slightly defocused. "Maybe soon all the Lords'll have fallen" he muttered. "Then there'll be peace." He snorted. "But of course there'll also be no one to pay our keep."

Athas grasped his Captain's shoulder. "The lad had gold" he implored. "Real gold, in Imperial currency. More too. He only wanted a bodyguard. Stupid not to even consider it."

Kiva turned to look his sergeant in the eye and Athas recognised the steel in it.

"The lad thinks I'm Caerdin and that's not something any officer wants to hear, least of all me. He's either crazy, stupid or reckless or all three at once. Any way you take it, we're better off without him. I don't care, I just want to get through tomorrow and then we'll think about the next step."

Athas smiled sympathetically. "That's crap sir" the big sergeant said. "You want your men to get through tomorrow, not you. *You've* never wanted to get through the next day. You've just been looking for a way to get yourself killed for twenty years now. Problem is: you got so damn good at surviving, it became second nature. I doubt if the Gods themselves could kill you now."

Kiva pulled away from his sergeant's hand and pointed down the hill. "He's coming back, damn him." The Captain picked up a small pebble and hoisted his arm back to throw.

"I don't think you should do that sir," Athas said quietly.

Kiva sighed as the lad ran up toward the wall.

"Come on lad, piss off. I told you the answer's no." He rolled the pebble in his palm for a minute and then dropped it to the floor.

The young man stopped and rested his hands on his knees, gulping down air. As soon as he stopped heaving, he spoke in a breathless rush. "There's ... there's an awful lot of soldiers ... in dark ... green down there, creeping along the ... gully. Thought you should know."

"Green?" Kiva asked sharply. "Dark green?"

Athas glanced for only a second at his captain and then turned and leaned over the wall, cupping his hands round his mouth.

"Stand to!" He called, his voice echoing round the ruined building. "Enemy sighted."

In a testament to the training and the fighting spirit of the Grey Company, every man was upright and arming in a matter of seconds. Kiva nodded at his sergeant and then vaulted over the wall, grasping his swords from where they still leaned against the crumbling stonework and sweeping them from their scabbards one after the other.

Athas turned to the young man. "Thanks lad" he uttered. "Now get inside behind the walls and keep yourself out of sight."

As the young man walked across the threshold into the ruined building, Athas stopped him and handed over the hatchet that had been left on the wall. "Just in case."

Moments later all twelve members of the Grey Company were at the wall. Like mercenary units everywhere, no two of them wore the same armour or bore the same weapons. The one thing that *was* uniform was the charcoal grey of their gear, from tunics to breeches to shield faces. Grey was the colour. Indeed, when fully ready, they were barely visible in the darkness, an army of ghosts in the flickering firelight.

Athas took his position at the far left as Kiva took a place on the right. The sergeant drew a long, curved southern blade from his back scabbard and stuck it point first into the ground near the wall before removing half a dozen arrows from his quiver and planting them into

10

the loose mortar on top of the wall in a similar fashion. With a creak of his recurve bow, he prepared himself and then nocked an arrow. Kiva nodded at Thalo next to him and the dark haired archer put down his bow and struck a flint and tinder, sparking until the dry substance on the ruined wall caught light and blossomed. He put a few small sticks and knots of dry grass on it and then, nodding at the captain, took up his bow once more. Kiva hefted his two gently curved swords and gave them a practice swing. He'd never taken to using a shield and had never been a great marksman. Along the wall, between the sergeant and himself, a number of men drew their own weapons of choice, three more of them bows.

An eerie silence fell across the ruin as the Grey Company waited for battle. Ten of the company waited at this wall, while two others kept positions at the opposite corners where they could watch for any kind of flanking action.

The only sound that announced the arrival of the enemy was the scrape of a boot on rock as a man tried not to fall foul of the treacherous slope. Kiva nodded a second time to Thalo next to him, and the small archer dipped the tip of his arrow into the burning tinder before lifting and firing it deep into the thick undergrowth. There had been no rain now for almost three weeks and the brush was so dry that they'd already started three small fires accidentally and consequently could be fairly assured of a burning oil-covered arrow triggering a blaze. Indeed, the moment the arrow hit, orange flame leapt up from the flora, throwing back the curtain of the night and crawling along the intertwined branches at breathtaking speed.

As the fire spread among the bushes at a phenomenal rate, Kiva was beginning to ponder on the wisdom of his plan when a scream announced that the fire had taken its first target. The horrible crisping, gurgling sound of a man suffering an agonising death by fire was something that Kiva had never truly come to terms with. He'd hardened himself such that he could usually ignore it, but in the depths of night when dream came in his black robe, with unbidden images of fire and death, to take the remaining fractured shards of his soul, then the flames still ate away at his conscience.

Moments later a number of agonised voices added to the tumultuous roar as the flames took man after man, dragging Kiva's attention back to the fight.

Almost a minute went tensely by before the first intact figure appeared from the brush, looking startled, having exited the smoke and the undergrowth and come face to face with the waiting Grey Company.

11

They barely had time to register the surprise on his face and hear his brief monosyllable before Athas' first arrow took him in the throat. The man toppled backwards, his blade clattering to the floor, and disappeared once more from view into the roiling thick black smoke. Glancing round, the big sergeant spotted another smoke-wreathed figure ghosting out of the brush.

"Here they come!"

Shapes began to appear, those who'd managed to find their way around the edges of the ever-growing conflagration and stumble through the smoke. The company let fly with arrows as fast as they could, each marking a single target as it appeared and announcing their shot to preserve their companions' ammunition. Few of the attackers managed to move more than a couple of feet from their cover before being struck, invariably with instantly fatal results.

Gradually, fewer and fewer of them appeared until at last there was just the crackle of flames and the groans of the few who lay bleeding their last. Athas waited for a moment to be sure of the lull and then called down the line "count off!"

"I took three," shouted Scauvus.

"Five," Thalo called, nocking another arrow ready.

"Four for Marco," called a light voice, "but only three for Alessus!"

There was the sound of a punch landing on an upper arm somewhere along the wall and a carefree laugh.

Athas nodded as he carried out his mental arithmetic. "And I took five." He added. "That's twenty down to arrow shots, plus however many dead in the flames. Not enough to turn a full brigade away, sir."

Kiva strained to see into the distance. "They won't come that way again until the fire's gone out" he confirmed. Turning to face his unit, he added "three groups! One remaining wall each."

As the dozen men split off to watch the walls, Kiva walked over to where the young man in white cowered, hatchet clutched in equally alabaster knuckles.

"Make yourself useful," the captain barked, "long as you're here. Stand and watch the fires. If a single living thing comes towards you up that hill, shout me or Athas, right?"

The young man nodded, the look of a startled rabbit about his eyes. Kiva returned to the rear wall, shaking his head, and looked up the hill toward yesterday's field of battle. He glanced across at Athas and beckoned to him.

"We'd see them if they came at us from there, but we still don't know how many of 'em there are. I can't run an effective defence without knowing what's happening or what we're up against. Get Scauvus to make a run to the top and see what's going on."

Nodding, Athas ran across to a side wall and spoke to a small, wiry looking man with dark, close-cropped hair and at least four days' growth of facial hair. Scauvus dropped his bow next to his shield and walked across to the other side of the ruin. Dropping to a crouch and taking a couple of deep breaths, he tore off at high speed for the crest of the hill. The company watched as he ran, fast and nimble as a mountain wolf, up the steep incline and to the top, where he slowed considerably. A bad sign thought Kiva and, as the scout reached the crest and dropped to his stomach, his worst fears appeared to be realised.

"Ahh, shit" the captain groaned.

Athas appeared to have had similar thoughts. He began to nock and store arrows, gesturing to the men to be ready. Kiva strained his eyes once more to see Scauvus hurtling back down the hill as if the hordes of hell were at his heels his form disappearing momentarily from view as a brief change in the wind drove the column of choking smoke across in front of him. A couple of seconds later, the scout appeared out of the grey and jogged back up to the wall, out of breath and wild-eyed.

"The other camps are..." he gasped "all on fire and the enemy ... are everywhere. I think ... we're the last."

"Shit! Fuck!" The captain spat. "They've done this deliberately to catch us!"

Kiva stood for a moment, fighting the obvious decision. He hated abandoning a contract, but if the rest of the army had gone, what chance did twelve men stand against thousands? He sighed unhappily and gestured once more at Athas.

"Get the kit together as fast as you can" he ordered. "We're leaving, and we're leaving *now*!"

Without questioning, Athas relayed the orders to the men. As the company gathered their gear, two men still on watch for the enemy to reappear, Kiva jogged back to the young man in white, crouched by the wall and keeping a close eye on the burning mass.

"We gotta move, so you're on your own, lad" he said. "Surrender fast and they'll probably just rob you; they can't mistake you for a soldier."

He turned to retrieve his kit bag just in time to see Athas glaring at him.

"What?" he growled.

The sergeant merely shook his head and then returned to his work. The company's bags were already shouldered when one of the lookouts called out the warning.

"Here they come again!"

Athas waved Kiva away. "Take the rest and get to the farmhouse, sir. I'll keep Thalo. We'll cover you for five minutes, then follow on ourselves."

Kiva nodded. The two were quite capable of taking care of themselves. Better to risk two than to condemn twelve. He followed as his men started moving out, and then stopped. Some strange need drove him to turn at the last minute and look at the lad in white, standing by the wall with a look of defiant despair. There was something hauntingly familiar about that look and Kiva tried very hard to push it to the back of his mind. Deliberately turning his back on the boy he joined his men as they rushed down the hill, around the perimeter of the forest fire and into the concealing darkness.

Chapter II.

The marble columns wreathed in fire. The purple and gold
drapes blazing and falling away into burning heaps on the floor. A
chalice of wine on a small table by a couch, boiling in the intense heat.
The panicked twittering of the ornamental birds in their golden cages as
the room around them was consumed by the inferno. And in the centre
of the room, standing in robes of white and purple, a man. He doesn't
look frightened, though the flames lick at his whole world and his face
is already grimy with the smoke. What he looks is disappointed, his arm
extended toward the sealed and barred door separating him from a
future and a life. Extended toward the figure standing behind that door,
turning the final key in the final lock.

Kiva woke, the grimy soot and dirt on his forehead running
down and into his eyes with the sweat. Despite the sweat, he felt so cold
and so agonisingly sad. Of all the thoughts jostling for a return to his
mind after the horror of the nightmare, strangely, his first and most
insistent thought was 'did the birds die?'

He glanced around the room. The farm had been unoccupied for
three or four days at most. When they'd made their way to the field to
meet up with the rest Lord Bergama's army, they'd found this building
the night before the battle, already empty. There had still been half-
eaten meals on the table and the fireplace had been warm. Yet another
case of the constant feuding between Lords disrupting the lives of the
ordinary folk. This family had probably heard tell of the armies
descending upon their district and fled, hoping to return after the trouble
and find their home intact. He clicked his tongue irritably. He was
starting to think like Athas. Screw it. They made their way and he made
his. Every man has a path and some are easier than others. He'd move
on to the next contract; the next battle. Kicking out in irritation at a
table leg, he scraped the chair back and stood. The night was old, with
dawn not far off. They'd reached the house around an hour ago and set
up shifts for watch. Kiva had immediately surrendered to exhaustion
and would still be in the arms of dream had not the old problem driven
him to wakefulness. It was no wonder really that his once proud blond
hair was now almost entirely grey and that his face had taken on a dark-
eyed, haggard look. Sleep was neither a friend nor a comfort to Kiva
Tregaron.

He had been the only one in the kitchen, seated by the thick
wall on a heavy bench padded with a blanket. He approached the door
to the main living space and peered round into the darkness. The

15

slumbering forms of the Grey Company filled the floor. Trying not to disturb their rest, he rounded the corner and climbed the creaking stairs to the upper floor. On one side of the upper room Scauvus sat on a stool, peering out of the upstairs window and watching for any stray scout that might stumble on their location. At the other side, Brendan and Marco sat on the balcony, keeping the rest of the valley under surveillance.

Touching his brow in recognition to Scauvus, Kiva made his way to the balcony.

"Morning. Any sign of Athas and Thalo yet?"

Brendan, a bulky man with a shaved head and greying whiskers nodded and pointed down into the grounds of the farmhouse.

"They got 'ere about 'alf an hour ago an' collapsed into that 'ay. If yer listen real 'ard, yer can 'ear Athas snorin' from 'ere."

Kiva followed the soldier's gesture and growled, leaning so heavily on the balcony rail that the wood creaked threateningly and a shower of dust drifted down into the yard.

"There's a boy in white down there" he uttered through gritted teeth. "Did they bring him with them?"

Marco turned, a piece of straw jutting from the corner of his mouth. "Nah, he came in a few minutes later. They let him join 'em though."

"Idiots" Kiva snarled.

Ignoring the questioning look from the two on the balcony, he snatched a piece of broken wood from the edge of the rail and hurled it down into the hay. Despite his almost legendary lack of prowess with aimed weapons, he noted with satisfaction the thump of the wood hitting something hard and a groan. Athas sat up suddenly, his hand reaching for the sword slung over his back. He spun several times, eyeing every dark corner of the farmyard and then looked up. Kiva made an angry gesture, motioning him toward the house. As the heavy sergeant walked toward the door, the captain turned and padded back through the room and down the stairs. He reached the bottom as Athas entered and he gestured toward the kitchen. As soon as they were both in, he closed the door and jabbed a finger at Athas' chest.

"I told you before," he growled "we don't need the kid."

The sergeant looked around to make sure none of the other soldiers were listening in on their conversation and then grasped Kiva's gesticulating finger and, jerking his hand aside, brought his angry face very close to that of his captain.

16

"I've had enough of this" the big sergeant rumbled in his deep voice. "The kid needs help and he's got money. We've no contract and we need the money." He waved aside Kiva's protests and continued. "I agreed never to gainsay you in front of the rest, but I've known you far too long to tiptoe around something like this. I know you think I'm a soft touch, but the fact is that I still care about things. You may be bitter and burning with resentment at everything fate's thrown at you, but you can't take that out on the innocent. You *think* you're cursed, so you make your own misery." He gestures with his hand open-palmed at the captain, but anger jammed up the words in his throat. With a sigh, he waved the arm dismissively. "Ah, fuck it."

Athas turned away angrily and raised his arms in irritation, seething silently for a long moment before spinning back round and jabbing his finger at the captain.

"All right, if there's no soul left there to appeal to, at least wake up and smell the money. If you don't help that lad, you're turning down easy cash for the sake of helping yet another petty claimant to the throne and I *know* you don't give a fig about *them*."

Kiva knocked the sergeant's hand aside and leaned forward, his face almost touching Athas' and his voice croaky. "Don't underestimate the shit I go through each and every waking day and the crap I live with in between. You of all people know why I am what I am. We don't *do* bodyguard. We never have. It's not the way we work. First over the wall and last off the field, remember? We always take it to *them*!"

Athas reached out gingerly and placed his hand on the shorter man's shoulder.

"I don't want to make it difficult, but you know that we're starting to get a reputation. A lot of the Lords won't touch us anymore and after tonight, we're unlikely to be heroes. We're a unit and you know that not one of us would contemplate leaving; we've been together since before the collapse, so you *know* that. But your whole attitude to battle frankly scares our employers. You're a risk. We could do with some steady work to help us with funds and maybe even boost our reputation."

Kiva sighed. "Look, I know we run a lot of risks, but you tend to do that when you fight a war. I won't do anything the easy way if it means…"

"I know that" Athas interrupted. "Gods, of all people, I know that. All I'm saying is you need to give the boy a break and you need to think of the men. They've fought five campaigns this last three months. They need a rest, but we keep getting stitched up over pay, so we can't afford one and here's your golden opportunity to do what's right on both sides. Speak to the boy."

Kiva sucked air through his teeth, turning over the idea in his mind. "Athas…"

"Speak to him" the big man interjected again.

Athas and Kiva stood little more than a foot apart, a determined look on the sergeant's face. The captain sighed. In the face of the sergeant's logic, he was running out of excuses. He folded his arms and exhaled.

"I don't like it," he muttered, "but you may be right. Ok, bring him in and I'll see what he's got to say."

Athas nodded and wandered out through the door. Kiva watched through the window as the big man went to the pile of hay and gently shook the other two awake. He spoke for a moment and as Thalo made his way into the main room to sleep among the rest of the company, Athas and the boy made their way into the kitchen. Now that he felt calmer, Kiva noticed as the two entered the large cut down Athas' arm and the wounds on the boy's shoulder and leg. He looked up at Athas and gestured to the bench upon which he'd slept. While the two made their way across the kitchen, Kiva leaned through into the main room and looked around. Spotting the company medic next to the cold, burned-out fire, he threw one of the worthless tin coins he seemed to be permanently saddled with across the room and bounced it off the man's head. The medic sat up, startled, and looked around the room.

"Mercurias, bring your bag into the kitchen."

The medic followed the sound of the whisper and spotted Kiva standing in the doorway. Muttering miserably, he returned Kiva's gesture and stood, stretching. The captain made his way back into the kitchen and took a seat on the rickety wooden chair opposite the other two on the bench. Moments later Mercurias entered, his usual sour, miserable look compounded by lack of sleep and a rude awakening.

"What the fuck d'you do that for?"

Kiva pointed at the other two and growled at the medic. "Enough lip. Take the sergeant upstairs and see to that arm. And when you've finished, come down and have a look at this lad."

Still grumbling, the medic turned abruptly and walked out. Athas shrugged at his captain and then followed. A moment later, Kiva was alone with the young man. He looked the lad up and down for a long moment. The stranger made him feel uncomfortable, and he'd felt uncomfortable with no one but himself for so long that the feeling was unpleasant and unwelcome. He cleared his throat.

18

"Alright, lad" he began. "I'm Kiva Tregaron and these are the Grey Company. Athas and Thalo you've met, and the man who'll be looking at your wounds in a minute is Mercurias. Now you know us, but I don't know you. If you want any help I want to know who you are, what you're doing in the middle of a battlefield, who was with you when they all got killed, where you're going and how much gold you have and are willing to spare. *And* why you would suggest anything as dumb as you did when we met on the hill." The captain sat in silence for a moment, and realised the boy was waiting for more. "Go on" he prompted.

The young man slouched slightly.

"Ok, my name's Quintillian. I'm a scholar from a small off-shore community. I was sent with two colleagues to find an art dealer in Calvion. They knew where we were going and we had with us a cart containing some very rare and beautiful works. We need the money to help support the community. With the constant warring, things have become very expensive, and we don't deal with the mainland very often. Our elders arrange delivery of what goods we can afford on a twice-yearly basis. We were on our way back to the island when we accidentally stumbled into those men in green. They killed Tomas and Enarion before we could even speak. They put me in a cage because I had gold and I suppose they figured there must be more somewhere. Fortunately the knots on the ropes that held the cage shut were childish and facile. I got them open as soon as it got dark and made my way away from their camp. Good thing, too; I believe they were planning to torture me to find out where I got the money. They took most of what I had on me and you saw what they didn't take, but most of the gold is hidden in a bush somewhere on the other side of that battlefield. I need to get back to the coast near the city of Velutio and take a boat from there to the colony, and I need someone who can escort myself and the money to there. Before the battle, we had three hundred corona. I suppose I needn't tell you what that's worth to us?"

The boy looked up again at Kiva, but the Captain had a far-away look about him, as though he was paying only the slightest of attention. In fact, the boy thought he looked slightly sad; haunted even. He tapped a gold coin on the desk and the Captain focused his attention once more on the conversation.

"Three hundred corona?" he mused. "That's a lot of money for a scholarly community. How much were you thinking of sparing?"

"A third of it?" the boy suggested with a shrug.

Kiva had been rocking his chair slightly on its rear legs as he listened. Suddenly the chair came down to the floor with a thud.

"A hundred corona?" the captain barked. "That's crazy. You'd hire an army for that?"

Quintillian smiled.

"I don't need an army, captain. I just need a little help to get home. A hundred corona *is* a lot of money, but if I take two hundred back to the island, it'll have been worth it. Without your help none of that money will get back. Do we have a bargain?"

Kiva smiled an unpleasantly predatory smile that the boy thought didn't suit him.

"What makes you think we won't just get you a few miles out into the wilderness and gut you for the whole lot?" Kiva asked.

A laugh. Quiet, but with true feeling.

"I don't think that's who you or your men are, Captain Tregaron" Quintillian replied. "*If* that's who you really are."

Kiva growled.

"Knock that off" he spat. "I don't want any more of your fantastic theories as to my origin. I *do* know the area round Velutio very well and you're right. You'd never get back on your own. The Lord of Velutio's probably the most powerful claimant in the Empire. And he's not a very nice human being. Less pleasant than me and a lot less forgiving. Ok. You've got a deal. We stay here until Celio's men have cleared the area and stopped patrolling for survivors. Then we'll go get your money and take you to Velutio."

The boy nodded at the captain.

"Agreed."

"We'll have to kit you out in some better gear though" Kiva said thoughtfully, tapping his finger on his chin. "Dressed like that you tend to stand out a bit. I'll ask Athas to sort you some kit; I think we've got a few spare tunics here and there. You'd best head upstairs and see Mercurias before you bleed out completely. Get him to send Athas back down here. Oh, and that's another thing before you go: as long as you travel with us, you're part of the company. You follow any orders you're given, whether they're from me, Athas or any of the others."

The lad, standing to leave, opened his mouth to object, but Kiva held his hand up.

"That's the rule" he said with an air of finality. "Think of it as for your own good. If we give you orders it's because we all rely on those orders for our survival. Also, it's because you're going to *be* one of the company as far as any outsider knows. If you don't like the rules, feel free to piss off and find another unit."

Quintillian stopped and then smiled as he turned back and made his way to the stairs.

"Aye, captain" he said with a grin.

Kiva sat in the dark and silent room, grumbling to himself. It was more money than the Grey Company had made the entire last year, and it'd only take a month at most to get him to Velutio. It was good business sense, but he couldn't shake the feeling that the lad was going to be trouble and he was starting to get very edgy and fidgety. The first ray of sunlight appeared at the window, with a shaft of light that fell across the ceiling by the window. Kiva rose and paced back and forth for a moment.

He stopped and idly examined a large kitchen knife on one of the cupboards for a moment, before growling and storming across to the door. He was about to call upstairs for Athas, when he saw the bulky southerner turn the corner at the top on his way down. He was holding his arm gingerly and, as he reached the bottom and was more clearly visible in the pool of light from the kitchen's lamp, Kiva could see the fresh stitch marks on his arm. They were not very neat. Mercurias really *was* in a bad mood. He gestured impatiently toward the kitchen and followed Athas inside and to the seats by the table.

"I'm very uncomfortable with this" he reiterated. "I've agreed to take the job on but I'm very uncomfortable, and not for the reasons you think. D'you notice anything familiar about the lad?"

Athas shook his head, blankly. "Nothing particular. Why?"

Kiva leaned heavily across the table and grasped Athas' shoulders, pulling him close. The sergeant winced as the stitches pulled. Kiva ignored the look and gritted his teeth.

"I noticed it almost immediately" he whispered. "He looks so like his uncle it's untrue."

"His uncle? Who do..."

Athas tailed off and slapped the side of his head in irritation.

"It's true. He even talks like the Emperor."

Kiva motioned for quiet with his hands.

"Don't use that word" he replied. "It's dangerous around the wrong ears. Anyway, I don't think he knows anything about his uncle. He's got to have been a newborn when Quintus died. He looks like him; he sounds like him; he's a scholar from Velutio. Hell, he said it was an offshore community, so I'll bet they're even on the Imperial Island. And he called me Caerdin, so he knows his history."

Athas frowned.

"Not too well, though" he said. "He'd never have trusted someone he thought was Caerdin if he knew what the General actually did."

"True. Still, I'm not sure there's much hope of us covering him by using a different name. He's a bit naïve and he'll make mistakes. We'll just have to hope no one else makes the connection. There aren't many people who met Quintus in those last few years, so they won't click the same way we did. He'll be safer when he's dressed like one of us. Can you see to that? Maybe a short sword or something too?"

Athas nodded. "No problem, captain. The only problem I foresee is the men. A lot of the Grey Company will remember the Em... Quintus from the old days. They're not daft and I'll guarantee you some of them'll have worked it out very quickly."

"We'll have to act fast" Kiva replied. "Get the lads together and explain things to them. Explain most of all that forgetting the name Quintus and any past affiliations is going to be worth eight corona each. That should shut 'em up."

As Athas nodded, stood and made his way back into the main room, Kiva wandered up the stairs to find Quintillian sitting on a stool and being treated by the ever-surly Mercurias. The burly and thick-set Bors stood by the fireplace watching the medic at work. Kiva glanced around and gestured at Bors and the lookouts by the window and on the balcony.

"Get downstairs and see Athas."

The three made for the stairs, leaving Kiva, Mercurias and the boy together. He watched as Mercurias cleaned out the shoulder wound. The young man had delicate, pale skin and dark, curly hair, cropped short. His eyes were a light blue, probably piercing when seen in a better light. Strikingly familiar. Kiva cleared his throat.

"Quintillian..." he began.

He noted the pause in Mercurias' work and the sharp glance the medic gave him. He shook his head barely perceptibly and returned his attention to the boy. Athas had been right. Most of the company would make the connection with the name pretty fast.

"Lad," he began again, "I need to know a few things before we go any further. Are your family still in this community, what's the name of the place, what's the aim of the community and who's in charge? "

The boy's eyes narrowed.

"I can't see why any of that matters, but I was orphaned. Brought up by the community on the island. I don't know much about

22

my parents, except that they died during the civil war. They must have been supporters of the Emperor; they *did* name me for him."

Somewhere inside, Kiva heaved a sigh of relief, though he didn't show it externally. It would have been nice to doubt the validity of the boy's heritage, but he'd known the Emperor Quintus far too well for that. The boy could have been a model for Quintus' earlier statues.

Quintillian continued "the island's called Isera. We're a community of scholars and holy men. The leader's a man named Sarios. A very intelligent and kind man who used to be a priest and scholar in the days of the Empire."

Kiva reached out and grasped the boy's arm.

"It's not a good idea to go round shouting out words like Emperor or names like yours. There are far too many bloodthirsty Lords out there, claimants to the throne, and talking too much would just get us noticed. Isera's probably not a name to use either..."

Again, that intuitive narrowing of the eyes. Quintus used to do that too.

"Why do you not want to be noticed?" the boy replied. "You're just mercenaries. You've not done anything wrong. Have you? Or have I?"

This was going to be hard work. Truths Kiva didn't really like to divulge were going to have to be shared. Damn Athas. Why couldn't they just have left the boy and found another Lord in need of troops? He sighed and looked the lad in the eyes.

"Quintillian," he sighed, "why do you think there *are* so many mercenary units or private armies? There were over two hundred thousand men in the Imperial army before the civil war. Most of us over the age of thirty-five have served with the military before the collapse. My entire unit here were all soldiers then. The Grey Company weren't always grey. They wore military green once. And a number of us met the Emperor on occasions. It's a very complicated political landscape right now and there are some things that are best left in the past. Deal with it."

He sighed again as the boy's innocent face contorted with the effort of coming to terms with lies and half-truths. Just like Quintus in the early days; before the rot set in.

"It's not much of a problem here in the Provinces," the captain explained, "but when we get near Velutio, things will be a whole lot different. The world's a different place there. You have to be *very* careful what you say. The Lord of Velutio and I are 'acquainted' and we don't see particularly eye to eye. He won't take very well to someone with your name, either."

Kiva reached into his pocket and withdrew a small silver flask. The container had a wolf's head engraved on it, and an inscription, but Quintillian barely saw it as the captain moved his hand to grip around the decoration. Lifting the flask to his lips, he took several deep pulls on it before lowering it once more and replacing the lid. He leaned back and closed his eyes, exhaling deeply. Quintillian watched him as did Mercurias, the first to speak.

"Don't you think you're hitting that a little hard?" the medic queried.

Kiva flicked one eye open.

"I'm not your worry. Keep your mind on your patient. I'm going down to see Athas and the rest."

He stood, swaying slightly as his knee almost gave way and then, righting himself with the support of the chair, squared his shoulders and started down the stairs. Once he was safely out of sight and with the rest of the men below, Quintillian turned to face the medic, his voice full of uncertainty.

"Should he be drinking strong liquor when we're all still in danger?" he asked.

Mercurias turned the lad back round and continued work on the shoulder, his hands remarkably light and gentle, considering his general disposition.

"It's not liquor" the medic replied. "It's Mare's Mead."

Quintillian's brow creased as he sought out memories.

"I've heard of that" he said brightly. "One of the priests at home kept it for something."

Mercurias raised his brows in surprise.

"It's quite rare and not very well known" he said quietly. "Your priest must be well versed in the medicinal arts. Mare's Mead is an extremely powerful pain suppressant. It's very acrid and bitter in its normal pollen form, which is why people mix it with mead to take, hence the name. Problem is, it also has a number of side-effects that vary from person to person. Kiva takes it for a pain in the side, legacy of a wound he took a long, long time ago. I dread to think what it's doing to him, 'cos he'll never let me examine him. I *do* know he averages about three hours a night sleep in a *good* week and he's a very troubled man, but then he's always been like that, ever since the days of the collapse."

"I don't think he likes me very much" the boy added.

"He doesn't like anyone very much. Just don't antagonise him."

"Done." With a short, sharp tug, Mercurias tied off the thread and then cut the spare away. "Try not to wave your arms around over your head for a few days, or I'll just let you bleed next time. If you're getting kit from Athas, can you give me your tunic afterwards? It's quite good quality material and I could turn it into good bandages with some washing."

Quintillian nodded, wincing as the activity tensed muscles in his neck that pulled gently on the stitches. He craned his neck in an attempt to examine his own shoulder, but couldn't see far enough round and the movement hurt. Instead, he examined the smaller wound on his leg.

"Your stitching's very precise" he complemented the medic. "Did you ever practice in one of the major hospitals or temples?"

Mercurias shook his head.

"I've always been in the army" he replied. "Thirty some years I've been with these men. I've treated everything from splinters to deep slashes to gangrene to trench foot. When I joined I knew nothing, just apprenticed myself to one of the combat medics. In the old days there was a lot of activity on the northern borders. Particularly with Kiva's unit. I was well and truly dropped into the shit at the deep end."

He frowned.

"You have a habit of asking earnest, simple questions and getting more truth out of people than they should be willing to give. I don't think you're half as naïve as you act, Quintillian. I think you play people to find out as much as you can."

The lad raised his hands in defence, but the medic continued. "Oh, don't get me wrong. I don't think you're sly or devious or manipulative in any bad way. It's just how you deal with people, isn't it. People find themselves telling you things that they perhaps shouldn't. I *know* that I told you things I wouldn't, and I think the Captain did too. That's a useful talent to have, but it could get you into a lot of trouble. Be careful. I've known people just as incisive who've fallen a long way because of their wit."

Quintillian smiled benignly.

"My tutor always told me to find out everything you can about a subject before you pass any kind of judgement on it."

"Wise words," the medic replied, "but bear what I said in mind. Now stay here while I go and get a tunic from Athas for you."

Mercurias reached the top step and turned to look at the young man, standing at the window with his hands clasped behind his back.

This boy was really something; much like his uncle used to be. Maybe that's why Kiva'd agreed to take him on. Sighing with the weight of the world, he turned back and descended the stairs.

Quintillian stood at the window and gazed out into the dawn light. The farmyard was in shadow on this side, the sun still barely rising above the horizon. Perhaps two miles away, over the crest of the hill would be a bag of coins hidden beneath a thorny bush. Many miles beyond that was the city of Velutio, and beyond that: the sea. If he tried hard, he thought he could almost smell the brine and hear the gulls. Below, whatever meeting the company had had must have broken up. Two of the men he didn't know left the house, moving out toward the hill. For a moment, he pondered the possibility that the captain had sent them after the gold but, even if they'd had the faintest idea where to find it, these men were not the sort to do that. The two men would be scouts, out to see whether the enemy army had left and the coast was clear.

These men, for all their brash roughness and mercenary cause, were men of honour. He'd played a dangerous game earlier with the captain to test that, impugning the man's honour. Most of those who'd served under the Emperors were dutiful and honourable and, despite the changes the world had undergone around them, many of them would not have changed in their hearts. The army had had a code. Oh, Quintillian hadn't been born during those glory days, but he read so much. Voracious, his tutor had called him, and he read far too much to wander this world innocently. Darius would be so jealous when he returned to the island with all these stories of adventure.

Stories of the Grey Company and their leader, Kiva Tregaron.

Quintillian chuckled and whispered quietly to himself.

"Tregaron indeed." Caerdin had had a reputation to be sure, but he'd been the stalwart of all the military in the days of his uncle and while grey hair and a lack of insignia might fool some of the power-hungry Lords of the realm it had not deceived Quintillian, nephew of Quintus the Golden, Emperor, genius, and God.

Chapter III.

The sun was now high, having beaten the darkness back and flooded the world with the hope of a new day. Kiva was first out of the house and into the farmyard. He stood in the bright sunlight, crossing his arms behind his head and pulling on his elbows to stretch the shoulder muscles. Behind him the rest of the company wandered out, blinking, into the sun. Athas grunted and squinted into the yellow fiery globe. It struck Kiva often that, for a man born in the searing desert lands of the south, Athas seemed to be generally uncomfortable in direct, warm sunlight.

Kiva wandered as far as the gate in the wall and examined the farmhouse. Under more long-term occupation, it could be made quite defensible. The yard was fairly narrow, but very long and level. The perimeter wall stood around three feet on the inside, and the same on the outside at the western end. The eastern end had been bolstered up as the ground fell away sharply into a small valley. At that side the wall was high and as secure as a fortress. He wondered whether it had ever been used as such. Perhaps if he had time, he would wander round and take a look. It was always worth knowing of defensible positions in case they ever found themselves in the area again.

He looked around at the unit and saw the runner adjusting his footwear. He turned to Scauvus and cleared his throat.

"You ok? Clear on directions?"

The scout nodded. "Yes sir" he replied. "The lad's got a good grasp of map making."

Just behind him, Quintillian smiled.

"Cartography and Geography lessons. Every day from three until four" the boy smiled.

Scauvus grinned. "I never had time for any kind of –aphy, but I *do* know how to find places. I shouldn't be more than an hour; two if it's too well hidden or I bump into trouble. If I'm not back in two, presume I'm gone."

Athas looked over at Kiva and than back at Scauvus.

"*Be* back in two" he said vehemently.

The scout dumped the majority of his pack by the perimeter wall of the farmyard and, taking only his sword and small bow, jogged out of the gate and off across the fields. Kiva joined Athas at the wall and together they watched until the scout was out of sight. Bors stood a short distance away playing dice with Pirus and Alessus, two of the older men.

27

Once Scauvus was no longer visible, the captain turned to look at the company's latest recruit. Quintillian stood in the sunny yard, wearing a grey tunic only marginally too large for him. Over the top was slung a harness of leather straps to help protect him from blows. Armour was too cumbersome a thing for a constantly-mobile mercenary unit to carry spares, so Athas had suggested that they make their way to the nearest village or town of any size and speak to a blacksmith. In the meantime, a few strips of leather would have to do.

Thalo had donated a bow, which now hung across the lad's back diagonally, a quiver slung at his side, and Athas had given him two long-bladed daggers and the rest of the standard kit, from tinderbox to canteen. He was actually beginning to resemble a soldier, albeit a pasty and thin one.

"Starting to look like one of us now, lad" Kiva said thoughtfully. "Next thing is: we might as well train you how to use those weapons."

Quintillian tapped the pommel of one of the daggers; long, straight-bladed steel knives with dark iron handles and red velvet grip.

"I'm not very good with these, but I *can* use a bow" he replied. "We had morning training at the colony. My friend Darius was always better with swords, but I could outstrip him with a bow."

Kiva glanced across the group with a sceptical look until he saw the sergeant.

"Athas, come over here a moment."

The burly dark-skinned officer put down his sword and the whetstone that he'd been using and wandered across the farmyard to stand by his captain. "Mmm?"

"The lad reckons he's good with a bow" Kiva said, a trace of disbelief in his voice. "I'm not exactly the best judge. If I set up a couple of targets, you and he can spar for a bit. We've a couple of hours to kill."

Athas nodded and retrieved his bow from where it stood propped against the wall, while Quintillian unhooked his weapon from around his shoulders. Kiva called over the others and between Thalo and himself they manhandled two large pieces of wood along the full length of the farmyard. Once there, the wood was propped against the perimeter wall. The two squinted back toward the house and made out the figures testing the tensile strength of their bows. Marco grinned.

"Best get along before they mistake us fer the bloody targets, eh sir?"

With a nod, Kiva joined Marco and the two jogged back along the wall to where the company had gathered to watch the sparring archers. Taking a seat on the wall, Kiva cleared his throat.

"One target each" he announced. "Six arrows. See how many you can get in the wood. Fire in your own time."

Kiva sat back and the others joined him at the wall where they could observe the results. Brendan offered him a chunk from a loaf of bread, which he declined. He turned the other way to see Marco chewing on a piece of dried beef before returning his attention to the competitors.

Athas exhaled and released the first arrow almost before Kiva had finished speaking. The arrow sailed in a low arc and, even at that distance, they could hear the splintering of wood. The sergeant drew another arrow from the quiver and turned before setting up his shot, watching the lad. Quintillian pushed his shoulders back in a stretch and then flexed the bow. Reaching to his side, he drew an arrow and nocked it in one smooth, flowing movement. Staring down the length of the arrow's shaft, the lad tensed, his breath held, and released the missile. The arrow arced through the air, considerably higher than Athas' had, and yet came down with great force and splintered the wood of the second target. The sergeant nodded at him and nocked his arrow.

Kiva and the rest of the company watched as the two archers nocked and released arrow after arrow, Athas in short, sharp motions; Quintillian in fluid, graceful sweeps. As the last arrows hit home, Kiva stood and wandered across to the two archers.

"No need to go count 'em" the captain addressed the archers. "I think we all heard them strike. Five each, I believe?"

Athas and Quintillian both nodded and the large sergeant, having leaned his bow against the wall, patted the lad on the shoulder.

"Damn good shooting for a scholar" he complimented his competition.

"Plenty of practice" the boy smiled as he replaced the bow around his shoulders.

The captain and the two archers strode across to a free area of the wall and took a seat. Athas looked at the lad and sighed.

"What you do, though," he added, "is sport or hunting archery and I presume that you learned using seabirds for targets. That kind of archery has two practical uses: hunting, where your targets are often far off or high up and at low speeds, and large scale warfare. It's true that in the days of the full regiments we'd have had archers firing high and far, but that was when there were hundreds of archers firing at a time

29

over our own men and into the mass of the enemy. We're a unit of a dozen men. You simply don't have the luxury of being able to set aside a unit to fire from distance. If you want to learn how to fight the way we do now, you have to learn to aim your shots low and direct and to be able to release a number of them in quick succession."

Quintillian raised one eyebrow and the sergeant went on.

"Your preparation and firing's pretty to watch, but it's quite slow. I daresay I could get three arrows off in the time you fire one if I'm on form. Thalo'd get four. He *is* good. Your arrows arc too high; too indirect for a modern battlefield. Remember your targets are on the ground, probably too close for comfort, and they'll be moving. The lower the arc you can manage, the less chance there is of them getting out of the way in time. Speed. A lot of it's about accuracy, but a lot's about speed."

Athas picked up his bow and an arrow and began flexing it and demonstrating to the lad. Kiva yawned and stood. Since he'd never been able even to hit a building at ten paces, the whole conversation was way above his head. The principle was ok, but when they started demonstrating technique it was time for him to move. Stretching again, the captain wandered off along the yard toward the wooden targets. The day was bright and becoming noticeably warmer. Flies buzzed around the dung in the farmyard and the smell was more than a little pungent. With a look at the two wooden targets it took Kiva some time to work out which arrows were whose. Whatever Athas thought about the lad's technique, each archer had struck home five times of six and the grouping was fairly good. The results had looked much the same.

To say Kiva didn't trust the lad would be to make too much of it. Quintillian was naïve and young. The deeper problem was that, as far as Kiva was concerned, he was a disaster looking for someone to happen to. One day someone who recognised the boy would capture and use him. Then everything would explode and the world would probably go to shit. He was too valuable a piece in the eternal game of power and politics and, as the last living descendant of the late Emperor, he would be important to some factions alive, but to a lot more dead.

Following the perimeter wall, the captain wandered away from the increasingly unpleasant smell of warm dung. With the farmer and his family having fled, no one had cleared the yard for several days and the acrid aroma at this end where animals had obviously been fed was too strong for prolonged exposure. Scanning the distant tree line for any sign of activity, he walked around the building and to the rear gate.

30

There seemed to be plenty of time. Even at best it would be three quarters of an hour before Scauvus returned. He exited the gate and wandered down the gentle gradient alongside the farm wall. As he moved toward the north western corner, the ground began to slope away toward a stream and he brought his attention back sharply, almost losing his footing on the loose earth and stones of the slope. Concentrating hard on not sliding down the hill, he reached the corner.

His years of combat-honed alertness saved Kiva at the last minute. He heard the stretch of a bowstring and a couple of skittering pebbles as he rounded the heavily buttressed corner and allowed himself to slip along the loose ground as he passed. The arrow, loosed in perfect time to pass through the air where Kiva's chest would have been, whistled off into the distance. The captain arrested his sliding descent with a kick and rolled to one side, coming back up into a carefully balanced stance for his next move.

Four men stood in a small knot, one fumbling for another arrow, while the other three hefted their swords menacingly. They wore the pale green tunics of Lord Celio, a lighter shade than the old Imperial Green. They also had the look of professional soldiers, rather than mercenaries. As always in situations like this, instinct took over, leaving no time for practical thought. As he came up and before he'd fully registered the situation, already his hand had wrenched his two throwing knives from the leather thong on which they hung and had brought them up in a sharp, underhand throw. The knives; straight, chisel-tipped steel blades with bone handles, hurtled through the air and hit the bowman in the left shoulder and the left leg. Athas had tried time and again to teach him with the best weighted knives available but, regardless, Kiva would never make a marksman. Still, the bow was effectively out of commission. The archer grunted and stumbled, the bow dropping from his suddenly spasming fingers.

As one of the four soldiers opened his mouth to speak, Kiva was already diving into his next move, rolling between them with his fingertips touching the pommels of his swords.

"Captain Tre..."

The soldier's voice tailed off as Kiva's blade tore through his hamstring. As the Captain had dropped and somersaulted, he'd whipped both his slightly curved blades out to the sides and had come up half a sentence later behind the middle two, having sliced neatly through the tendons at the back of the knees. From rounding the corner to standing behind them and watching them fall had been mere seconds.

With a sharp cry of pain the speaker collapsed in a heap, his blade flailing out at random. The man on the other side had slid to the ground, whimpering and clutching his knee. The archer began to back away down the hill, while the remaining enemy soldier stood facing the captain, looking somewhat startled. Kiva lifted one foot and kicked against the high perimeter wall, spinning in a half circle and lashing out with his swords as he turned. Before he even saw his opponent, he heard the slicing sound of carved meat and felt the slight resistance tugging at the blades. As he landed, catlike, on his feet before the man, he watched his victim's torso slide gently off the pelvis, the spine entirely severed. He looked down at the half body, registering with distaste the startled look still on the face as the lower half of the body toppled slowly backwards. Kiva stepped back.

He looked down at the two crippled but active men flailing around on the floor and clutching their wounds. They looked a great deal less smug now than they had a moment ago.

"The problem with full-time soldiers" he noted coldly as he trod carefully among the viscera, "is you tend to stand there and bluff and bluster when you could be busy actually killing."

He kicked the half-body out of his way and strode over to the two.

"Another problem is that you're hampered by certain codes" Kiva said with a feral grin. "I'm not."

Stepping on the hamstrung knee, causing another scream of pain, he leaned forward and thrust his blade into the second man's gullet. As he pulled the sword back out, he twisted and a large piece of the soldier's neck came with it. The gush of dark blood washed over his companion who was now visibly terrified.

"I don't like leaving a live enemy" he continued as if instructing a new recruit. "They tend to come back to haunt you."

With a heavy slash, he beheaded the remaining man and, turning, shaded his eyes with his hand, trying to spot the archer. The severed head rolled past his feet and off down the hill. The archer hadn't got very far, clutching his painful, bleeding leg and stumbling down the slightly treacherous slope toward the stream. Kiva growled. He hated having to chase people down.

"Can we help, sir?"

The captain turned and glanced up at the top of the wall. Three of the company were peering over the parapet at the grisly scene and he could hear the others scrambling across the farmyard now. Athas gestured down the hill.

32

"I might miss at that distance," the big sergeant admitted, "but it's a shot I'd bet the lad could make. He's more of a huntsman."

Kiva merely nodded and then set about the job of looting the bodies below the wall. Athas and Quintillian appeared at the top and the lad looked down. He squinted for a moment as he tried to make out the details of the scene below and then the colour slowly drained from his face. Muffled gagging sounds accompanied his desperate attempts to hold in his breakfast. The captain crouched, grey and unconcerned, among the severed pieces of human beings, busily rifling through their pouches. Athas grabbed a handful of the boy's tunic and hauled him back upright.

"I know it's not nice when you're not used to it," he told the lad soothingly, "but we haven't got time for this. See that man in green? Down near the river?"

Quintillian continued to stare blankly at the sergeant, his face white.

"Can you hit him or *not?*" Athas queried, his voice more commanding.

The boy turned robotically to look down the hill, trying not to catch the huge splash of red beneath him out of the corner of his eye. The archer had almost reached the stream. It would be a very long shot, but he'd hit worse. He nodded, gulping in air rapidly.

"Then do it."

Athas stuck three arrows in the wall while the boy unhooked his bow and tested the string gingerly. As the sergeant looked across, he saw some colour returning to Quintillian's face. The lad plucked one of the arrows from the wall and nocked it, aiming carefully. Steadying his breath, he released the arrow.

The shaft arced up into the sunlit air and curved down, picking up speed as it fell toward the river. Athas realised he too was holding his breath as the arrow narrowly missed the soldier and splashed into the water. The lad let out his breath in a huge rush and slapped his hand on the wall in irritation.

"It's too far" he shook his head. "He's almost out of range."

Athas plucked the second arrow and thrust it towards Quintillian, who accepted it reluctantly. The sergeant gestured to Thalo, who nodded and proffered another bow. In return, Athas held the arrow to him. Thalo stepped up to the wall, stretched out the bow, took the arrow, nocked it and fired with barely a pause to aim. Quintillian's carefully-aimed shot flew out away from the wall a mere fraction of a second later.

33

Even Kiva stopped and turned to watch as the two arrows reached their apex and then began their descent. Thalo's came down first, remarkably accurate considering his lack of aim, punching deep into the man's calf, splintering the bone and jutting out of his shin. Before the figure even hit the water the second arrow, quintillian's, struck him in the back, entering just below the shoulder blade. The distant figure crumpled into the stream, quickly staining the slow-running water red. Kiva stood back and looked up at the wall.

"Whoever goes down there to get my throwing knives back gets to keep anything they loot from his body."

As Kiva stretched and made his way back along the wall toward the gate, Marco and Thalo turned and raced toward the gate in the wall. Athas slapped Quintillian on the shoulder.

"Not too bad" he said admiringly. "That was a hard shot."

The lad was still very pale and shaky. He smiled weakly and then leaned forward over the parapet and retched convulsively for the best part of a minute, though nothing actually came up. Wiping his mouth with an exceedingly shaky hand, he leaned heavily on the wall, letting the bow fall to the ground, unheeded.

"He... the captain... butchered them all himself, didn't he?"

"He did, lad" Athas answered mildly. "He's very good at it. You could be that good one day with enough training and practice. Unfortunately, like me you've got a conscience and they tend to get in the way. He hasn't. Not any more."

The rest of the company had drifted back toward the main door of the farmhouse. Kiva had continued on round the wall of the house, and Thalo and Marco were racing for the body in the stream. The sergeant and the young man were practically alone. Quintillian looked up at the huge warrior.

"What made him this cold?" he asked with true feeling. "You've known him a long time. He must tell you everything, yes?"

Once again, Athas raised an eyebrow. The boy was always prying; probing for information. In another man it might be indicative of a spy, but for some reason Athas was sure of the lad's trustworthiness. The sergeant rarely pried too deeply into peoples' lives, tending to rely mostly on gut instinct. He sighed; gut instinct was good, but some things weren't his to tell.

"I'll tell you a lot of things you need or want to know lad, but not things like that." Turning, the big sergeant fixed Quintillian with a direct glance. "You want to know about the captain, you'll have to ask *him*. And I'd recommend you get to know him a lot better first. D'you drink?"

Quintillian smiled. "I've been known to have a few glasses of wine after lunch."

"Hah. Well never mind." Athas grinned and proffered a flask. The boy took it curiously, unplugged the lid, and sniffed delicately at the contents. He recoiled in horror.

"What in the name of ... What *is* that?"

The sergeant grinned.

"It's something they make in the northlands" he laughed. "The captain introduced me to it many years ago. It tastes like someone scraping their boot on your tongue, but it grows on you and there's nothing better for hiding the smell of fresh carnage and the taste of bile."

Quintillian took a slight pull at the tip of the flask and the look of horror intensified. He made a hollow throaty noise, reminiscent of his earlier retching.

"That's foul!"

"Isn't it though?" Athas beamed. "Have more. It'll do you good."

The sergeant glanced down once more at the scene below the wall.

"Come on" he sighed. "Let's get back to the house."

The two of them wandered along the farmyard until they reached the front gate, where Athas collared Brendan.

"Can you take someone and dispose of the mess below the wall. I don't think we want the kind of attention that brings. Let's not leave a trail for anyone to follow."

Brendan rubbed his shaved head unhappily, but nodded nonetheless.

"Aye" he said reluctantly. "S'right. We'll sort it sarge."

Kiva wandered back in through the gate as two of the soldiers left to deal with the mess. He eyed Athas and the boy thoughtfully.

"They were pretty good shots" he said to the boy. "Care to get up in one of those windows and keep watch for us? Four of Celio's men were looking for our unit, so I'd bet there'll be more out there."

Quintillian looked up at Athas questioningly, and the sergeant nodded. The boy frowned.

"I don't mind keeping watch sir, but I'm not sure I'm the right man for shooting people. I've never shot anything animate before other than rabbits and birds. I'm not really sure how I feel about what I've just done."

Kiva narrowed his eyes.

"What you just did helped save the company" he replied, his voice firm but understanding. "Get used to it. There'll be times in your life when you'll need to be capable of acts of brutality."

His frown deepened as his thoughts raced and the monologue continued inside his head '…and your family carry the most brutal of all madnesses.'

Instead, he forced a smile and slapped Athas on the shoulder.

"You'd best go with him and talk" he added. "You're the sensitive sort. I just border on 'don't give a shit!'"

As Kiva wandered off to sit in the shade of an old haywain, Athas escorted the young man up the staircase to the top floor of the farmhouse. The wide balcony let in a great deal of light, though the window on the far wall stood shuttered, blocking the worst glare of the sun. Athas gestured to the balcony and the two chairs that sat there. The pair wandered over and made themselves comfortable, the sergeant with his feet up on the worryingly rickety balcony. He shifted his weight and dust and fragments of worm-eaten wood drifted down into the farmyard.

Quintillian glanced out of the corner of his eye at the now relaxed-looking sergeant. Athas rubbed his nose and then drew out his flask of brew. Taking a slug, he recorked it and returned it to its accustomed place on his belt.

The young man cleared his throat nervously and Athas realised another difficult question was looming over him.

"What now?"

Quintillian sat up straighter in the chair and turned to face the older man.

"Your flask" he said, "has some engraving on it, yes?"

"Mmm. So?"

"A wolf's head and some writing?" pushed the boy.

Athas narrowed his eyes. "What are you getting at lad?"

The boy shuffled uncomfortably.

"I saw the same markings on the captain's flask. The wolf and the lettering. Does it have meaning for the Grey Company? The flask you issued me doesn't have it on."

Athas let out a long sigh.

"You've got to stop asking questions" he implored. "They make everyone feel uncomfortable. We're a mercenary unit and that means that there isn't a single man here that doesn't have *something* to hide; usually something he's ashamed of in his past."

Quintillian smiled.

"Just one more, then."

"What?" replied the sergeant.

"Was the captain ever married?" the boy asked, one eyebrow raised questioningly.

Athas growled and turned to face him.

"All right," he answered, "but this is the last time you ever mention that subject, and I'm only telling you so you don't make a mistake and ask him. Yes, he was. She died just after the collapse. It's not a very nice or happy story and it's one I *never* want to hear you ask the captain. Understood?"

Quintillian nodded and shuffled back to face the countryside over the balcony. The sun was glorious, lighting the green and gold fields as far as the eye could see.

"I'm just interested in what makes him what he is" the boy continued. "I've never met anyone who seems so bitter and yet I can't get over the feeling that that's not really him. D'you know what I mean?"

"Story closed. Ok?"

The two sat in silence for a long moment and finally the sergeant sighed.

"Tell *me* something for a change" he said, rounding on Quintillian. "You studied in that community. I find it hard to picture a scholarly community getting by these days. It was ok in the old days before the Emperor went m... Before the collapse. But now? There's precious little room in the world for quiet thought and study. What kind of people are they?"

The lad smiled.

"So now you'll interrogate *me*, yes?"

Athas merely raised an eyebrow and made a beckoning motion.

"Ok" the boy began. "Well, I suppose the most important person to *me* on the island is my best friend Darius. I suspect you'd like him. He's about the same age as me, but a little more active. He doesn't study as much as I do. Well he does, but only really history, war, geography and politics. He *is* good at sports; and at fighting. We used to be trained in all sorts of fighting, even unarmed, and the only thing I ever regularly beat him at was archery. I can usually trick him into things though."

37

"So why wasn't he sent out instead of you?" the sergeant queried, his eyebrows raised in genuine interest. "Sounds more like someone you want charging round the countryside with money, no offence intended."

"None taken" the boy replied. "The honest answer is that I don't actually know. He *would* be better in truth. And he would fit in much better with the Grey Company. Still, I'm here on the orders of the elders and he's not."

A shout from below drew their attention to the grassland before the farm. A figure was jogging down the hill at some pace. Athas had the bow at the ready but, after a moment he laughed, dropped the weapon and leaned over the balcony.

"Scauvus is back already" he grinned. "He looks happy and he's waving something."

He turned and smiled at Quintillian as he began to make for the stairs.

"Conversation's now for another time. Gotta go. Coming?"

The lad returned the smile.

"I'll follow on in just a moment" he replied.

Quintillian had always thought of himself as a lateral thinker; a planner. He hated having to lie to people, but he knew when he had to and he was good at it. He'd *always* been one step ahead of the game, his entire life. And yet no matter how much he tried to think it through he couldn't figure out why they'd left. They'd put the rest of the community in danger and fled in the middle of the night to gather money for heaven knows what purpose. No matter what reasons the elders had given him, he was well aware of the island's status and the complete isolation from the world in which they were kept. Darius would have been much better on that dangerous night-time boat trip; much better at the hiding and travelling by night they'd have to put up with before they'd reached a safe enough distance from the island. Why was *he* here then, and not Darius? Why *did* they need money when they'd never have the opportunity to buy something? With Tomas and Enarion dead, there was little hope of finding anything out until he made it back to Isera. The elders were too clever by far and their reasons escaped him. As he turned and followed down the stairs to see his gold returned, he couldn't help but wonder what the whole point was.

Chapter IV.

Quintillian sighed and rounded his shoulders before reaching down and removing his boots with a great deal of relief. It had been a long and arduous march since leaving the farmhouse and he'd watched with growing frustration as they'd passed four villages that the captain had considered too risky to enter. After twenty miles or so Tregaron had begun to relax a little, since they were out of Lord Bergama's lands and considerably safer. A further ten miles had brought them to the small town of Acasio and its warm, welcoming tavern. In fairness, he'd been allowed to spend a great deal of the journey in the cart with the equipment; a cart that he was fairly sure the captain had stolen from a nearby farm. Of the thirty-some miles they'd travelled, the lad had probably walked between ten and fifteen, but then he wasn't used to such long distance hiking, and especially not with weapons and kit.

The moment they'd arrived in the town, the Company had set eyes on the small market and had dispersed to purchase various goods leaving the captain, the sergeant and the boy standing in the street. Tregaron had raised an eyebrow and nodded his head in the direction of a tavern called 'The Rapture'. Athas had shaken his and gestured at the boy.

"Need to get him some armour" he'd explained. "We'll get along to the nearest smith and meet you in there afterwards."

So saying they'd turned and walked on, leaving the captain to enter the tavern alone. Athas had consulted Quintillian only very briefly on the subject of armour, more a confirmation of his own ideas than a real enquiry, and had then turned his attention to the smith and struck up a conversation about the folding of steel. It seemed that the big sergeant had both the knowledge and the skills of a smith. Quintillian had stood and listened for a few minutes until he was thoroughly bored and had then made his way from the smithy out into the street, browsing the few shops with interest. He'd spent his entire life in seclusion on the island and even such remote parts of the outside world still held interest for him in almost every corner. A minute or two of browsing and he'd made a surprising discovery: a scribe and bookseller. That was unusual to say the least in such a small provincial town. He'd perused the reasonably meagre though good quality range for around a quarter of an hour before his eyes lit upon a treasure: Carso's treatise on the collapse of the Empire. He'd read sections of it in the library on the island, but it was considered too valuable to leave in the hands of youngsters, so he'd never had a chance to read through from cover to cover. He'd been forking over the change for the purchase and complimenting the scribe who owned the place when an angry looking Athas had flung open the door and drawn him painfully outside by the ear.

"Where the hell have you been?" he'd demanded. "You can't just go wandering off whenever you want, you know?"

Athas had taken in the wide-eyed expression of the lad and the way he clutched the book tightly to his chest and had sighed.

"The armourer's going to take the rest of the day to put your stuff together, so we're heading for the tavern. Now." With those few words, the burly sergeant had hustled Quintillian across the street and into The Rapture.

Since then he'd had a reasonably good and filling meal and two glasses of beer. The Company had refused to order him the watered wine he wanted, just spirits or beer. He sighed again as his eyes strayed from the plate of chicken bones to the book lying open before him. He like Carso's writing. The style was fluid without being over-elegant; factual yet readable. He smiled as he turned the page. It was strange to think that he'd read so much history in his young life and now here he was, among the men who'd actually *made* that history. The Grey Company had been there when the Empire had crumbled; had seen it fall, even been involved in it. His eyes flicked around the room taking in his companions and finally lit on Mercurias, heading for his table and carrying a small tray.

"T'aint no good sitting drinking on your own" he grinned, his teeth flashing surprisingly white in the lamplight. "Solitude drives a man mad."

Quintillian returned the smile.

"I find solitude gives me time to read and think. I'm used to it."

The medic sat heavily in the chair opposite the lad. He unloaded the contents of the tray onto the table, a brooding unlabelled bottle of some unknown spirit and two small slightly chipped glasses, and then reached out to the book. The boy drew in a sharp breath involuntarily and the medic stayed his fingers as he touched the cover.

"You value this too much" Mercurias sniffed. "Books are for entertainment. Food and drink and company are worth a great deal more. You'll learn that in time."

Quintillian frowned.

"The written word" he said haughtily, "is far more important than the mere vulgarities of physical existence. We'll be long dead when this text is still illuminating and educating generations of scholars."

Mercurias smiled sarcastically and patted the book once before turning it to see the spine. His smile broadened as he read the title.

"Carso: Empire in Ashes" he chuckled. "Utter crap!"

Quintillian bridled and snatched the book from under the medic's hand, cradling it in front of him. His voice had risen in pitch when he addressed the medic.

"This is a work of genius" he argued. "Well written and accurate, from a man who was well placed in the Imperial bureaucracy at the time of the fall. I'll bet you haven't even read it!"

Mercurias smiled.

"Don't take offence lad; none's intended." He sighed. "Probably *is* well written, but it *is* also crap. You've got to stop taking things at face value. True, I haven't read it, but I'll guarantee you its inaccurate. Carso was no better placed to document the collapse than your average provincial farmer. He *may* have been in the bureaucracy, but that means nothing. The man was harbourmaster at Rilva, way over in the east. I shouldn't think he set foot within a thousand miles of the capital during the entire time. Carso'll have done what most historians do and pieced together bits from other people's writing; people who really *were* there."

The lad continued to hold the book defensively.

"But it's corroborated so well by everything else I read."

"'Course it is" the medic continued. "All these writers use each other for information. They're bound to all be the same. Don't take 'em as gospel. Personal experience is the only thing worth paying real attention to."

Quintillian narrowed his eyes.

"So you mean that *you* could tell me the truth?"

The medic shrugged and poured a slightly cloudy pungent spirit from the black bottle into the two glasses.

"I *was* there, it's true" he said softly. "The wars were all close to home by then and there was more need for doctors in the homeland than on the frontiers. Most of the medical corps was based in the capital at the time, in fact. I can tell you *some* things. Others are best left buried. What in particular do you want to know?"

The boy leaned forward, considering whether to drink the spirit. He clicked his tongue a few times and then picked up the drink and sipped it. The face he pulled made Mercurias laugh loudly.

"Slam it down," he grinned, "For heavens' sake don't sip it. It's not wine."

41

Quintillian wiped his eyes and rubbed his burning lower lip. His voice came out little more than a wheeze.

"What I *really* want to know is about the Captain and the unit. You were all there, weren't you; not just the medics. You were all in the capital at the end; when it happened."

The medic narrowed his eyes.

"What the hell makes you think we were there?" he said defensively. "There were a lot of units spread across the central Empire then. I think the Captain and most of the lads were out to the west."

Quintillian smiled.

"Do you have a canteen?" he asked.

The medic nodded and, slowly withdrawing the object from his pack, placed it on the table between them. The lad smiled knowingly and turned the flask over to reveal the engraved wolf's head on the other side. He pointed at the decoration.

"You all have them" he pointed out. "The Captain's very intelligent I know, but he's not doing a very good job of hiding who he is. Or the rest of you for that matter."

Mercurias leaned across the table, his face inches from the boy's. His voice issued in a threatening whisper.

"If you really did know what you were talking about, you wouldn't be doing it so loud."

Quintillian's voice dropped to the same level.

"Kiva Tregaron, Captain of the Grey Company" he said. "Kiva Caerdin, General of the Empire and Commander of the Wolves. It's not a great leap to work it out. It may be all nice and good and sentimental for you all to carry your old regimental flasks, but it really is a gaping hole in any kind of cover you're all trying to achieve."

Mercurias frowned and slugged down a little of the spirit before he spoke.

"Ok. You're bright. I knew that. Question is: how bright are you? Time for you to tell me what *you* know about *us*."

"Not all that much" Quintillian shrugged. "I know that he *is* the General. No one could make that mistake given the evidence. You're all so tight-lipped about it, I can only assume that what constitutes the grey company are, in fact, the members of the Wolves from before the fall, you included, yes?"

"Not all of us," the medic conceded, "but most, yes."

Quintillian nodded.

"The rest of what I have is questions."

The medic frowned.

"Alright" he said, taking a deep breath. "I have just one question for you and I want you to answer it truthfully. There are dozens of ways to tell if a man's lying and I know a lot of them."

He glared at Quintillian until the boy nodded, hovering between nervousness and excitement. At the nod, Mercurias leaned forward and spoke in a low voice.

"Why us? Were you actually looking for us?"

The boy shook his head.

"I know it seems odd," he said, "but I assure you it's entirely coincidental. I'm just grateful to get the chance to travel with heroes; legends even. That's worth a hundred corona alone. I've read about the Wolves since I was first able to pick up a book."

Mercurias narrowed his eyes and his voice dropped even lower, barely audible among the sounds of the bar.

"One more thing then" he murmured. "You *do* know about your family, don't you? You're too clever not to have made the connection, even if no one's ever told you. Your books would tell you. And the Captain tells me that your head-man on the island's a priest called Sarios. I'm assuming that's Minister Sarios. In the old days, he controlled all varieties of medical practice in the Empire. Hell, I took my oath in front of the man!"

Quintillian smiled.

"Yes" he replied, "but as the 'captain' keeps telling me, such connections are things best kept secret. Until I know more about him, he need not know more about me. I think that's fair."

Mercurias opened his mouth to rebuke the lad, but whatever he said went unheard as a loud voice from the other side of the bar cut through the general hubbub.

"I don't like darkies!"

The medic's head whipped round and he half rose from his seat. Quintillian craned his neck to see past the older man. A large brute with a shaved scalp and dark leather armour all but eclipsed the door to the street. He looked angry. Craning the other way, the lad could see Athas standing by the bar close to Kiva. He didn't even glance elsewhere to find the 'darkie'. It occurred to Quintillian that black-skinned warriors weren't all that common these days and were still considered 'exotic' and yet he'd barely registered the colour of the sergeant's skin. Perhaps his standing as a sergeant of the Wolves had overshadowed his mere physical presence. Athas stood away from the bar. In the fluid motion of a natural tide, the occupants of the main room drifted to the

43

periphery, leaving a clear passage between the sergeant and the new arrival.

Athas folded his arms and glared at the man in the doorway.

"I don't like mindless assholes," he replied evenly, "but I notice they let *them* in here."

The medic sat back down and turned, fleetingly, to look at the lad.

"This should be good."

Kiva hadn't moved from the bar; merely took a calm drink and smiled a frightening smile.

The bulky visitor stepped inside the bar, away from the door lintel and unhooked a heavy mace from one side of his waist and a long-bladed sword from the other. Behind him several other men entered, but stood by the doorway. Quintillian tapped the medic on the shoulder.

"If there's going to be trouble, shouldn't we be ready?" he asked.

Mercurias shrugged.

"Trouble?"

The second man to enter was a great deal smaller than the first. He wore armour very similar to the Kiva's and a bear skin over his shoulders. One of his eyes was permanently closed by the scar of an old blade wound. The man grinned and Quintillian shivered at the sight. 'Bear skin' stepped forward a pace and spoke to his bulky friend loud enough to be heard across the bar.

"Jorun, I don't think you want to mess with this 'darkie'!"

His words went unheeded as the large man continued forward, his two weapons ready and swinging as he moved. Athas stood still, arms remaining folded. Quintillian tugged on the medic's arm.

"This isn't good" he said urgently. "Why isn't the captain helping?"

Mercurias grinned back at him.

"He doesn't need any help. Can't you see that?"

The large man finally broke his slow advance and ran at Athas, the mace high and ready to drop and the sword jutting forwards at chest height. Athas continued to stand until the last moment, when he shifted his weight slightly to the left, stepped forward inside the reach of the blade and, unfolding his arms, jammed the fork he'd been holding into the man's throat. The momentum carried the two forward a couple more paces, the fork tearing skin as the movement jarred them both. As they stopped, the big man stared down in shock and the weapons toppled from his hands. He reached both arms toward Athas, who merely waggled the fork, still buried in the man's neck. His other finger waved in front of the enemy as though scolding a naughty child.

"Ah Ah. Play nice" he said sweetly.

The big man's hands dropped slowly to his sides. Athas smiled at him.

"I'm now going to remove the fork" he said slowly and clearly. "You're going to have to reach up very quickly and grasp your throat to prevent too much blood loss. After that you're going to leave. We have a medic in the corner, but I doubt he'll feel inclined to help you."

Mercurias laughed as Athas continued. "I noticed an apothecary on the way into town. If you can get there without too much blood loss, you'll be alright, but it'll cost you a packet and you may never speak again, coz I think I touched your voice box. Be happy. I could have stuck your windpipe. Ready?"

The big man, a stunned and stupefied look on his face, nodded, causing him to wince as a fresh gout of blood pumped out around the fork.

"Go!"

Athas removed the utensil with a bold, sweeping stroke and a great quantity of dark blood splashed onto the floor. A fraction of a second later, Jorun was out of the tavern, one hand clutching his throat very tight. The sergeant bent down and gingerly, trying to avoid the bulk of the blood, picked the two weapons up from where they lay. He tossed the mace onto the bar.

"Sell it to pay for the cleaning" he said loudly.

As Mercurias continued to grin and Quintillian sat dumbfounded, the sergeant stepped to their table and placed the sword on it.

"Clean it up lad" he said. "It's reasonable quality and it'll do you better than the two knives."

The other men by the door hadn't moved except to step inside. Now Athas turned to them. Quintillian gritted his teeth waiting and watched with bated breath as the large sergeant reached the group. Athas stopped in front of 'bear skin'.

"Captain Tythias" he smiled. "It's been just far too long."

He reached out a hand and the scarred warrior took it warmly.

"Athas?" he replied. "Nice fork. Yours, or just handy at the time?"

The entire band of warriors now entered the bar and Quintillian realised he hadn't released his breath for too long. As he gratefully

45

exhaled, he looked up in wonder. He was remarkably surprised to find someone that didn't actually want to kill them all. The group wandered around the bar and settled themselves among the men of the Grey Company who were already here. Captain Tythias reached the bar and leaned next to Captain Tregaron.

"Kiva" he greeted the leader of the Grey Company warmly. "Sorry about that. Should hire soldiers not gorillas, I suppose. Still, he'll not do that again and at least he'll shut up now."

Kiva smiled a rare genuine smile.

"Tythias" he replied equally warmly. "Nice to see you. Thought you were out east somewhere."

The scarred captain nodded.

"We were," he said "but the only lords with enough power and cash to pay my extortionate rates are round the gulf here, so we came back. I was actually on my way to see Lord Bergama. I gather he's in need of good men and he's one of the least dislikeable employers at the moment."

Kiva scowled.

"Was" he spat. "*Was* one of them. We've just left his lands and I think we were the only ones who did. Lord Celio's in residence now and he *is* a bastard. Bergama's probably been broken in the streets by now. Shame you weren't here a couple of days ago. The Grey Company and the Lion Riders would have stood a better chance together. It's been a long time since we've worked in concert."

Tythias slammed his fist on the bar.

"Damn!" he cursed. "Who the hell else is going to be willing to pay us? I'm not working for that vomit-bag Celio and the only others worth joining are halfway round the gulf or more. Don't forget, I charge more than you."

Kiva shrugged.

"Depends whether you're picky" he replied. "Velutio's hiring and he pays best of all. I know he hates me, but I'm not aware of anything he's got against you."

Tythias made a 'so-so' motion with his hand.

"I'm not entirely sure I want to be 'enslaved' to that man, but I suppose we could sign a short contract and then move on. Where are you headed next?"

Once more Kiva shrugged.

"Think we might go north and see how much the tribes are paying for training. We could do with a little time off and I've got a new recruit to train too."

Kiva pointed at Quintillian and he and Tythias crossed the bar, drinks in hand, and approached the table where Mercurias and the boy were sitting in silence, cleaning the blood off the fine new blade with a bar cloth.

"You know Mercurias of course" Kiva smiled.

Tythias grinned and rolled his good eye.

"Dear Gods yes" he said as he leaned forward. "How are you, you miserable excuse for a human being?"

Mercurias returned the smile.

"Not too bad you smelly, hairy old goat!" the medic replied.

Tythias then turned to the table's other occupant.

"And this is?"

Kiva gestured expansively at the lad.

"This is our newest recruit" he announced loudly enough for all around to hear. "Septimus. He's a bit of a bookworm, but good with a bow."

Tythias laughed.

"As if you'd know" he snorted. "You missed me last year at Parthis and I was standing perfectly still and not far away from you! What the hell are you doing here, lad? No offence of course."

Quintillian forced a smile. If the captain were going to the extent of giving him a pseudonym, he'd have to come up with a half-decent story.

"My father wants me to learn how to protect our lands," he lied, "rather than just reading about them. He's signed me over to the captain for a year to train me. Paid him quite well I thought."

"Ha!" Tythias laughed. "Should've come to a *real* unit instead of these jokers."

Kiva smiled.

"He's not particularly a natural," he admitted blandly, "but we'll make a mean-spirited killer of him yet. Why d'you think we leave him in the company of this miserable old bastard" he added, gesturing at the medic.

Mercurias reached up and tugged on Tythias' sleeve. As the two of them entered into a deep conversation filled with insults, Quintillian took the chance to stand and move close enough to Kiva to be heard quietly.

"Captain," he said in a low whisper. "I need to talk to you privately."

Kiva shook his head and slugged down the rest of his mug of drink before leaning forward and returning the whisper.

47

"No time tonight. Not with Tythias' lot here. We'll have to grab your armour from the smith and head out early tomorrow as well. We've got to change our route now, cos Tythias'll be heading that way and I don't want him to get in the way. I was never all that happy about going through Velutio anyway. Too much trouble there. If you really need to talk, it'll have to be when we're away from here."

Quintillian nodded and returned to his seat, deep in thought. How was the captain intending to get them onto the island without going through Velutio? Tomas was the only one who knew the way through the reefs and he was dead. Out of the corner of his eye, he saw Kiva stop on the way to the bar, wincing and leaning on a table with his mug in one hand. The captain looked around to make sure his moment of weakness had gone unnoticed and spotted only Quintillian watching. Straightening, he pulled out the flask of Mare's mead and took a large pull on the thing before he reached the bar and bought another drink.

Something in Quintillian's considerable memory clicked into place for just a moment and the lad made his excuses to Mercurias and Tythias, neither of whom were paying him any attention anyway, and approached the bar. The innkeeper, having just served Kiva his drink, wandered down the serving table and reached Quintillian.

"Yes?"

"Do you have a back room that I could use to read in?" the lad enquired. "A storeroom would be fine if there's light."

The barman looked him up and down.

"Septimus of the grey company, yes?" Without waiting for confirmation, the innkeeper pointed to a doorway. "You've all got accommodation upstairs. Any one of the first four rooms. Help yourself."

Quintillian smiled gratefully and, turning, pounded up the stairs to the room. As he disappeared into the next floor, Mercurias cast a glance up the stairs after him and frowned. The first door opened into a comfortable room with three beds warmed by a brazier and lit by candles. The boy approached the small table near the window and gathered several candles together to light the table's surface, upon which he laid Carso's history. So Carso wrote crap did he?

Feverishly, Quintillian flicked through the book, looking for something. It had been a long time since he'd read some of these chapters, but if he could just find those few words, he was sure it was what he wanted to know. Forward and back he flicked, scanning the pages and the section headings until he finally lit on the correct chapter.

Here it was: "The Death of Wolves". He only vaguely remembered it, but some of the events tied up too well for it to be falsehood. He pored over the first page, documenting the few actions the Wolves took an active part in after the death of his uncle. He continued over the other pages and then... There. The death of the Caerdin. Two of the Lords had been fighting over the lands near Serfium and the campaign had ended with the Lord of Velutio, chief claimant to the throne, ordering the destruction of lands and the burning of properties. Caerdin's own villa had been put to the torch with his wife and family and all their servants trapped inside. Her name had been Livilla and she'd been related to the Imperial house. A beauty by all accounts and, in a revelation that threatened to make Quintillian laugh out loud, a distant relation of his. That would make Kiva a distant relation by marriage. He smiled for a moment and wondered how he might broach the subject with the captain. Probably best not to. He didn't want to reveal too much and he was damn sure that neither did the captain. After all, that would be the most delicate of subjects: his wife and children.

Returning to the text, he flicked quickly through the next couple of pages which told of the revenge of Kiva Caerdin on the men who were responsible for his family's death. Even in the graceful and objective tones of Carso, Quintillian saw horror and violence on a hitherto undreamed-of scale. Caerdin had not been kind. Not merciful. In fact, barely human in his quest for blood. There was a reference to a duel with the Lord of Velutio in which Caerdin was badly wounded. Would this be the same Lord Velutio now, or his son? Despite all his time on the Island, Quintillian had never seen the man and knew precious little about him.

It was after this revenge was enacted that Caerdin disappeared from history. There was no mention of him or the Wolves from then on. Closing the book, Quintillian cradled his chin in his hands and stared out of the room's window into the night sky behind the inn.

"I presume that's why he doesn't want us to go through Velutio then."

A voice behind him spoke quietly.

"I told you not to take them as gospel."

Quintillian turned to see the medic standing in the middle of the room. Dear Gods' the man was quiet! The lad hadn't heard him climb the stairs or open the door.

"What d'you mean?" he asked the medic.

49

"I told you it's crap" the man replied. "Oh a lot of the facts are there, but not the meaning or the heart. It's not enough just to know what happened without knowing why; causes and consequences."

Quintillian scraped his chair back so that it faced into the room while the medic dumped his pack under one of the beds. He then sat on it and frowned. Quintillian coughed.

"Then why don't you tell me?" he asked. "You know I'm going to find out anyway. Better to have the truth of it from his close companions than to misread something."

Mercurias shook his head.

"No. It's not my story to tell" he said firmly. "The only person who'll be able to tell you it all is the captain, and he won't do it unless he thinks you need or deserve to know. The only way you're going to ever get any deeper with the captain is if you come clean with him completely. Tell him everything you know and all of your suspicions. Then he might feel remotely inclined to discuss some of this with you."

Quintillian sighed.

"Are there actually people out there in the world who *don't* want to kill him?" he asked.

The medic grinned.

"You met Tythias" he laughed. "*He* doesn't."

"Ah but they have in the past, haven't they" Quintillian replied. "You're not always on the same side. The captain shot at him last year, I heard."

Mercurias shook his head sympathetically.

"Don't be daft boy" he said. "Kiva's not the best archer in the world, I'll admit, but even a blind man with the shakes would be able to hit Tythias from around eight feet. Tythias is old school; one of the better officers from before the fall. I remember him in a Prefect's uniform. He fought alongside the Wolves in the days it all made sense. No one in the company would ever try to get rid of him. Athas dotes on him."

He patted Quintillian on the shoulder.

"It's the Lords that are the problem, begging the pardon of your humble Imperial blood. The Lords'll tear the world apart for their own greed. It's just there's no alternative for us these days. The common soldiers who hail from the pre-downfall army are all comrades of old and a lot of them remember that."

He leaned back and slumped onto the bed.

"Except in Velutio of course."

Chapter V.

The sun was starting to project some heat at last. It had floated, watery, above the horizon for perhaps an hour and the Grey Company had been on the road an hour before that, leaving Tythias and his unit slumbering in the inn. Last night Mercurias had collapsed into a heavy sleep early, leaving Quintillian to read his text. The rest of the company had barged noisily up the stairs some time after midnight, finding their rooms while Tythias' men made their way to the bunk room at the end of the floor. Almost an hour after the unit had succumbed to sleep, Quintillian had closed his book and, pushing back the chair, stood to retire, when some sixth sense made him glance out of the window. The solitary figure of Kiva could be seen walking slowly around the yard behind the Inn. The Captain had spoken little when the unit arose this morning and remained quiet and detached all through the march.

Athas had taken charge of the unit today and had announced a breakfast halt a few minutes ago, once he'd spied a grassy hollow by the side of the road. The dip was comfortable, with a higher ridge around the edge scattered with crooked rocks that formed an excellent defensive line. The company sat around the dell digging deep into packs for their dried beef and pork rations and the bread and cheese purchased from 'The Rapture'. Kiva, less companionable even than usual, sat on guard by a large rock near the road. Quintillian laid down his kit, taking great care to prop his new blade against a tree. Turning, he stretched his shoulders, wincing at the weight and discomfort of the metal plates and leather jerkin that chafed between his shoulder blades. Athas had taken him to collect his armour while it was still dark and had helped him in to the heavy plated tunic. He *did* feel more like a soldier now, but it would be a long time before he could wear the heavily armoured tunic with as much ease as the others. Throwing his arms out to his side, he wandered around the edge of the dell until he reached the captain, who spoke without even turning.

"Now's not a good time, Septimus."

Quintillian frowned. It would take a long time for him to get used to a different name. He'd assumed the pseudonym would vanish once the unit were alone again, but no one had called him by his real name this morning. He gritted his teeth. There was never a good time with this man. He continued to walk until he reached the rock, where he turned and faced the captain. Aware as always of the difference in the way he was treated compared with the easy familiarity between the others, he attempted to adopt a more relaxed and professional attitude in front of the older man. He leaned back against a tree trunk and pulled a piece of dried blood sausage from his pouch. He'd never have believed people would eat such a thing when he was on the island. The sausage was bitter and thick and cloying and Quintillian had to struggle not to gag, though he was proud of the way he was now managing to take these discomforts in his stride. He looked up at the captain as he swallowed the mouthful and fixed him with a steady look.

"Captain," he began. "I don't think you'll ever find the time. Frankly, although I realise that everyone thinks I'm spoilt, I'm the one who's trying to clear things here. I think you need to start to speak to me as an equal. The amount of money I paid for your company at least deserves that, doesn't it?"

Kiva raised an eyebrow.

"You want me to treat you like an equal, hmm?" the older man replied. "I can treat you like an adult, true, but don't try suggesting to me that we're equals in any way. You and I have nothing in common, lad. I'm not saying that I'm a better man; In fact I damn well know I'm not, but we're far from equal."

There was a moment of silence and Kiva gestured with his palm.

"You wanted to speak to me?" the captain relented with a distant look in his eye. "Speak."

Quintillian sighed. The captain may well be the most infuriating man he'd ever met. How could Caerdin manage to make him feel so small and petulant when he *knew* he was in the right? There was nothing for it now but to plunge in headfirst.

"Captain, are we safe enough from prying ears to talk? I don't mean the unit, but we can move away from them too if you wish. I think you might want to."

Kiva said nothing but shook his head and waited for Quintillian to continue.

"Hear me out, then" the boy continued, "and don't fly into one of your off-hand dismissals without giving me the chance. Firstly, I feel it's only fair to admit that I do know full well who I am. I know my family; my heritage; my uncle. No one's ever told me and no one expects anything of me, but I'm not stupid and I am a great reader."

The lad stopped for a moment and looked up at the captain again. Silence.

"Secondly," he went on, "I'm well aware of who *you* are, and these other man around you, so there's really no point in going on with this masquerade in front of me. There are too many glaring holes in your cover. I can't believe any of those who served in the army all those years ago like Tythias did haven't made the connection. Why do you persist in using your own first name? In keeping your Wolves canteens?"

He waited for a retort but once more, nothing came.

"And thirdly why, when you must have known about me, and I made it clear that I knew about you, wouldn't you come clean with me? Why all this dance?"

This time he stood and waited, creating a silence for Kiva to fill. They sat for some time, staring at each other before the captain shifted on the rock, the discomfort of his position finally getting to him. Quintillian wasn't sure whether he'd pushed the captain further than he should have. The man looked both angry and tired in equal quantities and his voice sounded weary when he spoke.

"Alright Quintillian" he began. "First: our names. You may not be aware of this, but Kiva was a very common name in the days I came out of the north. There were three Kivas just in the intake when I first joined up. Kiva Tregaron, in fact, was a good friend of mine in our first year in the army. He died from an arrow in the throat while protecting my back at the battle of the Galtic Narrows. I got promoted and decorated for the action, but I would have ended my days there with a spear in my spine had Tregaron not been present. He saved the day there more than I did, and it seems fitting in a way to take his name. Besides, taking on an assumed name is something of an art. It can take a long time to get used to something new and not react to your old name. You've been Septimus for around seven hours and I'll bet you keep missing calls to you. I chose a name I could easily get along with "

As he talked, the captain leaned forward, away from the rock and toward Quintillian.

"Second: the flasks," he continued. "Yes, we still carry the flasks of the Wolves. We don't show them around. Yes, *you've* seen them, but then *you've* been in the thick of the unit. We don't wave them around in front of strangers bringing attention to the symbols."

Quintillian opened his mouth and drew breath, but Kiva held up a finger and cut him off before he could speak.

"You wanted to know so I'm telling you. Third: if you really know who you are, then there are a whole number of questions that open up about you. I'd be disinclined to place too much trust in you until you or I can answer some of them. If you really do know your lineage, why do you even want to know me? D'you know the history as you claim?"

Quintillian bridled.

"I know my history General," he said sharply. "I know that you were the stalwart general of the armies. Of the four Imperial Marshals, you were the renowned one. You were the one my uncle loved as a brother and exalted. You were the only one who came to his defence when he was unjustly imprisoned in his Palace on Isera. You fought tooth and nail to put him back where he belonged, on the throne in Velutio. Of course I want to know you. You were a great man and possibly the only friend my family had. How can you ask such a question?"

Kiva was on his feet now and, as the lad looked around, he could see the company getting to their feet. They were paying attention. He and the captain had been raising their voices gradually and now Quintillian realised he was looking more and more foolish and petulant. Damn this bunch, why did they always make him feel like such an idiot. There was no choice but to push this as far as he could now.

"General..."

Kiva cut him off angrily, his eyes narrowing. "There's the most important question left for me to ask you. What is it that you want?"

Quintillian was momentarily thrown. "What?" he stuttered.

Kiva rounded on him, stepping forward.

"You've the Imperial blood," he said, his voice rising in volume. "The only man in the world now who does. You know what that means: some of the Lords would kill you if they knew about you; others would use you. In fact, I'm assuming you were imprisoned on Isera anyway; last I heard Velutio was using the place as some kind of base. You've come out here into the middle of a war zone and found us. Why? Are you wanting power? Protection? What is it that you want?"

Quintillian backed into the tree he'd been slouched against earlier. He felt like he'd been punched in the gut. What *did* he want? Why had he never asked these questions of himself? Then he'd have been in a considerably better position to answer them.

"I don't have a plan," the boy blurted out. "I want to go home. As for the future, I don't know *what* it holds, but I know I'd rather have people like those who risked their lives for my uncle running the world than the Lords of the big cities now, who tax and torture and press the populace into their armies. They're killing the Empire. You think I want to rule in place of my uncle? You're wrong. I don't want to run the damn world! I can't even run my own life. I'm a scholar and I just want to *be* a scholar."

54

Now the whole company were looking at him, but he felt less foolish than he had before, the conviction and the anger rising and eclipsing his uncertainty. He planted his feet firmly on the turf and pointed angrily at Kiva.

"What about you?" he demanded. "What do *you* want? Does what Captain Tregaron want differ from that of General Caerdin? Are the Wolves destined to limp from the pages of history?"

He stopped, ruddy faced and drawing ragged breaths. Kiva looked around, only now noticing that his men were watching. He ground his teeth.

"Boy," he growled, "you live in a fantasy world built around what you think the Empire was like. It wasn't like that. What do I want? I want to live until tomorrow. Tomorrow I'll want to live to the next day and so on. I don't want any of my men to fall, but that's about it. The Wolves 'limped' as you put it from the pages of history twenty years ago. Now there's just the Grey Company and we're renowned and feared in our own right. What would you have us do? March against the world and rebuild the Empire? Fiction! Stupidity!"

Quintillian's shoulders slumped.

"I don't want you to march on Velutio and claim the throne, General" he said, his voice taking on a pleading tone. "I'm not asking anything except that you have a little pride. Pride in what you were and what you are. There's no one around who would take offence at General Caerdin and the Wolves except Velutio, and he doesn't like you anyway. You've lost all your pride and your glory. That may not worry you, but how do you think these men feel?"

He waved his arm, taking in the rest of the company.

"They have constant reminders" he continued. "D'you think they'd use their Wolves flasks still if they had no pride?"

"The world has changed, little boy" Kiva growled. "The glory's gone. What we use to respect and protect has gone."

Quintillian stepped forward, bringing his nose just inches from Kiva's.

"It *hasn't* gone" he growled; "it's still there, but it's fading. If people don't care anymore then it really *will* go. Look around you General. Your bitterness is blinding you to what there is."

He gestured around the hollow. Kiva actually stopped for a moment and followed his gesture. The company stood in silence, their faces grave as they watched. They wouldn't interrupt; not on this subject. Other than them, there was just the grassy dell.

"What are you talking about?" the captain demanded.

55

Quintillian rushed over to the rock the captain had been leaning against. "Look!" he replied, anger and hope vying in his voice. "Actually look at it."

Kiva turned and looked down at the rock. He hadn't actually noticed the carving before. The rock was the fractured torso of a large statue, the robes and breastplate all but worn away. The captain stepped back.

"What *is* this place?" he asked, his voice now low and unsure.

Quintillian grasped the captain by the elbow and turned him, pointing into the deep grass nearby. The head of the statue stared back up, weathered, but better preserved. Despite the weather damage, the resemblance to the boy was uncanny.

"How many temples have you been in during all that time you commanded the army, General Caerdin?" the boy asked. "How many sanctuaries to the Imperial Cult? Don't you recognise my uncle when you see him?"

The lad immediately regretted his words. Though it was barely perceptible, he could swear that the captain was shaking a little, with his shoulders hunched over. For a moment, Quintillian actually believed that the man was shedding a tear, but then he turned again. The look on his face was one of cold, calculated anger.

"That's it, boy" he barked. "You've lectured me enough. I'm entirely the wrong man to appeal to a sense of nostalgia. You'd have been better targeting Athas; he's still a romantic at heart. You may be the last of the Imperial Line and by all the Gods there's a lot of your uncle in you, but that's just the problem, isn't it?"

"What do you mean?" Quintillian asked, with a rising tone of apprehension.

Kiva had fallen quiet, his hands shaking slightly. "What do I mean?" he continued. "Have you never read your histories? I thought you prided yourself on your reading? Your family are prone to the most brutal insanity, Quintillian. Never read about the madness? The death and mayhem this dynasty caused? Your grandfather had to be put down by priests of his own cult so he could be buried and ascend to the Heavens. He tried to bite them as they held him down frothing at the mouth, while they cut his throat in the fountain of his own temple. But that wasn't until after he'd had a thousand heads removed just for his amusement. Soldiers, senators, peasants, anybody. Hell, even one of the Marshals fell foul of Basianus the fair when the Emperor started to get paranoid thinking people were plotting against him. Problem is: by the time his madness was becoming obvious, they were! And your uncle? I couldn't believe your uncle would succumb; I knew him so well. Yes, he was my best friend, and I tried to save him when the Senate condemned him for his insanity. I didn't believe the rumours, but it was with my own ears that I heard him command me to crucify a city. A whole city, Quintillian. Men, women, children. Even the cats and dogs!"

The boy realised that Kiva was shaking now, whether with anger or some other emotion, he couldn't tell. The captain drew his sword and Quintillian's eyes fixed in fear on the deadly point. Kiva gave the sword a couple of idle, angry slashes.

"And do you know why?" he challenged. "Why they were all to die?"

In a panic, Quintillian stuttered. "N.. no."

"Because they couldn't afford to pay his new fucking taxes!" Kiva shouted.

The captain thrust the sword, narrowly missing the lad's shoulder and digging the point deep into bark before turning and speaking as he walked away.

"*That's* the problem with Emperors" he said without looking back. "Power curses you, or drives you mad or something like that. Look around you. The other Lords are all going the same way. They all want to rule and look at what it does to them. Better we stay as we are: mercenaries, and wait for the day the Lords have all killed each other. Then we can have some peace."

Quintillian stood stock still, his eyes on the hilt of the sword by his side, still shuddering with the force with which it had struck the tree.

"But you were his *friend*" he cried. "You still helped him. You saved him."

Kiva stopped abruptly. He turned and walked very slowly back toward the boy. Once he reached him, he put his hand on the lad's shoulder, almost comforting. To Quintillian's astonishment, there really *were* tears in the captain's eyes. Kiva pushed hard and, as the lad dropped to his backside on the grass, he drew the sword from the tree.

"I was more than his friend, Quintillian. He was like my brother."

Sheathing his sword, he stood, looking down at the boy.

"But it was *me* who locked him in his palace" he said, his voice cracking slightly with raw emotion. "*Me* who dismissed his guard." His voice sounded choked; clotted, his face bleak and more open than Quintillian had seen since they'd met. The captain cleared his throat.

"*Me* who set the fire and killed him."

Kiva turned his back on the boy, who had blanched and was gasping for breath. As the captain reached the edge of the hollow, he turned back one last time.

"It had to be done Quintillian. For the good of the Empire."

And with that the captain vanished from sight over the lip of the hollow.

The boy sat stunned in the grass, shaking uncontrollably until suddenly a large hand appeared beneath his chin, holding a Wolves flask that contained something that smelled revolting. Athas crouched next to him.

"Drink lad" he said comfortingly. "You've never needed it more than now."

Quintillian took a grateful pull on the spirit and coughed repeatedly. His throat spasmed and he leaned to one side, towards the bushes and vomited until he was dry retching. The face of his uncle stared up at him from the grass. Still shivering, he looked up at Athas, his face streaked with the tracks of his sorrow.

"It *can't* be true" he begged of the big sergeant.

The hulking, coloured man placed a blanket around the boy's shoulders and sat beside him. He took a swig from the flask and then passed it back to the lad.

"Quintillian," he said, "there are some things you have to understand."

"About him?" the lad said, his voice beginning to harden again. "A regicide? The man who murdered my uncle? I feel like such an idiot. Why should I need to understand?"

Athas shook the boy by the shoulders.

"It's not that simple" the sergeant said quietly. "Your uncle had lost his wits. We were the last to see it and the last to believe it. There were other officers, even Generals who had wanted to execute your uncle in public. The nobles were calling for it in the city, but no one could decide what to do. You can't kill a God without repercussions and who the hell would do the deed? It was Kiva who stopped them all. He tried to reason with Quintus, but there was no reason left in the Emperor; none at all. It had to be done, otherwise Quintus would have ruined the Empire or a mob would have got to him and torn him to pieces."

Athas sighed.

"In the end, history remembers that he died in a fire in his palace. He went to the Gods deified and pure and died a hero, albeit a lunatic. People don't talk about it. Most people are frightened to speak ill of a divine figure, so his name goes unsullied and that's the way it should be. He'd been a great man for a lot of years before he started to slip. And when the time came and there was no other choice left to us, Kiva did it all, from dismissing the guard to locking the door, starting the fire and watching until it was over. He had to, don't you see? He wouldn't let anyone else do it. Couldn't let them. To kill the Emperor was to kill a God. He would be cursed for the rest of his miserable life."

"Cursed?" the boy queried.

"Can't you see that in him?" Athas sighed. "A curse? Whether he actually *is* cursed or just believes it to be so, it's affected his life ever since. Personally I don't believe in curses; those of us from the desert lands never really held with the Emperor being a God anyway."

The burly sergeant grasped the boy's shoulder.

"Kiva did what he had to" he said. "He brought down the Empire with his own hands, but he had to do it; there really was no other way. Hate him now if you must, but try to remember this: you never even knew your uncle. Kiva treated him like a brother. He's had to live for twenty years with the knowledge that he personally brought down the Empire, destroying the dynasty and executing a friend. You might begin to understand why he sleeps so badly."

Quintillian had stopped shaking and, to his great surprise, had also stopped crying. Athas grasped him once more by the shoulders and hauled him to his feet.

"Perhaps now at least the two of you can talk as men, without all this carry-on" the sergeant said. "And now you need to stand up and straighten out. You're one of the Grey Company and you need to act like one, or I'll have to have Marco lash you."

The lad managed a weak smile.

"I wonder if he knows how much damage he just did?" he said quietly.

Athas sighed.

"I wonder if you realise how much pain it causes him just to look at you?"

Chapter VI.

The sun beat down heavily on the baker's dozen as they trudged along the road toward the coast. Now that late morning had arrived the heat was becoming unbearable and the dust from the mud and shale road was churned into throat-clogging clouds. The men sweated under their leather and steel armour, grateful only that the cart followed at the rear with the rest of the pack and gear aboard.

Quintillian plodded, his feet and his heart heavy as lead. He'd have refused to climb aboard the cart if they'd asked him, but no one had spoken to him as they'd set off once again on their route. Once in a while he'd raise his face and see the unit stretched out in front of him on the gravel road, chattering inanities as they marched. He'd tried hard to fall behind and bring up the rear of the column, but Marco had taken the position of rearguard with the cart and maintained a steady pace at the back of the unit. Quintillian occasionally turned to make sure that Marco was still there and the man winked at him every time. Far from being in a social frame of mind, Quintillian returned each wink with a scowl and faced front again. He shrugged and the leather tunic settled into place, distributing the weight better. He was starting to yearn for the days of simplicity on the island. Nothing had perturbed him there. People were learned; deferential to each other; calm.

On the island it'd been him and Darius. There had been no one else the same rough age, mostly ageing ex senators or bureaucrats or their young children or grandchildren, teaching and learning and farming to eke out a living. The island had once been a complex of palaces where the central power of the world was wielded. Now some of the palatial buildings had been converted into living, teaching and working areas and the once-proud gardens of the Imperial Palace were vegetable plots and pig pens. He and Darius had spent much of their time since reaching an age of truly conscious thought exploring the island and their own skills, interrupted by sessions of teaching and training and of hard, gruelling physical labour when the masters could actually find them. A horrible thought crossed his mind that the shattered and charred ruin where the two of them hid so often from the elders would have been the last place his uncle and the General had seen each other. Quintillian reflected that he'd never really grown up until he'd left the place, though Darius had seemed older and worldlier than he even when they were together and playing. When had the world…?

His train of thought shattered as he felt a hand on his shoulder. With a slight involuntary jump, he turned to see Marco grinning at him, a piece of roadside wild grass jutting from the corner of his mouth. He repeated his general scowl, but the infuriating man just scratched his chin absently and then grinned some more. Quintillian turned to face ahead once more.

Ah yes, the island. Darius...

"You really got to learn to relax, kid" said an easy voice from behind.

Quintillian spun around angrily, causing Marco to bump into him as the two oxen continued along the path, heedless of the lad's obstruction. The olive-skinned mercenary hauled on the leather strap until the cart slowed and stopped. The smile had slipped from his face.

"I mean it" he said. "Relax. For fuck's sake, you nearly got run over by a damn heavy cart."

Quintillian shrugged his shoulders uncomfortably as he spoke.

"Don't tell me to relax" he replied petulantly. "I'll relax when I get back to the island and not until then."

As the lad turned again and started to walk off after the group of men, Marco hauled on the strap and made the oxen begin their lumbering advance once more. He smiled again; this time a smile of sympathy, aimed at the back of the boy's head. Marco would be the first to admit that he was probably the most innocent still of the Company and he could still remember what it felt like to have such a simple view of the world; such a simple view of oneself. He spoke softly, expecting no reply.

"Quintillian, you've had a shock. You're disappointed. We all know that, and we do sympathise, but there's two ways to get over it. Either you confront it, beat the shit out of your problems and come out the other side happy, or you surrender to it; let your emotions run their course and it'll come out anyway it feels. Otherwise all you're doing is moping and sulking and that does no good for you nor for nobody else. People'll just treat you like a kid."

The lad walked on ahead of him in silence. Well, Marco'd done all he could to convince him. Someone would have to. The Captain damn well wouldn't make the first move and they all knew it.

He glanced up ahead. Being considerably shorter than some of his compatriots, all he could see was a mass of bodies in a haze of dust. Hauling on the side of the cart, he pulled himself up to where he was standing on the lower boards. The group was getting a little too strung out along the road, partially due to having to halt and restart the slow, lumbering oxen. Spying the Captain way ahead at the front, he dropped back to the gravel with a crunch and slapped the leather strap on the rump of the oxen to gee them up.

Kiva was already aware that he was further out ahead of the company than he should be, but the territory was fairly open and they'd be able to see anyone long before they became a threat. Besides, Clovis would be on point about half a mile ahead and would give plenty of warning. And he was still angry. Angry with the lad for refusing to drop a subject that he shouldn't have known about. Those scenes from that last hellish year may visit the Captain with soul-shattering regularity in his sleep, but he'd managed for a long time now to keep the past locked away in his nocturnal journeys and the rest of the time had been devoted to keeping his men alive through another day. Now, thanks to the prying youth, the line had been blurred and he was being forced to confront his own personal demons around the clock.

Admittedly, he was just as angry with himself for having said it all. He could have talked his way round it and let it lie as unfortunate, but he'd suddenly found himself angrily pouring out the truth. He hadn't spoken of these things for so long, he'd habitually lie or hedge around the subject and yet he'd revealed the cancer at the centre of his very soul to the one person in the entire world it would hurt most. Damn it.

The Captain had been pondering his outburst for the last two hours along the Serfium road and could not find a way to resolve the problems. There was nothing for it but to get as far as they could and then cut the boy loose. If they could get to Serfium, maybe they could pay a fisherman to carry him across the bay to the island. It'd be excruciatingly dangerous with all the hidden reefs and sandbanks, particularly coming from as far away as Serfium, but it would be just as dangerous, though for entirely different reasons, to go through Velutio. Perhaps he'd ask for fifty corona and leave the other fifty with the lad at the coast. Yes, that would probably be best. Cut him loose at Serfium and go their separate ways.

He glanced over his shoulder but could only see Athas and Mercurias at the head of the Company, stomping along, deep in conversation. Kiva growled. Without being able to overhear their talk, he knew damn well what they were discussing. Him. Or the kid. Or both of them. Athas would be fussing around them by tonight like a mother hen trying to resolve problems and force everyone to make friends. Problem was: Kiva didn't want any more friends. All the friends he needed were already long-serving members of the company, along with the odd acquaintance from other units with whom he shared a certain bond due to their history of service in the Imperial army. More friends just meant more people to rely on you; more people you had to watch out for. Besides, a cursed man couldn't afford friends, for their own good if not for his.

Still grumbling, Kiva pulled out his flask and took a quick swig. The mead warmed and sweetened his palate while the sharper aftertaste went to work on his nerves. Within moments relief swept through his system, down through his throat and past his lungs, easing the slight sting from the dust, into his gut, where it settled and numbed. The nagging pain just below his bottom rib gradually faded as the soothing drug deadened the flesh.

As soon as they got to Serfium he would…

Something sharp jabbed him in the calf. With a start, he glanced down and saw the dart protruding from his leg.

"Shit!"

Behind him he heard thuds and clangs as other darts ricocheted or found their target.

"Cover!" he yelled to the column.

The Company sprang into life as each member looked around until they spotted somewhere they could dive to remove the missiles from their flesh and evade further attacks. Most of the group ran off the path to their left, into a pile of rocks and low gorse bushes. Kiva dived ahead and to his right, behind an old milestone, the inscription long-since covered with graffiti. Momentarily, he glanced back to see only Marco and Quintillian visible on the road, ducked behind the cart Reaching to his calf, he dislodged the needle and flung it into the grass. Momentarily, his eyes burred. Shit. The damn needles were drugged. Best hope it wasn't poison. He glanced around again and spotted Athas and Mercurias behind a large boulder and beneath a cypress tree. The large black Sergeant looked around hurriedly, saw something move on the other side of the road and called out in a booming voice.

"Melee!"

The Company began to come out of cover, running onto the track and heading in Kiva's direction as the first two figures appeared. Julian, the youngest of the Company, though still in his thirties, and one of the quietest and least assuming, sprinted along the gravel toward his Captain, a short curved axe in his left hand and a long serrated dagger in his right. From seemingly nowhere a figure sprang, somersaulting in the air and landing mere inches behind the young man. Covered from head to foot in black cloth and armed only with two smaller knives, the figure immediately dropped to waist height as Julian spun around, his axe at chest height. The black figure made one small move with one of his knives and nicked a tendon in the back of Julian's knee as the other knife struck his knuckles and the axe spun away into the undergrowth. Julian collapsed, his knee unable to bear his weight, and tumbled forwards. The man in black grasped his hair as he dropped, arresting his momentum, and brought the knife around as if to slit his throat.

Julian closed his eyes, fumbling with his long knife in an effort to change his grip in time as there was a thud and a wet tearing sound. The black-clad man toppled gently forwards over Julian, who looked up just in time to see Quintillian, haloed in a shower of blood, still running, bringing his new sword up for another strike. With a surprised smile, Julian blacked out.

Kiva was unaware of the lad's activities as the moment Athas had shouted the call to arms, three more of the black figures had appeared from the brush like ghosts and launched themselves at the Captain. His vision was blurring uncomfortably and an unpleasant weight was beginning to settle on his limbs. Fighting like a demon he struggled, warding off the blows of knives and ducking as best he could, but despite his best efforts, he was already wounded in at least three places, particularly in his shoulder where he could feel the warm trickle of blood down his arm. Unless the others came to his aid, he wouldn't last too long.

Further along the road, Marco caught up with Athas and Mercurias. The large Sergeant looked around again for Kiva, spotted Quintillian facing off against one of the black assassins, and started to run. At his shoulder as he ran, he heard Marco call out "he just went off his bloody rocker."

Another assailant dropped from one of the rocks towards the three of them, and Mercurias thrust his blade into the air, catching the man in the side as he fell. The two of them rolled off into the grass as Athas and Marco caught up with Quintillian. The boy was already wounded, a fair gash running down his thigh. He was fighting with the ferocity of a wolverine, but his inexperience and lack of training would be his downfall the moment his rush faltered. Athas glanced ahead to see Brendan and Scauvus bearing down on the Captain. Quintillian was rushing into a group of five or six of them who were deep in a brawl with men of the Company. Behind him, the man he'd just gutted with his blade proved to be far from dead. Unbeknown to Quintillian, the man rolled onto his side, bringing the knife back and in a swing for the lad's hamstring.

Athas leapt forward and stamped his heavy hobnailed boot onto the man's arm, causing an audible snapping sound. The knife skittered away from the assassin's hand, now useless. The big sergeant was just reaching down to finish the man when Marco he ran past.

"Leave him Athas" the other shouted. "We need a survivor."

Athas looked up after his compatriot, already right behind Quintillian once more. With a sigh, he looked back down at the black-wrapped man and smiled.

"This is your lucky day" he said.

With a swat of his huge hand, he knocked the consciousness from the attacker and rose to his feet to join the others. Ahead, Quintillian launched himself at another man, literally flinging himself onto the man's back. As the assassin broke off the combat he was already involved in, he raised his knife to his this new threat, trying to reach round behind him, but the boy was already there and had drawn his arm back and thrust, plunging the blade into the man's back. The man arched his spine in pain, falling backwards like a sack of sand with the boy still on his shoulders. The two hit the ground, the lad pinned and struggling to retrieve his blade, the bulk of which was visible through the assassin's chest. One of the other attackers dived for the boy's face, his dagger gleaming in the sun.

"Oh no you don't." Marco swung his leg out and caught the diving assassin with a driving kick to the throat. The man collapsed over to one side and, as Marco helped heave the body off Quintillian, Athas arrived and delivered a hard punch to the man's temple. Marco finished heaving the body away and looked up at Athas. The big Sergeant was grinning like an idiot. He shrugged and then remembered the boy. The two of them looked back down at the floor through the gathering cloud of dust, but the boy was already gone, hacking away at the next man, one of those who faced Kiva.

A noise cut through the din of battle; the sound of a horn echoing around the rocks. Athas and Marco turned in the direction of the sound and took a moment to spot the figure standing on the hill through the dust cloud. A shadowy figure, silhouetted against the late morning sun. As the two watched the figure made a slight bow and then performed a perfect Imperial military salute, before climbing onto the horse beside him. Athas turned back to the melee, only to discover that the attack had ended. None of the black-clad assailants were to be seen, even the wounded or dead. They'd all vanished in a few mere seconds.

Athas rushed forward, Marco at his shoulder. Kiva was leaning against a milestone, his face exhausted and bloody, and Quintillian stood only a yard away, his sword and his teeth bared. Athas looked around. Mercurias was back along the track, dealing with Julian where he lay. Marco, Brendan and Scauvus stood nearby and Kiva and Quintillian faced each other, neither smiling. Of the other five there was no sign.

Marco stepped forward toward Quintillian, his hand held out in a conciliatory manner, but the boy ignored him, his attention riveted on the Captain. Kiva looked up at his opponent, his eyes still swimming, and challenged him.

"Come on then boy" he invited. "You want me? You'll never have a better chance."

Marco smiled and laughed nervously, his eyes flicking between the boy and his Captain. He cleared his throat and addressed them both. "Come on now. We've just fought off a whole bunch of fuckers. You're *comrades…*"

Kiva still looked up at Quintillian.

"Is that what we are boy?" he asked in a hollow voice. "Comrades?"

The first blow when it came, came so fast and unexpectedly that Kiva truly wasn't prepared for it. Quintillian's sword arced down towards Kiva's head and only a desperate thrust with one of his own blades deflected the blow off to the side. It had, however, cut a section of the Captain's hand guard away and taken the skin off his knuckles. Blood ran onto the blade as he hauled himself shakily upright just in time to stop the second blow from landing. Again the lad's sword was turned away, grating across the top of the milestone and throwing off sparks. Now Kiva was up and, despite the woolly feeling in his head and the heaviness of his limbs, his instincts were still good. The lad advanced on him like a charioteer at the races, sword held in both hands and falling with hammer-blows time and time again. Again and again Kiva turned the blow, giving ground as he backed across the light, springy summer grass. Soon he would have to deliver the lad an injury or he'd succumb to one of the blows.

Thalo appeared from the brush at the other side of the track. Behind him, Bors appeared, his long sword and shield held on one hand and a scrap of black cloth in the other.

"We were…" his voice trailed away as he took in the sight.

Back the two combatants tracked across the grass, the lad grunting with effort and punctuating each downward swing with bitter venom.

"Bastard!"

The crash of steel on steel.

"Murdering bastard!"

Another crash.

"Why can't you just die?"

More blows.

Athas and Marco followed the two, the rest of the unit close behind, with the missing men gradually returning to the road. Athas was truly unsure as to what to do; the Captain was clearly weakening. Another downward smash of the sword caught Kiva, too weak now to lift his own in time. The blow smashed into Kiva's body armour and knocked him backwards. The Captain struggled to pull himself to his feet as Quintillian stared at the sword in his hand and the rent in the banded plates of the Captain's armour. Kiva pulled himself into an upright position and readied his two swords once more.

Quintillian stared at his sword for a moment longer and lunged forward again, his sword raised above his head.

"Fucking Murderer!" he screamed.

Athas was close now. Close enough to help if needed.

The lad swung the sword once more, but the blow was not aimed down at the Captain's vitals, but wide. As the sword reached its apex, Quintillian released his grip and the blade whistled off into the grass. The momentum still carrying him, the lad hurtled forwards and down, crashing to his knees in the grass below the Captain. Mercurias, who had caught up with the group, made to approach the two, but Athas held out his powerful arm and stopped him, nodding toward the boy.

They could hear him now. Quintillian let flow the grief that had threatened to drive him mad over the last hours. His sobbing turned into a heart-rending wail as he grasped Kiva's knees. The Captain dropped his swords to the grass and left them where they lay, stepping back with one foot so that he too could kneel. He placed his hand on the boy's shoulder.

"Let it out, Quintillian" he said quietly and calmly. "Let it all out."

The boy looked up, tears streaming down his face.

"Why?" he pleaded. "Why you?"

Kiva grasped the boy by both shoulders and hauled him up to face height.

"Because it *had* to be me" he replied. "You know that. The hardest thing I could ever have had to do, but who else could have done it? You know that. And for it I'll spend the rest of my life cursed. You can't kill a God without paying the price. I've been doing that for twenty years and I'll do it to the day I die and probably beyond. I had to break the Empire to save its people."

Kiva coddled the boy's head and then pushed him upright with a great deal of effort, the drug was still working in him and he felt sluggish and weak.

"You're a good man" Kiva said softly. "The blood of divine Emperors flows in you and, Gods willing, you'll never succumb to the rot that afflicted your uncle. We're clear, you and I, and I'll make sure you're safe but I'll hear no more of your ideas about glorious futures. There's no glory in my future, so I forbid you to talk to me about it. Beyond that, we'll be ok."

He looked up at Mercurias and nodded. The medic wandered over to the boy and put his hands on Quintillian's shoulders as Kiva stood, slightly woozily. The captain smiled wearily at Marco, who wandered forward.

"Sir?" he responded.

"The boy's got both guts and strength, but he lacks expertise" Kiva said. "Train him."

Marco nodded and crouched down beside Quintillian and Mercurias.

Kiva wandered back across the grass to the milestone, where he sat, heavily. He glanced around for the others and spotted Athas and Bors, who were rummaging in the grass.

"Where are the rest?" he called.

Athas stood, cradling something in his large hand, his brow furrowed. He realised the Captain was speaking and raised an eyebrow. "Hmm?"

"The others?" Kiva rolled his eyes. "Where are they?"

Athas sighed. "They're all accounted for. Pirus has gone to look for Clovis. He never warned us and that bodes a bit. I hope he just got hit with darts and nothing worse. The other two never really got into the fight. Mercurias said they'd been hit heavily with the darts straight off and they'll be out for a few hours. You will be soon too. You must have the constitution of an ox to take that and still fight."

Kiva smiled and waved his flask at the Sergeant.

"Mare's Mead has its benefits" he explained. "It's a hell of a lot more powerful than this shit and I've been taking that for years."

Athas had returned his attention to the object in his hand and merely nodded. Kiva sighed.

68

"Well before I finally pass out," he said, "we'd best get the men out searching for those lunatics and their amazing vanishing corpses."

Athas turned and tossed the thing he'd been holding to his Captain.

"They won't find anything" the big man said.

Kiva looked down at the black dagger hilt in his hand, with the blade sheared off just below the guard. On the pommel, the embossed golden figure of a winged horse constituted the weapon's only decoration. Kiva's brows furrowed.

On a hill above the road, a tall figure, wrapped head to foot in black silks with a huge curved blade slung across his back, laughed lightly as he compacted his telescope and placed it in a large thigh pocket. He watched with keen eyes as the small figures moved around near the road and the big dark-skinned man was among them. He laughed again; a rich, velvety laugh, and scanned the valley until he saw the black-clad figures converging on their prearranged spot. With a last glance in the direction of the Wolves, he mounted his magnificent mare, saddle-less, with only a surcoat; black and decorated with a golden winged horse.

Part Two: Swords and Ploughshares

Chapter VII.

The small vessel rocked and shook as it rode the troughs and crests of waves in the narrow channel that led to Isera. The island had been a place of fortification and safety long before the days of Imperial power due to the treacherous system of reefs and rocks that formed a horseshoe around it. The only safe route for a vessel was through a narrow channel that led from the main dock on the island to the Livia Port in the city of Velutio, once the Imperial capital. Even in that channel the journey was hazardous enough that only the most stout-hearted sailor would attempt the journey in anything but the calmest of seas. At the height of its power, the Empire's engineers had created sea-walls that calmed this single passage with a complex system of rest stops and windbreaks. In those days the Emperor's pleasure barge would ply the channel with no fear. The days of Imperial surety were long gone, as were the sea defences. Now only a madman would make the journey.

Or a man with a job to do. Commander Sabian stood at the prow of the boat, his crimson cloak speckled and bleached by the salt in the constant spray. His red military scarf was wound tightly beneath his helm's neck guard and pulled up to his eyes, covering the majority of his face. His eyes stung and watered with the effort, but he couldn't trust anyone else on the boat to keep an adequate watch. Despite his position as senior officer in the army of Velutio, he had travelled this evil heaving channel more often than any sailor in the port. Realistically, very few sailors who had made this trip would be able to speak of it. Secrets were important to Velutio, and those sailors who'd shown more than the slightest curiosity over the island's contents had been blinded and had their tongue and hands removed. Sabian grimaced at the memory of the last poor seaman who'd asked questions. He could see the necessity for the preservation of secrecy but, had it been his decision, he would have at worst executed the men swiftly and efficiently, not left them to starve and eke out a beggar's existence, crippled on the dank streets of Velutio. That was no way for a man to go.

Sabian cursed himself for his wandering mind as the ship lurched sharply and he slammed into the rail. His hand was bound in a leather strap attached to the rail and his foot wedged beneath a solid plank for safety. He'd seen too many people go overboard here and should be paying attention to the rocks, even though the journey was almost over. Any time now. He blinked away the salty discomfort once more and turned gratefully to bellow toward the helm.

"Land!" he informed the helmsman. "Bring us to starboard a fraction. The channel opens up into the bay in a hundred yards and you're clear then."

The sailor bellowed something unintelligible back, a comment lost in the teeth of the gale, and the vessel jogged slightly to starboard. The last formation of rocks on the right passed almost within arms' reach of the boat; Sabian recognised that collection of jutting spikes that reminded him so much of a pleading hand raised in supplication. As the rock passed the waves died down almost instantly, the calmness of the bay as much a shock as a relief.

The clouds of stinging spray gone, the commander allowed his cloak to fall back behind his shoulders and pulled his scarf down to his neck. Briefly, he removed his helmet and examined the cranium. The salt had wreaked havoc on the polished steel. He would have to have one of his men spend a few hours tonight working on it. Replacing the helm, he glanced up at the shore. The dock stood deserted and dilapidated, a wooden platform covered with rot and rubble, jutting out into the water. No matter how much work the island's inhabitants put into their own accommodation, none of them had ever dealt with the dock. What would be the point? They'd not be leaving anyway.

A tall figure in a grey robe stood by one of the orchard's plum trees not far from the shore, reaching high and plucking ripe fruit from the branches and placing them into the large basket on his other arm. As the commander watched, the grey-clad figure finally noticed the vessel cutting through the waters of the bay. It stopped for a long moment, staring out across the intervening distance and then turned with an unconcerned gait and ambled up the path to the large gatehouse building.

By the time the boat was finally nearing the dock and the sailors were coming afore to work the ropes and boarding plank, the grey figure had reappeared from the huge gate with two others and began the stroll down the gravel path to the jetty. Sabian watched as they approached. With a crunch the boat bumped up against the dock, the beams and planks making alarming noises as they groaned under the pressure. Without waiting for the sailors to finish tying off the boat and extend the plank, he hopped over the rail and onto the slimy jetty. Taking a deep breath, he strode purposefully forward to meet the three as they neared the shore and nodded at the central figure.

71

"Minister Sarios" he said loudly. "It's been a while. May I request your hospitality for a few days?" The phraseology was formulaic. The inhabitants had little choice in the matter and Sabian held all power on the island at that moment. Even addressing the ageing Cleric as Minister was an unnecessary courtesy, the man having held no real power since the fall twenty years ago. Sarios narrowed his eyes and Sabian had to remind himself once more just how shrewd the old man really was. Idle courtesy was unlikely to hold any real weight with him.

"Commander Sabian" the man replied quietly. "It's been six months since we've even heard from the mainland. I hope you've come alone this time. The troops you brought with you last time demolished our food stores in short order."

Business-like and cold. What else could he expect?

"Minister" the commander replied, "I am alone. I'm not here to cause you any trouble, just to make my bi-annual report. I'll need to be here two days; three at most. I've brought some extra supplies; some luxuries for you. I know you're a bit cut-off here."

He regretted the last, an opening for a jibe from the island's leader, but Sarios merely smiled humourlessly; sarcastically even.

"Commander," he said, "I'll have a room prepared for you in the Peacock Palace. We've done some work there these past months and it's quite habitable again now. I'll have one of the brothers show you to the place immediately."

Sabian smiled. "Not necessary. I remember where it is and I can make my own bed. I'll wait until my gear's unloaded and the things for you. I've got two sergeants on the boat. They'll stay on board, but I'll get them to bring your supplies to the Ibis Courtyard first."

"Very well." Sarios nodded once, his only gesture of respect, before turning and making his slow, ambling way back up the path towards the gatehouse.

Sabian stood for a moment gritting his teeth as his sergeants unloaded gear onto a pallet. He hated having to deal with the island. He knew they were helpless; prisoners even; but he still felt admiration for the Minister and what he'd achieved with his prison. He still felt compassion. He sighed and gestured to his men to take the goods up the path as he set off.

The Gorgon Gate had been designed by the great architect Himistes in the reign of the Emperor Elander; a pleasing mixture of stout defence and imperial grandeur. The building stood three stories high with thick walls softened by arcading of marble, many of the alcoves still retaining their original artworks: Osos and the Victory Bull,

72

the winged Harpies, the Gorgon of Germalla. To either side of the gateway itself, the gatehouse stood proud in the form of drum towers, again punctuated by arches and columns. Beyond that high walls with a wide walkway stretched away, encircling the palace proper. Sabian glanced upwards involuntarily as he passed beneath the threshold, taking in the murder holes for pouring hot metal or oil on attackers and the huge, defensive bronze plated doors fastened back against the walls. They'd not been closed in more than ten years, though they appeared to still be polished regularly.

Sabian pointed ahead to the courtyard and the two sergeants strode on ahead, carrying the pallet of goods. The commander stopped inside the gatehouse as he noticed in the shadows an old man in a green-grey robe sitting on a boulder and carving a piece of wood. He cleared his throat and the old man looked up, a far away look on his face.

"I see someone's keeping the gatehouse in good order" the commander said jovially. "Not intending to keep me out, I hope?" He smiled. The old man lowered his eyes to his work again and spoke quietly.

"Jobs don't just go away" he said absently. "Gotta keep 'em polished or they gets knackered."

Sabian frowned and, biting back a retort, walked back out into the brightly-lit Ibis Courtyard. The bird carvings that adorned the stone seats and fountains were now long gone, but someone had evidently mastered the science of hydraulics. Two of the four fountains poured their sapphire blue water into the wide, alabaster bowls and the yard filled with splashes. The commander was never sure whether he should relax on one of these visits but every time the palace was a little more revived, a little less shabby. There seemed to have been serious work going on this past half year, though, beyond the level achieved in previous years. The two sergeants stood at attention by the pallet of supplies. Sabian returned the salute and then gestured back through the gate with his thumb.

"Off duty unless I need you" he said easily.

The two men fell into a more relaxed pose and sauntered off down the path towards the dock. Sabian gestured at a middle aged man reading a scroll on a stone bench. The man raised his head and wandered unhurriedly over to the commander. Sabian tried to contain his frustration at the obvious tutting sound that had issued from the man when he stood. As the cleric stood before him rolling the scroll back tight, Sabian reached down into the pallet of goods and pulled his pack from the pile, shouldering it.

"Everything else there is for your community" he commented. "Be real careful, though. There's some glassware and a few books."

The man blinked and looked up at the commander.

"Books?" he said uncertainly.

Sabian smiled. "Last time I was here I was led to believe that the one thing the island truly lacked was books. There are around a dozen. Mostly treatises; scientific, philosophical, that kind of thing. Hope they're what you want."

The man nodded greedily and reached into the centre of the mass, withdrawing a thick, heavy volume. "Deratius's 'On Aqueducts'!" the exclaimed. "Astounding!"

Sabian opened his mouth to speak, but the man reached out and grasped his hand firmly, shaking it hard enough to cause pain in the commander's shoulder and repeating "perfect" and "thank you".

The commander grinned and answered "Thank you" to the man's back as he hurtled off through a door to give the good news. He sighed again and his shoulders sagged. At least somebody here was going to treat him as something other than a jailor.

Walking through the now empty courtyard, he made his way through the decorative Arch of the Four Seasons with its three remaining carvings and its trellis of creepers and out into the great court. The neat grass had been recently tended and, despite being punctuated with vegetable gardens and ploughed areas, it still retained its feel of spacious beauty. Ahead and to the right stood the doorway that led to the Peacock Palace. The commander nodded absently to a few of the inhabitants fulfilling the roles of farmers and gardeners as he disappeared into the Hall of the Swans.

The long vestibule had once been the passageway between the Peacock Palace containing the Emperor's private apartments and the main bulk of the Imperial Palace. The arcades with their thick windows looked out across the gentle slope, with the palace walls at the lowest reach towards the sea and the waves with their white horses leaping over the sharp rocks surrounding the island and dashing themselves against the shore. The slope had once been a lawn decorated with statues and gazebos but these days it was the province of the farmers and goats roamed the slope, grazing. The corridor itself had once been lined with busts and statues of the Emperors and Empresses and the great statesmen of the old republic. These days, its star-painted ceiling was green with mould and the bright white walls were stained and crumbling. Along the full length of the hall, old wooden cupboards and shelves had been employed for vegetable and fruit storage.

The commander shifted the weight of his pack and walked purposefully down the length of the vast corridor, trying not to think about how many Emperors had walked this very route so many times a day. He'd seen the crumbling wreckage of the curiously oval Peacock Palace from the apartments of the elders and was interested to see what they'd done with it. It was not hard to see how the Empire had functioned so well under the kind of men that had turned a crumbling palace into a fully-functioning farming and scholarly community in so few years.

Exiting the corridor, he found himself in a circular stair hall with a beautiful enclosed broad marble staircase. He vaguely remembered being told about this by one of the elders a few years back. One of the Emperors who'd no love for his wife had had the stairs devised. There were two entrances to the circular stairwell on each floor, but they ran independently of each other, and people who took different doors could not meet on the stairs and could only see each other through windows across the central well. Ingenious. Wasted on the last dynasty, though. He made for one of the entrances and began to trot up the stairs. At the first landing, he was puzzled for a moment until he realised that he'd only come halfway round the circle in one floor and there was no door. This floor would be reachable only from the other staircase. He grinned. The Emperors may have been mad, but they had an interesting sense of humour. Trotting up the rest of the steps to the third floor, he wandered out into the hallway.

The floor had been recently repaired, new oak beams in place of the rotten ones and a good coat of varnish over the lot. The carpet was still very threadbare. They perhaps had not yet managed to start weaving on this scale. He made a mental note to come back before the next six months were up and to bring a few carpets with him.

Strolling along the curved hallway that surrounded the staircase, he peered into some of the rooms. This was obviously the floor they were currently working on. Several of the rooms were totally empty apart from plastering and painting gear. He continued on round the edge until he found one of the finished rooms. It was far from the glorious majesty of an Imperial apartment, but as comfortable as an army officer could ever expect. He dropped his pack gratefully onto an old chest near the door and flung himself onto the bed, not bothering to shut the door behind him. He lay for long moments before sighing and sitting up; too much to do to lounge around lazily. He stood and wandered over to the window, glancing down across the complex. The view from this side looked out over the Temples of the Divine Triad, the Imperial Shrines and in the distance the ruin of the Golden House, the last palace of the Emperors, built by the ill-fated Quintus the Golden. His eyes settled on the burned hulk of stone and rubble and a flash caught his eye. As he watched, it came again and again. Long years in the army left Sabian in no doubt as to the source of the twinkle. A blade.

Removing his helmet and cloak he dropped them on the bed, searched for a key and, finding it, closed and locked the door. Walking steadily round the hall, he jogged quickly down the steps and back out into the Great Court. Across the intervening space with the gravelled path was an archway, blocked with a badly-constructed timber fence. As he approached, he saw the gap at the side where the obstruction had been shifted to allow access. Last time he'd examined this ruin was on his very first visit here, more than ten years ago and there'd been no such obstruction then. Nothing had been organised then on the scale it was now.

Lifting the wood aside, he scraped past it, fretting at the sound of his cuirass grating on the archway's stone. Once past, he walked carefully down the dark corridor and trod gingerly among the fallen stones and puddles until he emerged, blinking, into the light. The ruins of the grand scheme that had been the Golden House lay sad and mouldering in the midday sun. As he pondered where to start, there came the sound of sword ringing on metal. He carefully made his way through a crumbling passageway, treading carefully among the uneven blocks of fallen masonry. Reaching out to steady himself, his hand rested on a support from a vaulted roof and the stone came away loose in his hand, crashing to the floor. Regaining his balance, he examined his hand and wiped the unpleasant reddish-brown slime from his skin with disgust.

Minutes later, as he carefully edged his way through the bones of the palace, he found himself at the entrance to an octagonal courtyard. He glanced around and realised that this huge space would have been enclosed long ago. The vaulting for a large dome was still visible at the periphery. In the centre of the space stood a young man of perhaps twenty years of age surrounded by wooden stakes driven into the ground, each bearing a piece of scrap metal, dented and torn. The young man was dark haired, with a neatly trimmed beard, surprisingly tall. He wore grey tunic and breeches with soft leather boots and swung a long, straight sword in practice swings with every bit as much skill as

76

any of Sabian's NCOs. He smiled. It had been six months, but young Darius was unmistakeable. Rather than interrupt, Sabian tested the strength of the charred door frame and leaned against it, watching the young man with curiosity and interest.

Again and again the boy rained blows down on the various targets, ducking, spinning and leaping to simulate different moves as required. After one particularly heavy downward swing, he landed light on his feet facing away and placed the tip of his sword down on the ground, leaning on the hilt and breathing heavily. His voice was steady and deep though it came in gasps as his chest heaved.

"Thanks for not interrupting," he said. "Concentration's very much a part of the game, as I'm sure you know."

Sabian smiled again; Darius had the makings of a good soldier. Shame he would grow old and die without ever leaving the island, but then there were worse places to grow old and far worse places to die. The commander pushed his feelings deep down and spoke light heartedly.

"How'd you feel about a bit of live practice?" He tapped the decorative hilt of his blade idly, but the young man shook his head.

"Think I'm about done for now, commander" he replied. "I have to get the sword back to storage before it's missed anyway."

Sabian frowned.

"I thought sword practice was one of your daily duties" he queried.

Darius sheathed his blade and turned again. "It is, but only at appointed times. Right now I'm supposed to be studying Edro's comedies in my room and it's only a matter of time before they check on me. I'll see you around" he added.

He extended his arm in a gesture reminiscent of a traditional Imperial salute and picked up his bag from where it lay by a shattered column before turning to leave through one of the other exits. Sabian stepped quickly across the room and followed him, catching up easily as the lad navigated the obstacles of fallen masonry in the passage. He fell in beside him, hands clasped behind his back. Darius looked sidelong at the commander with a quirky smile and raised an eyebrow.

"You'd be better to keep your hands free here," he offered; "you never know when you might fall through the floor tiles."

The commander unfolded his arms, keeping step with difficulty due to the obstacles. He glanced at the young man.

"Mind if I tag along?" he said. "I've nothing urgent on until I meet with the elders tonight."

Darius merely shrugged and kept walking. After a few minutes, they left the ruinous palace by a rarely used exit, clambering round the bole of a large cedar tree and onto a deserted section of lawn. The young man made straight for a small door in what Sabian recognised as the student dormitory, shared by everyone from the age of five to twenty and once the slaves' quarters serving the main palace. A brisk walk across the lawn and they entered the building. Darius made his way down the corridor within and opened a side door. Sabian followed with interest and peered through the doorway. The lad crossed the room and, removing the sheathed sword, leaned it against a cupboard. Reaching up to a glazed weapon cabinet, he tapped the wooden frame with the side of his hand and the cabinet came away from the wall a little. Supporting its weight with one hand, he lifted the sword with the other and slipped it round the frame into its allotted space before pushing the whole assembly back against the wall.

The commander grinned as Darius turned to leave. "I see you've developed the art of theft in recent years" he laughed.

The young man shrugged again.

"Is it thievery if it's yours anyway?"

Without waiting for an answer, he edged past the commander and continued on down the corridor. Sabian followed once again, taking in the flaking plaster and peeling paint in the passage and stairway as he glanced around. This building could do with a little work. Stairs led up from the storage area to the dormitory proper and the two made their way to the end of the dorm vestibule where a large window looked out over the manicured lawns. Darius turned the handle of the last door on the left and swung it open before turning to the commander.

"I probably ought to get on with my studies," he said uncertainly, "but I've a bottle of elderflower wine if you want to join me. I don't get many visitors. Except those who want to teach me rubbish or have jobs for me" he added as an afterthought.

Sabian thought for only a moment.

"I'd be happy to" he smiled. "I was hoping to get in some social time before I started all the assessments." He followed the young man inside and sat on one of the chairs at the desk beneath the window. "I'm quite impressed with the progress you've made since last time I saw you. There are trainee officers in my army that couldn't hold their own against you."

The mechanical shrug again.

"I practice a lot" he replied absently. "In fact, it's most of what I do when I'm awake; that or reading treatises on war or combat. Or maybe politics."

The commander nodded and picked up a textbook, examining it briefly and speaking as he flicked through the pages with little interest in the content.

"I can understand that," he said. "I could never be bothered with all this drama crap myself. It's all a bit of a shame really, as I've the feeling you'd make a good officer."

Darius' face darkened.

"All I'll ever manage though is to end up like one of the elders here, running the island for the younger generation." He held up a dismissive hand. "Don't try and sweeten it all for me commander, I know what I am; what we all are. We're prisoners and with no hope of release. I'm not aware of why most of us are here. Some of us were even born here."

Sabian sighed. This was never a duty he'd have chosen; he was a soldier, not a jailor, and the lad was absolutely right and knew it.

"Darius," he began, "I know it's not a perfect world, but it's no better out there…"

He gestured at the door. Darius' eyes followed the motion and then returned to the floor. "I'm not a child, commander. I know a pointless platitude when I hear one, but bear this in mind: empires and princedoms come and go all the time. Nothing lasts forever; not even Velutio. One day your precious master's little empire will fall like all the others before him and we'll find our way off the island. I might not live to see it, but it'll happen."

Sabian stood, placing the book back on the desk, and made for the door.

"Very well, Darius" the commander said coldly. "I think perhaps we should end this discussion for the moment and I think I'll turn down that wine after all."

Darius looked up at him. "It might make you uncomfortable, but you know it's true. Velutio's by far the strongest of the Lords, but that just makes him a juicier target for the rest of them. Not listening to me talk about it won't make it go away."

Sabian's brows creased into a frown.

"Darius, we'll talk about this again, but when I've done the job I came to do. Maybe tomorrow. For now I'd best go and meet with the elders. Where's young Quintillian by the way? You two are usually together."

79

Darius' face darkened and he lowered his eyes.

"Quint's gone, commander" he said bleakly.

"Gone?" Sabian straightened, his hand falling automatically to the pommel of his sword. He'd no real idea who many of these people were himself, but his Lordship had always impressed on his jailor the importance of these boys. Darius had been so matter-of-fact. "Gone how? When? ... Where?"

The young man looked up and Sabian noted the tear crawling down his cheek.

"Dead, commander" he replied sharply. "Dead along with two of the better teachers. They were doing some restoration work when the Fortune Fountain collapsed on them. They're all buried in the cemetery by the orchard, ok? Now I think I've said all I really want to about that. I think you'd best go."

Sabian realised that he'd back-stepped slightly again and was now in the corridor. While he was trying to formulate a reply, Darius shut the door in his face. He stepped back again and sank down onto the chest beneath the large window. Glancing over his shoulder, he could see across the well tended lawn and to the orchard and the cemetery beyond. This changed things. He'd have liked to have got the tasks done first, but now he'd best get a message to Velutio. His Lordship would want to know about this immediately. Standing once again, he jogged down the corridor and descended the stairs. If he got to the dock fast, the ship might have time to get back to the city before it got too dark and dangerous. His sergeant'd have to deliver the message while he stayed here.

Formulating his plans he picked up speed, gathering surprised looks as he ran, gleaming and clanking through the corridors and courtyards of the palace and down to the dock.

Darius' chest heaved from the effort of running as he pushed open the door of Sarios' chamber, gasping for breath. The old man sat with a scroll of parchment and a quill and looked up in surprise at the unexpected interruption.

"Darius" he reprimanded the boy. "Do you not know how to knock?"

The young man gasped.

"S... sir. I had to tell Sabian they were dead. He... he's gone to the boat."

Sarios moved his left hand and the scroll contracted into a coil, the still wet ink running and blurring. He took a deep breath.

"Then I hope you've been studying your drama, Darius" the old man said with deep feeling. "We're going to need to play this very convincingly and if he's sent for Velutio, we'll have a most attentive audience."

Chapter VIII.

Commander Sabian stood on the turf by the dock, watching as the ship bumped along the wood, sending spray into the air. Velutio stood in the prow with Crosus, the captain of his personal guard and a few of the guardsmen. Sabian ground his teeth; Crosus irritated him intensely. As head of the army, Sabian theoretically outranked the captain, but Crosus served directly under his Lordship and thus treated the commander as an equal and made every effort to undermine his authority with the troops. Velutio's steely eyes alighted on Sabian, his severe iron grey hair remaining unruffled in the strong breeze and his helm held by his side. He rarely wore armour these days, except on ceremonial occasions, but when he did it was always very traditional and practical armour rather than the decorative rubbish that some of the lords preferred.

With a crunch, the ship came to rest and Sabian's sergeants rushed to extend the boarding plank. He was relieved to note that the unit forming up on the deck was his own veteran unit and not one of Crosus' guard. He'd sent specific instructions with his senior sergeants as to who to bring with them, but had half expected Crosus to have overridden the instruction. Fortunately, his Lordship had had enough trust in his most able commander to abide by his advice. The plank was extended and the colour party alighted on the dock. Velutio stepped forward to face Sabian, who noted that Crosus had placed his hand on the pommel of his sword and strode ahead to remain at his chief's shoulders. Velutio's voice when he addressed the officer was cold, hard and business-like.

"Sabian. Show me the graves."

No preamble, but the commander was prepared for this.

"Yes sir" he replied, equally professionally. "Would you prefer to meet with Minister Sarios first? He's awaiting you in the dining hall with his staff."

Velutio shook his head, already stepping past the commander and starting up the gravel path so that Sabian was forced to step quickly and fall in beside his Lordship. He cleared his throat.

"I've not had time to run all the assessments I need to" he reported. "By the time we were ready last night, it was already getting dark. I've had the entire population of the island report to the dining hall for your inspection. I've run a head-count and only the three are missing."

Velutio's only response was a grunt. Crosus kept close, not more than four steps behind his lord, watching his opposite number with narrowed eyes. Sabian's unit were assembling on the grass by the dock before they made their way to the palace. As the command party approached the great gate house, it struck Sabian as odd to see the place with no wandering life, everyone having been sent to the hall. He'd never seen the island empty before. It felt sad and hollow.

"I've visited the graves sir," he continued, "but I'm still not sure why they're so important. We've had deaths here plenty of times." Sabian continued on a step automatically as Velutio came to a sudden halt and turned to Crosus.

"Go back to the commander's unit" he ordered his captain. "Have them form in the Ibis Courtyard and keep them at attention." He turned to Sabian and frowned as Crosus gave one last suspicious look at the commander while he descended the path toward the dock once more. Once the two were alone, Velutio fixed the commander with his resolute gaze. His voice was tight.

"Sabian, have you ever given any thought to who these people are?"

The commander shrugged. "I know who some are," he replied, "but I've never made it my business to find out. A prisoner's a prisoner sir and who they are makes no difference to how they're treated."

Velutio nodded and his posture relaxed a little.

"Commander," he said patiently, "these are all political prisoners and are all of importance. Every man, woman or child on this island has a history in the machinery of the old Empire. They may be useful to me one day and that is why they are allowed virtual autonomy here and to get on with their lives as they wish so long as I always know where to find them and no one else can. Sarios may appear the most dangerous because of his past position and knowledge, but the two boys are far more important in the grand scheme of things."

Sabian merely raised a questioning eyebrow in response and his Lordship continued.

"Quintillian? You must be able to make something of the name."

The commander shrugged. "He's named for Quintus the Golden sir. The son of some minor officials in the palace who died years ago, or so he told me once."

Velutio shook his head and his voice lowered. "Quintillian *was* the son of a palace official, but there's nothing minor about it. His father was Quintillus, master of the Horse and brother to the Emperor.

It's the same blood and that makes him the nephew of Quintus." Velutio sighed. "Last survivor of the line."

Sabian whistled through his teeth and rubbed his hair. "I'd always assumed some kind of distant connection sir, but I've never read anything about a survivor. They were supposed to have all died."

Velutio rounded his shoulders as he went on. "The very existence of Quintillian has been a closely guarded secret since the day Caerdin burned the madman in his house. Quintillian was just a baby then and fortuitously came into my possession when his parents died."

Sabian's eyes narrowed. "What about Darius then, sir?" he added. "Is he a distant member of the line? Why's he important?"

Velutio shook his head and gestured for the two of them to start walking once again.

"If anything, that boy's probably more dangerous than Quintillian, but for entirely different reasons" he said darkly, and after a pregnant pause: "and as closely guarded a secret as his friend. I imagine that I and Minister Sarios are the only people who know his surname and I think that's one secret I wish to keep commander."

For a moment, Sabian's step faltered again. A light dawned in his mind, but to speak of such a thing to Velutio could be to open a poisonous subject. Darius was perhaps twenty years old, very much the same as Quintillian. He was officially an orphan on the island and no one ever spoke his surname if they knew it. There were only two or three names in the Empire that were important enough to conceal, and only one of those had particular relevance to Velutio. Caerdin. Darius had to be the Caerdin child.

Sabian was thirty four years of age and had only been young when Quintus died, but he remembered the tales of Kiva Caerdin and knew all too well the story of that fateful battle that raged around the Caerdin estate at Serfium shortly after. They'd said that the Caerdin woman and child had died, but then who was it who'd walked away from that battle a victor but Velutio and the truth was his to keep. Of course Darius had to be Caerdin and that also explained a great deal about him. Time and time again Sabian had read the three campaign diaries Kiva had written and he knew a great military mind when he read one.

He glanced sidelong at his silent superior as they walked, his mind racing down unexpected channels. Caerdin had not been the only Imperial marshal; the commander was walking next to another this very minute and there was a history between these men. He wondered what it would have been like if Caerdin had been the one to come away from that fight. A man with intelligence and charisma like that? Hell, he'd have been Emperor by now if he'd lived.

Sabian returned his gaze to the path ahead and continued to mull things over silently as they walked through the courtyards and corridors to the orchards on the south of the island. He'd always considered Caerdin the most impressive of all the great generals of the Imperial past. The man had been a tactical genius and an impressive individual combatant by all accounts, eclipsing all his contemporaries; even Velutio. Sabian had modelled his battlefield strategies on Caerdin's Northern Campaigns and with the benefit of hindsight, he could see how Darius came to be the clever and athletic swordsman he was. Dear Gods, if he'd known this island held such blood he might have spent more time here. Still, Darius should be no real threat to Velutio's power even if he knew who he really was. Perhaps Sabian should try and persuade his Lordship to allow the boy a commission in his army.

The commander shook himself from private speculation as they entered the orchard. He cleared his throat and addressed Velutio, pointing between the trees. "The graveyard's just beyond that row of cherry trees, sir" he said. "You can see the three freshly-dug graves from here. They're the closest."

Velutio nodded and, as they left the shelter of the branches and moved from a floor of twigs and fallen fruit onto neat turf, the lord of the most powerful city in the Empire stared down at three meagre wooden gravestones with a look of deep concentration. He came to a halt by the last of the three and folded his hands behind his back, rocking on his heels. He glanced over his shoulder toward the palace and then back at the commander. His voice took on an edge harder than before.

"Detail a company of your men to exhume these graves."

Sabian blinked.

"Exhume sir?" he asked in surprise.

Velutio rounded on the commander, beginning to look a little angry.

"Yes, exhume," he repeated himself, impatience making his voice deep and sinister. "I want all three bodies on display and my personal physician brought from the ship to examine them. I don't like this one bit."

Without needing the command repeated again, Sabian saluted and jogged off back to the Ibis Courtyard. As he passed through the gate toward the palace proper, Crosus appeared in the archway and stopped, folding his arms. His lip curled into a sneer.

"Bit of a mess you've made of this one, Sabian."

The commander bridled. "I'm no jailor" he replied, "but I'm a soldier and a good officer and anytime you feel the need to put that to the test, duelling's still legal. I've always thought your throat would look better with three feet of steel jutting out of it." Without waiting for another pointless comment, he pushed past the guard captain and as he entered the marble enclosure his sergeants came to attention, though Sabian waved aside the discipline with a half-hearted salute.

"Sergeant," he said, his face devoid of expression, "detail ten men for duty exhuming graves and have them get to the graveyard as fast as they can." He continued as the sergeant nodded. "Have a runner sent down to the ship for his Lordship's physician and have him sent to the same place. Then fall the rest out and relax for a while. I have the feeling it'll be some time before you'll get to relax again."

The sergeant saluted and turned to the unit, bellowing orders. Leaving the logistics in the hands of his officers, Sabian jogged back through the archway and off to the graveyard. He had a horrible sinking feeling. He'd automatically trusted these people and assumed that everything was as it seemed. If Velutio doubted it, though…

A few minutes later, he slowed to a walk and came to stand beside his liege. Velutio was staring off into the distance across the sea while Crosus stood on his other side, glaring at Sabian. Velutio cleared his throat and addressed Sabian without a glance.

"The graves are likely empty commander," he said with cold conviction. "If there *is* anyone in there, my physician will check them and I'm absolutely certain you will find that they are not who they are supposed to be."

Sabian frowned.

"How can you be so sure sir?" he asked.

Velutio folded his arms and nodded toward the graves.

"You don't know the histories of these people, commander" the older man said in a matter-of-fact manner," but I know every single one. Apart from Quintillian, these three were Tomas Castus and Enarion Stavo. Castus was harbourmaster for the imperial island and Stavo was Quintus' personal courier. I don't know how they managed to find a way to get off this island without using the channel to Velutio. It's theoretically impossible, but if anyone could do it, it would be those two."

86

Sabian frowned and scanned the walls with frustration. At most places on the island the turf met the water and the walls were far enough down to afford a good view of the sea from the palaces, but here were cliffs and the walls were too high to see the water beyond.

"Sir," he began, "I've spoken to people who used to sail the passage in the days when the Imperial engineers kept it safe; I've spoken to architects who've done studies of the palaces; I've read a number of books on the place since I took on this jailor's job, and never anywhere have I found a sign that there is any other navigable route to Isera than through the narrow."

Velutio turned once more towards the commander. He looked a little tired now.

"Sabian," he sighed, "just because no one has ever documented a thing doesn't mean it's not there. *Someone* knows a way through the reefs; a safe channel. Never assume you know everything. If I'd thought for a minute that this island was completely secure, would I ever have assigned you to keep an eye on the place?"

He provided his own answer before Sabian could speak.

"No, commander. Though I don't want you to think that I hold you in any way responsible for any of this. It had to happen eventually."

Sabian blinked. It hadn't occurred to him that blame might land with him anyway. He was guiltless. Gritting his teeth at the unpleasant smile Crosus was giving him from behind Velutio, he glanced back over his shoulder and saw the exhumation party and the doctor making their way to the graves.

Stepping back beneath the cherry trees, he leaned heavily against the bole of one of them while he watched his men digging. If they found nothing, he'd have to take charge of the situation pretty damn quick. Praying to fortune for all to be in order, he cleared his throat and addressed his Lordship again.

"Sir, unless you really need me right now, I ought to go and address my men. They'll be draped around the Ibis courtyard waiting for orders."

"Do that Sabian," Velutio nodded and raised his hand, "but be back here in ten minutes and have some of your men bring the elders down here with you."

"Yessir."

Sabian trotted off once more toward the main palace and the Ibis courtyard. His two senior sergeants stood by the Arch of the Four Seasons, deep in conversation. They came to attention as Sabian jogged into the yard and slowed to a halt. He glanced around.

"Where are the men?" he asked. "I told you to fall them out for now."

The sergeants nodded and the younger of the two addressed his commander in a clear, sure voice.

"Yes sir" he replied efficiently. "Four companies are fallen out and are relaxing on the grass outside the gate, two of mine and two of Cialo's. The other two have been set on guard at strategic points as best as we can manage; none of us know the layout of the place very well sir."

"Nice job lads," Sabian smiled. "Now Cialo, go get your two resting companies and bring them back here." He pointed to a set of windows high up on one side of the courtyard. "I'm going to fetch the elders."

The sergeant saluted and ran off through the great gate toward the sloping lawn. Sabian sighed; he had a really bad feeling about today. Entering through a decorative archway, he pushed open a heavy oak door and slowly climbed the stairs. This had once been the Raven Palace; the administrative centre where the senior Imperial officials had lived and worked. Minister Sarios had spent most of his free life here, controlling the intricacies of Empire, and had continued in the same building for a further two decades of captivity. With a sense of foreboding, Sabian climbed the stairs, trying to gather his thoughts and formulating his words before he reached the huge wooden double doors to the dining hall and pushed them open.

"Good morning" he addressed the assembly. "His Lordship wants the elders to join us at the graveyard, so please gather yourselves and make your way down to the courtyard. The rest of you'll have to wait here for the moment."

He turned on his heel and started back through the doors to the stairs as the room behind him erupted with muttered conversation. He stopped at the head of the stairs and sighed. Without turning, he cut through the murmur with a loud clear voice.

"Now!" he shouted.

As he started down the beautifully crafted marble staircase, he heard the inhabitants shuffling toward the door in confusion. Pausing a second at the bottom with his hand resting on a slightly damaged ivory carving of an elephant, Sabian waited for the elders to catch up a little. He stepped to one side of the door, noting with satisfaction the companies forming in the Ibis Courtyard. Gesturing to the small crowd to continue on into the open, he made a mental count as they shuffled past. All the elders he could think of seemed to be present, as well as a few people he only vaguely recognised. Toward the rear of the group came Darius. For a moment Sabian considered hauling the lad out of the line and telling him to go back, but the realisation of the importance of the boy both in intrinsic terms and to this particular situation got the better of him. If he didn't take Darius, he was fairly sure his Lordship would ask why he hadn't. The group assembled in a small knot in front of the two companies of soldiers and Sabian took one last glance up the stairs before he ventured out into the sunlight.

The companies of men were at attention and the islanders stood silently, their intent eyes locked on the commander. Sabian gestured toward the arch with one arm and the courtyard began to empty. The commander fell in alongside the rear company of soldiers, side by side with the sergeant. He walked with his back straight and his arms by his sides, every inch the military commander on a mission. Within, however, he was still hoping that the graves would contain the bodies of those they declared and that the island could be left to its own devices while he went back to his house in Velutio. Hope, but not belief. He shaded his eyes and saw the small group standing around the graves. His Lordship turned and looked in their direction, his attention presumably drawn by the racket the companies of men and the group of muttering elders made.

He picked up a little speed and bypassed the group, coming to the front just as they arrived at the burial site. Sabian noted with some distaste the twisted forms of three bodies that lay on the grass, surrounded by fragments of burial gear and small piles of earth. They were not pleasant to look at, damaged as they had been by falling masonry and then eaten by worms for many months. He realised that while he had his hands clasped behind his back, his fingers were crossed. Shaking his head a little, he uncrossed them and addressed the men with him.

"Fall into formation, four deep!" he barked, turning back to Velutio. The Lord glanced around at Sabian while his physician continued to examine the bodies he knelt beside. He shook his head barely perceptibly and the commander's heart fell.

The physician stood, brushing dust, earth and much worse from his hands, and addressed Velutio.

"You say these men died some time in the last six months?"

With a brief look at Sabian, who had been here half a year earlier, the lord nodded.

"They were alive at the last head count here, yes" he said.

89

The physician shook his head. "These three have been dead much longer than that," he pronounced confidently. "I would estimate two or three years ago. They do have reasonably fresh damage, however. There have been a number of wounds inflicted on them with blunt objects, possibly masonry, within the time-frame of which you speak, my Lord."

Sabian stood still as a statue. He daren't move. Velutio was almost always a calm man, but like all tightly controlled individuals, when something got past that implacable exterior, an explosion was bound to follow and the commander was determined to avoid being the target of the blast. Instead, his Lordship merely shrugged.

"Then these were the three who drowned two and a half years ago whilst fishing among the reefs" Velutio said. "I remember it clearly; as I'm sure do you, Sabian."

The commander nodded; said nothing. Waiting for the explosion still.

Velutio turned and sought out Minister Sarios in the crowd. Locating him, he strode forward. "Sarios, I would ask you to explain yourself, but I think I see your mind clearly enough. Useful for you that you'd had three deaths of people roughly the same ages as Quintillian, Castus and Stavo eh? I'd never realised that you were capable of such calculated callousness."

With no warning, Velutio swept his hand up and across Sarios' face with a resounding slap. The minister staggered and almost fell, his nose fractured and blood running in rivulets down around his mouth. Sabian lurched forward for a moment, intending to intervene, but remembered the likely consequences of such an action and forced himself to stand, impassive. Crosus craned his neck and grinned at the commander.

Sarios grimaced at the steely grey lord. "I am a prisoner for no crime" he announced loudly and defiantly. "Do what you will."

Velutio sneered. "Where are they now?"

The minister continued to glare at him. "I have no idea" he declared with deep determination.

Reaching down to his belt, Velutio drew out his gauntlets; leather gloves protected by interlocking bronze plates after the fashion of the East. Not taking his eyes off the minister, he drew the glove onto his right hand and flexed his fingers.

"I say again only once: Where is Quintillian?"

The minister held his head high and spat a large gobbet of clotted blood onto the lord's boot. Velutio clicked his tongue and then

90

brought his right hand round in another back-handed slap. This time the sound of breaking bones was audible even where Sabian stood. The commander closed his eyes, but not quick enough to miss the minister falling to the floor and the spray of blood that dampened the grass.

Velutio reached down and wrenched a length of cloth from Sarios' mantle, wiping the blood from his gauntlet. He looked up at the assembled group, as Crosus leaned across and whispered something into his ear that Sabian would have killed to have been able to hear.

"Doctor?" the lord addressed his physician without looking around.

"My Lord?" the man replied.

"Take this old fool away and make sure he doesn't die" Velutio said coldly. "I will have need of him yet."

He then finally looked around at Sabian. The commander couldn't read his master's expression and that was a bad sign. Sabian drew a sigh inwardly but kept his back rigidly straight and his features deadpan.

"Commander."

"Sir?" he responded. He knew he wasn't going to like whatever came next.

"Take the rest of this rabble back to the dining hall and lock them in" Velutio commanded. Sabian sighed in relief as he turned to his men, but too soon.

"And Sabian?"

The commander froze.

"Pick three of the young ones at random and have them crucified on the lawns" the older man said calmly as he turned on his heel and strode off in the direction of the palace. Crosus stood still a long moment savouring the look of distaste on Sabian's face before giving a brief heartless laugh and striding off after his master.

Sabian winced. Again he'd contemplated intervening but there will little chance of Velutio's mind changing and somehow, though the reason escaped him, he seemed to be slipping from Velutio's favour at a rate of knots. Instead, he walked over to the minister who lay on the grass, barely conscious, with the physician fussing around him. The commander craned his neck to see what it was the doctor was actually doing and regretted it as he saw the man pop an eyeball back into its socket. The old cleric strained to look up at him, but the pain of his damaged eye was too much and the lids closed. Sabian sighed.

"Minister," he said very quietly,"you know me as a fair man, yes?"

There was no response from Sarios, not that he'd expected one.

"I beg of you," he went on, "tell his Lordship what he wants to know. The boy's probably in great danger wherever he is. There are dangerous wars and feuds in almost every corner of the Empire and this place is at least safe, for all its nature." He sighed. "Or it was anyway."

Sarios opened his better eye painfully and the orb swivelled up to Sabian.

"You know I cannot do that" he replied. "You know who he is and you know who I am. Can you imagine I ever stopped serving?"

Sabian nodded. He could understand commitment and loyalty, particularly between this man and that boy, but the whole thing was foolish and with no worthwhile goal. He realised the physician was looking back and forth between them in curiosity. He growled at the man "this is not your concern. Just tend his wounds."

"Sarios," he continued turning back to the old man. "I sympathise, but his Lordship is going to have me crucify the young men of your island if you don't tell him and I've no wish to be a part of that. I'm a soldier not an executioner."

The minister actually smiled through the blood and bruises.

"Then you serve the wrong man, commander."

Sabian continued to crouch silently for a long moment as the old man collapsed back to the grass, his eyes closing and his breathing erratic. With a sigh of resignation, the commander stood and turned to his men.

"Sergeant Cialo," he commanded. "Have a detail produce the timber and set up three crosses on the lawn. Find some rope."

The sergeant, a long-standing member of Sabian's command and a man that could only be described as a 'grizzled veteran', nodded and turned, barking orders at his men. Sabian returned his attention to the crowd.

"Everyone back to the Raven Palace."

The elders shuffled onwards, silent now with despair settling over them. Sabian walked behind them all the way, the rest of his unit with him, barring those left to re-bury the dead. Once they entered the Ibis Courtyard, he pointed to the door leading to the dining room and, needing no verbal command the group of islanders made their way inside. Had he been less preoccupied, Sabian might have noted the absence of young Darius from the group.

As the commander contemplated how to deal with this most onerous of jobs, his sergeant and four men marched past, carrying lengths of rope and bags that clinked with a metallic sound. Sabian waved at Cialo to get his attention.

"No nails!" he ordered.

The sergeant nodded and Sabian thought the man looked a little relieved. As the five soldiers exited the courtyard through the great Gorgon Gate, they stepped respectfully aside and Velutio once more entered the courtyard, two of his private guard at his shoulders. He spotted Sabian and made directly for him. Sabian noted the absence of Crosus with trepidation. What was the wily bastard up to now?

"Commander," Velutio announced, "I am returning to the city. I have many resources at my disposal and I intend to find the boy. I'm very much afraid he will have to be killed now. I'm leaving my physician to tend the minister and I want you to crucify the three you select tonight and then ask Sarios each morning from then on where the boy is. If he actually answers you, though I can't imagine that he would, you may take down the children. If not they stay up there until they rot. I don't care who's chosen with the exceptions young Darius. He is not to be harmed. Is that clear?"

"That's clear sir," Sabian replied through gritted teeth. "When will we be returning to garrison my Lord?"

Velutio shook his head. "I've not decided yet. Certainly not for a while." he declared. "For the foreseeable future you are the garrison commander here! I want you to be hard. Fear is the most useful weapon you can have here."

As Sabian glared, anger and disgust rising in him he saw Crosus standing in the archway watching him. Something was going on here that he didn't like and being away from the rest of the army for any length of time would just tighten that bastard's hold on things. He growled.

"My Lord," he said, stressing the word unnecessarily, "I'm not a prison warden. You hired me for my skills as a commander and you're wasting them. What happens if one of the other lords launches an attack while I'm playing nursemaid here? Crosus may look like a bear, but he's not got anywhere near enough experience on the field of battle to lead your army. This is ridiculous!" He realised that he was doing exactly what he'd vowed not to earlier, but the situation was becoming increasingly untenable.

Velutio glared back at him. "*I* am the one who gives the orders commander" he growled, "and you will do what I say when I say it or by the hells I'll have *you* on a cross before I leave here. Do I make myself understood?"

Sabian stood at attention, shaking slightly with anger and gritted his teeth to bite back every retort that came naturally and unbidden. "Yes sir" he uttered, again stressing the word. Still shaking, he watched the lord turn on his heel, the two guards at his shoulders, and make for the dock. Waiting just long enough for Velutio to be out of earshot, he ran to the gatehouse and looked out over the grass to where his sergeant was erecting a 'T'-shaped structure.

"Cialo!" he called as loudly as he dare, and the sergeant turned at the sound of his name and jogged up the slope toward his commander.

"Sir?" the man reported as he came to a halt, saluting. Sabian looked around to make sure there was no other within earshot. He could see Velutio on the dock, climbing into the vessel to make his way back through the channel, his ever present guard at his shoulders. He would personally gut Crosus one day and, if the man wasn't very careful, Velutio too.

"Cialo, I have something very strange but very important to ask..."

The sergeant nodded, waiting quietly.

"You've served me for half a dozen years," the commander went on, "and I've always considered you one of the most professional and reliable soldiers I've ever known."

"Thank you sir." The sergeant didn't even smile.

Sabian sighed and leaned back against the wall. "I've sixteen sergeants under my command and four staff officers, but there are few who've seen proper service and show the signs of professional soldiering. In the old days, a soldier took an oath of loyalty to the Emperor, to the Gods and to his General. I assume that you were a member of the Imperial army?"

Cialo nodded. "I had that privilege sir. I was only a young recruit mind, but I took that oath and proud of it I was. Even fought in some of the last engagements for the Emperor."

Sabian nodded in turn.

"And have you ever taken such an oath in Velutio?"

"Well..." the sergeant thought for a moment. "No. I suppose not. His Lordship was my commander when I was in the Imperial army, so I guess he's never needed another oath?"

The commander smiled. "With whom does your allegiance lie, Cialo?"

The sergeant came further to attention, rail-straight as he replied. "My loyalty is to you, my men and the unit's insignia, sir" he announced. Sabian hushed him with lowered hands.

"For Gods' sake Cialo, not so loud" he implored. "This isn't a parade ground." The commander's smile began to broaden. "And what of your men?"

Cialo nodded. "They're yours, sir; at least as far as I know. I've never noted a word spoken against you."

Sabian nodded and continued. "Very well. I'm putting you in direct charge of the prisoners. I want you to look after them well." He gestured at the construction on the lawn. "That thing is to be finished, but not to be used, do you understand?"

Cialo nodded, a look of uncertainty on his features.

"Sir?"

The commander grinned. "As I said before," he replied, "we're soldiers, not executioners. I'll kill any man in war, but I've absolutely no intention of slaughtering young people in the hope that the minister will break when we all know that he won't."

Cialo's shoulders slumped a little. "I appreciate the sentiments sir," he added, "really I do, but his Lordship will likely have *us* executed if you do this."

Sabian smiled. "I'll work it out; you let me worry about that. All we have to do is make sure that there are no mistakes." He registered the worried look on the face of his sergeant and smiled reassuringly. "I have no intention of betraying my lord or my contract. I am a General of Velutio" he added vehemently. "But I know the value of human life and of live prisoners and it's also my job to protect his Lordship from himself when need be."

He grinned as he saw acceptance swim across the sergeant's face.

"I need to go and address the prisoners" the commander said. "As soon as his Lordship's craft is out of sight, form up all the men on the island and bring them to the Ibis Courtyard. We have a lot to do."

The sergeant saluted and as he turned to complete his task, Sabian stood for a long moment gazing out into the bay where Velutio's ship was already bucking among the waves. A second set of eyes peered out into the bright sunshine from high on the palace wall, though this pair were intent on the commander himself.

95

Chapter IX.

"Four days" Cialo commented. "No supplies; no gear; no word even! Begging your pardon sir, but can I speak freely?" Sabian nodded and the sergeant went on. "There's some who say there were raised voices the day he left. You haven't pissed him off have you sir?"

The commander shrugged. "I very possibly have, Cialo, but even if his Lordship is incensed with me, he's still bright enough to know that we'll need supplies. These people here barely grow enough to feed themselves, let alone a score of soldiers too." He sighed. "One thing that's certain: we're going to have to come to some arrangement with the islanders." He'd refused to call them prisoners, despite their evident captivity, and had encouraged his men to do the same. After all, until another ship came, the soldiers were in much the same position as their wards.

The gruff sergeant cleared his throat as the two of them walked, side by side along the wall walk. The westerly breeze carried a hint of salt but did little to temper the heat of the summer sun.

"The 'islanders' don't talk to us, sir" he grumbled. "I know they speak to you, cos you've got the power and all, but we're the enemy as far as they're concerned. They do things when we tell them, but they don't ask or answer unless they have to. Not that I can't see it from their point of view" he added quickly with a sidelong glance at his commander. "What his Lordship did to that old man made us all very unpopular, sir. Hard to see how we can come to any arrangement."

Sabian shrugged, his red military cloak fluttering in the light sea breeze. It really was a spectacular view from here. He could actually see Velutio, spread out on the lower slopes of Monte Bero and plunging out into the sea like a swimmer taking his first stroke. In the days when this was a palace complex full of glittering life, it must have been a paradise on earth.

"We're going to have to do something Cialo" the commander sighed. "No supplies and no way to reach or contact the city. How many men do we have on the island?"

Cialo made a 'harrumphing' sound again.

"Six companies, sir" he replied. "Just over a hundred men all told." He grinned. "Plus me and Iasus, 'course!"

Sabian smiled. The beginnings of a plan were forming.

"I'm going to have to go speak to the islanders." He made for the wall stairs but turned to Cialo as he reached them. "You need to find Iasus and assemble all the men somewhere out of the way, say the old bath house down by the shore. Don't keep them at attention or anything, just have everyone there by the time I'm done."

The sergeant nodded and walked back the way they'd come along the high, thick wall. Cialo had seen warfare first-hand many times and had the scars both physical and mental to prove it. Some of the men grumbled about their role here as guards, but from a veteran's point of view, what better way to live out your last few years of service than here. The place was beautiful and for the first time in years, the grizzled sergeant strode happily along the wall, a spring in his step.

As Cialo went off to round up his men, Sabian jogged down the steps and strode across the turf toward the rear doors of the Raven Palace. He couldn't work out why supplies hadn't arrived. Surely Velutio'd not be pig-headed enough to withhold their supplies just because he'd spoken out of turn. He dreaded to think what Crosus would be making of that.

His train of thought was broken by a shrill whistle. He stopped in his tracks and looked around for the source of the sound, and then up, where he spotted the figure in the tree. A young man sat with a leg hooked over one branch and his elbows resting on another.

"Morning Darius" the commander issued. He forced a smile, though his thoughts were still elsewhere. "Thought you'd have been at sword practice again on a lovely morning like this."

The boy laughed mirthlessly. "Your men impounded all the weapons, didn't they."

Sabian grunted. Of course they had. He may have cancelled the crucifixions, but he had no intention of rebelling against his command and had issued all the standard orders for prisoners of war. This would have to change of course, in the circumstances.

"True" the commander admitted. "Probably unnecessary, but an automatic response."

The boy nodded once and then unhooked his leg, swinging from the branch and releasing to land light on his feet next to the soldier.

"Ferastus, yes?" Darius inquired. "From 'on captivity' in his collected essays."

Sabian smiled, a real smile this time. "You really do know your stuff, don't you?" He squared his shoulders. "However, I don't think this place really applies to the Ferastian rules. After all, there's no way off for you or us. We're in very much the same position and perhaps some of the standard rules need to be relaxed or even changed."

Darius shook his head and the commander raised an eyebrow in surprise.

"You don't believe so?" he asked, unconvinced.

The boy shook his head again. "We're prisoners and you're an officer of our captor. You've already put yourself and your men in considerable danger by refusing to crucify our people." He smiled. "Now that's a good gesture and makes us believe in you a little, but if you relax things too much, you'll only end up bringing trouble for yourself and we'll get someone like that other captain as a replacement. I don't think that would be at all good for us."

Sabian blinked. The boy made a great deal of sense, but the commander had already made his plans. "Thing is Darius," he said, "I have no intention of becoming a jailor. I'd rather you all carried on as if we weren't here. I have a permanent lookout stationed on the gatehouse and one of your less sociable companions removed an obstructive tree for us. We'll have best part of an hour's warning when a ship appears in the channel."

He gestured for them to walk and Darius fell in beside him.

"As it happens," he added, "I'm on my way to see the elders now with a few ideas. Then, perhaps we can arrange for you to be able to continue your sword practice, eh Darius?"

Darius didn't answer. In fact he'd gone rather quiet and subdued all of a sudden as they walked toward the Raven Palace. Sabian glanced sidelong at him and cleared his throat.

"Is there something you want to say?" he asked.

Darius shook his head. "No" he replied. "Not yet at least."

Respecting the young man's decision, but eyeing him suspiciously, Sabian thought about Darius for a moment. He'd not seen the lad around since the day Velutio left and Darius was usually visible enough. He frowned, wondering what the young man was up to, but surprised himself as he realised that Darius was actually one of the few people he still trusted, despite his being a captive. Still frowning he changed the subject. "How's Sarios? I've been meaning to get in to see him since he's been awake again."

Darius shrugged. "The two doctors are arguing over him. Velutio's physician says he'll never see with his left eye again. Our own doctor disagrees and thinks he can help, but your one won't let him. It's all a bit stupid really. If someone needs help you help them in my opinion."

They had reached the door to the Raven Palace, a single wooden side door, very ornate and with carvings of serpents and gods in

98

armour, though now in a sad state of repair. Darius stopped talking and reached out, pulling the door open for Sabian to pass. The commander nodded his thanks and walked inside with the young man following. In the lower hall of the palace, Sergeant Iasus, young and fair haired, was giving out duty passwords to three soldiers. The sergeant and his men came sharply to attention as they spotted the commander. Sabian waved the salutes aside.

"Iasus, I've asked Cialo to gather the men at the baths" Sabian called. "I'd like you to do the same. Don't worry about duty passwords right now."

With a sharp bow, Iasus waved towards the door and the three soldiers exited in short order. Sabian started toward the staircase as the sergeant exited the building, but suddenly realised he was walking alone. He turned, only a few steps up, to see Darius standing still in the doorway, glaring out after the exiting soldiers. The commander's brow furrowed.

"Darius, what the hell is wrong?"

The boy shook his head as if to clear it from a daze.

"I don't know," he replied, walking toward the steps." Maybe nothing, but I'm just not sure." Sabian frowned. The boy had good instincts and if he had suspicions then Sabian should know about them.

"Darius, talk to me."

Again a shake of the head. "I'll tell you when there's really something to tell" the boy said quietly and began to ascend the steps, his gaze still fixed on the doorway to the courtyard. Sabian shook his head. Caerdin had been a complicated man by all accounts and if he was the man's son, then it obviously ran in the blood. Reaching the top of the stairs the commander walked toward the open double door that led into the ancient dining room. Though once the administrative staff of the Empire had eaten in this room, it served more these days as a senate for the elders and if Sabian ever wanted to speak to one of them it was rare he would find the room empty.

He stepped inside and admired the décor. Unlike most of the structures on the island, this room retained much of its original wall painting and decorative plaster, creating scenes of hunting and nature, garlands of flowers and beautiful solitary columns and arches. A mosaic covered the central square recess in the floor, depicting frolicking nymphs with jars of water. On the raised floor around all the edges would once have been recliners where the powerful men of Empire would lie to eat. These days they were rickety wooden chairs and tables full of documents and lists. Three of the elders whose names escaped him stood at just such a table, arguing over a list.

As Darius reached the top of the staircase, Sabian cleared his throat loudly. The three elders stopped mid-sentence and turned to face the newcomers. The commander smiled. "I'm not sure who I need to speak to in the absence of the Minister?" He left the question hanging. One of the three, a man of some fifty five or sixty years of age, stepped away from the table.

"I am Turus, also a minister, once in charge of the treasury. You can speak to me."

Sabian stepped across the room and brought himself up in front of the man.

"Very well Minister Turus." His voice took on an efficient, military tone. "It has been brought to my attention that there is no interaction between your islanders and my men. This is a sad state of affairs when we are forced to live in such close proximity and I feel it's time to change the way a few things are done around here."

Turus narrowed his eyes. In a face not much given to humour, his appearance hardened. "I'd imagined this was coming, but I'd expected it sooner commander. What are we to do now? Be herded into one building and restricted in our movement perhaps?"

Sabian smiled again, but the smile was tight and hard.

"You would be wise, Turus," the commander said, "to take lessons in courtesy and observation from your leader once he is better. If you had opened your eyes you would be well aware that I am carrying out my orders with the loosest possible leash and trying to make the best of a bad lot for all involved."

Turus opened his mouth with some retort, but Sabian cut him off before he could begin. "I think you'd better stay quiet and listen Turus before you get yourself into trouble." He relaxed his stance a little and became aware of Darius standing by his side, almost supportively. Good. That might lend extra weight to his words in this place. "We need to work on our interaction. Our supplies have not arrived and, while I have absolutely no intention of letting my men starve, I also refuse to commandeer all the goods you have put so much work into. There is precious little need here for guards right now and I shall put my men to work for the benefit of the community, in return for which, you can pay us in food and goods."

Turus stared at the commander and then turned to look at the other two elders by the table. Sabian couldn't see his face, but could imagine how it looked. He drew another breath and finished his

100

proposal. "I need you to run an inventory along the same lines that I do on a biannual basis and detail the quantity of all your supplies so that we can work out a reasonable and fair split. In the meantime, I must go to address my troops. With the exception of blustering and complaining have you any comments?"

The minister turned once more to face Sabian.

"Are there any engineers among your men?"

The commander smiled.

It was late afternoon by the time Sabian finally reached the bathhouse and he imagined that the soldiers had probably waited over an hour. Still, it had been worth it. Once he'd actually got through the stubborn shell of Minister Turus, the man turned out to have a more than able command of administrative duties, as one would expect of someone who once held such an important position. As soon as Turus had started questioning, the other two elders had joined in and the ideas had begun to flow thick and fast. Darius had spent most of the time sat on one of the tables to one side watching with interest, but had occasionally piped up with his opinion, though only where it mattered and was of use. As Sabian had finally managed to excuse himself, the elders had continued to plan and prepare and had sent Darius to fetch the rest of the council.

The bathhouse had not been used since the end of the Empire and, though it was still intact, was sadly neglected and dilapidated. As the commander approached, he could smell the rank odour of fetid scummy water and damp plaster. It came as no surprise then when he rounded the corner to find his troops sat in groups on the lawn close by; he couldn't blame them for not waiting inside. The spot itself was actually rather nice as long as the wind stayed how it was, carrying the aroma of decay away from the men. The bathhouse was one of at least four on the island, none of which were still in commission. This particular one was the largest; the one designed for the general community in the palace. There were two in the actual Imperial palaces that had served the Imperial household and there was one that had served the palace guard, but these were all also currently out of commission. This particular complex was next to the sea, with a fresh water channel that ran down from the cisterns in the palace proper. It stood outside the walls, with a small postern gate allowing access.

The troops struggled to their feet to come to attention as they saw their commander come round the corner of the bathhouse, but Sabian waved it aside and announced "at ease everyone."

As the soldiers fell back onto the grass smiling, Sabian looked around. Spotting an old altar to the Goddess of hygiene leaning against the wall, he walked over and took a seat on it, crossing his legs. He was in uniform but unarmed and unarmoured, his equipment being locked away in the chest in his room.

"Gather round lads" he said and the men shuffled forward into a semicircle around their commander. "Ok" he began. "As of now you can consider yourself off-duty as soldiers. I'm sure you're already sick to death of patrolling empty walls and grounds when you know there's no enemy and no trouble, yes?"

There was a murmur of agreement and a small amount of joking and laughter.

"So we don't really need guards or soldiers, yes?"

Again a buzz of general agreement.

The commander smiled. "So what we really need at the moment are skilled civilians. Supplies have not arrived as I'm sure you're aware and we can't keep living off the islanders' supplies or in the end we'll all starve. Whether our supplies arrive or not, we may be here for a long time and anything we can do to improve conditions on the island will improve things for us as well as for them. I take it you all see that, yes?"

The buzz returned, but died away as sergeant Iasus held his hand high.

"Sir," the sergeant offered, "I know we're being lenient on these people and there are to be no crucifixions or beatings, but is it really our job to help them improve their prison? Aren't we just giving them false hope?"

Sabian smiled again. "False hope is better than no hope sergeant" he replied. "I for one want to be able to bathe. That's going to be one of the first things to attend to, I think."

He addressed the crowd in general once more. "I've spoken with minister Turus already and he's preparing me a list of the islanders who have specialised skills. I need to do some working out with you lot too. I know that in the old days the Imperial army taught skilled trades to the soldiers as well as just fighting skills and I assume that some of you older ones are the product of that army, yes?" The murmur went around again.

Sabian sighed and produced a scrap of parchment that had seen better days and a stylus. "Firstly, have any of you got any kind of engineering background." Three hands went up, including sergeant Cialo. Sabian grinned. "Well done, Cialo. You've just volunteered to command the engineering section. Looks like you've two able seconds as well. That's handy, cos I've three duties lined up for them."

Cialo craned his neck to see two older veterans at the back with their hands raised. He turned back to the commander and returned the smile. "Let me guess sir: the bathhouse, yes?"

Sabian nodded. "First duty of the engineering detail. Clean out, repair and restore this bathhouse. You'll need to do a lot of repair work on the aqueduct channels that run down to here as well as on the drainage pipes to the sea. The actual water source at the top must be in working order as the fountains in the courtyards have been repaired, though I gather as a source of fresh water rather than for decoration." He took a deep breath. "Which leads me to the second engineering duty. The actual water-carriage system around the entire palace needs looking at. If they've had to restore the fountains for water, then there is some kind of blockage preventing the water from entering the buildings. This can be taken care of and then the buildings will have clean water again and maybe be can even work on the internal baths then. The third duty will be to survey the entire island. I want to know every piece of dangerous masonry, every conceivable landing point on the shore, where fishing jetties can be constructed and so on." He coughed. "Are there any questions?"

Cialo grunted. "That's a hell of a lot of work sir. Just how many people are you thinking of assigning?"

Sabian smiled. "I want you to ask for volunteers. Take forty men; the best you can find for the job. There are several locals who will be joining you, including the man responsible for the fountains. He probably knows this water system better than anyone. It's up to you how you split the duties. They can all be done at once if you want to split them into three squads, or one after the other if you think that's best. You're the engineer."

"The second detail," he announced, returning his attention to the group as a whole, "will be responsible for repairs and decorating in various buildings. One of the palace elders already has a schedule of works that the islanders have been adhering to, so I see no reason to deviate from that. I'm thinking of maybe twenty men for that detail. Preferably those with some small level of skill in the area, but I don't think we'll be too fussy." He pointed at a short rather plump soldier at the front. "Even Crispin here can wield a brush!" The group laughed.

"The third detail has the hardest work I think, but the most important job. Any of you who aren't assigned to a group will need to join the workforce on the island and involve yourselves in farming, fishing and all other sources of food production. I'll warn you against fishing until we've surveyed the coast unless you've a stout heart and you're a damn good swimmer, but I'll leave that up to you and your individual skills."

He sighed and leaned back against the wall. "Now, I intend on keeping a small group still as guards and lookouts. Maybe a dozen men in three four-man rotating squads on eight hour shifts. That'll be the last. Everyone should be involved then." He looked down at Iasus. "Which of the other details do you want to take sergeant?"

Iasus looked up at the commander, distaste showing on his face. "I think I'd be happier leading the guard detail sir. It's what I'm trained for."

Sabian nodded. He couldn't imagine Iasus the farmer anyway.

"Very well." He handed the papyrus and stylus to Iasus and addressed the entire group. "The two sergeants will call for volunteers and assign squads. I'll be joining the island's council at least until Sarios is capable of the role again. When the groups are chosen and you've picked out a few leaders or representatives, get your men together and start planning. First thing in the morning I want a small deputation from each detail to come to the council of elders in the Raven Palace and discuss how we proceed."

Leaving the group muttering and arguing, Sabian held his breath as he walked past the door of the bathhouse and toward the Water Gate on his way back to the palace. If nothing else at least he would be able to bathe soon and the troops would be kept busy and occupied. He remembered in the accounts of Caerdin's northern campaigns that the army had been garrisoned throughout the winter and the troops were becoming increasingly restless and lazy. The general had set his entire army to building a wall of turf and timber that stretched fully twenty five miles across the Galtic Narrows that he'd defended a decade earlier. This was much the same principle though the conditions were greatly different. Thoughts of Caerdin inevitably led his mind back to the subject of Darius and he wondered where the boy was. There were a few hours before he needed to interrupt the elders, but other jobs he could be doing. He stopped for a moment by the dilapidated Imperial shrines and pondered where to go first. Probably best to visit Sarios he thought and, sighing gently, headed for the Raven Palace once more.

The minister was being kept in his rooms at the palace on the top floor, above the continually-used dining room. Sabian wondered whether they'd been the rooms he'd occupied twenty-some years ago. Probably, knowing the man. He made his way to the small rear door once more and turned left inside along one of the marble corridors whose windows looked out over pleasant greenery. At the end, a spiral staircase led up through both floors and down into the cellars. He climbed the steps, formulating in his mind a greeting for the leader of the island's community and at the top made his way to the suite at the end of the corridor. The door was ajar and he could hear raised voices within. He paused before entering, listening to an argument in full swing inside. Two doctors disagreeing about treatments. Although he had precious little understanding of the detail of their conversation, one thing shone out clear: Velutio's doctor was advising some safe slow course of action that would result in no harm to the minister but would leave him permanently blind in one eye. The island's doctor was advocating some radical treatment that sounded very visceral to Sabian that might save the eye, but could put the man's life in danger. He grunted. Not a conversation he felt inclined to stand in the middle of. Taking a deep breath again, he pushed the door open. It took a few moments for the two red-faced doctors to notice him and the argument stopped suddenly.

"Good afternoon, gentlemen" Sabian greeted them. "If I may, I would like to see your patient if he's conscious."

The island's doctor, 'Favio' the commander seemed to remember, cleared his throat. "He's conscious but resting in the next room." He then turned and glared at the other doctor, who returned the look.

Sabian's patience was rapidly wearing thin. He stood for a moment until they both looked back at him. He gestured angrily with his thumb and the two filed over to the door. Once they were standing before him he spoke, his tone a low menacing whisper. "Don't you think you should be discussing things like this out of earshot of your patient? He's half-blind, not deaf!" The two doctors looked at each other sheepishly and Velutio's physician nodded. Sabian stepped to one side while the two doctors filed out into the corridor. He waited until they'd exited and slammed the door early, hard enough to hit one of them in the back.

He sighed and made his way to the bedroom door, which was shut. This room was less than opulent and mirrored the personality of its occupant perfectly. Functional would be Sabian's description. He drew a long breath and rapped lightly on the door.

"Yes?"

Turning the handle, Sabian wasn't sure what he'd expected from the inner sanctum of the island's leader, but this certainly wasn't it. The room was well-appointed but bore more of a resemblance to a shrine or a storage room than a chamber. Busts of the Emperors and great men lined one wall on innumerable shelves. The wall behind the bed was decorated with a fine mosaic map of the Empire at its height. A third wall bore more shelves containing numerous artworks of the highest quality, all of which had presumably been removed from places on the island and brought here to preserve them. The floor bore a huge mosaic of a raven surrounded by the incarnations of the old Provinces and the final wall contained three huge windows that lit the room. The only furniture inside were the bed, a small writing desk covered with documents, a chair and two altars, one to the protective spirits of the household and the other to the Imperial cult. In the midst of this veritable museum lay Sarios, half his head bandaged, propped up on pillows and cushions. The minister managed a weak smile as he recognised his visitor.

"Commander. It's good to see you. I hear good things about your command of the island."

Sabian shrugged. "I'm glad you're looking better now. As for 'good things', I'm not so sure about that. I just don't like to see needless cruelty." He smiled. "Actually, I'm just embarking on a few projects around the island. I don't like my men to get lazy."

Sarios smiled again and tried to pull himself a little more upright on the pillows. Sabian rushed to the bedside and helped the old man pull himself up. Sarios gratefully relaxed in a better position and then looked up at the commander with his good eye. "Thank you. I feel so useless, but it's a terrible thing when you get old and feeble. He only hit me twice, but I feel like I've spent a day in the arena entertaining the crowd." Again the smile. Sabian couldn't help but admire the man.

"I just really dropped in to see how you were and how they were treating you. I take it you were listening to the two idiots outside your door?"

Sarios nodded. "It's hard to avoid it when all there is to do is to lie here." He beckoned to the commander with his finger. "Actually, I'd like to ask you a favour." Sabian nodded, silent, and the minister continued. "I want our own doctor to deal with me. I know it's a risk, but he really does know what he's doing, I assure you."

Sabian tapped his finger on his lips. "Perhaps" he muttered. "I'm loathe to put you in any more danger though."

The minister nodded. "Still, I would wish it." He glanced over at the table near the window. "I actually got up yesterday for a few minutes and strung some thoughts and ideas together. Perhaps you'd be good enough to take that top sheet and see the council of elders with it?"

Sabian nodded again. "I'd be happy to. Unless you need me for anything though, I'd better get on. There's a lot to do" he added. Sarios nodded gently. "I'd better sleep anyway. That's one of the few things both doctors can agree on."

Without another word, the commander bowed and retrieved the top sheet of paper from the table. Glancing at it briefly on the way out, he noted a list of things that needed to be done, including a priority list for the upcoming vegetable harvest. He smiled. Great minds, eh? As he left, he made sure the chamber door was shut tight and opened the outer door to leave the apartment. The island's doctor stood in the corridor still and he turned with a start as Sabian appeared.

"Ah, commander" the doctor said. "Darius was by here and wants you to go see him when you're free. He said you'd know where."

Sabian nodded. "I think I know. By the way, I'm inclined along with the minister to ask you to deal with his treatment your way. If you see Velutio's doctor, please tell him to find me tonight. I would warn you though that I will be *very* unhappy if anything untoward happens to Sarios, so make sure your treatment works." To add weight to his words the commander had bunched one hand into a fist and was rubbing the knuckles with his other hand as he spoke. The doctor nodded solemnly with no trace of fear. "I'll do my best," he replied.

Sabian fixed him eye to eye for a long moment and then stepped around him and continued on down the corridor to stop and collect something on the way.

The ruins of the Golden House mouldered and smelled dank even in the late afternoon sun. The day was wearing on rapidly now and the sun was diminishing behind the high perimeter walls even as Sabian, once more armed and armoured, picked his way among the rubble. Turning the corner, he immediately spotted Darius seated on a timber in the centre of the octagonal room, idly twiddling a short dagger in his hand. He looked up as the commander appeared in the shattered doorway and nodded a greeting. Sabian strode into the centre and, reaching down to his belt, unhooked an extra sword from his left side. Holding the sheathed blade out to the young man, he nodded.

"I've talked to the elders" he smiled, "and I want you to continue your training. In fact, I'm going to make sure you're not interrupted by things like poetry. You can keep this with you; it's not going back in the weapon cabinet."

Darius grinned lopsidedly back at him. "Thanks. Somehow it feels wrong not to have sword practice." Sabian inwardly agreed. He felt the same himself and imagined the boy's father was much the same. The lad unsheathed the blade and gave it a few practice swings. "This isn't the sword I was using" he noted.

Sabian sat on one of the fallen boulders. "No," he replied, "this is a northern sword with a heavy hilt and a slight curvature, like the barbarian tribes to the north use. It doesn't do to limit yourself to one blade. If you find yourself in dire straits and needing to use what's to hand, you might not be able to wield it effectively. Plus I have to say that the northern tribes designed one of the best weighted implements of war ever created." He smiled, patting the sheath still hanging by his side that carried a blade of very similar design.

Darius examined the slight curve thoughtfully. "That makes sense I suppose. It's a little heavier than the other one too, even though it's shorter. Going to take a bit of getting used to…"

Unhooking his own scabbard, Sabian laid his own blade across his knees. "I assume you were interested in some live practice? Is that why you asked me here?"

The young man glanced up and turned the blade, sheathing it very professionally. Sabian once more had to acknowledge what a natural Darius was.

"Actually I had other reasons" admitted the boy. "And I needed somewhere fairly private to talk to you. You weren't followed, were you?"

Sabian blinked. He'd not looked. Why on earth would he be followed? Seeing the commander's face Darius smiled and, reaching up to part of the ruinous vaulting hauled himself up to the wall level. Though the sun was now hidden by the fortress-like walls of the palace, at that height the boy's head was once more in bright light. He shaded his eyes and glanced around the ruin. Satisfied they were truly alone he dropped, cat-like to the floor.

"We seem to be fine."

Sabian frowned. "I don't think you should climb here; the masonry's too dangerous. And I think you'd better explain all this" he added darkly.

108

Taking his seat on the timber again with the blade across his knees mirroring Sabian, the boy nodded. "Don't worry about the walls. I've been here all my life and I know which ones are stable. As for the other, I think you've got a problem."

"A problem?" enquired the commander, one eyebrow raised.

Another nod from the boy. "I think some of your men may be less than trustworthy."

Sabian bridled. "Be careful what you say Darius, I..."

The young man waved his hands to dismiss the words. "I don't mean it like that. I..." He tailed off and looked down at the floor. "I actually trust you commander." He looked up again. "Have you any idea how difficult that is for me; for any of us here? We know you work for Velutio and that he basically owns us as though we were slaves, and yet *you* I can't help but trust. Perhaps it's the fact that you remind me so much of the military men I read about in the old days."

Sabian shrugged. "I try to be fair. Where are you going with this, Darius?"

Again the boy looked a touch uncomfortable. "The day Velutio left the island I was on the roof, watching him go. I also saw you talking to your sergeant. You were quiet but I could hear, and since I was in earshot, the man in the soldier's uniform on the wall certainly could."

The commander's shrugged again.

"What's odd about that?" he probed. "We had guards on the walls."

The young man shook his head. "I don't know who he was. I only saw his back and he was partially hidden, but definitely wearing a uniform and definitely watching you. He wasn't on any kind of duty though, cos he didn't have his shield or sword with him. Trust me. I know when someone's doing something they shouldn't. They move and act in a certain way. Anyway, that's only part of it."

The young man had piqued Sabian's interest now. "Go on..." the commander urged.

The boy sighed. "I've been doing some observing of my own over the last few days. I've not had my sword and the tutors have been wrapped up in other things, so I've had a lot of time to myself. A couple of days ago you were writing a letter in the Ibis Courtyard and I was on the gatehouse thinking when I saw you. And guess what? There was a soldier in uniform at one of the high windows of the Raven Palace watching you from above. Now you can't tell me that's right? The top floor of the palace is all apartments for the elders."

Sabian nodded. The boy was absolutely right. Had he found one of his soldiers up there he'd have disciplined him.

Darius went on. "Either he or some other man's never been far from you since then. There may even be two or more of them, cos to be honest when you're all in uniform, I find it hard to distinguish at first glance and I don't get to see them up close. That'd be too risky. I think there's several though and your younger sergeant might be in on it. The soldier or soldiers that I've been seeing are often with him. Sort of with him and shifty if you get my meaning." He frowned.

Sabian shrugged again. "It's a bit thin though Darius. It's not like they've been hunting me with their blades out or anything. I don't like the sound of it, but without any kind of evidence, they may just be bored. I wouldn't be at all surprised."

Darius shook his head. "True, but I followed one of them myself this afternoon. He went into one of the rooms people don't really use in the Peacock Palace. It's on the top floor and a bit dangerous. He was in there for about a quarter of an hour and then left and raced off to find that sergeant. After he left I went into the room and the only thing in there was a signalling lamp standing on the windowsill." The young man crossed his arms. "Now tell me *that's* not fishy!" he added.

Sabian frowned. Such news threw a whole new light on the subject. "Take me to this room Darius."

Chapter X.

The sun was floating lazily almost touching the sea to the west when Darius and the commander reached the main palace buildings. Within the complex walls the shadows had melded together and lamps had been lit in the palaces. Up on the main gate and at strategic places on the walls braziers burned where the soldiers on the night watch had just come on duty. Making their way through the Great court and along the Hall of the Swans the pair had seen not another soul. Everyone would probably be preparing for dinner at this time.

Sabian walked quietly but quickly, his hand gripping the pommel of his sword to stop it swinging as he walked. He wasn't quite sure why he was being so cautious, but for some reason his instincts told him to be careful and he had long since learned to trust his instincts. Besides, Darius was also treading quietly and the boy was equally intuitive. Moving into the intricately designed stairs they made their way up the six flights until they could see the wide vestibule at the top, dark but for the scattered patches of grey where the windows in the stairwell allowed a little light to penetrate the gloom. Sabian stopped.

"Lead on Darius" the commander whispered. The young man answered with a simple nod and turned to make his way along the curved hall. They made their way quietly, softly around the central well until Darius stopped and held up his hand. Pointing down at the floor, he shook his finger. Sabian looked down and realised that this floor must be hardly ever visited. The dust was thick and settled apart from several sets of footprints leading both to and from the door that now stood before them. The commander took a moment to examine the tracks. They were of an average size and bore all the hallmarks of military boots, though with little or no signs of the hobnails; whoever it was needed their boots replacing. He looked back up at Darius and nodded as the two pulled themselves up in front of the door. Darius was reaching for the handle when Sabian stayed his arm. The commander pointed at the cracks around the door itself and the younger man realised that a tiny amount of light was visible around the edges. Darius had assumed the room's window to be the source of the light, but it was possible that the sun was now beneath the horizon and this window would face east. Perhaps the window or... a lantern maybe? Slowly and with infinite care Sabian drew his well-oiled blade from its sheath. Darius raised his eyebrow and at the commander's nod drew his own sword, new and unfamiliar.

Stepping to either side of the door, the two took up defensive positions as Sabian reached out and, gently lifting the catch, thrust the door open and peered round the edge. Since he didn't flinch or pull back, Darius leaned forward and peered round to survey the room. Much like the corridor, the room with thick with dust. Old ramshackle furniture stood around the walls collecting dust and bird droppings. The ornate window had seen better days, much of its plaster moulding having fallen away both outside and in and the walls were shedding plaster in places, beautifully painted chunks lying on the floor in the dust and leaving just the bare bones of the walls. The only articles in the room that did not show a sense of neglect and decay were a small wooden table and chair before the window and as Darius had noted in his brief earlier visit, a signalling lamp standing on the table next to a flickering candle that had almost burned out. It took long moments for his gaze to pick out the other oddity in the room and, as he did, he joined the commander and they walked into the room, their swords still ready.

Not far from the table in the dust on the floor was a heap that Darius had at first assumed to be old drapes or wall hangings. In fact, with the low flickering candlelight, its nature became clear as they made their way closer: it was a body. Darius stopped suddenly and turned, his blade flashing in the dim light as he squinted to check the corners of the room. Sabian shook his head.

"No one here," he said, "apart from him." He gestured at the body and then turned to the young man. "Step careful. There are tracks in here we don't want to disturb."

As the commander stepped lightly toward the body, Darius remained where he was, watching the doorway. Sabian reached the heap and crouched.

"His name's Ursus" he confirmed. "One of Iasus' men." He sighed and, standing again, added "we need more light."

As Darius nodded the commander scratched his head. "I've sent word for his Lordship's physician to find me. No one else should be around for best part of an hour; it's dinner time." He gestured to Darius. "Are you alright guarding this room while I get some lanterns and find the doctor?"

Darius nodded again. "Don't be too long."

Stepping carefully to avoid scuffing the footprints in the dust, Sabian left the room and Darius heard him jogging along the corridor to the stairs. As the hob-nailed boot noises faded away into the distance Darius placed his sword on the table, hilt facing him for easy retrieval should it become necessary. Crouching he examined the footprints in the dust. He hadn't examined the ones in the corridor, but they were fairly clear tracks. Here there were at least two sets of prints crossing each other many times, one military boot and one light flat shoe. Darius frowned and crossed to the body. The man was probably in his late twenties; perhaps ten years older than he and powerfully built. A big man with a lantern jaw and a shaved head and wearing the full kit of a soldier. The young man considered examining the body himself but thought better of it. These things were best left to men of science.

Standing once more he walked past the table and peered out over the water. Velutio was visible in the distance as myriad twinkling lights in the shroud of darkness. How anyone signalling would know what to look for was beyond him, as it would be near impossible to distinguish between the lights.

He hadn't realised just how long he'd sat there, staring out at a world beyond his reach, but it must have been some time for he was shaken from his dreamy state by footsteps in the corridor. Retrieving his sword he came to his feet in a sweeping motion to face the door as Sabian and the doctor appeared in the open, framed in the doorway by the light of the lanterns they each carried. The lad relaxed, his shoulders dropping back and the sword coming to rest by his side. Sabian entered, stepping to one side to avoid the footprints and advising the doctor to do the same. Without a word, the physician reached out with his lantern and held it in front of Darius, expecting the young man to relieve him of his burden. Gritting his teeth in annoyance, Darius grasped the lantern and placed it on the table. Looking around, Sabian found a high wooden cupboard still in a reasonably sturdy state and placed his own lantern on the top. As the room was bathed in the glow of the two oil lamps, the commander wandered across and shut the door, sealing them in the room before he addressed the doctor.

"Alright. Tell me everything you can about him."

The doctor was crouched beside the body and with some effort rolled Ursus back and forth. "No visible wounds on the torso or limbs." He lifted the head gently and it rolled around threatening to become detached. Darius frowned as the doctor continued: "looks like someone broke his neck. I would suggest that the culprit you're looking for was not a natural fighter, as there are a great number of marks on the neck and the upper arms. It seems to have been quite a struggle." He cleared his throat as he gently lowered the head back to the floor. "Also, judging by the size of the victim I would suspect you're looking for a large or at least surprisingly strong assailant." The doctor stood, dusting his hands and with a distrustful glance at Darius, faced the commander.

"I would say you can rule out your men as they would have made a much neater job of it I'm sure. Is there anything else?"

Sabian shook his head. "I don't think so. I'll let you know if we need any more."

Nodding curtly, the physician made for the door, turning as he reached it.

"I think you are making a mistake commander," he declared, "in respect of the minister. This procedure that's planned could easily kill him and his Lordship will not be happy with that."

Sabian glowered at the doctor. "That's my concern, not yours."

With a shrug, the doctor left and Darius and the commander stood beside the corpse of the soldier silently. After a pregnant pause, Darius cleared his throat and threw a quick glance at the doorway before speaking.

"I don't trust that man."

Sabian sighed. "That's only natural really, but he does know what he's talking about. I need you to do me a favour Darius. Can you run and find my two sergeants? You know Cialo and Iasus?"

Without comment, Darius sheathed his sword and slipped out of the room. Sabian was starting to get that itch he always got back in the city when he knew something was going on. Oh, in the city there was always *something* going on. An assassination here, a plot foiled there, rivalry and vying for power and prestige. The commander had learned to live with it and to navigate his way through the dangerous currents of life in the biggest city of the Empire, but he'd never liked it. He was a soldier, not a politician, as he kept having to remind people including himself. He liked things clear cut and out in the open and to have come to this virtual banishment while games were played behind his back in the city did not sit well with him. To have orders to clamp down on the freedoms of a bunch of people who, as far as he could see, hadn't done anything wrong irked him just as much. And now, as an added burden he'd displeased Velutio and put himself in danger and to add to all his irritations and worries there was something going on here of all places. And no one seemed trustworthy. In fact, most of the people he had any inclination to rely on were prisoners like Darius and the minister. Apparently not even his own men!

"Shit!"

Sabian kicked a piece of fallen plaster in irritation and it ricocheted off the wall, causing further cracks to appear. He glared out of the window at the city twinkling in the distance and a bad taste filled his mouth. He'd always known he would be a soldier and he'd been damn good at it. After only a few years serving one of the petty lords further around the coast he'd become a commander and with only eight years service under his belt his record was good enough that Velutio had sought him out. Velutio's army was the closest thing in the world to the great army the Empire had once had and Sabian had leapt at the chance for a proper commission. These days he was starting to wonder whether it was worth it. Once the hazy view of exuberant youth had faded he'd realised that, despite Velutio's army being the largest and most organised of all the lords, it still bore no resemblance to the glorious military of imperial days. And with it came treachery and deceit. Perhaps when this was all over he'd resign his commission and sign on as a mercenary captain. At least they weren't beholden. If they found out they'd signed on to lunatics they could just walk away.

He sighed again and, pulling out the uncomfortable wooden chair, collapsed into it while he waited for the lad. He found himself once more musing on Darius and his background. If the boy really was Caerdin's son and had even a fraction of his father's wit and talent, which he appeared to do, he was truly wasted locked away on this island. Hell, had things been different, another ten years would probably have seen Sabian serving under *him*. Smiling at that last thought he drummed his fingers on the table and stopped for a moment. One thing he hadn't noticed before was the mark on the table. Something else had been standing on the table very recently, as there was a small circular patch among the dust. He shrugged; probably just a mug or glass.

He sat staring at the table for a few more minutes until the sound of several footsteps appeared in the corridor and Cialo and Iasus entered the room, coming to attention and saluting the moment they were inside. Sabian nodded and beckoned them forward, surprised to see behind them not only Darius but Favio, the island's doctor. He glared at Darius and raised on eyebrow. The young man just shrugged.

"He was looking for you anyway."

With a squaring of the shoulders, Sabian stood up.

"Well as long as you're here Favio," he addressed the doctor, "you might as well have a look at the body and tell me what you think. But," he added "what we say goes no further than the walls of this room." As Darius and the doctor wandered over to the body, Sabian examined the sergeants. Since they'd been here there was a notable change in his men. Cialo's only concession now to his uniform were the tunic and belt and he looked every inch the engineer. A stylus rested behind his ear and a wax tablet stuck out of his belt. He was covered in dust and spattered plaster which matted his hair in places. It was hard to look at the ageing sergeant and not smile. Iasus on the other hand was still in his armour and had polished it every night by the look of it. One might think he hadn't changed, but to those who knew him... He had a few days growth of facial hair and, despite beards being quite fashionable these days, Sabian had never seen him other than clean shaven. His helmet was tucked under his arm, but instead of the traditional skull cap beneath, a bandanna of crimson silk was wrapped around his forehead. And most of all, he smiled occasionally. That had never happened much. For a moment Sabian wondered what changes the others saw in their commander, but pulled himself together and tried to ignore the tutting and muttering of the island's doctor as he spoke.

"Ursus was one of your men Iasus, yes?"

"Sir" Iasus nodded confirmation.

"But he was working as an engineer under you, yes Cialo?"

The older sergeant nodded.

"What was he doing here?" the commander queried. "You've only been working for a couple of hours."

Cialo dropped from attention and addressed Sabian. "He was supposed to be hunting around for old damaged plaster sir."

Sabian frowned. "Damaged plaster?"

"Yessir," the sergeant went on. "Old plaster can be used as part of a base for mortar. He and a couple of the others are bringing me sack loads of old plaster from all over the island. Anywhere things have fallen down. We'll be using it in the mortar mix for the repairs to the baths."

Sabian nodded. "That explains him being here, but not what happened. I don't like this at all. You see this lamp..." he began but his voice trailed off as the muttering of Doctor Favio intensified and distracted him.

"Doctor, could you kindly keep your voice down."

Favio grumbled and beckoned to the commander with a finger. Biting his tongue to stop himself shouting at the insolent man, Sabian leaned down toward them.

"What is it, Favio?"

Favio shook his head. "What did your *doctor* tell you?" he enquired, heaping sarcasm on the word.

"That he was attacked by someone untrained in martial combat, there was a fair struggle and finally someone managed to break his neck. I can see the marks and the broken neck for myself."

Favio continued to shake his head. "Begging your pardon commander, but that's a whole heap of horse shit and unless your man was trained by a blind beggar with the mental capability of a sewer turd he knows it."

Sabian glowered at him.

"Go on..."

The doctor smiled. "Someone's trying to pull the wool over your eyes commander. This man was dead at least a half an hour before his neck was broken and all these bruises made."

Sabian leaned forward. His dark countenance had gone replaced by one of concern. "Are you sure of that Favio?"

The doctor nodded. "Absolutely. If you'll let me examine him properly, I'll tell you how he died too; my instruments are all in my clinic."

Sabian gestured back at Cialo and Iasus without even turning to look at them. "Take Ursus," he ordered the pair. "Follow the doctor and let him do whatever the hell it is he needs to do. Iasus, you stay with him while he does it. Cialo, meet us at the bath house. You and I and young Darius here are going to check something out." He added as an afterthought "and try not to be seen carrying Ursus. No one says anything about this."

The room burst into life as the two sergeants and the doctor collected the body of the soldier and carried him from the room. Darius was making for the door when Sabian called out to him and he turned.

"Darius, I want you to go find the doctor from Velutio. You and I and Cialo are going to have a little talk with him. Bring him down to the bath house. I don't really care what excuse you use."

With a nasty smile, young Darius carried out an elaborate sweeping bow and left the room. Sabian cracked his knuckles and then shuddered. It was a habit he thought he managed to break, that. Whatever was going on here, if the Favio was right, then Velutio's doctor had something to do with it. However Favio might talk or treat people, he really did seem to be an excellent doctor. He suddenly realised that Darius had said Favio was looking for him. Still, that could wait until later.

With a hard smile that closely matched Darius', Sabian left the room and made his way down the stairs. If the doctor was involved in any underhanded business, the commander would deal with it and do it his way and as soon as possible. He trotted along the hallways and across the courtyards until he reached the soft, springy turf of the gardens and strode down the hill and through the Water Gate. The bath

117

house was surrounded by wooden scaffolding and ropes and buckets and myriad tools lay strewn about. Cialo had been busy already it seemed. As he neared the entrance to the baths he almost smiled to note that the unpleasant smell of musty decay had died away a little. Cialo would have drained the baths first no doubt. A long plank of wood led down into the baths themselves, covering the various places where the floor had given way to the dark tunnels between the supporting pillars of the underfloor heating. At the doorway to the changing room, still close enough to the entrance to admit the low light of a sunset now all but over, two oil lamps stood in niches by the arch. Smiling, Sabian lit the lamps and moved into the room. The wide space was covered with tools and clothing and the various bric-a-brac of workmen. The niches for storing the bathers' clothing was filled with unidentifiable items, along with sawn planks and scribbled plans and notes. Cialo really was taking his work seriously. The commander wandered across to one of the less occupied niches and carefully moved its contents into the next one before taking a seat. Mere moments later, Cialo strode into the room and nodded.

"Sir. Got some news from the quack". He rolled his eyes upwards as though repeating a list he'd been made to memorize. "He said to tell you that Ursus' tongue was all swollen up and a right funny colour. He reckons he drank something poisonous, but he's not sure what yet. He'll let you know what he finds."

Sabian's face took on an even threatening look. There could be little doubt about the doctor's guilt now.

"What're we up to?" Cialo asked curiously.

Sabian smiled. "Sergeant, you are a soldier of the old school, yes?"

The sergeant nodded. "I would say so, sir."

"What," the commander enquired, "would you have done with a traitor in the ranks when you served in the Imperial army?"

Cialo's face darkened. "He wouldn't turn up at roll call the next morning sir."

Sabian nodded. "I've always thought of myself as old school you know? I was only a lad when you were out serving with the great generals, but I always thought that the Imperial army was the most organised and efficient force the world has ever seen and I've tried to emulate that in my time at Velutio." He sighed. "But when you think you're doing it right, and you still have to worry about loyalty, something's got to be wrong."

Cialo smiled and leaned back against the wall.

118

"Sir..." the sergeant began and then changed his mind. "Gaius... "

Sabian blinked. No one called him by his given name. Apart from the fact that a ranker addressing an officer like that was something that just wasn't done, he wasn't aware that any of the men even knew that name. He was so surprised he realised he hadn't even interrupted and the sergeant had gone on.

"You are Gaius Vibius Sabianus of a noble house and commander of the most powerful army to be found in the Empire. I don't like to speak out of turn, but I'm not a great believer in any of the causes for war these days and I'm not really sure why people even join the armies now, apart from the fact that it's better to live well and die young than to starve into old age. You have loyalty among your men because you're a good man and a good commander and you look after your own. If you'd been twenty years older you'd have been an Imperial officer of some standing in the old army I reckon."

Sabian smiled. Cialo was the quintessential sergeant and he realised he was coming to rely more and more on the man over the days here. He cleared his throat.

"Well, it looks like not everyone shares your opinion. Something's going on here. Someone's been secretly signalling the mainland from the room we were in earlier. I don't believe it was Ursus though. One of the guilty ones has to be Velutio's own physician, though he may have friends among the men. You and I and young Darius are going to have a word with the doctor and see just what he's been up to. Darius is bringing him now."

The commander was gratified to note the vicious look that flashed across the sergeant's face. The veteran growled "I'll rip his balls off!"

Sabian smiled and shook his head. "I want to make sure it was him and see if he has accomplices, then I'll decide what we're going to do with him. I'm not going to torture the man; that's his Lordship's way not mine, but I'm not particularly inclined to be lenient either."

The sergeant sat up straight. "You're not going to let him off?"

Again the commander smiled. "I doubt it, but I want to see what he has to say first."

The two sat in silence for a long time until they heard footsteps in the entry corridor. The doctor's head emerged around the pillar of the arch, peering with difficulty into the gloom of a large room lit only be two small oil lamps.

"Commander?"

The man edged into the room and Sabian spotted Darius standing behind him. The commander rose, aware instantly that Cialo was right beside him.

"Doctor, come in." Reaching out, Sabian lit another lamp he'd noted in the next alcove when he arrived. The light in the room increased to an easier level though the doctor hesitated, Sabian noted, before moving into the room. Darius, right behind him with a hand on his sword hilt, had a face like thunder. The doctor smiled uneasily but his voice betrayed no fear.

"You wanted to talk to me commander?"

Sabian's teeth flashed in the lamp light. His hand made two small, subtle gestures that only Cialo would understand and with quiet speed the man sidestepped the doctor and joined Darius in cutting off the exit. The sergeant folded his arms for a moment but then smiled broadly and picked up a heavy bladed shovel-axe from the corridor.

The commander stepped forward and grasped Velutio's physician by the tunic, gripping a handful of linen and twisting, bringing the man close to his face and lifting him onto his toes. If only the doctor could have seen the predatory smiles on the two men behind him blocking the exit.

"Doctor," he growled, "you will begin by telling me who you have been signalling from that room. You will then tell me exactly what you have said. I want to know who else on the island knows about you or is in league with you and how and why you found it necessary to poison one of my men. If you answer me readily and I think you're telling the truth, you may even leave this building with all your limbs. If you lie to me even once, I will give you to the sergeant, who knows how to deal with traitors."

The doctor swallowed nervously. Behind him, Cialo muttered something to Darius and they both grinned. The word 'gut' was the only one that Sabian caught and, but from the doctor's expression he'd heard also. The man spluttered; his face had gone red.

Sabian smiled and bunched the tunic a little tighter. "You can talk now, doctor. It's your turn."

The man shook his head as best he could in the tight clinch. "I really don't know what you mean commander. I'm just a doctor here with a pa..."

Sabian tightened the knot, almost cutting off the man's breath, but after a moment he let go of the tunic and the doctor dropped back to the floor. A wave of relief broke on him but too soon for when he looked up, Sabian was drawing a sword from the scabbard at his side.

120

"You can't do this," the doctor demanded. "His lordship will have you crucified!"

The commander smiled, looking up at the doctor with his head still bowed. The flash of his cruel eyes matched by the twinkling of the blade in the lamp light were truly menacing and Darius had to give the doctor some credit; some people would be weeping for mercy by now under that gaze. Sabian realised that the doctor truly believed he would abide by whatever the man said just because of their joint allegiance to Lord Velutio.

"Is that your last word on the subject?" he enquired. The next sentence would seal it so he waited, his eyes and blade still glittering unpleasantly in the guttering light.

"I'll see you pay for this" the doctor declared haughtily.

Behind the doctor, the sergeant's deeper voice said "I doubt it!"

Sabian saw Cialo raising the shovel blade in the light of the tunnel. The sergeant was clearly incensed and meant to bury the shovel in the doctor's head. Darius' sword was also out. The commander sighed. "Put your weapons down gentlemen. Neither of you're going to harm him."

He saw Cialo blink as the shovel faltered. Darius' sword dipped toward the floor and Sabian turned his back on the man with deliberate slowness, noting as he turned the sleazy victorious smile on the doctor's face. The smile was still there as Sabian picked up speed in his turn and the sword flicked out. The smile was still there as the blade cut through muscle and sinew and cleaved the bone. The smile was still there as the head bearing it rolled across the floor and into the gutter leading to the main drain.

He let the blade drop toward the floor and smiled coldly over the slowly collapsing body at the two in the archway.

"That's *my* job."

The rest of the corpse slumped against the wall, leaking out onto the floor. A torrent of red pumped from the neck and pooled behind dams of broken plaster and tile before running in rivulets into the drainage system. The commander stepped back toward the doorway, kicking the head gently and knocking it back toward the body.

Sabian cleared his throat. "Cialo, I'm going to have a little word with the men in the morning. I want to make sure that this piece of shit had no friends among our companies. Darius, you might as well head back and get something to eat. We're going to be quite busy tonight I think."

121

The young man shook his head. "I'll help you get rid of this first and anyway I think that whatever you're in now, I'm in too. You can probably rule out any conspiracy among my island kin. None of the prisoners would be reporting to Velutio, I can assure you.

Sabian stood still for a moment and then nodded. He wasn't so sure.

"Ok. Let's throw him in the sea and then go get something to eat while we talk."

A short while later the remains of the highest paid doctor in the greatest city in the world disappeared into the sea with two splashes unheard by any but those responsible and the few bats flitting around the trees. Out across the bay amid the twinkling lights of Velutio, one flashed repeatedly, invisible to the unaware and completely unanswered.

Chapter XI.

Sabian was in his full kit when he strode into the square, his armour gleaming in the bright sunlight and his sword swinging idly by his side. Darius stood, as seemed his automatic place these days, behind the commander's shoulder. He wore the standard kit he used for sword practice or hunting; brown and grey leathers. Cialo and Iasus snapped to attention and the six companies of men behind them followed suit with an ear-splitting crash.

The commander stood for long minutes, his countenance cold and dark. Behind him his new ally shared the commander's visage, as did the two sergeants. Sabian let them sweat at attention for a few minutes before he spoke.

"I've called this parade to give you some news and an ultimatum."

The companies didn't move but he had no intention of letting them stand at ease. A few cast curious glances in the direction of Darius without moving their heads. It hadn't escaped anyone how much time the young man was spending in the commander's company. Sabian paused a moment and then continued.

"The doctor from the city will no longer be treating you for any minor abrasions or construction injuries during your tenure here. He went for a swim last night without his head."

He emphasised the last words to increase their shock value and had the desired effect on more than a few soldiers. Without the commander having to utter a word, Iasus bellowed "Stay at attention!" Those who'd slumped a little came rail straight again instantly.

Sabian cast his eyes around the Ibis courtyard windows. No one. Good. He'd sent the elders to examine the bath house and the rest of the population had duties assigned elsewhere. This sort of meeting had to be conducted in some privacy.

He rounded his shoulders and began to pace slowly backwards and forwards along the line of men as he went on.

"The doctor betrayed both myself and the loyal troops of the army to someone back in the city. He murdered Ursus yesterday which is why you may have wondered where he was today. In the end the doctor paid the price traitors always pay!"

Again he fell silent, still stalking up and down the line.

"There is also some suggestion that one or more men in these six companies may be involved in this treachery."

A murmur of denial spread throughout the lines until Cialo bellowed "Quiet!" at the top of his voice. The commander paused again in the centre of the line and faced them, his hands clasped behind his back.

"I will not allow treachery and mutiny within the ranks. I've always been a good commander to my men and you've all benefited from my leniency. I don't want to have to stamp down on any freedoms we've granted, but enough is enough."

He glared at the men. "Rest assured I will find out about anyone who is involved. Anyone who comes to my attention will be summarily punished. If you admit your guilt, I may be lenient. If not, I will make damn sure that you suffer beyond the limit of your wits. Is that clear?"

Silence greeted his last words.

"Is that *clear*?" he bellowed.

The companies saluted in unison with an affirmative. The commander nodded and continued. "If I find out that anyone has been keeping any information from me, they will suffer the same fate. Am I understood?"

No hesitation in the response this time.

Sabian nodded again. "All work parties are suspended for two hours while the elders tour the bath house works. At noon, we'll be holding a service for Ursus in the graveyard and I expect everyone to attend. I had Minister Sarios informed of events first thing this morning and he will be performing the service for us. After that, work will begin again and you should report to your officers as normal. If any of you feels the pressing need to get anything off your chest in the meantime, you can approach either Iasus or Cialo or find me. I will be somewhere in the complex.

He nodded once at the sergeants before he turned and marched out in the direction of the gate with Darius at his shoulder. Behind him he heard the sergeants give the order to fall out and the men went their various ways. He stalked along angrily into the trees. The doctor had annoyed him so much last night that he'd dealt with the man without getting any real information or confirmation from him and now he had to threaten his own men which irked him all the more. He stopped beneath a tree with perfect lilac flowers and shrugged his armour back into position. Scanning the horizon, he lifted his cloak out of the way and sat with his back to the tree. Darius wandered across to a tree opposite and seated himself. Neither spoke for a long time. Sabian rubbed his hands and stared at them while the young man watched him intently before becoming the first to break the silence.

"Do you think anyone will come to you?"

The commander shook his head. "I really don't know. This whole thing is irritating me beyond fucking reason. I came here to do a twice yearly head-count and now I'm a prison guard and I can't trust most of the men around me. I don't even know why I trust you. I think the time's coming when we'll all need to take some oaths of loyalty again."

Darius nodded. "You can have my word that I have no involvement in any plot against you and that I'll do my damndest to help you sort this out."

Sabian smiled. "If only you were a free man Darius. I'd have had Cialo fit you for a uniform before you could draw breath."

The young man returned the smile and then spoke, tapping his fingers on the hilt of his sword. "What enemies do you have?"

The commander shrugged. "Enough that I know of, let alone those I don't. His lordship isn't altogether happy with me right now; I have an ambitious captain back in the city that I should have brought with me theoretically, since he's Cialo and Iasus's direct superior. Then there's three or four noble families whose noses I've put out of joint in the last few years, my previous lord who tried to have me killed to stop me taking a position with his opponent... the list goes on. You have no idea how irritating it is to live in a city like Velutio and to have to deal with all the conspiracies that go on there on a weekly basis. No one's really safe in that city but his lordship. There's no proof as yet, but I have absolutely no doubt in my mind who's at the bottom of this: Crosus. The one who commanded the bodyguard, when his lordship was here if you remember. Got to be him, the weaselly bastard."

He sighed and rearranged his sword belt to be less constrictive while Darius shuffled into a better position. Reaching into his tunic the young man produced a flask of earthenware, topped with a wax seal. He smiled at the commander. "I managed to lay my hands on some of the minister's plum brandy. With him being bedridden, no one's looking after his store.

His smile broadening, he broke the seal and took a swig from the flask, swilling it round his mouth appreciatively. The taste was both sharp and sweet. The island did make an excellent brandy. He proffered the flask to the commander who smiled and took it for a grateful swig. The morning was already gearing up to be a scorcher and the shade of the palace wall behind and the trees above was welcome. Down the hill between the dappled shadows of the branches a short stretch of grass sloped down to the sea. In the distance the city of Velutio was vaguely visible in a wavering heat-haze and between the waves crashed on the rocks surrounding the island and fish leapt, sparkling in the sun. In other circumstances it would be idyllic.

He resealed the flask and handed it back to Darius, who secreted it away again. With a grin the young man stood.

"Enough of feeling sorry for yourself commander. I haven't had a chance for sword practice today and I'd be grateful if you'd spar for a short while."

With a nod the commander stood and drew his blade as Darius drew his. Looking around, they stepped out from the area of cluttered trees and wandered across to the area of lawn before the sea. As Sabian removed his cloak and placed it on the ground to one side, the young man took up a duelling stance, his sword held at forty five degrees before him. The commander smiled and took up a similar stance opposite. Neither moved for a moment and then Darius stepped forward with some speed, swinging the blade at chest height in both hands. Sabian had been prepared and stepped to one side, his sword vertical and blocking the blow. He pivoted with the momentum of his step, his own sword coming back in a swing at head height, but Darius had already recovered. The young man ducked and lunged towards the commander's thigh. Sabian barely sidestepped in time, the blade catching his breeches and tearing along the seam. The two stepped apart again, breathing heavily.

"You know, Darius, you're better than I thought? You almost caught me good and proper there."

The young man nodded. "I get a lot of practice, remember?"

As Darius grinned, Sabian lunged forward and Darius came to meet the blow, only to discover it was a feint; the commander fell forward into a roll beneath the sweep of Darius' sword and the flat of the blade connected painfully against the young man's shin.

Darius collapsed to the floor, his sword falling from his hand as he sat clutching his shin. "Shit, that hurt!" he exclaimed.

Sabian dropped his own sword point to the grass. "You do have a tendency to over-extend. I think you've done remarkably well taking everything from the great writers and more from a couple of reasonable tutors here, but nothing beats field experience and live targets. Shame Ursus went; he's one of the best training officers we had."

Darius opened his mouth to speak, but was interrupted by a voice from the gate. One of the island's scribes was calling them and, collecting his cloak, Sabian and Darius strode up the hill. The scribe,

126

clad in a white tunic and cloak and with a scroll in his hand frowned at Darius before turning to Sabian.

"Commander" he said, slightly breathlessly, "Minister Sarios would like to see you in his chambers if you have the time."

Sabian nodded and thanked the man as he and Darius strode across the Ibis courtyard toward the doors of the Raven palace. He wondered momentarily whether to tell Darius to wait below for him as they approached the narrow spiral staircase that led up to the top floor apartments, but decided against it. As they strode down the corridor, he realised that the minister's door was open and spotted the old man moving about within. He paused at the door and knocked out of courtesy. The minister's voice, stronger than the commander had heard it in some time, called for them to enter and they did so. The sparsely furnished study was full of paperwork at the moment and Sarios stood at a desk, shuffling a large wad of notes and filing them away in a leather case. He turned and smiled. His colour was considerably better and, although he staggered a little as he turned he seemed generally in better health. His head was no longer bandaged, though the bruising and scrapes on his face were still clearly evidenced and he wore a hastily fashioned eye patch to cover his still blind eye.

"Commander, thank you for coming so promptly. I didn't want to interrupt anything important, but I think I may have something that could help you and I wanted to catch you before the funeral." He gestured to a couple of wooden chairs arrayed beneath a window. "Please sit down."

The two settled into the chairs and Sabian raised his hands, palms up, and shrugged questioningly. The minister wandered over to the corner of the room and picked up a lamp, bringing it across and placing it on the desk before them.

"Is this the lamp you found in the room?"

Darius and Sabian glanced at each other before they both nodded. The commander pointed at the lamp. "Where did you get it? I confiscated the one from the room and hid it in my own kit."

The minister smiled. "I know we're supposed to be cut off from the mainland here, commander and I have to admit that we've never used these; after all, who would we signal? But there were three on the island that had never been confiscated in the early days. All three have been locked away in a storage room for many years. As soon as Darius here told me what had happened, I went to check on them and I assume you can guess how many I found?"

127

Sabian cleared his throat, standing once again. "So this lamp we found was stolen from your secret store room?"

The minister nodded and a sour look crossed his face. "And that means that your doctor was being aided be someone from the island."

The commander glanced at the grim and bleak expression on Darius' face and moved forward to the dusty signalling lamp, tapping it with his fingers. "Who knew where that room was and what was kept in it?"

Sarios shook his head. "Several people knew of the room's existence and its contents, but only I ever kept the key." The minister watched a look cross the commander's face and continued hurriedly "there are a number of things in there that we keep very private and I'm breaking a rule of the council's just by telling you about it, but I would like to think that you would allow us the trust to keep the room hidden in return for what I'm about to give you."

Sabian frowned and raised an eyebrow as the minister continued once more.

"Since I have been incapacitated my affairs have been handled by Minister Turus and it is in his hands those keys have rested these past five days. I suggest that it's he you need to visit to pursue your enquiries."

Sabian smiled, though there was precious little humour in it. "Minister, I *am* grateful, and my men and I will find the good minister and deal with him accordingly."

As he stepped back, however, he held out his hand. "I would like to think you trust me and I would hope I can trust you, but if you have a room containing such things as signal lamps, I do need to see the room and its contents. What I do after I've seen them is something I'll have to think on, but please pass me the keys."

The minister's face fell but he held out the key without another word and dropped it in the commander's palm.

"You'll find the store room on the ground floor along a corridor past the rear entrance" he said. "At the very end of the corridor is a locked door. I hope I can rely on your discretion and although I realise that Turus has betrayed both you and us, but I would still ask you to inflict no harm without him being brought to the council first."

The commander nodded. "I imagine that Turus is just a tool in this and I'll abide by your wishes for now. What happens after the council sees him remains to be seen." He turned, leaving an unhappy looking old man watching after him.

As Sabian left, Darius cast a quick glance at the minister and nodded once before following the commander back along the corridor and down the stairs. He hurried to catch up as they crossed the main floor and entered a corridor that the commander had never used before. The young man strode at Sabian's shoulder and cleared his throat.

"Commander, is this important right now?"

Sabian continued to walk, talking without turning. "Darius, if Turus and the doctor had access to lamps in there, I can only wonder what else they could have found. I need to check the room out for myself before I confront the minister on it; besides, I want to know what's in there for my own satisfaction. I can afford to be lenient in my command here, but not blindly so."

As he finished speaking they arrived at a heavy wooden door. The commander reached out and turned the key in the lock, pushing the handle hard. The door barely moved, scraping along the floor with a spine-tingling noise. He put his shoulder to it and the heavy portal suddenly gave way, swinging inwards. He recovered himself quickly and glanced around the room; it had obviously been visited rarely and dust lay thick on everything. The window to this room was high and of opaque glass casting strangely wavering, almost submarine light around the interior. He made his way to the desk directly opposite on which sat a signalling lamp of the same style as the two he'd already encountered. Two bare circles in the dusty surface betrayed the existence of the other two. Biting his lip in concentration he began to survey the contents of the room.

Picking up a small soft leather bag from the desk, he tipped it gently upside down over a tin plate. A number of small gems of remarkable quality tumbled out onto the plate with a rattling noise. He blinked and whistled through his teeth. He was no expert on gems, but he'd be willing to bet that this small pouch would be worth enough to keep him in luxury for over a year. These must have been found in the wreckage of the palace just after they'd been made prisoners here. A glance around told similar stories and his eyes wandered across the desk as he poured the gems back into the bag and pulled the draw-string tight.

Items abounded here that he knew would be confiscated if Velutio had known of their existence. A large chest of dried foods carefully packed and sealed would be very useful on a long journey; signalling lamps that could keep the islanders in contact with someone on the mainland; a bag of gems that could keep a traveller for some time. Oh, but they were by no means all forbidden items though. Some had obviously been stored here due to their precious nature. A number of delicate and very rare books lined a shelf each covered in linen to protect them, a jewelled knife bearing the imperial crest on the hilt, a portrait of the last emperor, a little faded but otherwise well preserved. Sabian whistled again. Now that he gazed at a good portrait of Quintus the Golden, the resemblance to the missing Quintillian was unmistakable.

He quickly reached across the desk and pulled over a set of scrolls, six in all, unfastening the silk tie and unrolling them. The moment he saw their contents, he let the scroll go and it rolled back into a coil. He glanced over his shoulder to check on Darius, but the young man was poking around another desk in the corner. Unrolling the scroll again his eyes strolled across the genealogy of the Imperial bloodline and there, clearly labelled at the bottom was Quintillian. He was about to roll it back up carefully when another name caught his eye that made him blink in surprise. Tracing the lines on the chart from Quintus the Golden, he double-checked, but there it was: Livilla Dolabella, a cousin of the Emperor and her husband clearly marked next to her: Kiva Caerdin. He frowned, for there was no mention of a child. With another furtive glance at Darius to make sure he was occupied, he rolled the scroll once more and tied it, fumbling with another. Another genealogy, this time showing the ancestors of a man named Pelius; a name vaguely familiar to the commander from his roll calls on the island. A third scroll revealed another familiar name, and he glanced briefly at it before unrolling the fourth and smiling broadly. The Caerdin line. This short scroll showed Darius clearly enough along with his mother and father and some of the members of the non-direct Imperial family. Caerdin's father had been added but presumably the northern tribes he came from didn't keep records of ancestry beyond their father. The maternal line went back a long way, though and very high-born. His suspicions finally confirmed, along with a connection of which he'd been previously unaware, Sabian allowed the scroll to roll up once more and then placed the six back in their container. He turned to Darius.

"I think I've seen enough here" he said and the young man turned, pulling himself away from some dusty book. The commander went on. "I'll speak to the minister later, but I can't imagine any of this presenting a problem for me at least. Shall we go and have a word with Turus?"

Darius nodded and left the room, waiting in the corridor as Sabian heaved the door shut and locked it.

They strolled down the corridor in the direction of the great courtyard, the commander walking ahead lost in his own musings. Behind him, Darius carefully shuffled into his breeches the one item he'd removed from sight in the room while Sabian had been otherwise occupied. He placed a great deal of trust in the commander, but showing him the only map they had of the island's reefs and safe channels would be taking that trust too far.

Sabian stood in the octagonal room of the ruined Golden House tapping his fingers on his bronze-plated belt, his eyes darting around the various shattered entrances to the room. Behind him Cialo leaned yawning against a crumbling wall and Iasus stood stiff and upright in what was once an alcove, his sergeant's vine-staff jammed under his arm. No one had said a word for more than five minutes but impatient sounds abounded. How long would it take the young man?

Footsteps in the ruins announced the arrival of their guest. The commander heaved a sigh of relief and Cialo pulled himself upright off the wall. Minister Turus rounded the corner, picking his way gingerly among the fallen masonry with Darius at his shoulder. The minister spotted the soldiers and gave a crooked smile as he gratefully crossed into the clear area within the octagon.

"Commander," the man said slightly breathlessly, "young Darius said that you need to see me? A strange place to meet."

Sabian nodded. "Somewhere quiet... out of the way." He grinned an unpleasant grin at the minister. "Easy to clean..."

The minister opened his mouth to say something, his eyes surprisingly wide, but the commander rode over the top of whatever comment he intended to make.

"I would assume, minister, that due to your complicity in the affair, you are aware of what happened to the good doctor yesterday?"

The colour drained from Turus' face. He made strange burbling noises and spun around, finally taking in the solitary location in which he now found himself and the four armed men around him. Eyes so wide they looked like they might burst, he collapsed in a heap on the ground.

"This can't be happening..."

Darius, only a couple of steps behind him dropped his sword point to the ground a foot away from the minister's knee. "Oh but it can" he said.

Sabian reached down and grasped the slightly portly man by the tunic and hauled him to his feet. He was surprisingly heavy.

"Save your breath with denials" the commander said plainly. "We know about the doctor and we know about you. The doctor's gone because he wouldn't talk to me. I'd assume you're more intelligent than that."

The minister said nothing, still pale and frightened, but he nodded vigorously. Sabian smiled inwardly. This was easier that Velutio's damned doctor. He released his grip on Turus and the man sank back to the floor.

"I'll give you a very simple choice, Turus" the commander said. "Either you stand brave and irresolute and protect your fellow conspirators, in which case we cut you into several pieces to fatten the fishes... or you tell me everything you know right here and now and I turn you over to Sarios to deal with."

As he finished speaking, he became aware that the minister was whimpering. The man reached up and there were tears in his eyes.

"I didn't want to, but ... my family! You must understand."

Darius looked over the broken minister at the commander and cleared his throat. "The man's daughter lives in Velutio."

Sabian remained stony faced. "I'm waiting, minister."

Pulling himself together as best he could, Turus hauled himself to his feet.

"Someone in the city. I don't know who, but he must be powerful. The doctor came to me with an offer; said he could get me off the island and to my family. How could I not? I didn't know he was going to kill anyone; that was never part of the deal."

Sabian nodded. "I know who the someone in the city is and I know about the doctor and you. You're not telling me anything. I know there were soldiers involved; *my* men. Tell me who they were and what was sent." To emphasise his words, he drew his sword and tapped the flat of the blade against his shin. The minister's eyes bulged again.

"I don't know what the messages were; I was just to get the lamp. There are three men though... three that I know of anyway. Don't know their names, but they're all on the guard duty under him." He pointed at Iasus. Sabian turned and nodded at the sergeant. The young martinet stepped forward and reached out with his vine staff, placing it beneath the minister's chin.

"Descriptions" he said. "If you can't give us names, give us descriptions."

The minister tried to nod, but the vine staff inhibited him; the position looked very uncomfortable. Sabian glanced briefly at Iasus. Sometimes a strict military disciplinarian had his uses. Turus gulped.

"There's a tall one, fair haired. I think he's probably in charge."

Iasus nodded and spoke to his commander without taking his eyes off the minister. "Rufus. Got to be Rufus. He's officer of the night watch. Go on minister…"

"One with a black beard, quite curly."

Iasus tutted and lifted the vine-staff, almost choking the minister. "No one in my duty with a black beard" he said.

The minister's eyes bulged again, but Cialo piped up from the other corner. "He means Carbo. Carbo was assigned to guard, but I swapped him for one of my crew this morning after we had a minor accident."

Iasus nodded and loosened his grip on the stick again. "And the last?"

"A fairly plain man" the minister said. "A bit thin, brown hair, quite pale…"

"Kasta" spat Iasus. "Never did trust northerners."

Sabian squared his shoulders and put his sword away.

"Ok minister. I'll assume you've told us everything. We've got to go prepare for Ursus' funeral. Darius will deliver you back to Sarios and he will decide how to proceed with you."

As Darius herded the man back out of the octagonal room, Sabian turned and called after him "and bear in mind that if there's anything you haven't told me, I'll be back for you." He turned to the two sergeants. "Come on. We haven't got much time."

Making their way out of the ruined palace as hurriedly as they could, Sabian almost walked into one of his men who was trying to get past the barrier they'd replaced after they'd entered the ruinous building.

"What are you doing soldier!"

The man came to attention instantly. "I was sent to find you sir. There's a ship in the channel; should be here in a bit over an hour sir. Lookout says it's his lordship, sir."

Sabian smiled. "Good. Now get everyone but the lookout to the graveyard."

The vicious smile stayed riveted on to his face as he marched through the orchard. If Velutio was on his way, the lack of signal last night must have irritated someone. For an instant he wondered whether his lordship himself were behind this, but dismissed the thought after a moment. This was definitely the work of Crosus and, if Velutio was on his way now, that walking dead man would be right behind him.

133

Chapter XII.

The funeral was short and Spartan, but well-attended and with full honours. Sarios had dealt with every funeral here in twenty years, so Ursus was in good company. Throughout the whole thing, however, Sabian's mind had been elsewhere. He'd watched the three men the minister had named throughout the entire service but none of them had betrayed any sign of nerves. His real problems were how to go about the legality of proving treachery in the guard Captain and how to disprove anything the man accused him of. After all, his lordship was hardly likely to be in a welcoming and forgiving mood. The last lines of the prayers to the local spirits brought him back to the present. Velutio would be here in about half an hour.

Cialo and Iasus stood at attention, awaiting the command to fall out. Most of the island's population were in attendance despite their lack of connection with the man, but they stood still, perhaps unsure of whether to leave before the soldiers. Well let them watch. He turned to the six companies of men and cleared his throat.

"Soldiers Rufus, Carbo and Kasta! Front and centre!"

The three men fell out of their units and stepped out to the front, lining up shoulder to shoulder though, Sabian noted with some satisfaction, unhappily and a little hesitantly. He drew breath to speak again.

"These three men are guilty of treason and mutiny. In conspiracy with the doctor from Velutio and one of the island's elders who will be dealt with under local law, these three men have been undermining my command on Isera, feeding information to an outside source and disobeying orders. As co-conspirators they are also a party to the murder of trooper Ursus."

He paused to let this all sink in. To their credit, the three soldiers continued to stand at attention, unwavering. He folded his hands behind his back and addressed the men again.

"I'm sure I don't need to remind you that I encourage traditional values in my army and I expect most of you can tell me what the punishment was for both treason and mutiny in the ranks?"

The blood of the men was rising now. Sabian had a good reputation among his men and he knew it. Those who betrayed him, betrayed them, and in the current setting the murder of Ursus hung over them like a cloud. A number of voices cried out "stoning" or "death" among the general murmur of outrage and disgust.

134

There was some wavering among the three now, but they still didn't break. Sabian nodded. Very well, he would give them the black news now.

"Stoning. Indeed." He rocked on his heels. "Unless anyone else would like to speak up in favour of these three?"

The silence was deafening. Sabian nodded.

"Very well, according to military law you're all three hereby sentenced to death. I'll give you one chance to make it quick, though. Tell me what information has been sent to whom so that I can confirm my suspicions and I'll grant you a clean soldier's death, by the sword. Otherwise your comrades will take you away for a slow and painful way out. Now is your time to decide."

The three dropped from attention as Kasta glanced across at the others.

"We're going to die anyway!" he growled in a thick accent of the Northern provinces.

Carbo held his arm out to the mousey-haired northerner. "'ave you ever seen a man stoned to death? It's a fuckin' nightmare." He turned and took a step toward Sabian. "Give me the sword sir." A moment or so later, Rufus joined him, nodding. Sabian eyed them coldly and then glanced across at Kasta, who was scanning the crowd around him, his head moving wildly and a panicky look in his eye. The commander spied Iasus behind him and the sergeant nodded.

The moment Kasta broke and made a run for the orchard, Iasus and two of his men were already on his heels. Sabian cast his eyes across the other two who daren't even look after the escaping soldier. He gazed behind them at the troops.

"Cialo and four men with me. The rest of you know what to do!"

The grizzled sergeant and four of the men behind him stepped up to join the commander, while the rest turned, their fury still high and empowering their blood as they chased down the fleeing man. Sabian paid no attention to the cries and shouts among the trees. Kasta would be caught long before he ever reached a door and Iasus had both the authority and the will to carry out the appropriate punishment. The commander brought his attention back to the two in front of him.

"I've never had a problem with either of you? Why then?"

Carbo hung his head. "It's not you sir. You're a good man an' no one was meant to get 'urt." He stopped but Sabian just let the silence reign until the soldier spoke again. "We nearly came to you anyway after the doc told us what 'appened to Ursus, but we reckoned we was

135

too deep in it by then." Again a pause filled only by the man continuing. "It was that Crosus sir. 'E 'ates you sir."

Confirmation at last. Quietly, Sabian replied "I know."

Rufus picked up where his friend had left off. "He was going to get us commissions in the guard, what with him being their commander..."

"*Captain*," corrected Sabian.

"Yessir. Anyways, they get paid about four times what we do and they live in the palace. Crosus just wanted you to look bad. I think he wants you to look sort of soft sir. Think he wants your job."

Sabian nodded. "He *does* want my job. And I suppose it was the doctor who sent all the information, yes? He seemed to be very tight-lipped with it all."

The soldiers nodded and Sabian took a deep breath. "Well I'm sure my leniency here has armed Crosus with more than enough ammunition to cripple me. You all did your job quite well."

He looked across them at Cialo and nodded. "Take them somewhere private. Make it clean and fast and they're to be put next to Ursus."

The gruff sergeant nodded and the two soldiers, resigned looks about them, trooped off towards the Water Gate accompanied by Cialo and his men. He watched them go and suddenly realised that the island audience had not moved since the funeral. Inwardly he cursed himself for not having dismissed them before he talked to the traitors. Still, they already knew he'd been lenient and one or two of them were perceptive enough to have guessed he'd landed himself in trouble. Well he may not make is past Velutio, but he'd sure as hell make certain Crosus saw the sharp end of it all first. He turned to the assembled islanders who were all watching him intently, some curious, some approving, some even horrified. It took him a moment to notice Sarios standing deep in huddled conversation with Darius. He sighed.

"It would be a good idea for you all to go about your business. Lord Velutio will be here presently and I very much suspect you'll then see a change of command in Isera."

Without waiting for comment, he turned and strode off into the orchard, following the sounds of violent affray. It was not hard to find the scene. Kasta hadn't even made it out of the edge of the wood, as a trail of blood made clear. Iasus had had the taste and presence of mind not to do this among the islander's fruit-bearing trees. He found the hundred or so men by the south wall on the cliff. The broken, tattered and bloody remains of the northerner were in a pile against the stone wall base. There were blood, brains, guts and chips of bone in an arc around the unrecognisable pile of offal. The last few stones were still being thrown now, despite the fact that the man had probably been dead after the first volley. This was an expression of the loathing of a unit for betrayal in their midst and for all the unpleasantness of the sight, Sabian felt a rush of pride in his men. They were proper soldiers, not poncy fair-weather troops like the guard. Still, he was running out of time. He cleared his throat loudly and the companies fell silent and parted to allow him through. Iasus stood at the front; for the first time Sabian could remember the sergeant looked weary.

"Sergeant. Detail a few men to get a sack and fetch the remains across to the other orchard. I want them nailed and tied to that crucifix Cialo built last week."

Again the pride in his men. Not one of them argued or questioned. Iasus didn't even have to detail someone, as several people went for the body straight away. Nodding in satisfaction, he turned to head out toward the dock. If he was going to fall from grace today, he was going to make a blazing statement out of the whole event, and he'd take certain people with him.

A quarter of an hour later, Sabian stood on the path before the Gorgon Gate. Four companies of men in full gear stood at attention on the lawns, two on either side. The rest manned the gate and the top of the walls. The islanders all stood in the Ibis Courtyard, with Sarios at their head. The commander hadn't wanted them out front in case things went too sour too quickly and his Lordship merely landed troops to make a clean sweep of it. To his left, just a few yards off the path, an unrecognisable mass of body parts and innards was tied and nailed to a T-shape. If one looked for a while it was possible to pick out an eye; a hand; a foot. Doctor Favio had suggested the wood be smothered with some oil or other and flowers placed at the base to help cover the smell that threatened to make them gag. Sabian had refused. He had a message to put over as plainly as he could.

And now Velutio was striding up the path. No shock to Sabian to see Crosus at his shoulder along with a dozen of the personal guard in dress uniforms. He almost laughed. To think some of his own men had wanted to be that. He could only imagine how quickly those men would get butchered on a real battlefield. He stepped forward as Velutio reached him.

"Your lordship."

137

Velutio had been walking with his head lowered but now he raised his face and his pure rage shone in his face. He'd never seen the lord like that. Velutio got cold and calculating, not red and furious. His lordship thrust an accusing finger into Sabian's face.

"Tell me why I shouldn't have Crosus here kill you where you stand!"

Sabian almost laughed; this was too surreal. If he was that deep in, why not just ride the wave of insanity. He spoke lightly and with a humorous lilt.

"Firstly, because you need me considerably more than you need him. Secondly because I am in the right and I've done nothing wrong." His gaze came to rest on Crosus. "And thirdly, because if this trained ape tried to spit me I'd have to hand him back to you in slices my lord."

It was amazing when you knew it was a lost cause how easy it was to speak your mind. His words did nothing to mollify Velutio, but they'd provoked a huge anger in the captain. Sabian almost laughed again when he saw the purple colour of Crosus' face and the whitening of the man's knuckles on the hilt of his sword.

Velutio squared his shoulders. "Commander, you've picked up a very nasty habit of gainsaying and back-talking me since you came to this place. That is not the attitude of a trusted officer."

Sabian raised an eyebrow. "Indeed my lord? I would have thought that was exactly the attitude you need from a trusted officer? Yes-men will just nod and agree as you slip all the way down the slope. You need someone who argues. I have never done you disservice."

The lord turned his iron grey head and glanced at Crosus who was still shaking with anger and then back to Sabian again. "Nevertheless, the captain went to a great deal of time and effort to get a spy working within this community and suddenly last night, we stopped getting reports. Why is that I wonder, and where might my personal physician be?"

Sabian felt the ground gradually slipping away beneath him.

"The spy, *your* physician my lord, murdered one of my men and had been feeding you reports in a bad light in order to augment this shit-head's ever growing reputation and power base." He pointed at Crosus. "This man's been buying off my troops, bribing islanders and having good men murdered just to get him that little bit closer to my job." He suddenly realised an opportunity open to him here.

"And he can have it. By dead man's boots if he cares to try."

Crosus actually lunged forward, but Velutio held out an arm to stop him.

"I will not have you duelling or even besmirching the name of my guard while you stand under such taint. You deliberately disobeyed my orders at every turn and appear to have 'gone native'." The last phrase almost caused him to spit. "You never sent one person to the crucifix, which was a direct order." As he spoke, his eyes strayed to the mess on his right. A startled look crossed his face, which pleased Sabian no end. In fact the Gods might be with the commander after all today for, as Velutio noticed the crucified pulp, so the wind chose that very moment to double back on itself and carry the reek across both his lordship and the captain. Velutio merely turned back to the commander, his nostrils dancing in the miasma, and raised one eyebrow.

Sabian grinned. "One of Crosus' turncoats. I don't like traitors in my army."

He watched the changes of expression and colour in the captain's face with immense satisfaction while Crosus battled against the smell, the anger and now the uncertainty. Without letting either of them recover, Sabian continued. "The two men who sang me a whole long story died well and they're buried next to the veteran that Crosus had killed." His smile widened. "As for your doctor, he wouldn't cooperate at all, so I'm afraid I had to send him fishing without a head. Probably a good thing for you though my lord."

Velutio had not moved. "How so commander?"

Again Sabian smiled. "I suspect if you tell me what reports you've had and I tell you the truth, you'll find glaring errors. You see I rather think that the doctor was receiving a higher wage from Crosus than from yourself. In fact" he said, tipping his head to one side with a thought that hadn't occurred to him before, "I wonder whether the captain's long-term plan doesn't involve knocking me out of the game and then having you poisoned? Perhaps the murder here was a test-run was it Crosus?"

Again the big captain, his features red and furious made a lunge for Sabian and again Velutio prevented him. Sabian opened his mouth to rile the captain further, but a voice behind called out "commander!" Sabian's head swung around and he spotted the minister standing in the shadows of the Gorgon Gate with Darius at his side. Sarios was still in his priestly garb from the funeral and the white robe accentuated the black eye patch disconcertingly. He wondered when the doctor was going to try and deal with that. Darius was still wearing his leathers and bore the sword at his side. He smiled. Why not go the whole hog? This would make the lord and the captain as angry as anything.

"Excuse me for a moment my lord."

Even as Velutio opened his mouth to order Sabian to be still, the commander turned and strolled slowly and unconcerned up to the gate. Once in the shadows and out of earshot of the others he looked back down to see Velutio and Crosus in a heated debate. Good. Friction would help. He turned back to the minister.

"Well timed gentlemen. Can I help you?"

Sarios thrust his arms out to the sides. "What the hell are you doing commander? You're going to get yourself killed!"

Sabian smiled. "I think that's kind of academic now. Velutio's got too much on me and I've got no defence. I just want to make them angry enough that I get a chance to gut Crosus before I go."

Darius and the minister exchanged glances and, with a saddened look, the old man nodded at his charge. Darius turned back to the commander and withdrew something from the recesses of his tunic, thrusting it into Sabian's hands, keeping his back to the scene below.

"What's this?"

Sarios let out a long breath. "The one thing we have kept from you at all costs." Sabian began to unroll the battered scroll and his eyes widened as he recognised the island on the map, the reef systems, and finally several marked safe channels. He whistled through his teeth. Sarios continued "and the only thing that might save your reputation here.

Sabian thrust the scroll back at Darius. "I don't even want to know this exists."

Sarios grinned. "You don't think I haven't made a copy, do you?" Watching the slow smile form on the commander's face, he added "and I assume that Velutio will be on the track of young Quintillian by now."

Sabian nodded. "Velutio has spies and mercenary units pretty much everywhere. If they haven't found him yet it won't be long."

The minister stood for a moment tapping his chin with his finger. He seemed to reach a decision. "Tell Velutio that Quintillian and his companions landed just outside Serfium a little over a month ago." He dismissed Sabian who was waving his arms trying to shut the minister up. "The three of them then went to Calvion to acquire money. After that they were to get as far away from the sea as possible."

Sabian shook his head. "I'm not going to do that. I'm not going to be the one responsible for you betraying your people.

The minister smiled. "It's not the whole truth commander, but enough of it to get you off the hook. I doubt it will make any difference to Quintillian's chances."

140

Sabian stood for a long moment staring at the pair. Finally he nodded and, tucking the charts away beneath his cloak, strode back down the hill to where Velutio watched him impatiently.

"Nothing wrong I trust commander?" his lordship said coldly and sarcastically.

Sabian smiled. "No sir. Just conferring on a point of law with the minister. He does, after all, have a remarkable command of legal knowledge. It seems that I'm quite entitled with the amount of evidence and the number of witnesses I have to demand trial and punishment for the captain here."

Again Crosus' face went purple as he spluttered angrily. Velutio raised an eyebrow. "You're going to ask me to put my personal guard on trial?"

Sabian grinned. "Actually no. I'm going to demand he face me in trial by combat. Then we'll see how much he really matters."

Velutio shook his head. "I'm still trying to decide whether it's you who should be on trial here."

Sabian nodded. "Then let it be that way round. *My* trial by combat. So long as I get to face this armoured monkey I'll be happy." He reached into his cloak and withdrew chart Darius had given him. "You might want to hold this though my lord. It's quite important and I'd hate to see it get skewered."

Again Velutio's brow arched as he took the scroll. Unrolling it, Sabian was gratified to note genuine surprise on the face of his master.

"Where did you get these?" Velutio demanded.

The commander smiled. "I know you want me to be a despot, but I prefer to be fair. Being fair gets results too you know sir." He flexed his fingers. "I don't care whose trial it is my lord, but only one of us is leaving this place: him or me."

Behind Velutio, Crosus nodded, his hand around the hilt of his sword.

The lord stopped for a moment and then finally, nodding, stepped aside. As Sabian and Crosus both drew their swords and swung them a couple of times, Cialo and Iasus gave orders and the four companies on the grass fanned out into a circle of shields around the two officers. Crosus, armoured in a shiny steel cuirass with leather strops protecting the thighs and upper arms, swung a long, straight sword in wide sweeps. Sabian in his very traditional cuirass, much like that of Crosus but less ornate, swung his slightly curved blade in figure eights.

141

The first lunge came from Crosus, disguised initially as another practice swing of the sword. As the blade came to the top of its arc, he took a massive step forward and brought the sword down in a one handed sweep toward Sabian's head. The commander saw the lumbering move from the start and neatly sidestepped the heavy blade. As the point dug into the turf, Sabian trotted past his opponent, flicking out once with his blade and carving a line across the captain's thigh. Pieces of four of the protective leather strops dropped to the ground and blood welled up beneath the breeches within. Crosus growled.

Sabian came to a halt directly behind his opponent but made no use of the obvious opening created as the captain wrenched his blade from the ground and tottered back to face him. He was determined to make this as slow and painful as possible for Crosus. He'd like the opportunity to make him bleed from every surface and maybe even die from that before he could deliver a killing blow. He also had to prove a point about superiority to Velutio. He smiled.

Crosus took a couple of slow steps toward him and swung the blade out to one side. Too slow and too obvious by far. By the time the sword came swinging back toward Sabian's side, the commander dropped to the floor and came up from a roll behind the swinging edge, jabbing once with the point of his own sword and drawing more blood from the same thigh. He was rewarded with a grunt of pain from the burly captain. If this was all the man had, it'd be a short task. Crosus staggered with the weight of his swinging blade on his injured leg and had to allow a couple of steps back to regain his balance.

The captain righted himself and took up a defensive stance. He was learning from his mistakes. There would be no more stupid lunges. Sabian took a couple of steps forward, daring Crosus to strike again and the captain fell for it with no prior thought. He swung the sword, but in a much tighter, more controlled arc and Sabian raised his own blade, parrying with a flash and a scraping of steel on steel that set the watchers' teeth on edge. With a quick recovery, he struck again and Sabian parried once more, knocking his opponent's blade to one side. Again he flicked out quickly with his blade, drawing a red line across the captain's extended forearm. Another grunt.

Taking the advantage, the commander pushed forward with a swing over his shoulder. The captain parried clumsily, but turned the blade aside. Good. He'd not expected to connect, but to gauge the reactions of his opponent. What he didn't expect was the blow that landed. Although the sword had gone wide, the captain had swung around with his fist and punched Sabian in the jaw. The commander staggered back across the grass, his face throbbing with the blow. Damn he should have been more careful. Shaking the daze from his head he righted himself, realising that Crosus had followed up on the blow and was bringing his sword around and up in an arc. Despite his wounded leg, the captain was still moving surprisingly steadily. Sabian leaned heavily to one side and the blade whistled through the air where his shoulder had been a moment before. He gritted his teeth. The captain was starting to get a grip now, so he'd have to either unbalance the man again or pick up the pace and actually finish it.

Crosus came back into a defensive stance again and grinned at him.

"Come on you cheap whore. Fight me like a man."

Sabian shook his head. There was no way he was going to let this idiot goad him into doing something stupid. "Whatever you say ape man."

With a smile, he flicked the sword out to the left and withdrew it in a blur, sweeping out to the right with it. He was rewarded as Crosus pulled back to parry a blow that never came, the sharp edge instead slicing deep into his other arm. There would be no more punches from that arm. Crosus shambled back into his stance once more, starting to look less balanced. The loss of blood was working on him; his leg and arm were both drenched in scarlet rivulets and pools on the grass told of how much strength he was losing.

Enough was enough. It was no real effort and there was no glory in this. Dragging it out no longer mattered; time for a coup de grace.

With deliberate slowness, he raised the sword for an overhead blow. The captain saw the blade rise and, turning slightly, brought his own up for an overhead parry. Just as the blade reached its apex, however, Sabian spun to face away from his opponent and changed his grip on the hilt. The surprised captain didn't have time to bring his own sword back down before Sabian's came thrusting out behind him, gripped in both hands, shearing up through Crosus' leather strops and deep into his armpit. Sabian fell backwards with the blade and drove the length of steel deep into the man's chest until the sword stopped, point lodged against the opposite shoulder blade. Crosus stopped, going momentarily rigid, the blade still held aloft in his hand and his life essence pumping wildly from his armpit. He stared at Sabian in surprise and died where he stood, still transfixed by the commander's blade. As life fled the body and the muscles relaxed Sabian staggered under the weight, withdrawing his sword with some difficulty and allowing the corpse to crumple to the grass, blood pooling beneath it.

Heaving a deep breath, he straightened and turned to face his master. Velutio stood with his arms folded, his face expressionless. Digging his sword point first into the turf and leaving it swaying gently, Sabian walked slowly towards him.

"My Lord. I am innocent of any wrongdoings this heap of shit made you aware of. His own power games required that he make me look weak and take my position from under me. You may not be happy with what I've just done, but in the long run I've done you a favour."

Velutio merely stood watching the commander intently, so Sabian cleared his throat. "I also have some news about the youngster, Quintillian."

The older man shook his head.

"I'm glad to hear that, but it's irrelevant now. I already have leads on him. He's travelling with a group of mercenaries of some reputation to the north. I have a number of my own mercenary units tracking them down so they won't be at liberty for long."

Sabian nodded, trying to keep his own thoughts at the back of his mind. Today wasn't the day for brooding sentimentality. "So what happens now?"

Velutio turned and began to walk slowly up the path toward the shade of the Gorgon Gate where Darius and the minister stood. "Now I need you back in the city. There are no problems here and plenty of people on the trail of Quintillian. There's been some speaking out against me in the city of Helus and rumours of a rebel army massing in the hills above the place. As a vassal state of mine any hint of an uprising is unacceptable, so I want you to take the army down there and put down any resistance you meet." He stopped and faced the commander, who had been matching his pace. "Here's your chance to show me what you really *are* worth commander."

Sabian nodded. "And the island sir?"

"I think," replied the lord, "that you should leave three companies under one of your sergeants here as a permanent garrison. I don't want anything like this happening again."

Another nod. Cialo would relish the opportunity, he was sure. Equally, Iasus would like to get back to the city. The commander glanced up at the gatehouse and the two figures watching them intently as they approached. The island would be fine now, though he'd miss the opportunities to talk and spar with Darius. Still, who knew what the future held in these days.

144

Part Three: Heroes and Villains

Chapter XIII.

Kiva leaned back against the farm gate and sighed. Bees buzzed around him, congregating among the multicoloured wild flowers by the roadside. The low hills above the coastal plain were one of Kiva's favourite areas, though he rarely got a chance to spend time here. In fact one of the greatest battles of his career had been only a few miles from where he stood right now, around thirty years ago when the tribes of the Pula Mountains had finally managed to pull together under one leader and make a serious push into the Empire. It had been high summer then too, with bright golden sunshine pouring over the lush green hills and the sounds of bees and meadow fowl playing through the air. He scanned the horizon, a single piece of hay jutting from the corner of his mouth; he'd been around Marco far too long.

The rest of the unit sat on the grass verge opposite the stone farm building, sharing bread and flasks of who knew what while they rested their tired limbs and chattered away meaninglessly. Athas was the only alert one, keeping an eye on the road whence they'd come. Things had been quite comfortable on the journey toward the sea and no unpleasant surprises had caught them unawares in the last month of travelling. They'd had the best of the weather for the journey as in a couple of weeks the climate would become much more changeable and unpredictable as summer slid into autumn. Still, they'd be on the plains and in the towns long before then

A voice caught his attention. Turning his head toward the path he saw Quintillian jogging toward him. It amazed him how adaptable the young man was. In just a month he'd become so entrenched in the life of the Grey Company that it was becoming difficult to remember what it was like before they'd found him. To look at him now one would hardly recognise the pasty, permanently unhappy youth that had crawled out of a thorn bush seeking aid and safety. A month of travelling in the summer sun had somewhat bleached his hair to a dark bronze and given his previously pale complexion a healthy glow. His muscles had bulked out considerably, largely due to the two hours of weapon practice a day the lad endured under whoever had time to tutor him. Indeed, the way he wore his swords; the hang of his armour; the comfortable pace when he ran all spoke of a man of arms. He'd become a soldier, there was no doubt about that.

"Captain..."

Kiva heaved himself from the wall.

"Septimus" he acknowledged Quintillian by the name the unit used on a daily basis. "Something amiss up front?"

Quintillian shook his head.

"Not amiss I think." He smiled. "There are at least a dozen men about a mile away down the hill. Some of them are staying off the path in the bushes, and I think they're waiting for us, but not in ambush."

Kiva cocked an eyebrow. "And why's that?" Obvious to him, but the lad needed testing every day in every way. The worrying thing was that he was progressing as a scout and a tactician faster that Kiva and the others could really teach him. He had a voracious appetite for learning.

Quintillian grinned. "A test, sir? Very well. Five of them are waiting on the path itself in the open. There's so much cover in the area that they could easily have remained unseen to the last minute. Moreover, their horses are tethered in plain sight and without a guard, so they expect no trouble and aren't preparing a quick escape route. I only counted two bows among them and they're both on the road, not in good positions for picking travellers off. Shall I go on?"

Kiva laughed. He hadn't laughed a lot in the last couple of decades, but for some reason Quintillian brought out something in him he hadn't seen in a great length of time.

"Ok, I believe you. You know what you're doing."

Quintillian sheathed the knife he'd been carrying, a curious habit he seemed to have picked up from Mercurias, and his grin widened. "There's one other give-away about them..."

Kiva raised his eyebrow again and the lad continued. "Two of the ones in the road are rather familiar. Big man with a shaven head and a heavy scarf round his neck and a smaller man sweating his life out under a bear skin cloak."

The captain grinned. "So Tythias caught up with us after all. Still, it's taken him a month. Wonder what he wants?"

Quintillian squared his shoulders and placed his hands on the weapon pommels at his hips. Shall I run out ahead? I wonder if he'll recognise me."

Kiva smiled. "I'll get the rest of this lot and follow on. You take Athas down with you." He turned in the direction of the bulky sergeant who remained transfixed on the path behind them and opened his mouth to call out but the sergeant pre-empted him without looking.

"I know... I heard. I've been traded to the boy."

146

The big dark-skinned man turned and his white teeth shone in a warm smile. Again Kiva pondered. While his own relationship with Quintillian had improved and the two of them talked as though they were members of the same unit, there was always a strained undercurrent. He knew the boy wanted something more from him but the conversation had never arisen since that day in the temple ruins. As long as he and the lad travelled together, there would always be an element of discomfort that they would have to ignore.

The captain had always tended to spend the nights separate from his men. Not far away but separate nonetheless; he slept little and had a propensity to wander. Quintillian, on the other hand, seemed to have hooked up particularly with Athas, Marco, Brendan and Bors. The five of them were always together in the evening playing dice, telling stories or just talking. Kiva was fairly sure that the lad had been working his ideas of a return to glorious Imperialism on the company, since he was forbidden to speak of it to the captain. Still, that bunch were prone to romantic notions anyway so what difference would it make?

With a shrug, the captain watched the sergeant wandering off down the path with the young man by his side amid the flowers and bees and the gentle heat haze. It was hard to imagine two more physically different individuals. He cleared his throat. "Ok you lot" he shouted. "Pack up; time to move. There's some old friends down the road waiting for us and I want to get to Carmana before dark."

The company stood, stretching their legs and hoisting their armour and packs into position. As he turned back to the wall to collect his own swords, he caught Mercurias for a moment staring at him in an odd, curiously knowing way and made a note to ask the medic about it later.

By the time the rest of them were on the move, Athas and the lad were already down in the dip with Tythias and his men. Kiva crested the hill with Thalo at his side and was intrigued to note that still not all the 'Lion Riders' were on the path and in the open. A number remained in the bushes and, despite Quintillian's good eyes, he'd missed three more that remained on watch around a half mile out from the meeting. What the hell was Tythias being so careful about? Who'd he angered this time?"

As Kiva approached the group on the road, he motioned Thalo and Scauvus to either side and the two ran off toward the scouts away in the trees.

"Tythias," he said as he came to a halt. "Nice to see you again. What's all this in aid of?" He gestured around at the Lion Riders among the bushes.

The scarred mercenary reached out and clasped Kiva's hand. Curiously his customary smile was absent. Kicking himself for his over confidence, Kiva's smile faded too in anticipation of the worst.

The captain of the Lion Riders stood beside the big brute he remembered from the Inn at Acasio. The mute made a hollow whistling noise and nodded.

"Tregaron." There was not a hint of the usual humour about Tythias' greeting and Kiva's hand found its way unconsciously to the hilt of his sword, where his fingers played on the pommel. Tythias folded his arms. "I could have saved myself a lot of work if I'd paid more attention to your young 'Septimus' back in Acasio. I've been looking all over for him for a couple of weeks now without really knowing who it was I was looking for."

A quick glance to either side confirmed that the Grey Company were all ready for trouble, though no blade had actually been drawn yet. "Go on..." prompted Kiva.

"We're here for him, I'm afraid. Velutio's paying a thousand corona for the boy that travels with your company and he's not particularly fussy over the state he's returned in. In fact, I think he suggested a preference for dead."

Kiva reached out with his right hand and pushed Athas' hand down, forcing the blade the big man was starting to draw back into the sheath.

"Whoever you think he is" Kiva answered, "he's one of my company and you can't have him."

Tythias shook his head and held his hands out. "I was kind of hoping you'd have dumped him by now. I can't pass up on a thousand, but there's five hundred more for the unit he travels with that I'd prefer not to collect."

Kiva smiled, though there was no humour in it. "Tythias, don't start this. You won't win. We've never fought each other; not properly. Anyway, you were a commander of men in the noblest service on the planet, man. We're old comrades. You took an oath, remember?"

Tythias shook his head. "I remember the oath. Hell, it was under you I took it, but the world has changed Kiva. If I don't claim the reward someone else will and they won't be half as reasonable about it as me!"

Athas stepped in front of Quintillian. The boy had said nothing so far, but his hands were twitching around the hilts of his swords and he was glaring at the captain of the Lion Riders. The big sergeant frowned at the mute in front of him. "How about you, whitey? You feel like another try?"

Jorun shook his head and made an "Ah... aghk" noise as he pointed at the boy. He turned to Tythias and shook him by the shoulder. "Aghk! Ah... ah... ah!"

Tythias ignored him.

"Kiva, what's happened to you? A thousand gold for him? You've never passed up an offer like that in your life. I could be persuaded to split it..."

The burly barbarian continued to shake his captain until Tythias' head snapped round angrily. "What is it you great idiot?"

Jorun pointed desperately at the boy. "Akk!" he shouted.

Athas stepped to one side and with only a momentary glance at Kiva, addressed Tythias. "I think what your big friend here is trying to tell you is that he knows who the boy is."

Kiva turned sharply and gave Athas a barely-perceptible shake of the head, but the sergeant shook his own in reply. "It's no good captain. Now his hair's changed colour, he's unmistakable."

Kiva's attention was drawn back to his opposite number by a whistle.

"Hell and fucking Gods!" exclaimed Tythias. "You mean..."

Athas nodded. "Why else do you think Velutio would pay that kind of scratch for a boy? He's not that way inclined."

"Holy Hell!" Tythias swung round away from them, throwing his hands onto his head and rubbing his scalp as he considered the situation. One of the younger members of his group shrugged. "Who is he?"

Tythias laughed and Kiva was pleased to spot a note of hysteria in there. "Who *is* he? He's the fucking Emperor! Or he would be. Or will be. Or something. Shit, Kiva. How'd you land yourself in this?"

Before Kiva could reply the young Lion Rider piped up "There's no Empire any more so does it matter who he is?"

Tythias motioned to Jorun and the big barbarian slapped the young man round the side of the head with a hand the size of a dinner plate. The outspoken mercenary collapsed to the floor, his eyes rolling up into his head as he fell.

Tythias laughed again. "Does it matter? Does it *matter*?"

Kiva smiled. "See the kind of shit life throws at me Tythias?"

Again Jorun tugged on Tythias' sleeve and made a hollow questioning sound. Tythias turned to him and nodded. "We all used to take the oath, of course I took it. And it still damn well applies now, yes." He fell silent as he glanced back at Kiva. "Of course it might not apply to you."

Kiva growled and the other captain shook his head. "Never mind. We can't take this bounty; we'll have to head west again around the coast. Can't have Velutio find out we've let his prize escape or he'll have the next bounty out on *us*." He stepped close to Kiva and his voice dropped to a whisper. "Be very careful now Kiva. We'll get out of here, but you're walking into a world full of trouble. There must be fifteen or twenty mercenary units between here and the city looking for you at the moment, and then there's plenty of ordinary folk who'll drop you in it for Velutio. He's offering too much for you to rely on friends."

Kiva shook his head. "There's one place I know I'm safe. Just need to get there."

Tythias looked at him silently for a long moment and then nodded once. "I'm going home for the time being, so if you run into too much trouble you know where to find us." Kiva nodded. 'Home' to the Lion Riders meant the old Imperial fortress of Vengen in the North West; Tythias truly was getting out of the way. The scarred captain turned and then stopped as a thought crossed him. "You're heading to Serfium I presume?" Without waiting for an answer, he shook his head. "Fair enough, but don't go through Carmana. I presume that's the way you're heading, but Janus and his Spear Company are waiting there in the hopes you'll pass by. Find another way around."

Kiva nodded. "I'll do that." As the two clasped arms and smiled, Tythias lowered his voice and said "what are you going to do with him?"

Kiva shrugged. "I really don't know yet. Maybe take him back home."

Another nod and the two captains separated. Kiva raised one eyebrow as Tythias drew his sword and walked across the path towards his horse. Halfway across the cracked dirt track, he paused and thrust the blade down between the shoulder blades of the unconscious young mercenary from his unit. He turned briefly as he wiped the blade and noted the quizzical look on his opposite's face.

"He didn't understand the oath. I won't have men of no morals in the Lion Riders. See you on the other side, General Caerdin." Grinning, he climbed onto his horse and called to the rest of his men, who also began to move. Jorun, the big barbarian with the wrecked

150

throat paused, staring at Athas and the boy. Tythias frowned. "Come on you big ape."

Jorun looked back over his shoulder momentarily and then grinned at the big black sergeant. He stepped forward and held his hand out. With a smile of genuine surprise, Athas took the hand and shook it, releasing as the big man stepped away. As Jorun backed up next to his huge cart horse he stopped, looking at Quintillian and bowed deeply before straightening and climbing on to the horse. Tythias looked across at Kiva and smiled. "You northerners are all far too bloody sentimental you know that?"

With that the Lion Riders cantered off into the scrubland and were gone in minutes. Athas motioned to the unit to prepare to move out, just as Thalo and Scauvus returned from the bushes. Kiva stretched his back and called out for the unit's attention. "We're changing route again. Tythias is right: Carmana's too dangerous. There's a village about three miles from here and we're going to make for it and stay at the small inn there. There'll be no carousing though, cos I want everyone asleep long before sunset. We're going to leave again at midnight and travel in the dark from now on. It'll be two or three days from there to Serfium and I'm damn determined to make it there without running into any of Velutio's dogs. Now move out!"

And with that the Grey Company began to move once more, with Marco and Quintillian heading out to the front as scouts. Athas walked alongside Kiva for a while in silence until he suddenly turned to the captain.

"You really *don't* know what to do about him do you?"

Kiva sighed. "Do we have to have this conversation again?"

The big sergeant grunted. "You've got to decide before we get to Serfium. You know you won't cast him adrift to fate there."

"For fuck's sake Athas," Kiva rounded on him, "what do you want me to do? Adopt him? Crown him? You know as well as I do that there's no way we can face off against the big lords. It doesn't matter how noble a cause you follow if your enemy has a hundred times your number. Now give your jaw a rest and forget about it."

Without a word, Athas glared at his captain and then dropped back to play rearguard once more. Kiva's sigh of relief came too soon as Mercurias glanced over his shoulder and then slowed his pace, dropping back to walk alongside the captain. Kiva frowned at him.

"What is this, some kind of nagging relay?"

Mercurias prodded Kiva in the shoulder and pointed out to the grass at one side of the path. "Get out of line. We'll catch up with them in a minute."

Kiva looked for a moment as though he'd argue, but in the end shrugged and stepped aside onto the springy turf. As Athas went past frowning at him and the column slowly trooped on along the road, Mercurias stood face to face with the captain and pointed his finger at him, inches from Kiva's nose.

"You listen here Kiva Caerdin. I'm a little bit older that you and a hell of a lot more sensible. Athas is absolutely right: you need to make some decisions before we reach Serfium. Your men are slipping away from you, you know?"

Kiva raised one eyebrow as he folded his arms and the medic went on. "Quintillian is the most important thing any of us has seen in more than twenty years and he's got the touch. The sentimental and the optimistic are already forming their own ideas and making their own decisions about him. If you can't control the situation, you're going to lose men at Serfium and I won't allow that."

"*You* won't allow that?" interrupted Kiva.

"No. They're my unit and my friends as well as yours. You're a good commander. Hell, you're one of the best, but the time's come to stop being bitter and pessimistic and actually strive for something. Tell me honestly, do you still have even the faintest intention of sending him off in a boat at Serfium?"

Kiva glared at the grizzled medic for a while and eventually shook his head. "Mercurias, I don't want to see the lad sent back to his island. Hell if we did that he'd be dead in a week, as soon as Velutio found out he was back. On the other hand, Velutio wants me dead, so I'm a liability to him. Where can we take him? He might have been better going with Tythias up to Vengen. At least he'd be safely out of the way there."

Mercurias nodded. "At least now you're thinking. So you don't want to send him back to the island, but you don't want to travel with him. You're ruling things out... keep going."

Kiva glanced across in annoyance, but the medic was absolutely right, and so was Athas. He'd apologise to the sergeant later. "I know what the men want to do. I heard Brendan the other night when he'd had a few too many battering on about a war and a new Empire and so on, but that's just not feasible." He held up his hands in supplication. "There'll be a new Empire soon enough, but it'll be Velutio's, and then the rest of us'll have to find places of exile.

Velutio's the only one with enough of a power base. Every war we fight makes the other lords weaker, while he just keeps getting stronger. Every month another lord swears fealty to him and it's almost got to the point now where he's more powerful than all the others put together. It doesn't matter how good our cause is, we've no hope of going up against someone like him and time's almost up."

Mercurias nodded. "Fair enough. You can't send him home, you can't keep travelling with him and you're not ready to start a war. What's left then?"

"I really don't know. Why d'you think I haven't made a fucking decision? I'm just hoping we can get to Serfium safely. I've got plenty of friends there and we'll find out a lot more about what's going on then. We can't make any kind of move, but we can't delay forever. What would you do?"

Mercurias shrugged. "I don't make command decisions. I'm a medic, remember? If I could plan like that, I'd have been a commander."

The two began to walk fast, catching up with the unit, already a long way down the path. As they walked in silence with Mercurias quietly humming an old tune, Kiva's mind churned possibilities constantly. It was true that the unit suddenly felt different these past few weeks. They'd always got by as they were, but now the men were adrift and looking for some kind of purpose and he really couldn't work out what direction that should be. If there were some way to break Velutio's power then the world of opportunity would open up in front of them, but that was such a massive undertaking with no real chance of success. Hell, he was a cursed man; a deicide. The fates were unlikely to be kind to him.

Perhaps he could go home. He'd not been in his native northlands since he was young and energetic. He couldn't even remember how to speak their language these days, but at least the boy should be safe there. Maybe he could leave him there and then the company could get back to its business. He grunted in annoyance and reached down, clutching his side. The pain was back. For some reason it always got worse when he was angry, but it was getting noticeably more regular and more painful as the years passed. He reached into his tunic and pulled out his flask, taking a swig of the nectar within and feeling the numbing warmth envelop the sharp sting beneath his ribs. He looked up to see Mercurias watching him.

"You never let me look at that" the medic complained.

Kiva shrugged. "Nothing you could do. Nothing anyone can do."

"How the hell do you know?"

"I spent a while in a temple when it happened, remember? A very good surgeon looked me over and decided it was too close to my liver to touch and the muscle was healing around it. Even if I sneeze it grazes me. Can't be removed, so I've just got to live with it."

Mercurias snorted. "Just like you then."

Kiva glanced sidelong at the medic and smiled humourlessly. "I'm going ahead to talk to Quintillian. You just keep your funny comments to yourself."

With that he jogged on ahead, wincing with each step as the pain hadn't quite subsided yet. As he passed the rest of the unit and they acknowledged him with nods and salutes, he noted once again the subtle change in the men. They looked different, and not necessarily in a good way. The carefree smiles they habitually wore had been replaced by looks of concern and thoughtfulness. Perhaps it'd have been better if the boy had never found them.

Quintillian was only a hundred yards ahead of the group. He and Marco were walking side by side deep in conversation when Kiva dropped to a walking pace beside them. With a quick glance at the boy, he nodded to Marco. "Go back and join the others. I'm taking point until we get to the village."

As Marco nodded and slowed to let the rest of the unit catch up, Kiva settled in to walk along side the lad.

"I've been thinking about what happens when we get to Serfium. You want to go back to Isera. Now I know Isera. Used to spend quite a lot of time there and I know that it's part of the demesne of Velutio. Going back there is just going back into captivity and, worse, Velutio now has your death warrant ordered, so he's unlikely to let you live even if you go back voluntarily. I assume you used one of the old Imperial escape routes to get off the island. If we're very lucky I might recognise the route since I've used them before, but very few know of them. There are a couple of people in Serfium that'll know how to get there, but it doesn't solve the problem of why you'd want to go back. Tell me."

He looked ahead as they crested a hill and spotted the smoke from the chimneys of the village around half a mile away. "And give me the short version."

Quintillian sighed. "I'm not going to be safe anywhere now captain. It strikes me that the safest place for an escaped prisoner to

154

hide is in his cell. It is, after all, the last place the guards would look. Sarios and the elders would hide me away. It may not be a permanent solution, but it's the best I can think of."

Kiva nodded. "In theory it's all well and good but now that Velutio knows you escaped from the island, you can bet there's a garrison there and though Sarios is a very subtle and clever man, he can't hide you for long on a patrolled island the size of Isera. There's got to be another way forward, but I just can't think of it yet."

Quintillian smiled. "Well while that tactical brain of yours is coming up with a solution, what better place for us to be than in Serfium, where you used to live and on Isera where I have many friends." He frowned. "Are we on terms where I can ask you personal questions yet captain?"

Kiva sighed. It was another one of those trying days. "Go on. If it's too personal I'll tell you, don't worry."

Quintillian swallowed nervously. He'd been avoiding certain subjects for so long he wasn't sure whether he was comfortable asking about them. "It's about your estate there. In Serfium" he added with an inherent question.

"Not a subject likely to endear you."

"No." Quintillian raised his brows. "But I think you owe it to me to tell me something. I know that we're related you see."

Kiva frowned. "We're not related. You're related to... her."

"Livilla." Quintillian nodded. "But that makes you a relation of sorts. "I want to know what happened when my uncle died. I've read the histories, but Mercurias keeps telling me that they never give the whole story, and it's the story of my family and their friends, so I'd rather like to know the truth.

Kiva glanced aside at the boy. His speech had become noticeably easier and less fancy during his time with the company. It made him easier to listen and talk to.

"Livilla was your uncle's cousin; she was quite a woman. Had all the power and intelligence of your family, but no pretensions." He realised how insulting that must sound. "Sorry. No offence meant, but it's hard to wield infinite power without acquiring a few pretensions. Your uncle was like a brother to me; had been ever since the early days and I spent a lot of time on Isera with him and his court. Well I'm not going into too many details, but Livilla and I were wed in the spring and in the winter I was sent on campaign in the west. When I came back during the thaw I couldn't help but note a decline in Quintus. He spent a lot of time alone brooding and the palace servants began to disappear. I

155

guess I just kept fooling myself into thinking nothing was wrong. I was distracted at the time, you see, as Livilla and I had a son that month. I called him Quintus after your uncle, you know? They were good days for me, but it didn't last long. Over the next couple of months things just got too bad and a number of the Emperor's close advisors began to turn against him. He was seeing plots and conspiracies everywhere and because of the way he reacted to them, they came to be real. The court members who were frightened of your uncle spoke to the senate and they condemned him for a madman; imprisoned him on his own island. The man they sent with an army to deal with him was one of my peers, General Avitus. I was outraged when I heard and I left the training camp at Munda and marched on Velutio with my men. We routed Avitus' rebels and restored Quintus to the throne in the city. It all looked good again for a month or so, but then even I had to admit there was something very wrong. There were accusations of treason and random executions in the city. People started to live in fear like they had under the Emperor Basianus. That's when I was sent on a punitive expedition and told to burn a city. I disobeyed my orders and marched back to the city, demanding your uncle withdraw his order, but he wouldn't. He accused me of conspiring against him and tried to have several senators and senior officers, including me, executed. In the end, I sent my army back to Munda, dismissed the palace guard while he was relaxing in his new Golden Palace and put an end to it. You and your mother were safely away in the city at the time."

He took a deep breath. Quintillian realised how much speaking of this was hurting the captain and held up his hand. "I'm sorry captain. I shouldn't…" Kiva waved him aside.

"You should know" he replied, "and I've not told the story in two decades. They say a trouble shared is a trouble halved, yes?"

When the lad nodded, Kiva took up the story once more.

"I left the island, probably by the very same route you did, and went back to Serfium. I was quite distraught as you can imagine, and went to spend time with Livilla and the boy. Unfortunately Avitus had been vindicated by what I did and he came back to power very quickly, getting one of the other Marshals on his side. He started killing people off in the city; anyone who opposed him in any way met the sword. I was a recluse while all this was happening but the last Marshal, Covis, took up his troops and went to stop Avitus. They ended up fighting just north of the city around Serfium. I was out at the time…"

156

Kiva swallowed and Quintillian looked up at him in concern. He was about to ask the captain to stop once more when the story tumbled out again.

"I went for a ride in the hills to think. I only realised something was wrong when I saw all the smoke, so I turned and charged back to the town, but I was too late. Covis' army were annihilated around the town and the damage was immense. I'm probably selfish to think of it in the terms I do, cos a lot of villas were torched and many of the people in the town itself were killed out of hand, but it was my villa that I couldn't take my eyes off. It was an inferno when I arrived and Avitus' troops were marching away. It was nearly four hours before the house was safe enough to get into. They were all there. All of them. The servants, the animals and in one of the dining rooms Livilla and the boy." Again the captain stopped, his voice having deteriorated to a croak.

Quintillian, his face deadly serious, grasped Kiva's arm. "I read about the rest, you don't need to tell me."

Kiva smiled weakly. "I'll not go into detail. You know how I fight, so you can picture the scene. I went back to the city. He was still calling himself Avitus then; didn't change to Velutio until he dismissed the senate a few months later and took control of the city. He'd had most of the people of any power killed, including your mother and, as far as we all knew, you. To be honest, until you mentioned him I'd presumed Sarios to be among the victims. I wonder how many others are still alive on your island that were supposedly killed in the city. Anyway, I sought out Avitus and we fought for quite a time. I was always better than him, but I wasn't in my right mind at the time and not as capable as I should have been. I let him get the better of me and he stuck me in the gut with a knife. I fell off the wall we were fighting on and somehow managed to land in a midden, so I didn't hurt myself further. By the time Velutio got down there to finish me off, I'd gone. I made my way back to Serfium and to the temple there. I don't know how long I spent there, but it was probably a month. The knife came out easily enough, but he'd chipped a shard of bone off my rib and it'd worked its way in to rest on my liver. Never been right since, but I'm still alive."

He turned and looked down into the boy's eyes.

"I think that's pretty much it. You know more now than most people, as much as the rest of the company. Athas found me in the temple, you see. The Wolves had come looking for me after they heard

157

about the fire. After that we left the lowlands and disappeared from the world of Velutio." He smiled and added "until now."

Quintillian nodded. "Velutio should pay for everything he's done. And one day I'll make sure he does."

Kiva smiled at him and looked up and around at the outskirts of the village. "Right now let's get into the inn and have some food. And maybe a drink. I once introduced your uncle to a drink my people make in the mountains. It used to be hard to get, but it's a lot more common now, so we might get a shot or two."

Quintillian grinned as they headed for the inn door. "If it's the stuff that Athas drinks, I've tried it. It tastes like it's already been drunk once."

As Kiva laughed and opened the inn door a voice from within called "General Caerdin. I thought you must have got lost."

Chapter XIV.

Kiva's hand went straight to his sword hilt, as did Quintillian's by his side. The interior of the inn was dark despite the sun still being high, and in the shadows to the side of the door a single figure sat behind a heavy oak table, cradling a glass between his hands. He appeared to be the sole occupant apart from the innkeeper who remained behind the bar, nervously polishing drinking vessels. Kiva allowed a moment for his eyes to adjust and could hear the rest of the Grey Company approaching the door outside. He squinted into the low light and his eyebrow rose in surprise.

The figure at the table was tall and thin, turning the glass back and forth between long elegant fingers. Dressed in a knee-length surcoat and robe of black silk, with a winged horse picked out in gold, he was an imposing sight. His face was swarthy and clean shaven with dark, piercing eyes that peered out beneath straight, perfect brows and Quintillian found it extremely hard to place his age. The stranger's hair was long, dark and straight, held back from his eyes with a thin, plain coronet of gold. He smiled in a predatory fashion.

Kiva frowned, his hand not leaving the pommel of his sword.

"I thought it might be you when you launched that attack on us back near Acasio. Athas found one of your men's weapons. You're as subtle as ever, my Prince."

The swarthy man nodded slightly.

"And you, Caerdin, are not as subtle as you once were." The man's eyes drifted to Quintillian and the smile widened showing perfect white teeth with curiously prominent canines. "And this is the boy. First time I've seen him up close." His accent was noticeably eastern, but with perfect tone. Quintillian spoke to Kiva without tearing his eyes away from the stranger.

"Captain, who is this man?"

Kiva's gaze also remained on the black figure as he replied, still not smiling.

"This is Prince Ashar Parishid, nephew of the King of Pelasia."

Quintillian nodded. "I've read a lot about Pelasia; used to be one of the Empire's staunchest allies, yes? I've also read a lot of unflattering material."

Ashar smiled still. "All of it untrue I'm sure."

Athas' voice joined them from the doorway. "Untrue my Prince? That your people spied for the Emperor? Carried out

159

clandestine assassinations? There's a reason for the old saying 'the only Pelasian you can trust is a dead one.'"

Ashar's smile faltered for only a moment. "Say what you like Athas, but we only ever served the boy's uncle. It was his own people who betrayed him." His gaze moved back to Kiva. "Enough of this bantering. We haven't spoken in over twenty years and the only thing we can do is insult each other? Ridiculous. Come. Sit."

The prince turned and waved to the barman. "Bring me whatever it is you keep in reserve under the counter. Price will not be a problem."

The rest of the company were now drifting in through the door. Quintillian glanced at Kiva for direction and the captain nodded. He and the boy took a seat opposite the prince. Athas pulled up a chair at the next table and the rest of the men scattered themselves around the bar at tables close by. Brendan stood by a window and turned to Kiva.

"Want me to set watch, captain?"

Kiva shook his head. "Hardly worth it. There'll be two dozen assassins out there in the shadows. If his highness wanted us dead, they'd have jumped us on the way in."

The prince laughed. "How little you think of me. Perhaps I trust you implicitly and my men are carousing and taking advantage of local hospitality."

Kiva smiled now, but with little humour. "And perhaps the winged horse on your cloak will take flight and drag you across the rooftops my Prince. How did you know we'd be here? Even we didn't know we were making for the village until an hour ago."

Ashar placed the glass on the table as the innkeeper brought over a tray of varied bottles, some of surprisingly high quality wine. "You are about as difficult to follow as a camel train of bells and gongs. You move slowly and noisily. We've been tracking you since your battle at Bergama's lands and I must say that if even your friend Tythias can find you with his one eye, then be sure we will always know where you are."

Kiva nodded. "You're absolutely right. Enough bantering. What do you want and why did you attack us outside Acasio?"

"Straight to the point as always" the prince smiled, pouring himself a glass of wine and motioning for everyone to help theirselves. "Refreshing after dealing with my countrymen for so long. I yearn for those days I spent in Velutio with you and the boy's uncle."

160

Quintillian stopped in the middle of pouring a glass and interrupted. "You keep referring to my uncle. How do you know who I am?"

Kiva answered before the prince could speak. "The prince here knows everything that goes on everywhere. Hell, I'd bet he knew you were leaving Isera before you did."

Ashar nodded. "It was his escape that brought me back, it's true. But it *is* good to see old friends also. Very well." He drew a deep breath. "We had to have a little go at you on the road; I was intrigued. I haven't seen you all in twenty years. To be honest, we weren't sure it was even you until I spotted Athas; you've changed rather a lot, you see. I wondered whether age had slowed your wits and your blade. I was pleasantly surprised to find that you're as good now as you were back then."

Kiva nodded seriously. "And you haven't changed at all. Shit, you even look younger than you did then. Why were you tracking us then? Tell me you don't want to claim the boy for Velutio. I can't imagine *you* working for him."

A laugh, rich and deep. "No. No I can't see myself allied with that man either. He's less trustworthy than any of ours. No." The smile dropped from his face. "I do want the boy, though."

Quintillian stopped, a glass of rich wine almost at his lips. Thalo and Marco rose and moved to the door and other window without the need for orders. Indeed, the whole company moved up to the alert, Mercurias playing with his knife on the table top and Bors with his longsword in his hands, point down on the floor. Kiva shook his head. "The boy's not going anywhere and you'll have to kill all of us before you can harm him."

Trying not to betray his surprise at himself, Kiva wondered when that had happened. When had Quintillian become such a focus of concern that he would consider placing the Wolves in jeopardy to save him? Curious the effect the boy had on people without them even noticing, but then his uncle had been much the same.

Ashar smiled again. "You misunderstand me, Caerdin. I don't want to harm the boy. In fact, quite the opposite. I want him to assume the title that is his birthright."

Kiva blinked. "What?"

The prince looked around the inn at the readiness of the company and shook his head sadly. "It's such a shame that the years have turned you over-cautious, Kiva. You don't trust me anymore. I tell

161

you your men can stand down. My soldiers and not within a mile of us at the moment."

Kiva snorted. "Don't flatter yourself highness. I never trusted you, even in the Palace when Quintus ruled. I *liked* you, but that's a whole different matter; I never trusted you. And I still don't. Why is the boy any of your concern? What's in it for you?"

Ashar shrugged. "The Empire was ever a good neighbour to Pelasia. Our trade has declined; we have to suffer the stings and bites of small raiding parties from your petty lords on the border that would never have happened under Imperial rule. And of course, there's family. Don't forget that my grandmother was of the boy's house."

"Sentimental crap" announced Kiva, taking a slug of something expensive and refilling the vessel.

"Alright" answered the prince with a curious smile. "You tell me why I want him."

A voice from the other side of the room interrupted. "You've lost your position, haven't you, highness?" They turned to Mercurias who'd put down the knife and was peering at the Pelasian. Ashar grinned.

"Your doctor was ever the most perceptive of the Wolves, Caerdin."

Kiva raised an eyebrow at the medic and Mercurias shrugged. "His uncle's been usurped. Why else would he be interested in the power struggles of the Empire? Why else would he leave his lands and come this far on a fool's errand like this?"

Ashar nodded. "He's quite right. Very bright for a man who shuns the learning of our own doctors. You *know* we're centuries ahead of you in medicine, Mercurias." He turned his attention back to Kiva and Quintillian. "Yes, my uncle is no more. His head now graces the tip of a lance over the Moon Gate at Akkad and the twins are buried in an unmarked grave somewhere in the desert. I am the last of the Parishid dynasty. Pelasia is slipping away into chaos in much the same way the Empire has."

Athas shrugged. "That means nothing; you have no small power yourself. You should be able to take the throne back without too much effort."

Kiva turned and wagged his finger at the sergeant. "Not that simple though," he turned back the prince, "is it? You could take it back, but you couldn't hold it. Not now that the Satraps have seen how possible it is to remove a King. It's not easy to kill a divine power, believe me, but once you do everyone gets ideas."

162

The captain patted Quintillian on the shoulder. "That's why he needs you. Got to put the Empire back together so that he can have Imperial support when he retakes the throne. No Satrap would stand against him then. Otherwise he'll stay on the run out here."

Quintillian frowned. "I still don't understand. Velutio's close to becoming an Emperor himself now and I'm the perfect bargaining chip, yes? From the prince's point of view, giving me to Velutio would get him the support he needs anyway."

Ashar grinned. "Don't believe for a minute that I didn't consider it either."

Kiva shook his head. "Velutio would never ally with a Parishid ruler. They were close to the Imperial family; they even share the blood. No; Velutio wouldn't stand for Parishid interference."

Mercurias piped up once more. "This is getting us nowhere. The fact remains that he wants Quintillian and he can't have him…" he turned and gazed questioningly at Kiva "can he?"

The captain sighed. "I'm afraid not, your highness. I appreciate the fact that you're the first person we've come across that wants to support him and not to kill him, but I'm not actually ready to let go of him just yet. We might be able to come to some arrangement though, if you tell me your plans for him."

Ashar frowned. "I'm not in the habit of revealing my strategies before they're carried out, Kiva. You know that, for you were ever the same."

The captain smiled back at his opposite number. "Just for once, it sounds like we're working to the same end. Let's not spoil it."

"Very well" the prince replied. "For all your harsh assessment of my people, you are correct that we have the finest assassins in the world, and I intend to use them against your old nemesis. Velutio has the most powerful army in your empire, but that won't help him if his head wakes one morning next to his body."

Kiva shook his head. "That's bad planning, Ashar, and you know it. You're more desperate than you let on, otherwise you'd have thought this through further."

"Explain." A simple demand from the Pelasian.

"If you kill Velutio," sighed Kiva, "all you do is take away the incentive for the lesser lords to behave themselves. If Velutio dies, the chaos will increase, not decrease."

The prince nodded. "I realise that that is a possibility, but it would be easier to put down the smaller lords than the master himself. Besides, what other choice is there?"

163

It was Athas who picked up the conversation now. "Did you ever play 'towers' when you stayed in the capital? It's a very good strategy game that the captain and I used to play regularly. The objective is to destroy enough of the opposition's towers that the remaining ones are too far apart to support each other. I was never all that good, though the captain was better… but Quintus was the best player I ever saw."

The prince narrowed his eyes. "I believe I see where you are going with this, but do go on."

Athas smiled. "He's the only player I ever saw completely demolish the opposition. He left not a tower standing. The game was nice and evenly balanced one minute and then he pulled a trick I'd never even thought of and in only three moves I had no pieces left. It was unbelievable."

Ashar nodded. "But this is no game and we have no Quintus. We have Quintillian and the towers are real and filled with armies and hungry lords. A nice story, but how does it apply?"

Athas coughed. "I'm not actually sure yet. The captain and I have discussed the future a few times though and it always comes back to the game. All the towers have to go at once, as we only have a couple of pieces ourselves." He glanced across at Kiva. "There's only one man here with the kind of tactical genius that Quintus had, so we'll have to wait until the captain here has a flash of inspiration."

The prince nodded. "It's up to you then Caerdin. If you have plans for the boy, I will not interfere. Perhaps we will work together when the time comes? I will wait upon your magnificent brain and when you think the time is right and your plans become clear, call my name. I will never be very far away." He smiled at the boy. "And we'll drink to the health of your future ruler and my future ally."

Raising his glass the prince stood, saluted Quintillian, and drained the amber liquid. Dropping the glass back to the table, he reached into his surcoat and spun around. A chisel-tipped throwing knife whistled through the air with an accuracy that surprised even Kiva and entered the innkeeper's throat just below the chin. Turning back to the table, the prince refilled his glass and smiled. "I told him price would not be a problem" he joked as behind him the innkeeper slithered down the wall leaving a trail of red.

Quintillian blinked. "Why him?"

Kiva patted him on the shoulder again. "If his highness hadn't have done it, I would have. Within a day Velutio would know you've been here and the barman would be able to retire a wealthy man."

164

The prince laughed loudly. "Unless you've undergone some miraculous training in the last two decades, you'd not even have hit the wall, let alone the barkeep!" Taking a sip of his drink and replacing the glass, he wandered over to the bar to retrieve his knife. Returning and wiping the blood on a bar cloth before sheathing the blade, Ashar raised an eyebrow and regarded Kiva as he sat. "What are you planning to do then until your miracle comes to pass? Remain on the move? In hiding?"

This was of course a question Kiva was ill-prepared to answer, having only the loosest idea himself. He watched the prince suspiciously. Still, the Pelasian would know what he was doing as he did it if not before and had as much at stake here as anyone. Sometimes the least trustworthy of people became the ones you had to rely on.

"We head for Serfium. I've friends there from the old days who'll keep us out of the way of Velutio's hunters. Quintillian wants to return to Isera though I'm loathe to walk into the bastard's hands like that."

Ashar nodded. "Foolish indeed. Perhaps some of my information will be useful to you, at least in preventing such insanity."

Kiva pricked up an ear. "You know about what's going on in the capital then? Anything you can tell us might help. I'm stuck at an impasse at the moment."

The prince laughed loud. "When was I ever in the dark about current events, Caerdin?" The smile faded and with another sip of wine he placed his hands on the table. "Very well. Velutio is well aware of how the three fugitives escaped Isera. He now has a chart showing the old Imperial escape route as his commander spent a week on the island with everyone there. I believe some harm came to the minister, though no report yet has suggested that he has passed away, so I presume he still runs the island. There was some altercation between the commander of Velutio's army and the captain of his personal guard and I believe a man called Sabianus is commanding both units. Other than that events on Isera are a bit of a mystery. It was hard enough gathering intelligence on the island before Velutio's troops landed there and my source on the island stopped signalling once Sabianus landed. All the information I have now has been gleaned from sources in the city."

As Ashar took a breath before continuing, Kiva held up his hand. "What kind of man is this Sabianus? Do you know anything about him?"

The prince shrugged. "Only a little. He has a good reputation as a commander and very highly paid. He's been sent to deal with insurrections by some petty lord to the south at the moment. Velutio's left a small garrison on the island and it really would be ridiculous to go there. Now that he knows about the escape route, you can be sure there's no secret way in any more."

Kiva smiled. "There's always a card up my sleeve, highness. There's more than one secret passage through the reefs. Just have to know them, that's all. Still, I agree." He turned to Quintillian. "Going back to the island is nothing short of surrender and probable suicide. We have to find another way forward, and I think I'm getting an idea."

The prince raised a questioning eyebrow. "Your mind works fast general."

"Sometimes." He drummed his fingers on the table thoughtfully. "Though this relies on stirring up a lot of trouble. Can you find out about this commander Sabianus for me? If he's a good commander, he might be someone from the old days. There were an awful lot of lesser officers I didn't know, but if he commanded in the Imperial army, you can be sure that I'll know someone who knew him. On the whole Imperial officers would tend to be more sympathetic, but I don't want to push anything until I know more."

There was a scraping noise as Athas pulled his chair across to their table. "Do I take it we're getting ready to act, captain?"

Kiva grinned. "Anything that stops you and Mercurias nagging me night and day has to be worth a leaping into the mouth of hell with a very long rope." He turned back to the prince. "Ok. If you're really in this the whole way, we might as well make some plans, but if we are going to actually commit to something I have to have absolute control. You have to submit to my command, alright? I want the old oath from you and from all your men."

The prince frowned. "I will not take your soldier's oath Caerdin. I will not be bound to you for the rest of my life, but I will remind you that I am still bound by an oath to the boy's uncle. We have an accord between our nations that supersedes anything you may ask for, and that oath stands for my men also, as it does to any Pelasian."

The captain nodded. "I'll accept that, though I want your men back here and I want to hear you all reaffirm that oath to Quintillian."

"Very well, general. I will submit to your command. What would you have us do?"

Kiva smiled and rummaged in his pack, producing a stylus and a wax writing pad. Scraping off the existing text, he started to scribble furiously. "This is a list of the few Lords I can think of who might consider joining us. They're all currently free men, but all live in the shadow of Velutio. You'll need to use my name and that of Quintillian to convince them." He slid the tablet across to the prince, who picked it up and rand down the list of names.

Another rummage in his pack and the captain withdrew three items. Two flasks emblazoned with the insignia of the Wolves appeared on the table, next to a ring with a seal. He passed one of the flasks to Ashar. "This should be proof enough you've spoken to me." Pushing the ring across, he stared meaningfully at the prince. "This is the only one of its kind left, so be very careful with it. The Imperial seal. They were all destroyed, but as a member of the family I have one as a keepsake. Do *not* lose it."

He turned to Quintillian whose face was aglow with wonder. The boy spoke in a low croak. "You still have a seal?"

"Yes." Holding out the second flask, the captain continued. "This is for you. You're not an Emperor yet, but you are one of the Wolves now."

He turned back to the prince. "Between your status, my name and the Imperial seal, you should be able to convince any lord that still has a yearning for order and peace. I do warn you, though" he added, "that if any of them will not give you their oath, they must be dispatched for the good of the cause. I know that won't be a problem for you."

Ashar nodded. "You gather an army. What am I to tell them?"

"Tell them to wait for the Winter Feast. We need a lot of time to pull everything together. Tell them to marshal their armies at Munda on the day of the Winter Feast. By then we should be able to act."

The prince frowned. "I can see how building a rebel army in secret is of use, but this is not the toppling of all the towers of which your sergeant spoke. How do you intend to even the odds? Even with this list of petty lords and your old allies from the army you'll still be outnumbered at least ten to one if not more. What else do you have planned?"

For a moment a dark look crossed the captain's face. "That is something I'm not ready to speak of yet. I have an idea that should help us seriously even the odds but a lot of this plan relies on reputation and appearance. We must be seen to be in the right, restoring something broken and longed for."

He drummed his fingers on the table once more. "Next, you need to send some of your men out and about. I want every scrap of information they can gather on Velutio, his commander, the situation among the lords of the central Provinces, potential rebellions and coups,

167

troop movements, barbarian threats on the borders and anything else they find out, no matter how trivial it seems. Any information can be passed to the priests of the temple at Serfium. Be sure it'll reach me from there. Equally, if you need to contact me, talk to them. If I need to get a message to you, I'll leave word there. Understood?"

Ashar nodded. "Understood general. Your mind is as sharp as it ever was. It is a pleasure to see you again." Kiva grinned as he noted the optimistic buzz among the Grey Company in the room. He turned to the others, rummaging in his kit for some of the coin that Quintillian had given him.

"Athas and Mercurias. Buy horses" he commanded. "Get after Tythias as fast as you can. Try to catch him before he gets all the way to Vengen. Tell him the same thing: Munda at the Feast. Tell him to get in touch with any of the other units from the old days that he knows and trusts. After you've spoken to him, head round the coast to the west. The last I heard, both Filus' and Sithis' units were employed round there. Find them, pass the word on and then get a ship back across the sea to Serfium and join us."

Athas grinned as he took the coin and turned to Mercurias. The grizzled medic smiled one of his rare smiles and accepted some of the coin, motioning again with his hand. With a sigh, Athas produced his flask of spirit and handed it over.

Kiva drew a deep breath. Brendan and Marco? Head to Munda and check out the lie of the land there. I don't think it's been occupied since the Fall, but I'd rather not have any nasty surprises. Anything that needs dealing with, we'll do it well in advance of the Feast. While you're there, find the old meeting place and get all our old kit out of storage. Make sure it's clean and polished. Half of this will be about appearance. Seeing the Wolves in full kit riding at the front of the army should be enough to boost the morale of our allies and frighten the hell out of a few of our enemies."

He stretched his arms. "The rest of us will head to Serfium with Quintillian and keep our heads down very low. Without myself or the boy, you shouldn't run into any serious danger. None of Velutio's men are looking for odd pairs of mercenaries on the move."

With a deep sigh, he reached out and took a deep pull of his drink, turning once more to the prince with a sudden thought. "I take it your men are actually around outside and you're just obfuscating out of habit?"

Ashar smiled. "Would I disappoint you?"

Kiva shook his head. "Do I take it they'll have dealt with anyone who could have heard or seen us?" The Pelasian nodded a reply.

"Very well, get your men back here so they can reaffirm their oath." As the prince nodded and stood, straightening his surcoat, Kiva turned back to the rest of the room's occupants and cleared his throat. "Same goes for all of us. We took an oath to a man who's been gone more than two decades and an Empire that went with him. Now we need to take that oath again." He paused as he turned to the boy. "This time to Quintillian."

As the Pelasian prince leaned through a window and imitated a strange eastern bird call, Athas and the others shifted the tables and chairs out of the way to the edge of the room. At one barked order from the large dark-skinned sergeant, the unit fell in as three rows, dropping to one knee. Kiva gestured at Quintillian. "You can't just sit there. This is important. In all your reading and studying, did you ever learn about the oath?"

With a grin, the lad stood and faced Kiva. "I know what's to be done, captain." He stepped into the centre of the room, squaring his shoulders and drawing his sword, which he held vertical next to his head, his other arm across his chest with a clenched fist in the old fashioned salute.

As the Pelasian soldiers returned to the inn, clad in black and moving lightly, they stopped in the doorway to watch an Imperial Marshal leading one of the most famous units in history in the traditional soldier's oath of allegiance. Somehow Quintillian looked larger and more imposing now than the boy they'd seen fighting among them a month ago in the hills. They watched silently as the Wolves repeated each line after their captain, and as the last line of the oath faded away, Quintillian held out his arm with the sword above their heads in the traditional Imperial benediction as he accepted their allegiance.

Minutes later the second oath was taken, and Kiva nodded in satisfaction as the Prince led his own men in their speech. As Quintillian's second benediction echoed, Ashar turned to the captain. "And so begins a new history, eh Caerdin?"

Kiva nodded quietly. He fervently hoped so.

Chapter XV.

Nine weary men trudged along the road on the outskirts of Serfium. Quintillian had found that his voice became quite choked that night in the village when he had to part from Athas and Mercurias, heading north on horseback as fast as they could go, and Brendan and Marco, heading south at equal pace. The captain had spent some of the nights' travel walking with him, but more on his own as his mind churned with ideas and plans for the near future. Instead, the big but ever quiet Bors had spent most of the time as Quintillian's closest companion. He'd become quite good friends with the gentle giant over the last few weeks, surprised as he was by how calm and intelligent the man was, despite his initial appearance.

Kiva walked with his head down, a wax tablet and stylus in hand, periodically scribbling notes in the dim pre-dawn light as something leapt to mind and occasionally tutting in frustration and scribbling them out again. Clovis and Scauvus spent most of the time as they travelled ahead and out of sight, scouting the wilderness for any sight of Velutio's mercenary groups, but had found nothing but occasional signs of units having passed. Now that they'd reached the built up area, the two of them had pulled back in and walked only a few yards ahead of the rest of the column. It would be at least another hour until sunrise and the streets were empty and silent. Kiva put away his writing materials as they passed the first building, far out.

Quintillian watched the captain looking this way and that as they walked in the eerie half-light. They passed a few recently constructed buildings on the very edge and then came to a long open stretch of road. Quintillian wondered for a moment why these houses had been built so far out with a long stretch of countryside between them and the main mass of the town, but then he spotted the shapes looming out of the dark; shells of collapsed buildings standing like land-locked shipwrecks, jutting wall fragments reaching toward the canopy of the night. Young trees grew within the ruins and many were covered with ivy. With a nervous swallow the lad realised why the captain had been so quiet recently and why his head turned constantly as they moved. He found himself wondering which one of the sad ruins had held Livilla and the boy named for his uncle while the flames had charred their bones. A shudder ran down his spine. Fire. It always came back to fire where the captain was concerned. Perhaps his family's death was the Gods inflicting their punishment on Caerdin for harming one of their own. He shook his head, angry with himself. He was of the

170

Imperial line too and he was damn sure he was no God, so Quintus the Golden had been naught but a man, which meant that none of this was the working of fate or Gods, and there could be no curse on the captain. In actual fact the man, and probably his uncle and Velutio for that matter, were only doing what they each believed in their own way to be right. A serious of unfortunate and sad accidents and necessities.

He almost walked into the back of the captain as he was deep in thought and hadn't noticed the man stop in his tracks. This must be the one then. About a hundred yards from the road a crumbled wall rose up out of a dip. Fragments of a roof were visible in the corner, where some kind of creeper had grown and held the fractured masonry and tile together. He swallowed again, worried that he might shed a tear if he pondered too much on the sight before him. Yet, unbidden the visions came: pictures flashing in his mind of screaming women and children, unable to escape the inferno as the soldiers surrounding the villa threw more and more lit torches in. A haystack flaming next to the wall perhaps. The roof collapsing when a fireball exploded into the sky as the flames found the fuel for the under floor heating. Quintillian cursed his imagination. He could see it clearly. Perhaps that was for the best though, since there were no tears in the eyes of Kiva Caerdin as he looked on his old home. His eyes were grown hard and a sense of furious purpose shone in his face. Quintillian understood. The urge to shed a tear was gone in him now, replaced by a cold anger. He would exact revenge on Velutio for everything the man had done in his life.

He was still seething silently and personally when he became aware that Caerdin had started walking again, past the ruins of the broken villas and into the town itself. The walls of Serfium were white and clean, even in this curious early morning light as they passed between high-walled houses and narrow side streets in the town that was once the centre of the summer villa locale for the Empire's elite. The sun was not far off now, and the light increased noticeably every few minutes. He shrugged off the feeling of loss and sadness from the burned villas they'd passed and concentrated on the town itself. Presumably the captain knew where he was going and what they were going to do, so he would just follow along.

They passed a corner with an ironmonger's that was closed as the shopkeeper would be still abed, and reached a wide crossroads surrounded by old buildings whitewashed and with red tile roofs. Kiva stopped at the crossroads and frowned. He beckoned to Clovis and Scauvus and then pointed up the side streets. "No point in being foolhardy. We're being looked for as a unit. Clovis? Take Julian that

171

way. Scout through the edge of town to the other end and then work your way back to the temple in the square. Scauvus? You take Pirus the south route and do the same. Move fairly fast. You've only got around half an hour before the streets will start to fill up, so I want you in the temple in twenty minutes at the latest. Stay out of sight and out of trouble." His face serious, he added "and don't go anywhere near the harbour. The town's still asleep, but there'll be people working down there."

The men saluted quietly and then started to jog off down the side streets until they disappeared around the curve of the road and out of sight. Quintillian glanced around himself. The Grey Company were diminishing rapidly as people were sent on errands missions and now only five men walked down the road into the centre of the town. Kiva and Bors walked on either side of him, with Alessus and Thalo behind, paying careful attention to every window, door or alley they passed. They really were running out of time. The light was coming up fast now and Quintillian could pick out colour in the windows of houses.

The street was long and straight and as the light continually improved, so did the range of vision. Quintillian suddenly spotted an edifice far ahead in the centre of the street: a fountain ten or fifteen feet high carved in the forms of the Sea King and his mermaids. He smiled. "Funny thing Captain, but I've come full circle now. I passed that statue months ago just after we landed on the mainland. We went out to the north so I haven't seen any of this part of town."

Kiva nodded. "I know Serfium quite well. The town hasn't changed, but the feeling of the place is different."

"How long is it since you were last here?"

The captain shrugged. "At least ten years. I try not to come back too often; it's not very pleasant for me and I'm a reminder of worse times to the people I know here."

The captain picked up a little pace as they neared the central square. It was saddening to see the town he knew so well, that he'd called home for years, so different now. Gone was the happy festive atmosphere that was the heart and soul of the community in the old days. Thirty years ago generals, senators, governors and other rich or important men had private villas around Serfium and with them came family and attendants, servants and slaves. The whole town had thrived and embraced its Imperial status. Now Kiva walked past a hollow, cylindrical marble stump used as a flower planter. In his mind's eye it still bore a magnificent bronze statue of the Emperor Corus the Great, conqueror of the steppes, dressed in the garb of a soldier. Without

172

looking, he could remember across the square the statue of Basianus the Fair in priestly garb. There was no point in looking for the statue of Quintus the Golden, once ten feet high in marble and bronze and towering on its pedestal in front of the Tribunal building. That had been one of the first casualties of the new regime. Velutio had torn down all the Imperial statuary across his demesne, shattering the marble and melting down the bronze to arm more troops.

He looked up to see Quintillian watching him with a look of concern. He smiled weakly. "Sorry. Getting soft in my old age."

Quintillian laughed gently. "Somehow I can't see that."

The captain stopped and the other four clustered around him. "What now?" asked the young man.

"Now?" Kiva repeated. He pointed ahead. "Now we go in there and hope there hasn't been a change of priesthood in the past ten years."

The temple of the Divine Triad dominated the square more even than the public Tribunal. Law and order had never been a great issue in Serfium, quiet coastal town of wealthy homes. The Tribunal had only really been used for regular public meetings and occasional minor disputes. The temple on the other hand, had to be grand enough to support some of the most important families in the Empire. There were only three cities in the Empire with larger temple complexes than Serfium, and one of those didn't count, being dedicated to strange eastern Gods in Germalla.

The temple itself was circular, but with a curved porch of high marble columns facing the square; a portico of impressive dimensions itself. A triangular pediment above showed the birth of the Gods in a marble frieze that had seen better days, much of the paintwork having faded or flaked off. Behind the colonnade stood two high embossed bronze doors. They would not be locked; the doors of the Triad temples were never locked.

Quintillian whistled through his teeth. "That's a big temple. The Temples of the triad on Isera are small comparatively."

Kiva nodded. "A lot of that's down to your grandfather. Basianus wanted no temple on the island to be bigger than his own. You see he may have been called 'the fair', but nicknames are rarely accurate."

Quintillian frowned. "I didn't know there was a temple to my grandfather on the island?"

"There isn't now" the captain replied. "You see, your uncle became very egocentric long before any serious slide into ... well anyway, you know what I mean. He had the temple Basianus built torn

173

down and his Golden House built over the site. In fact some of the stonework was reused; I remember him building the place. He had all the statues of your grandfather put to one side and the bases were re-chiselled. Your grandfather's name was removed from them all and replaced with his own. In fact, there aren't many Imperial statues left now, but any time you find one of Quintus, there's at least half a chance it's actually Basianus with the name changed."

Quintillian frowned. "You mean that even before he went insane he destroyed statues and temples of his own uncle?"

Kiva nodded. "Of course. It was standard practice when a previous Emperor had been condemned for anything in the public eye. He had to distance himself from Basianus you see?"

Quintillian nodded and stepped to keep up as the captain had begun to stroll toward the doors of the great temple.

They stepped into the shade of the colonnade and it was only then that Quintillian realised that the sun must actually officially be up now. A quarter of an hour ago there had been little difference in the grey half-light between being sheltered or in the open air. Now the eyes had to adjust as one stepped from the open air into the shade of a canopy.

The captain reached the doors and grasped a huge bronze handle, wrenching it to one side and heaving the doors slowly open. Normal practice was for the doors to be opened just after sunrise by the priests, but Kiva was in a hurry. The handle squeaked and screeched as it turned and strained and the veins stood out of the captain's forehead as he hauled on the heavy bronze door, pulling it gradually open.

The main room of the temple within was a domed circular span, with small chapels and rooms leading off in various places. The main area of habitation was to the rear, through doors denied to all but the priesthood. This alone was the public space, but what a space! The dome was perhaps forty feet high in the centre, with a huge diameter. The room itself could easily contain the entire population of the town of Serfium. A dark look crossed the captain's face. That very ability had been proved over twenty years ago while Velutio's army had rampaged around Serfium hunting down the remaining soldiers of his opposition while the frightened populace flocked to the one place they felt safe. Hundreds of terrified people crowded into this room, listening to screams and sounds of battle outside; to occasional sounds of collapsing buildings and the roaring of flames. The captain shook his head to clear it of such memories. Not his memories, for he had been miles away with his horse on a hilltop, but he knew well what had happened in the

174

town. Some of them had been his friends, and some of his friends had not made it to the temple and had been trampled, speared, burned or even raped in the streets before they could make it to sanctuary. A victorious army always had to be tightly controlled by its commanders, or it could easily become a mob, but it seemed that Velutio had *wanted* a mob once the battle was over. A mob would give him fear, and fear was a very useful weapon to a new power.

As they stepped into the wide open central dome, a figure in a white robe stepped forward from the rear doors. He was an old man, perhaps even what one would consider venerable, with a short and well-tended beard and white hair cut in the old fashion. With a slight limp he stepped up the stairs onto the circular central platform and held his hand up in greeting.

"Kiva, my boy, it really is good to see you. I had feared the worst. Messengers ride into town every day now asking whether people have seen you. It must have been hell out there."

The captain smiled and mounted the central platform himself, reaching out to shake hands with the elderly priest. "Pelian. You're looking good. I'm afraid I'm going to have to impose on you and ask for sanctuary for myself and the rest of the company."

The priest nodded. "Well you'd better come in the back and divest yourselves of your packs."

Quintillian stepped up onto the platform, but the captain just watched the priest turn and walk across the room. "Pelian..." Kiva said, "what's up?"

The priest stopped and turned. "Nothing Kiva. Why?"

The captain's hand went now to his sword hilt. Quintillian opened his mouth, but got barely a syllable out before Kiva interrupted him. "Shh!"

The priest smiled. "Come on, we have much to talk about." This time, Quintillian picked up on the look in the old man's eyes and realised that he hadn't actually agreed to the captain's request for sanctuary, more side-stepped it. The young man's hand now also went to his sword pommel. Something was very wrong here and he had the feeling the priest was doing his best to warn them. The old man turned again for the rear door and it was at that moment that an arrow whistled out of the air above and struck the priest through the chest. Quintillian drew his sword, as did Kiva ahead of him and the other three behind. A figure appeared on the balustraded gallery that ran around the circumference of the dome, with a crossbow in hand. Quintillian's sharp mind told him there were more than one, as his bow was loaded and

175

he'd not had time to reload. Before he could think what to do, the captain had wrenched his throwing knives off the thongs round his neck and hurled them up into the open canopy. More by luck than by judgement, one of them grazed the bowman on the shoulder, the other fell considerably short and clattered to the marble floor, skittering across to the wall. Behind them the huge bronze doors clanged shut with a sound that reverberated around the central room. Simultaneously, ahead of them the door to the priests' chambers slammed.

Behind him Quintillian heard the stretch of a bow string and the creak of the wood. An arrow whistled past his head as Thalo, probably the fastest and most accurate archer Quintillian had ever heard of, released. The arrow took the man Kiva had grazed directly in the forehead, slamming through the bone and knocking him backwards and out of sight on the balcony. Quintillian's smile crashed from his face as the whistle and thud of the arrow was answered by the snapping sound of four or five crossbows releasing. Turning in horror, he saw Thalo jerking this way and that as the bolts plunged into his torso and head, his arms and legs flailing and spasming as though he danced.

He heard himself shout something as he ran towards the company's archer, but had no idea what it was. Panic and grief hit him in waves and that horror amplified yet again as he saw Bors running for the stairs to the side that led up and onto the balcony. It was such a wide open space he'd never have stood a chance. Another two crossbows released, hitting the big gentle man at the same time, both in the back, and hurling him across the room, where he landed at the foot of the steps and lay there jerking rhythmically. Quintillian knew enough to know that the man was already dead but that his nerves wouldn't let him rest yet.

Kiva was already moving, though Quintillian was riveted to the spot. His life had turned upside down in a matter of seconds. He'd lost two of the group who mattered to him more than anyone, and he was in danger of losing the other two. He saw Alessus and Kiva making for the rear door.

"No!" he screamed. For just a moment, Kiva stopped running. Perhaps he thought the lad had been hurt but he stopped and, a moment later, so did Alessus. A shudder of relief ran through Quintillian as he saw a dozen crossbowmen leaning over the balustrade. There was precious little hope the two would have even reached the door, let along force it open before they were both exterminated as the other two had been.

Again, he found his head turning. The body of Bors lay still, the jerking having finished, his head and one arm on the stairs. The way he had rolled as he fell, the two bolts had been driven deep into his beck and then sheared off at the entry point. His long sword, the largest single handed sword Quintillian had ever seen, lay some six feet away where it had slid as he hit the floor. A pool of dark blood was slowly spreading across the white marble at the foot of the stairs. Too dark. One of the bolts had gone through his liver. Taking in the horrifying scene, his head still turned until he found Thalo, lying with an arm and a leg folded beneath him, the way he had fallen. His bow lay close by and his eyes stared at the centre of the dome, unable to close. His mind flickered through scenes from the last two months: Thalo nodding seriously at him as their arrows came down from the farmhouse wall and took down an enemy soldier before the archer raced away to beat Marco to the loot; Bors, only two nights ago, grinning and handing him a canteen he thought was water only to find it was filled with fiery, thick liquor. Other scenes of their travels, both happy and sad, but all of comrades; comrades now gone. Quintillian was angry.

"Captain" he called out. "They want me; you're incidental. Don't give them a reason to kill you."

A voice from high above echoed his sentiments. "The boy's right. I don't really care whether we take you in living or dead. In fact dead would be easier, but I think his lordship would prefer you alive."

Kiva stepped back. Unable to see over the balustrade from his position near the rear door, he walked backwards toward Quintillian, with Alessus close by. Not far from the centre of the circle he stopped and looked up at the figure on the balustrade: a thin and perhaps even slightly effeminate man. "Phythian?" he called. "That you?"

"Of course it's me Tregaron. How many other people make such a use of crossbows in this number? I told you a year ago in Burdium that you'd not stand a chance if we'd been on different sides."

The captain snarled. "Why kill Thalo and Bors. You know them for fuck's sake!"

The man he'd called Phythian smiled a dead smile. "You've got too much of a reputation these days Tregaron. We're all well aware of how dangerous the Grey Company are, so we all shoot first and then decide what we should have done."

The captain growled. "So what now?"

Phythian shrugged. "We wait for the other four and then take you all to Velutio and see how much the lord will give us if we don't have the full set. I don't suppose you'd like to tell us where your sergeant and the other three are, would you?"

Kiva snarled again. "Tythias got them back in the hills" he lied. "They won't be giving him any trouble. The murdering bastard had them knifed in their sleep."

Phythian nodded. "Very well. The Lion Riders will have to claim the rest. Still, we'll be sitting pretty just from what we have. I think by now you've traditionally dropped your weapons when you know you're surrounded and there's no hope."

Kiva dropped his sword. Quintillian blinked. He hadn't for a moment considered that there really wasn't a way out; the captain always had something up his sleeve. As Alessus also dropped his blade with a low growl though, he realised that he would die if he didn't join them. Swallowing back the misery he let his fine blade, the one that had once belonged to Jorun of the Lion riders, fall to the marble with a clatter. Two of the men from the balcony trotted down the stairs and edged round the three of them without getting too close, collecting up their weapons. The captain growled at them and then looked up at his captor.

"Do you have any idea who this boy is that you've laid your hands on?"

Phythian laughed. "Wrong question Tregaron. Do I *care* is what you need to ask."

"You might" replied Kiva "*if* you knew."

Phythian trotted lightly down the stairs to where the three of them stood. The other soldiers had collected all the weapons now and were busy dragging the bodies behind the stair case. He smiled that snake-eyed dead smile again as he walked round the three in a slow circle. He stopped in front of the boy. "Let me guess. He's someone important enough that you think it'll change my mind." He stared deep into Quintillian's eyes. "Ah yes. He has to be one of the Imperial line. Curious, since I thought they'd all died. Nice try Tregaron, but you see if he were a God, as they say the Emperors were, then this wouldn't happen, would it?"

He raised his hand and one of the archers above let loose a bolt that plunged deep into Quintillian's thigh, ripping through the muscle until it protruded from the flesh at the rear.

"Presumably Gods aren't indestructible then." Phythian gave a laugh that was as dead as his smile and cradles his hands.

"Get in the back chambers" he told the three.

178

Kiva and Alessus reached out to help Quintillian walk. He had gone pale with shock and, though the wound was far from mortal, a surprising amount of blood trailed along the floor as they half-supported, half-dragged the young man across the floor toward the rear exit. The captain stopped as they reached the door and it opened of its own accord. Beyond another six men stood in the priests' robing chamber, crossbows already levelled at them. Kiva's hope for an escape from the rear chambers faded instantly. The bodies of half a dozen priests lay strewn around the floor of their own chambers. Phythian was unlikely to be turned around with any kind of appeal to reason or honour if such sacrilege was not beneath him. He turned to look at the cold, mad man that had brought them to this and spat on the floor.

"When I'm back on top there won't be a fucking hole in the world deep enough for you to hide from me, Phythian."

The man just laughed again. "We shall see. I can't see you bouncing back quickly from this. Anyway, your friends are coming; I can hear them. Let's hope they don't do anything stupid, eh?" He motioned with his finger and unseen hands slammed the rear door shut. The heavy door cut off all noise from within the dome and Kiva growled again, furious with his impotent position.

He stopped in silence and could hear his heart beating. Where was his plan now? Where were the allies he needed? He glanced around at the six men training their weapons on them. Perhaps he and Alessus could take three each. The lad would be no use now with a leg than wouldn't support his weight. But then they had no weapons and would each take two or three bolts before they reached the archers. No, it was no use. There was no way they could get out of this for now. He frowned at the six guards. "We're going over to the corner. We need to get the boy comfortable. Ok? We're not escaping, so don't shoot."

There was no acknowledgment from the six, so he turned to look at the boy. Quintillian was now out cold. Perhaps the pain; perhaps the loss of blood. He and Alessus lifted the boy by the shoulders, eliciting a lifeless groan, and dragged him over to two benches at the room's corner, where they lay him gently on one.

Alessus made a harrumphing noise as he undid the scarf from his neck and tied it around the boy's leg just above the wooden shaft. "Wish bloody Mercurias were here."

Kiva shook his head. "No you don't, and neither do I. Just staunch it as best you can. There's no hope of us getting out of here now, but it's quite a long road to Velutio, and anything can happen

179

between here and the city. Perhaps Phythian might have a little accident."

Alessus nodded. "Wonder what the hell's happening out there?"

As if in answer, the doors were suddenly thrown open and the young Julian limped into the room, two bolts through his shin and one in his shoulder. Alessus looked up in concern and Kiva raised an eyebrow. "The others?"

Julian shook his head sadly and walked across to the other three in silence, lowering himself painfully to the bench and sitting as comfortably as he could.

Kiva rumbled deep in his throat. He was so angry now he could almost feel his heart boiling in his mouth. "Bors and Thalo, Pirus, Scauvus and Clovis. Five good men." They'd served in more battles together than he could count in the last twenty years and with rarely more than minor wounds. Only one fatality some ten years ago, after which they'd taken on Julian to make up the unit's numbers. And now five down in five minutes. Almost half the company, and things didn't look over hopeful for the rest either. That was what happened when you dealt with politics and blood feuds; battles he could cope with. He hoped to hell that Athas and the others would find out about this before they walked innocently back into Serfium.

Phythian and his archers marched into the room.

"Tie them" he ordered two of his men. "Securely."

As the two men came into the corner of the room with heavy cord and began to lash them around the wrists with their arms behind their backs, Phythian took a seat on a table and crossed his legs, kicking the air idly. "I often wondered how you got this awesome reputation, Tregaron, and now that I've actually fought you, I'm still wondering."

Kiva snarled. "You haven't fought me yet, Phythian. This was just using poor innocent priests to trap us, but don't worry; I'll let you fight me soon."

Their captor laughed again and then turned to someone without a bow, possibly his second in command. "Get them roped together and shackle each of their left legs onto a chain. I don't want any chance of these four going anywhere."

Kiva looked round at Julian, Alessus, and finally at the unconscious Quintillian. His mind raced as he tried to fathom a way out of this mess, but there seemed to be precious little chance of any escape. Perhaps Athas and the others would find them on the way to Velutio. Perhaps Tythias would head south. Perhaps even, and this seemed the least far-fetched of the three, prince Ashar would learn of their peril and do something about it. The only other hope would be to find a friend in the city, though it had been a very long time since Kiva had had a friend there. Perhaps this Sabianus would prove to be someone he could deal with. There were many possibilities, but all of them either relied on someone coming to their aid, or slim chances he would have in the city itself, providing Velutio didn't have them all executed the moment they arrived.

With a sigh, he wondered how such a promising week had produced such a bad day.

Chapter XVI.

Three days they'd been travelling in both light and dark to reach Velutio, with Phythian and his score of men on horseback and driving the wagon in the back of which the four of them lay bound tight. They'd tried to persuade the effeminate leader that their wounds were bad enough to demand they delay the journey until the healing process was underway, but Phythian would have none of it. He wasn't going to risk holding Tregaron any longer than necessary, knowing that the man had friends in the most unexpected of places. In fact, as Alessus had done his best to keep their wounds under control, Phythian had not allowed any of his men to get closer than a dozen feet from the prisoners, including their unit's medic. Alessus had complained bitterly at the lack of medical treatment and, while he was no doctor and knew only a little field medicine, even he could see that Julian's leg was infected. Unless there was a very good surgeon waiting for them in Velutio, and that seemed extremely unlikely, the leg would have to come off. The young Julian was facing bravely up to the possibility though, even when fever came on him and the smell from the infection filled his nostrils. Kiva had said hardly a word since their journey had begun. He spent every day and night watching the countryside, half expecting to see the Lion Riders or some other friends come running from the undergrowth to rescue them. Indeed it was gratifying in a small way to see that Phythian kept just such a look out himself.

And now he saw the first hopeful sign as the heavy stone south gate of the city of Velutio passed over the four of them as they lay in the cart staring at the sky. Kiva caught his breath and nudged Quintillian as best he could. The boy turned his head to look at his captain and Kiva raised his head very slightly to gesture upwards. Following his direction, the young man looked up and took only a moment to register a figure in black standing on the battlements and leaning over to look down into the cart. Something flashed a couple of times; a falling coin, flipping over and over and catching the sun as it plummeted into the cart, falling onto the captain himself. Kiva looked down his chest and could see a Pelasian gold sindar lying on his front. He looked back up at the battlements, now disappearing into the distance as they travelled along the south road toward the centre of the city, but the figure in black had gone. With some difficulty he shuffled back and forth until the coin finally rolled off his chest and into his bound hands.

He gripped it tight and then winced. Typical bloody Pelasians. They'd sharpened one half of the coin as either a tool or a weapon. Still, he thought as the warm blood trickled around his hands and soaked the bonds, he could use both a tool and a weapon at this point in the game. He settled back into the cart's bed. Whatever Prince Ashar had in mind, there was precious little the four of them could do about it right now. Due to the raised sides of the cart, he could see very little of the city as they travelled, though what he did see appeared not to have changed since the days he'd frequented the place. The looming walls of Basianus' Great Baths rolled by on his right, along with their surrounding parkland and the aqueduct that supplied them. A short while later, he saw the tops of the triumphal columns of the Calumnite Dynasty and the Avenue of the Gods with its temples in myriad shapes and sizes. All landmarks he recognised and remembered well.

Street after street slid by with a gradual increase in noise as they approached the centre until finally they neared what was undoubtedly their destination. They'd passed through the great markets and the lower forum, gradually climbing as they turned to head west. Then the triumphal arches began to appear as the cart and its escort rode beneath them, carved relics telling stories of campaigns long gone and celebrating Emperors than no one in these days would remember. This was the Imperial Way and, not far off at the top point of this mile long avenue of triumphs, stood the Palace of the Emperors on its rocky promontory overlooking the bay of Isera to the north and the ports to the south. Here the Emperors had ruled for three hundred years over the city of Velutio and the world beyond, long before the first villa had been built on Isera. Indeed in those days Isera was a watch tower and fortified island and nothing more, before one of the Emperors whose name escaped Kiva had decided he wanted a summer palace as a retreat from the city. The Emperors had begun to summer on the island while the rest of the government built their villas at Serfium.

And now the last arch rolled over the top of them and disappeared into the distance beyond their sight and the cart rumbled to a halt. He knew this place well enough. The sides of the wide avenue had closed in at the end and now became a three-sided courtyard with the fourth open to the Imperial Way. The walls of the palace, with their windows and battlements looked down from three sides into the cart where the four lay. Somewhere just ahead there was talking, but over the general din of a score of horsemen Kiva couldn't make out any of the details until one of Phythian's men unbolted the back board of the cart a minute later.

"Out!" he ordered curtly and stepped back. Lifting his head, Kiva could see four of them with crossbows aimed at the cart. Probably a little unnecessary considering where they were, but Phythian would be very careful right now since he hadn't been paid yet.

Struggling, Kiva helped Quintillian to sit up while at the other side of the cart, Julian pulled himself up with the help of the side board and Alessus. The four shuffled with difficulty to the edge of the cart, grateful that at least their ankles were no longer chained while they'd been aboard. Kiva hauled himself off first, turning to give Quintillian a hand. Julian dropped to the stone flags, but his leg gave way instantly and he collapsed to the floor groaning. Alessus helped him to his feet with a struggle and the four stood, their hands tied behind their back. Blood still dripped from Kiva's hands, though he continued to clutch at the coin until he turned and could deposit the item into his pocket. The man who'd ordered them to disembark gestured past the cart. "Time to go."

As they limped and shuffled around the cart, they could see Phythian with his second in command beneath the huge ornate gate of the palace, with a dozen guards around in the red uniforms of Velutio. Other guards stood atop the battlements with javelins by their sides. Even in the current circumstances, Kiva was impressed to note how closely Velutio's men emulated the old Imperial army. Their dress, kit and even stance spoke of the old ways, though they wore red instead of traditional green. This had to be the influence of their commander, for Kiva knew the lord of Velutio well enough to know how much he shunned the reminders of Imperial days.

As they reached the arch Phythian folded his arms and smiled. "This way. His lordship will be meeting us in the courtyard."

Uncomfortably and painfully they plodded through the dark, covered gateway with Velutio's guard ahead and Phythian's archers behind, crossbows still trained on them. Kiva swallowed. This was the moment of truth. If Velutio was on true form, the four of them would probably be executed in the courtyard without any preamble and then anything Prince Ashar could do wouldn't be enough. His only hope was to annoy his old adversary enough to make him keep the prisoners around long enough to suffer. The light dazzled them as they broke out from the gatehouse shadows and into the bright courtyard. This had changed beyond recognition. Gone were the statues and fountains, the flowerbeds and well tended walkways. In its place was a bare stone-flagged courtyard of immense size with two low stone buildings that had all the hallmarks of guard-posts. Around the beautifully decorated walls of the ancient palace now stood dummies for sword and javelin practice. In fact it reminded him greatly of the old Imperial training camp at Munda.

One thing that could not be mistaken though was the Lord of Velutio. He'd aged considerably since the last time they'd met, but then Kiva would be the first to admit that he'd seen better years himself. The lord's hair may have greyed and his features wrinkled slightly, but there was no mistaking that cold, calculating face and the mind like a steel trap behind it. His attention was drawn to the small unit of no more than ten men standing behind the lord. Like the ones at the gate they carried themselves in the manner of old fashioned soldiers. A sergeant stood with the unit, young but very military in his appearance and deportment, vine staff jammed under his arm and a red crest on his helm to denote his rank. And in front of them at Velutio's shoulder was a man that had to be this Sabianus. Wearing a very traditional general's gear, with a burnished helm and breastplate, he stood straight and tall. Kiva's heart fell as he realised this man was far too young to have been an officer in the old days. Probably no hope there then, though he obviously kept the old ways where it applied to his men. The commander was staring at him in a way that made Kiva curiously nervous. He shuffled his feet as he realised that blood from his hand was dripping onto his boot.

Velutio stepped forward and the commander followed him, staying at his shoulder.

"Kiva. You've looked better."

The captain was interested to note that Sabianus glanced at the lord and then resumed his interrogative stare at him. How was Velutio going to play this?

"Avitus" he answered the Lord with a grin. "Nice city you've borrowed."

Velutio's temper seemed to have calmed over the years. Instead of the angry backlash he'd expected from such a comment, the lord smiled a humourless smile and turned his attention to Quintillian.

"You gave us quite the little run around, boy. I've spent rather a lot of money finding you."

Quintillian cleared his throat and tried to stand straight, having previously been leaning against Kiva to support his weak leg. "You could have saved you money if you'd come looking yourself, Marshal. I'm sure we'd have given you a fitting reception."

Velutio laughed and Kiva was most surprised to hear a note of real humour in there.

185

"By all the Gods, he even talks like you Caerdin! You do have a curious effect on people. Has he been adopted into your unit, whatever they call themselves these days? I note he's wearing a soldier's clothes now."

Before Kiva could answer, the lad piped up "I'm a member of the Wolves now, yes."

Kiva smiled. Quintillian, ever bright, seemed to have cottoned on to what he was doing and was taking turns in helping wind the lord up. Couldn't afford to go too far though. There was something about the calm quiet way Velutio was taking the comments that unnerved him; reminded him of a volcano ready to erupt. He cleared his throat.

"So, Avitus, what are you planning for us then? A little jaunt round the bay? A social drink and a chat about old times?"

Velutio shook his head. "I haven't quite decided yet. I'll make sure you're shown to the best of quarters while I decide though." He turned to his senior officer. "Sabian? Take the four of them down to the Dalertine prison and have food delivered to them." He stopped for a moment and peered at the four. "And if you can *find* a doctor, send him to look at them."

Kiva's brain ticked away as he filed everything he heard and saw. There may still be hope here. The way Velutio spoke to the commander told an intriguing tale. There was some suspicion or disagreement there, and the way 'Sabian' as he appeared to be called reacted to the comment made it clear that the discomfort was with both parties.

Sabian saluted and called over his shoulder "Iasus. Send your men out for food and drink for four hungry men and a doctor. Don't worry about a guard. I'll escort the general down to the Dalertine." He glanced up at Kiva. "I'm assuming there'll be no trouble, general?"

Again that grating edge. To call Kiva a general in front of Velutio was bordering on insult, but the lord brushed it off. Definitely a change there from the old days. Behind Kiva, Phythian coughed.

Velutio sighed. "Yes captain, I have your money. Go through into the gardens and I'll be with you presently."

As Phythian and his men walked off through the next arch and Sabian's unit left the courtyard, Kiva glanced around. There were few guards here, but enough to stop anything foolish. Sabian wasn't risking anything, just giving Kiva a certain deference and respect though whether for his benefit or to irritate Velutio escaped him.

The lord turned to Sabian and frowned. "All the respected and feared units we have out looking for these men and the people who take

186

them are virtual unknowns. Perhaps they could be useful to the city on a more permanent basis?"

Sabian shook his head. "That captain's a short step away from complete madness and I wouldn't want him in my army. Better to use him a long way away from home I think."

Velutio glared for a moment and then shrugged. "Perhaps you're right." He turned to Kiva. "I must ask where the rest of your unit is. There are four of you here and Phythian informs me that he has the bodies of five more, but that still leaves four, including that sergeant of yours." He raised an eyebrow and leaned a little closer to Kiva. "You may as well tell me now. You know I'm not above having the boy tortured for the information and though I know you wouldn't break, I'd be willing to wager he would."

The captain glared at Velutio, meeting his gaze. "Tythias found us in the hills. He managed to jump us surprisingly well considering how well I know his tactics. We were forced to make a hasty escape. Athas and the others played rear-guard for us and were to meet us in Serfium, but they never turned up. I think you can assume that the treacherous one-eyed bastard will turn up before long wanting the payment for four of them."

The lord nodded contentedly. "Very well. I must go and deal with payments due, but I'll leave you in Sabian's hands and rest assured I'll be down to visit you as soon as my schedule permits."

With one last long look and an unpleasant smile, Velutio turned and walked away through the arch and into the gardens. Sabian squared his shoulders.

"Very well general. I apologise for the nature of your quarters, but the orders aren't mine to give." He gestured off towards a doorway.

Kiva smiled. "I know the way."

As they walked, Kiva looked around at the palace for the first time since Quintus the Golden had been resident. Remarkably little had changed about the majority of it, with the exception of the removal and destruction of all the Imperial iconography. He turned his head in interest as Sabian began to talk, but not to him.

"So Quintillian, I'm glad to see you're not badly wounded, though you'd have been better having never left the island."

Quintillian nodded. "The world's a big place though Commander, and the island's so small. I'd still be a boy if I'd stayed. Now I'm a soldier."

"Indeed," Sabian replied. "I'd never have imagined seeing you so weather-beaten and military." He smiled though his face betrayed his unhappiness. "You'd give Darius a run for his money now. They're all quite worried about you on the island and I very much suspect with good reason. You do realise that his Lordship's unlikely to ship you back off to the island now?"

Quintillian nodded. "As I said though Commander, the world's a big place and possibilities are endless."

Kiva broke in. "I heard talk of you Sabian, while I was north of Serfium. It seems you've a fair reputation. I suspected you might have been an officer from the Imperial days. I'm obviously wrong, but your men do remind me a great deal of the old times."

Sabian smiled. "I try to do things the right way. The Imperial army worked and, as they say, if it's not broken, don't try to fix it." He sighed. "I always regretted the fall when I was a boy. I have the suspicion I was born half a century too late."

Kiva returned the smile. "It's hopeful though."

"What?" the commander questioned.

"To hear people your age talking like that. There are few people who speak fondly of the old ways these days. In other circumstances, I have the feeling we'd have fought together quite well." Kiva's mind raced on. If there was any kind of division between Sabian and Velutio, he needed to apply a crowbar and push them further apart. Any ally was worthwhile at this point.

Sabian nodded as they opened a door and walked down a set of dank steps toward the cellars and the infamous Dalertine prison. "Perhaps. Times have changed though, general. I used to read your campaign diaries avidly. They're the foundation of all my tactical knowledge, but these days I only have the chance to field an army against a disorganised and inferior Lord or perhaps against rebels and dissidents. Nothing like the old glorious campaigns. There's no one left who could stand against my army and the little wars we do have are becoming less frequent. Soon there may even be peace."

Quintillian looked up into Sabian's face and interrupted. "How are the others?"

Sabian sighed. "Good for the most part. Darius is coming on well; if he were a free man I'd have commissioned him by now." He smiled. "Though you're getting that way too now. Minister Sarios was wounded when he refused to tell his Lordship where you'd gone, but he's having treatment at the moment and Favio thinks he may keep his eye. Minister Turus is still alive and well as far as I'm aware, though I was tempted to put an end to him at one point. All in all, things go well. There's a small garrison based there at the moment under my best

188

sergeant, but they're getting on quite well with the islanders. They're helping to repair and rebuild."

Kiva raised an eyebrow. "Velutio approves of your men fraternising with prisoners?"

Sabian shook his head and smiled. "I doubt it, but we've reached a certain understanding since I became sole commander in the city. He leaves military matters to me now and in return I try to stop him doing dangerous or stupid things."

Kiva nodded. "I'd heard something about you and the captain of his guard coming to blows. I take it he's buried deep now then?"

"The guard captain was a devious, conniving power-hungry megalomaniac. He wasn't a good commander and he wasn't a good man and he coveted my job. He tried to bring me down, but with the help of a few friends I managed to turn the tables on him. You are remarkably well informed for someone who'd been so far out of everything, General."

Kiva smiled. "I like to keep abreast of things."

They reached the lower floor and walked between the cellar doorways until they reached the prison, known in the days when Basianus had been incarcerated here by his own priests as 'the pit'. A bare room carved from the rock with no windows and no decoration. Two flat wooden pallets lay on the floor to serve as beds and a bundle of straw in the corner for warmth. No toilet and no front wall, just bars an inch thick and three inches apart that would require a team of horses to bend. A soldier sat on a stool at the opposite wall and came to his feet at attention as they entered before leaping forward to open the prison door.

Sabian sighed. "First time this has been used since I've been in command. Hopefully the last time too." Reaching to his belt, he withdrew a dagger and, leaning forward, cut the bonds on their wrists one by one. Ushering the four into the cell, the soldier closed the grill door and turned the keys in the two heavy locks before coming back to attention.

"I can leave a guard here if you wish" the commander said "though it's quite unnecessary from our point of view. Just in case you need anything?"

Kiva shook his head. "I think we'd value the privacy if it's in your power to grant that."

Sabian nodded and gestured up the stairs. The guard marched off.

189

"Sergeant Iasus will be down here shortly with food and drink and a doctor. I will stop by once in a while."

And with that the commander saluted them and then stalked off toward the stairs.

"A good man, commander Sabian" noted Quintillian.

"Yes," Kiva replied. "I'm not sure whether that's a good thing or a bad thing. At least bad men can be bought or bargained. Good men have the tendency to be incorruptible and to carry out their orders regardless."

He shuffled over to one of the pallets and sank onto it, opening and closing his hand. The blood was beginning to clot now. With a frown, he withdrew the coin from his pocket; around an inch across with one edge sharpened to razor point, the coin displayed the flying horse of Pelasia on one side and an image of the eastern Moon Goddess on the other. His frown deepened as he rubbed his finger across the coin, smearing the blood. Standing once more, he moved over to the bars of the cell and smiled ironically.

"What is it?" Alessus asked as he lowered Julian to the pallet and then sank to the floor himself.

"A pointless note from a friend." He smiled again. "Ashar's man dropped it to me from the city gate. There are marks on it, but they're in the linear script of Pelasia and I haven't the faintest idea what they mean."

Quintillian limped across the room and grasped the coin from the captain's hand.

"Careful, it's sharp."

Quintillian brushed the concern aside. "I studied several languages on Isera. This is fairly simple, much like the languages the eastern provinces used to speak before they were brought into the Empire." He grinned. "It's amazing how much text you can fit into such a small space with this kind of language."

Kiva tutted. "All very fascinating. What does it say?"

Quintillian turned the coin in the extremely low light.

"Four assassins. Twenty five archers. No chance. Wait for better timing."

"Ha!" exclaimed the captain. "So they've waited until we're in a cell. Very helpful."

He slammed his fist on the cell's bars in annoyance, but he knew the words were right. Ashar probably didn't even know they'd been captured yet. These would just be four Pelasians he'd sent to the city to gather information, and they stood precious little chance against Phythian or the army of Velutio. It would be down to him after all.

Quintillian handed the coin back to him. "What do you think's going to happen, sir?"

Kiva shrugged. "Death" he said with a cold certainty. "I'm surprised we made it past the courtyard to be honest; it's most unlike him. Perhaps he's having trouble deciding how gruesome to make it?"

The lad shuddered. "Then it's time we start making some plans. Shame Darius isn't here. All the best plans we ever put into action were made by the two of us together."

Kiva yawned. "There really isn't anything to plan. There's no way to get out of here. Nobody's coming to the rescue, and any time we actually get to leave the cell, we'll be in the middle of a palace guarded by an army in a hostile city."

"So there's no hope at all?" Quintillian asked, his voice incredulous. "That's not you. You always find a way round things. You're a survivor, captain."

Kiva rounded on the boy angrily. "If you think I'm that clever, why are we here? Do you think I can conjure an escape tunnel out of my pocket?"

He turned away. "Ahhh shit. We'll be lucky to see another dawn. I hope Athas and the others have been sensible enough to lose themselves somewhere. Our only faint glimmer of hope now is that we can drive a wedge between this Sabian and his Lord. It looks suspiciously like they're already on the way."

Alessus stood and walked over to join them. "Are there any escape routes from the palace? Plenty of Emperors have been paranoid."

Kiva shook his head. "I've heard rumours, but you can guarantee that Velutio's had every inch of this place checked and sealed. I wouldn't hold much hope out for that."

"What about the gardens? They're out in the open."

Kiva shook his head. "Almost one hundred and fifty feet of sheer rock face with jagged rocks and reefs at the bottom. Then there's his guards patrolling the edge and his men in boats patrolling the bay. And that's only if we could get out into the gardens. I think that's reaching. If we find ourselves out in the open at any point it's going to be a matter of taking any opportunity we see, rather than planning in advance."

Alessus opened his mouth to speak again, but Kiva cut him off. "Not worth asking. I've been through everything I can think of, but there's no way out without outside help. We'll have to bide our time and try and work on people we come in contact with."

His head jerked up.

"Now's not the time anyway. Someone's coming."

The three standing men retreated to the rear of the cell and took their seats on the wooden pallets as hob-nailed footsteps echoed down the stairs and along the corridor. After a few moments, the sergeant they'd seen in the courtyard appeared with a guard, two of the palace servants and a man in a white tunic with a leather case.

At a gesture from the sergeant, the guard unfastened the door and stepped back. The two servants entered the cell nervously, each with a covered tray and a jug. They placed them on the floor by the bars and then left in a hurry. The sergeant laughed at them as they ran up the stairs.

"Idiots" he sneered. "Did they really think you would attack them here?"

Kiva smiled at the sergeant with no real humour. "It's not all that farfetched."

The doctor entered and made his way into the dark. "This is totally unacceptable" he declared." I need light."

Without waiting, the sergeant picked up one of the oil burners from a shelf near the guard's chair and gave it to the soldier with the keys. "Light it and give them it."

The soldier did as he was bade and the flickering light was carried into the cell, though it did precious little to push back the oppressive darkness of this place. As the doctor began to examine Quintillian's leg by the guttering light, the sergeant straightened. "I'll leave you with him." As he spoke the soldier locked the door and stepped back to the seat. "When you've finished, doctor, tell him and he'll bring you back out."

The doctor nodded, unable to speak as he had some miscellaneous implement held between his teeth while he prodded at the flesh round the bolt with both hands. Kiva stood. "Thank you sergeant."

With a nod, Iasus left and climbed the stairs back to the surface world.

The doctor was mumbling and grumbling to himself as Kiva sat down among the others once more.

"What's wrong?" the captain asked.

The doctor took the tool from between his teeth and pointed at the bolt with it. "It's done considerable damage to the muscle, but it's

192

also chipped the bone as the head went through. I'm going to have to break off the flights and draw the bolt through by the head and it's going to be extremely painful." He produced a strip of leather. "Bite on this young man."

As Quintillian bit down, the doctor snapped the flight end off next to the skin. For the first time in days blood welled up thick around the wood. Accompanied by muffled howls the man gripped the head of the bolt and in one slow, agonising move pulled the shaft through, accompanied by a gush of blood.

"There's some infection here too. It may heal or it may not. If not, it'll become a very painful problem. In the meantime, I'll stitch the wound up."

As the doctor worked, Quintillian looked up at the captain, a frightened look. Kiva smiled back as comfortingly as he could. "Of all our worries right now, I'd not panic over-much about infections."

Chapter XVII.

Danis was a small town that had grown from a tiny village due solely to the old Imperial courier post there. These days, of course, the post served only as a tavern with a few rooms for rent. The serving girl dreamed of moving to the bigger cities where she could push the limits of her ability and perhaps become a dancer or a musician in one of the great Inns. She'd always had some talent in both and carrying trays of food and drink around tables and rooms to lecherous perverts was not how she'd seen her future. Take this group, she thought as she reached the top of the stairs and approached the door. The young one was nice in an exotic sort of way, but the others were just ugly, hairy and smelly. They must be brigands or something. She swallowed nervously as she reached out to knock on the door, but stayed her hand as she heard the words being spoken within.

"He's a fucking Emperor" the muffled conversation declared. "We can't just leave him to rot!"

Her eyes wide, Sathina placed the tray as quietly as she could on the table on the landing and leaned closer to the door, holding her breath.

"I appreciate your feelings, really I do and I would like nothing better than to be able to spirit them all away to safety, but you're talking about the biggest city in the world and the largest army in the Empire. Even with all of us, there are perhaps fifty or sixty men. Given time we could perhaps drum up a hundred more, but by then they'll be long dead. How long do you think Velutio will let them live. I would be very surprised if they're not dead already."

Velutio? Emperor? Sathina wondered whether to go and see the boss. She reached down to collect the tray and at that moment the door slammed open and a hand the size of a side of beef grasped her wrist and pulled her inside. The door slammed shut behind her before she had time to gasp and the big brute holding her gestured at the door. "Agkhh! Akh!" There was something wrong with his throat. She'd wondered earlier why he wore the scarf pulled up to his chin like that.

She glanced round in a panic. Four men sat at the table as well as the big man by her side. The young one was eastern, a swarthy dark handsome face and a graceful body clad in black. To his side sat a man in ill-matched armour with an ugly scar closing one eye. To the other side a large dark-skinned man sat next to an older one. Neither looked very savoury.

"Jorun, put her down."

194

The big man let go of her arm and Sathina turned for the door, but he reached out and held it shut.

The grizzled old one smiled at her. "I'm sorry my dear, but unfortunately we can't let you go right now."

"I didn't hear nothing" she blurted out. "Honestly!"

The smile stayed. "I'm sure, but you see we have to be very careful at the moment." He stood and crossed the room, fumbling in a pouch at his belt. She panicked and tried to back away, but the big one called Jorun wouldn't let her. She flailed as best she could with her arms to keep the old pervert at bay. His smile widened. "You really don't need to worry. I'm not about to rape you and I don't want to hurt you. In fact, I'm a doctor" he said, holding out something the size of a cherry tomato wrapped in dark leaved. "This will just help you sleep for a while."

She continued to flail and the smile fell from his face. "I'm running out of patience, woman. Either swallow this or Jorun will have to do it the hard way."

She stopped flailing, but her eyes held the same panic. Jorun held her arms and Mercurias popped the pill into her mouth and held it and her nose shut. Her eyes bulged in terror but, restrained and short of breath she swallowed involuntarily and the pill disappeared. Mercurias grinned. "Just like trying to get you lot to take medicine, Athas."

Jorun continued to hold her for a minute until it became obvious to him that her body was going limp. Gently he picked her up and placed her on one of the room's twin beds before opening the door again and retrieving the tray of food.

Taking his seat, Mercurias frowned. "Highness, your men are renowned for their subtlety. Surely there's something you can do? "

Ashar shook his head. Not at this time. I've been in contact with my men in the city. They tell me that two of them are wounded: the young one and Quintillian. They're unarmed and have been imprisoned in the bowels of the palace. If my men thought it was at all possible they would have said so. Gods, apart from Jorun, we've all been in that palace and we all know what we're up against. Our only hope is that they bring them out into the open. Do you think Velutio will want them humiliated publicly?"

Athas shook his head. "He won't want any publicity over there being an heir to the Empire, let alone the fact that he will be killing that heir." He frowned. "And of course, general Caerdin is a name to be reckoned with too."

The prince sighed. "Then we're at a dead end, but whatever happens we need to get to the city. I'll send orders for the rest of my men to recall and join us."

Mercurias shook his head. "No, don't do that. Tythias, you need to send a couple of men round the coast to try and hook up with Filus' and Sithis' units and we'll have to do with whoever we have. If we can get Kiva and Quintillian and the others out of there, we'll need everyone's support afterward." He glowered darkly. "And if we can't, we're going to need a sizeable force in order to separate Velutio's head from his body."

Tythias nodded. "I'll have two men ride out at first light. Have you sent word to Brendan and Marco?"

The prince nodded.

"Very well" said Athas, reaching out for one of the plates on the tray. "We'll get to the city and then see what we can do. Have your men found somewhere safe we can hole up there?"

Another nod. "We've had a safe house in Velutio since the days of Quintus. Let's just hope we're in time to do something about it."

* * *

In the poor light of the cell Sabian smiled. "What would you have done if they'd actually had cavalry though?" He proffered the jug to Kiva again, who nodded. The commander refilled the mug and then passed the jug across to Alessus, who refilled the other three.

Kiva shrugged. "They didn't. If they had by some miraculous method managed to get their horses through the forest in less than a day, they'd never have been able to field them effectively in such a confined space anyway. If I'd thought for a moment they could've done, we'd have had plenty of time to set some extra defences up, but sometimes it's better to give an army the night before a battle to drink and relax."

Sabian shook his head. "I tend to find my men get jumpy and nervous if I give them too much time to think before a battle."

"That's because your men are from the southern provinces, though" Kiva replied with a grin. "The two brigades I took with me up from Vengen were both formed in the fort there of northerners. Don't forget that you southerners like to drink watered wine and listen to music to relax. The people I came from drink a mixture of strong spirits and ox blood and fight each other for amusement. If it's that sort of blood in your army, letting them relax their way just makes them look

196

forward to a good battle. That's why I always tried to allocate the northern brigades to myself and left the southern ones to Avitus and Leus. Covis was a whole different issue. He was from Germalla and he liked his eastern cavalry. All well and good in open field, but they were precious little use at Serfium when he came up against the other two." The general went very quiet and gazed off past Sabian into the distance. That subject still haunted him and the commander knew well what had happened then.

Sabian leaned back against the bars and shuffled uncomfortably. He'd been coming down here three days now. It had begun as an unpleasant and stifled discussion. Caerdin had been understandably reluctant to talk and had continually pushed him for any information on what Velutio had planned. By the second visit though, he'd managed to turn the conversation to military tactics and the flood gates of the general's experience had opened. Since then he'd been several times, sometimes bringing food and sometimes drink. He'd supplied them with blankets instead of straw now. He wished he could do more, but nothing would change the fact that they were in prison with a very finite life expectancy, and that was shrinking by the day. He sighed.

"I realise that this is a bit personal, but I want to ask you something, general."

Kiva smiled indulgently. "I think you could safely call me by my given name now Sabian. "

The commander shook his head. "I'm sorry but I think I'd rather keep this by rank. I'm uncomfortable getting too familiar in the circumstances. Had things been different..."

Kiva nodded. He'd thought he was getting somewhere with the commander. He actually liked Sabian and had the distinct feeling it was this man's doing that the four of them weren't dead already. Sabian had a surprisingly strong influence on Velutio it seemed. "Go on then" he encouraged with a smile.

The commander shuffled again. "Why did you withdraw from public life? After it all happened, I mean. His lordship fought for his own position, Leus supported him until he came to an... unfortunate end." He remembered well the story he'd read about the revenge Caerdin exacted on Marshal Leus before he went after Avitus. He cleared his throat. "And Covis fought for the preservation of the status quo. But you? You went on a bloodthirsty revenge spree and then vanished for years. To be honest I didn't know you were even alive until his lordship told me who Quintillian was travelling with."

197

He sat and watched the various emotions crossing the general's face. The question was an uncomfortable one and he knew it. He'd briefly wondered whether to mention what he found out about Darius on the island, but it would be cruel to tell the condemned man that his son was still alive and also a prisoner of Velutio's. Especially when the general would never live to see his son. Besides, Velutio had forbidden any discussion about the occupants of the prison or the island with anyone not in his lordship's pay.

Kiva coughed. "It wasn't an easy time Sabian. I'd done some fairly unpleasant things and had others done to me. I lost my family, my house, my Emperor, my position; everything. On top of that, I knew it was me alone who was responsible for killing a divine power and bringing the Empire down. What was I supposed to do? Walk into the public square and declare it all. No. I just had to get away. Once the Wolves found me we just went north and disappeared. We'd still be anonymous and obscure now if it weren't for Quintillian's appearance. Against all the odds he managed to get us all fired up again and ready to do something about the state of the world." He sighed. "Needless to say, this is the result. I'm a cursed man; a deicide, and nothing I do will ever come right because of it."

Sabian shook his head. "Gods are highly overrated. I didn't think you northerners were all that bothered with religion anyway. It's come to this, general, because there are so few of you left now and my lord's resources are so vast. It was inevitable."

Kiva sat in silence for a moment, though he didn't look convinced. "When are we to die, commander?"

Here we go again, though Sabian. Every visit the question would crop up at least once and the truth was that the commander didn't know Velutio's intentions any better than the prisoners.

"I don't know, as I keep telling you. All I can hope is that when he does decide, it's quick and noble. By the sword I would prefer, as military men. Over in a second and the proper way for renowned soldiers to go." He frowned. "I'm not convinced that will be the way of it to be honest, but I myself won't be party to anything else, I assure you."

Sabian stood slowly and stiffly and stretched. "I must go again. His lordship wants to see me at lunch time. I hope…" his voice trailed away as the foolish words died in his throat. He turned to the door and motioned at the guard standing at the opposite wall. The young man stepped forward and unlocked the cell door, letting the commander out and then closing and locking it once more.

With a final bow to the prisoners, Sabian turned and walked along the corridor and up the steps to the outside. He crossed the courtyard and entered Velutio's private palace on the other side, the two soldiers at the doorway standing to attention as he passed. Through the man hall and up the golden-white marble staircase, he made his way along the corridor to the door at the end. With a swift rap on the door he paused and, leaning to one side, picked up an apple from the fruit dish and took a bite from it.

A voice from beyond the door called for him and he reached out and opened it.

Velutio sat in the bay window, a scroll unrolled on his lap. He beckoned to Sabian and the commander crossed the room and with a curt bow took the seat opposite.

"You wanted to see me, my Lord?"

"Yes" the older man said without looking up from the scroll. "There are remarkably few people who will speak their mind to me, you know? Perhaps half a dozen the world over. You have the privilege to be one of them and I do find that I value your opinion." He looked up over the edge of the scroll. "That doesn't mean you don't irritate me at times and it doesn't mean that I will always follow your advice, but I do like to hear it before I make my decisions."

Sabian nodded. He wondered whether this was to do with the fate of the four prisoners. If so, he may be able to do something at last.

"Thank you my Lord. I try to advise you to the best of my ability." He shrugged. "On military matters anyway."

Velutio nodded. He rolled the scroll once more and placed it in the tube before dropping it into the basket next to the seat.

"Sabian, what is your assessment of my position at the moment?"

The question was a surprise, but a welcome one. Here was a subject the commander knew well. "I assume you mean in a military way? There are perhaps seven or eight lords in the Northern, Central or Eastern Provinces that still have an army large enough that they could consider fielding it against you, but I very much doubt that any of them would, especially if you call in your various allegiances."

Velutio nodded. "Go on."

"Well, the Western Provinces are different. We've never really concentrated on the lords there, but once we have all those on this side of the Nymphean Sea under the yoke, the Western Provinces will fall in short order. I would give it three months of campaigning and there'll be no one left to stand against you. You'll have total control."

199

Another nod and an encouraging gesture.

"You're perhaps wondering what to do after that, my Lord?"

Velutio smiled. "I will be sixty years old this winter. My life has been a constant struggle to improve and control; to bring things to better order. People may hate my methods and praise the heroic and short-sighted general Caerdin, but they also forget that it was Quintus' dynasty that brought chaos and terror to the Empire and Caerdin and his loyal few that destroyed all we had of order and control. Between Caerdin and the Emperor they plunged the world into chaos because of their need to do the right thing. I have been called cruel, a tyrant, a murderer, unjust... many things, but I have taken a world gone to seed and brought order and control to it once more. There are no bandits in the Central Provinces now; no Pirates on the Nymphean Sea. The system of tax and tithe works again. You see I am rebuilding the Empire they destroyed."

Sabian blinked. He'd never heard Velutio talk like this. Moreover he'd never looked at it from that particular point of view and the idea was seductive. It was true indeed that the lot of many people and places had improved.

"I can see your point, but I'm not sure where it's leading..."

Velutio smiled again. He was smiling more often than usual and the effect was rather disconcerting.

"Commander, I intend to be Emperor within the year. I see no reason why not. All Imperial dynasties have to begin somewhere, and it's time the Empire was whole again."

Sabian nodded; a sentiment with which he wholeheartedly agreed.

"There is one problem though," Velutio went on. "I am old. I shall be sixty before we can safely declare a new regime. I have no family and therefore no dynasty."

Sabian shifted uncomfortably. This was a conversation he wasn't sure he wanted to be involved in. "In the old days, my Lord, some of the Emperors adopted their heirs with a fair level of success. Dynasties are not necessarily the most secure way to control an Empire."

Velutio nodded. "That is my thought too. The problem then remains when and who do I adopt? It needs to be before any Imperial control is declared. An individual Emperor with no heir apparent is an easy target for assassination among the greedy. If there is someone to inherit instantly the temptation is greatly decreased. But who?"

Sabian swallowed. "Why are you asking me these things? You have political advisors to deal with questions like this. I'm a military man."

He was answered with a smile. "That's exactly why it's you and not them I must ask. I believe that as a career military man you have no intentions toward political power yourself. You're also a sensible and honourable man. As such, who else should I trust the judgement of?" Without waiting for an answer, Velutio went on. "I cannot adopt Quintillian. That is plainly obvious. There must be a clean and complete break with the past."

Sabian leaned forward and cradled his hands. "By 'complete break', do I assume you mean the removal of all those connected with the last dynasty?"

"Yes."

Sabian sighed. This was something he'd seen coming for a long time and dreaded. "So no one from the island will survive your succession my lord?"

Velutio nodded. "It has to be so. As long as they remain they are a reminder of a past regime and can be used in plots and coups against anything we do. It is not enough then to imprison or exile them. We must start with a clean sheet."

Sabian frowned. "We?"

"Of course 'we'. I shall need a commander for the Imperial army. As such, you will be one of the closest advisors I can have. You've been instrumental in bringing us to this stage and it shall be greatly your doing when we achieve our goal."

Velutio gazed out of the window. "There can only be one heir as far as I can see. Only one real candidate."

Sabian sat straight again. "This is why you've made sure no harm comes to Darius?" The commander slapped his forehead in irritation. "Of course! You've been planning this for twenty years. That's the only reason you kept them all on the island this long isn't it?"

Velutio nodded. "Indeed. I needed Darius trained by the best people in every aspect of Imperial life. On Isera he's been tutored in the military arts, numerous fine arts, but also in politics, economics, geography, history, trade... everything a boy could need to take control of an Empire. He's probably been better trained than any Imperial heir in history." He smiled, and the effect made Sabian shudder. "But now things are almost ready. I have the monopoly and the world is bowing to me. When we have the last lords beneath us, I can bring Darius back from Isera and his education will be complete. At that point the rest of

201

the island become dispensable and Isera can revert back to its palatial status."

Sabian tried his best not to let his feelings show in his face. Darius would make a good candidate for Emperor, but there were so many problems his lordship hadn't accounted for. Darius carried the blood of both the parties Velutio was planning to wipe out and he couldn't surely believe that Darius would accept the adoption at the cost of the deaths of everyone he knew. The goal of a new Empire was sensible and reasonable and Velutio was the only man who stood a chance of actually doing this, but his methods spoke of paranoia. So many deaths of innocent and useful people were entirely unnecessary. Of course, there was no way to tell his lordship all this. Instead he forced a smile.

"What of all those across the Empire with leanings toward the old Imperialism?"

Velutio nodded. "Most of those are soldiers; mercenaries even. Mercenaries will become unnecessary once we have a united Empire again with one army. Mercenary units will be outlawed and those who do not resist can be split up and shuffled into our army. Those who do will have to be removed. In any case, the majority of the people of whom you speak are middle aged at least. By the time I have passed on and Darius is in control, there will be few alive who can remember the old dynasty."

His lordship smiled. "I do not really care whether I am remembered fondly or with bitterness, but I *will* be remembered as the man who rebuilt the Empire."

Sabian shuffled again. His discomfort was increasing with every sentence.

"I'm still not sure why you're telling me all this right now, my lord."

"Because," Velutio replied, "you will be my instrument in much of this and I need you to be primed for everything as it comes to pass and to think in advance of any stumbling blocks for which I have not already accounted."

Sabian leaned back again. "There's a lot to think on."

"Yes. Perhaps you'd best go and think on it. I want to meet again in a few days and go over anything you can come up with. I intend to be fully prepared for every eventuality."

Sabian nodded and stood. With a salute, he turned and left the room. As he trod the corridors of the palace on his way back down his mind reeled. There really was a lot to think on and very little of it was good. One thing was certain: he couldn't let Velutio execute so many innocent people out of simple paranoia. That was never a good way to start a new regime. It would be as likely to *make* him enemies as to remove them.

Leaving the palace proper, he walked out into the Imperial gardens. His men patrolled the low wall at the edge in pairs and he strolled out among them, returning their salutes and he passed flowerbeds and the few large old trees that dotted the lawns. Reaching the wall, he stood on the gravel path, with his arms folded and his elbows leaning on the stonework, gazing out over the sea. Across the bay, with the constant white froth of waves breaking on the reefs, he could see Isera like an emerald set in a sapphire sea. How could he let so many people die for nothing, so that the island they had worked to turn into a home could be used by a new dynasty of Emperors responsible for their death?

He straightened, a new sense of purpose flowing through his blood. He had to betray Velutio to save the man from himself, but then that was why his lordship placed such faith in him. He stared out across the water, trying to pick out the individual buildings there but with little success. There was nothing he could do about the four in the palace prison, but the islanders he could save.

* * *

Night flooded the corridors of the Imperial palace as the commander climbed the stairs. He'd passed no guards on his route. He knew the routine of his men well and which passages and rooms he could use to remain undetected. The small oil lamp in his hand illuminated just enough to see where he was going, but that was all. Reaching the top of the stairs, he turned and followed a long, dark corridor until he reached a small nondescript door on the left at the end. Reaching down to his belt he withdrew his set of master keys and unlocked the door after some struggling to find the appropriate key. Beyond, another stairway led up, but there was no portal at the end of this one. A cool night breeze washed his face as he began to climb.

Moments later he was on the uppermost roof of the palace, forty feet above the highest patrolled walk. Carefully making his way to the low wall at the edge, he leaned over and recoiled at the precipitous drop to the gardens below. Heights had always sent a shiver up his spine and he was now at the very highest spot in the city.

Reaching down to his belt again, he unhooked the lantern he'd brought and placed it on the wide surface of the wall. Carefully, he judged how far back the lantern would need to be to become invisible from the palace gardens below and, satisfied with his calculation, he lit the wick within. There was no way he could take ship for Isera without drawing far too much suspicion, so he must be subtle and find other ways. Well, playing the court games against so many good opponents in his time at Velutio, he'd become quite adept at subterfuge himself and, though he always hated having to be underhand at anything, there were times when it was required for the good of all concerned. He dredged his memory to recall the standard signalling codes and then flicked the shutter open and closed a number of times.

A tense wait for five minutes and he repeated the gesture. Someone must be there.

After almost an hour of signalling with no reply, he was tiring and wondering whether anyone bothered to use the lamps on the island since he'd discovered them when suddenly a flashing light on the island brought him to his senses once more. Cursing himself for his lack of alertness in realising too late to translate the message, he flicked the shutter again asking them to repeat.

The signal came once more. He raised an eyebrow. 'My prince?' What prince? He clucked in irritation. Why did everything that involved these islanders create more and more mysteries?

Working away madly at translating into the code, he sent 'No. Commander Sabian. I don't care who you are. Find Darius and bring him to the lamp.'

He leaned back and exhaled deeply. This was it. He'd crossed the bridge and then burned it down.

Chapter XVIII.

Tythias slammed his fist on the table.

"There must be something we can do?"

The leader of the Pelasian spies in the city shook his head. "We have no access to the palace proper. We don't know for sure where they're being held, but it seems likely to be the Dalertine prison. If that's the case there is absolutely no way out. We might be able to do something when they're brought out for execution, but we don't even know when that'll be. It's likely not to be publicised and it'll probably be carried out in the palace grounds with no access to outsiders. I really don't see what we can do. If we had more information from inside we might have other options."

Sathina's voice was lost in the general tumult as the eleven men in the room erupted into argument once more. She sat and sighed. All the way from Danis the big sergeant, Athas, had told her the whole story and despite her grogginess from the after-effects of Mercurias' medication, she'd absorbed every detail and her fear for the so important people at the centre of this was muted only by her sheer excitement at being involved in such earth-shaking events. They'd told her that they couldn't let her go until the whole thing was over and for obvious reasons, but she'd been insistent on staying by then anyway. To be here with such great men working toward the future of the world she knew, or to be in a dirty tavern in Danis, serving drinks while even dirtier travellers tried to reach up her skirts? Ridiculous!

She tried to be heard over the voices again, but these men were so loud, especially the two they'd met up with this morning, Brendan and Marco. Those two were determined to make themselves heard.

"We need ta get inside then! Gotta do somethin'"

Amid the fresh eruption of voices, Tythias stood and held his hands out. Taking a deep breath, he shouted "Shut up!"

The room fell silent instantly as everyone turned to look at the scarred captain. Sathina smiled as the man gestured to her. He and his associate Jorun had been the biggest surprise of the journey. For such hairy, dirty and scarred men, they'd looked after her during their whole journey and Tythias particularly had proved to be a surprisingly polite and educated man. In her presence anyway. She smiled and stood.

"It seems to me that the only way you gentlemen are ever going to do anything other than argue about what can't be done is for me to go work at the palace. I can do any servant's job they give me and I'll be able to find out a lot more than you can by watching the place."

Athas shook his head. "Too dangerous. If you got caught, Velutio wouldn't be kind. And then you'd also put the rest of us in danger."

Tythias nodded vigorously, but next to him Prince Ashar shook his finger, a thoughtful expression on his face.

"I'm not sure about that" the elegant easterner argued. "We're in a dire position now. Quintillian could be executed at any time now and if we don't have any more information, we'll still be arguing when it happens. I think this young girl may be our only hope."

Tythias and the others made disagreeing grumbling noises around the table, but in the end Athas sighed and leaned back. "He's right. We need to know what's going on and sure as hell none of *us* are going to get inside and look. If you're willing to do it girl, we'd be grateful."

Across from him Jorun nodded and made a questioning gesture at the prince.

Yes Jorun, I'll help her as best I can." He turned back to the rest of the crowd. "Shahar is my second here. I'll take the young lady away and we'll work on getting her safely into the palace. Shahar can help you make any other arrangements."

One of the Pelasian spies, a man with a neat pointed beard, nodded. "We must to plan next stage anyway; what we do when we manage get them out of palace."

As Ashar and Sathina made their way out of the room, Mercurias leaned forward. "Isera." The rest turned to look at him. "It's what Quintillian was saying before. The place they're least likely to look for an escaped prisoner is in prison."

Tythias nodded. "Makes sense to me. If they've got a small garrison on the island we can either avoid them or overwhelm them. Either way I like the idea."

Mercurias nodded. "Ok Shahar. Until we can learn more from the young lady, we need to work something out about the island. What do you know about Isera at the moment?"

The Pelasian shook his head. "Very little. We resume communications there recently, but three nights I get one last cryptic message telling us communications being monitored and would have close down. I not know what do about it."

Mercurias sighed. "So we're back to waiting for more information then."

* * *

206

Sergeant Iasus stomped down the steps to the Dalertine prison, his face contorted with disgust. Holding the oil lamp high, he approached the bars of the cell and saw the four inmates huddled on the wooden pallets.

"General Caerdin?"

Kiva stood slowly with some stiffness and made his way toward the bars.

"Sergeant?" he replied. "Is there a problem?"

The young martinet nodded. Placing the oil lamp on the shelf, he straightened. "Lord Velutio has made his decree I'm afraid."

The other three now stirred in the rear of the cell. Kiva nodded solemnly.

"Not good news then" he noted.

"No." The sergeant sighed. "His lordship has ordered that you be taken to the gardens in an hour's time and that you're all crucified. I'm personally not happy with this, but it's my duty to follow the orders."

Kiva nodded. "I'm surprised that Commander Sabian didn't come down to give us the tidings personally."

The sergeant's face shifted but Kiva couldn't identify the emotion.

"The commander refused to be involved and I can't say I disagree with him. He's left the city less than an hour ago and I'm not sure whether he'll be back. This isn't the way for a soldier to go... crucifixion's for criminals." Iasus took a deep breath. "You have an hour to make your peace with the Gods and then we have to carry out the sentence."

After almost two weeks in the dark, damp hole even death lost its sting if it meant seeing the sky again. Kiva nodded. "That's not necessary for me, but the others will need it. I'll await your return though sergeant."

Iasus nodded curtly and went to pick up the oil lamp. He paused for a moment without picking it up and then shook his head before walking off into the dark and toward the stairs.

Quintillian moved forward to join Kiva at the bars as the general mused to himself. "I wonder what Sabian's up to. Can't believe he'd quite his position over us, but would Velutio really just let him go for this? I think not."

"That's it then" Quintillian said, defeat in his voice. "We're going to die in an hour."

"I wish it were that good" replied the general. "It starts in an hour, but crucifixion takes days. You slowly succumb to hunger and thirst. Then there's exhaustion, the ropes and the spikes in your limbs. Chances are they'll beat us and cut us as well, but not too much. Velutio won't want us to die too soon or too easily. In the end the birds will start to peck at us, but hopefully we'll be dead by then."

Kiva glanced up and saw the look on the boy's face.

"I'm sorry Quintillian. I didn't think. But it helps to be prepared for whatever they have in mind. Velutio doesn't need to torture us now. He's won. But he *wants* to torture us; he wants to take it all out on us, and he can't afford to leave any of us alive." He patted Quintillian on the shoulder. "Now go pray. I'll stand watch here." He grinned. "The Gods don't listen to me anyway."

It was less than an hour, in fact, when Iasus and a small party of men came down the stairs and brought the four prisoners from their dark pit. The morning sun was dazzling as they were taken out into the main courtyard for the first time in two weeks. Their hands were cuffed once more and none could shade their eyes from the glare, causing them to squint as they walked and to tread carefully until their sight adjusted.

The half dozen guards split up and walked to either side of their charges, with Iasus behind, solemn and stony faced. The small group marched through the archway and back into merciful shadow for a few moments before they burst out into the Imperial gardens, with the morning sun halfway up the eastern sky and glaring directly into their faces. The gardens were almost empty. No grand execution for these four; their deaths would remain as unknown as their lives and their 'crimes' to the world in general. There were perhaps a score of guards in the gardens on patrol and at stationary posts and a party of four men standing by the few individual trees on the central lawn. Kiva made a quick count. In actual fact, only twenty two guards, but what chance would they have even if they made it to the cliff? He nudged Julian, limping alongside him, and gestured across the gardens with his head.

"Think we'd ever make it?" he whispered.

Julian rumbled deep in his throat. "Might make it to the wall, but could we survive the drop?"

"Then we've no choice but to be crucified. Is that any better?"

As the two silently mulled over their chances, Julian was suddenly pushed aside as Alessus started to run. The guards by their sides took a strangely long moment to notice what was happening, and then with a yell started their own run. Kiva stuck out a foot and watched the first guard go tumbling over onto his face. Julian had apparently had much the same idea, slumping and knocking the next guard out of line. As the six guards called a warning to their fellows around the garden, they hauled their other three prisoners back and restrained them painfully. Julian cried "run man!" and Kiva and Quintillian tried to join in the encouraging shout before the arms locked round their throats, preventing them from speaking and almost from breathing. Alessus, never a great runner, but a fit and tactical military man with thirty years of combat experience, slowed as he reached a small knot of trees and gardens. Kiva saw him disappear behind a box hedge and there was no sign for a moment until four more guards reached the same spot and started searching the various hiding places. As they entered, Kiva saw Alessus break out of a hedge almost where he'd first entered, doubling back and making for the low border wall. With a skip and a vault, he disappeared over the edge.

Tense seconds passed as Kiva, Quintillian and Julian craned forward for any sign of what had happened to their comrade. The guards were now converging on the spot he'd crossed the wall. From the shouts of consternation among them, Kiva could safely assume that Alessus had begun to climb the slow climb down the rock face. He smiled, but the smile slid from his face a moment later as another group of guards armed with short recurve bows appeared from a doorway at the other end of the gardens. Behind them Velutio himself appeared with a number of his personal guard. With shouts the lord directed them to the wall and, as the archers began to fire vertically down the cliff face, other guards began to collect stones near the path and to drop them over the edge. Kiva held his breath, shaking slightly.

And then there was a distant scream, becoming more and more distant by the second as Alessus, struck through with an arrow and battered by other missiles, came loose from the treacherous cliff and bounced down the jagged rocks far down to the sea and the reefs below. Kiva pictured for a moment the broken body splayed across the sharp watery rocks and had to shake his head to clear the vision. Hopefully the man had been dead before he was halfway down. He glanced round and Julian's head was lowered.

Iasus merely said "stupid" and ushered them all forward again. The three of them and their six guards, now holding them tight, shuffled forward toward the trees in the centre. Kiva looked up and noted the four soldiers armed with tools and an ominous bag. The ropes to fasten wrists and ankles were already looped over branches and ready.

Curiously there were only three trees set up. Either they were psychic or Velutio had other plans for one of them.

Once they reached the lawn and the guards brought them to a halt, Velutio and his personal guard were approaching across the grass from the direction of the perimeter wall. The old lord, unruffled and in civilian clothing, stopped several yards away from them and glared past Kiva at the sergeant behind.

"Can my entire army not keep four prisoners under control? Sabian's been gone for less than two hours and already you're falling to pieces!"

There was no answer from Iasus, so Kiva smiled and spoke. "So now you've driven Sabian away too."

Velutio turned his glower to Kiva.

"Caerdin, you'd be wise to keep your over-sized mouth firmly shut. The commander is away on a temporary duty and will be returning within the week. I do hope the birds haven't made you unrecognisable before he gets back." He gestured to the sergeant and the guards pushed the three forward again toward the trees. As they stood with their wrists bound the sergeant walked across to them with a small knife and began cutting away the ties and stitching on their clothing. Tunics were cut away, as were breeches, leaving only their underwear. Then Kiva and Quintillian were unceremoniously dropped to the turf like sacks of flour, while two other guards held Julian up by the shoulders and dragged him to the first tree. Quintillian lowered his head, but the guard next to him pulled it back up by the hair.

"Watch" he ordered.

The young man stared ahead to where Julian was being propped against the tree. He saw the man's hands being fed through the rope loops and heard the strange sawing noise as the ropes were hauled tight and Julian slammed back against the bark with a grunt. At that point Quintillian, aware that he couldn't look away, defocused his eyes and tried to think of something different. He was still vaguely aware of what was going on in front of him, but his mind wandered as he thought of Athas and Mercurias, of Brendan and Marco, wondering where they all were right now; of Prince Ashar, who he knew had men in this city, and Tythias, away to the west preparing perhaps for a glorious campaign to bring the Empire back to rights that would never happen. Well, this was it. The next Empire would be Velutio's and there was no way to stop it now.

His eyes refocused automatically as he was brought out of his daze by a cry of pain. Julian was now hanging from the ropes at his wrists, his shoulders separating painfully and his feet bound to the tree with another rope that ran around the trunk. The bark of the tree was stained red where the tough wood had flayed the young mercenary's back as he was hauled up the bole. For good measure they were using nails and the first one had been driven through Julian's left wrist. A spray of blood gushed out around the nail after the first heavy blow and splashed to the grass like a crimson fountain. Quintillian averted his eyes again, only to have the guard wrench his head back forward once more.

Velutio walked toward the gory scene, his boots making an obscene squelching noise as he walked into the red pool, and cuffed the soldier with the mallet around the back of the head very hard. The soldier staggered, taken unawares.

"You dolt!" shouted the lord. "Not through an artery! He'll die in minutes like that." He wrenched the hammer from the soldier's hand and passed it to the man holding the bag of nails, who took it reluctantly.

Julian managed a weak grin at the lord of Velutio as the blood continued to pump from his wrist. The other soldier stepped to one side and lifted a second nail. Carefully probing the mercenary's wrist for veins and arteries he placed the point and, slowly pulling back the hammer, drove the nail deep through the flesh and into the wood. A small puddle of blood welled up around the head of the spike and ran down the arm before the second blow knocked it flat against the skin.

The young mercenary seemed short of breath, but his grin deepened as he looked down at the soldier with the hammer, who was staring at his own hands in a sort of horror.

"Don't forget the feet. Don't want me running away."

The soldier looked across at Velutio, a question in his eyes, and the lord nodded. With a sigh, the soldier stepped forward and pulled the man's feet together, placing the third nail over the middle of both feet. The first blow knocked the nail in deep and broke most of the bones in both feet; the second drove it home. The smile gradually slipped from Julian's face. His flesh had become deathly pale as more and more of his life's blood rushed out onto the turf. He raised his head with some difficulty and focused as best he could on Kiva.

"Looks like I got it easy; no birds for me." His last words came out a low croak, fading into a sigh as the light went out in his eyes and the seventh Wolf passed from the world.

Quintillian risked moving his head now the spectacle was over for the time being, and glanced at Kiva. He expected the general to be shaking, furious, angry. Instead, all he could see was sadness and the sheer power of the expression in the old general's eyes melted into Quintillian's heart and brought out in him an overwhelming feeling of loss. He opened his mouth to say something, but at that moment, two more soldiers hauled Kiva to his feet. The general didn't even resist. Quintillian wondered at what point the man had given up hope. Looking up as the general was turned away, he searched the man's eyes for a sign of anything other than resignation, and that was when he saw it. There was a sparkle. Just a slight sparkle and then... a wink. The general's eyes looked down and Quintillian's gaze followed them to his hands, where something gold flashed in the sun. The Pelasian coin. There was some kind of plan brewing, but what use would it be now?

He watched as the two men hauled Kiva to the next tree and pushed him back against it. Again the ropes were looped over his hands and he was hauled upwards to the branches, scraping the flesh from his back and causing rivulets of blood to run down the bole of the tree. Quintillian stared as the second rope was hauled tight, the feet being placed atop each other. He couldn't believe this was actually happening. He'd never really expected to rule anyone; never wanted power as such, he just wanted the Empire back together and in the hands of the people who knew what to do with it; people like Sarios. And now, because of what he'd done, he'd killed himself and the Wolves. He just couldn't believe there was no way out and that providence wouldn't save them somehow. The general had a sharpened coin, but what possible use could that be now?

Kiva glared at Velutio as the tip of the first nail was placed on his wrist and Quintillian watched him grit his teeth and wince as the nail was slammed through and into the wood. Not even a whimper. Would he be as brave when it came to his turn? The nail was knocked home and the second put in place. Again, the teeth were jammed together as the nail was hammered home, blood welling up and dripping down the arms. A third nail was produced and hammered home in the feet with the sounds of breaking bone.

That's it then, thought Quintillian. The Wolves are no more. Oh four of them still existed somewhere, he hoped, but the unit was destroyed and their commander crucified. How long now before people like Tythias and his men became unnecessary and Velutio did the same to them, and then those on the island. A tear came to his eye unbidden as he watched the general settled gently against the wood, the muscles in his shoulders tearing as he sank down slightly. He thought of Darius and the elders, the people on the island. He should never have left and then none of this would have happened. His attention was caught by the general's voice as he addressed Velutio.

"I know you've wanted to do this for a very long time, but it makes no difference in the end, Avitus. The boy'll be rescued yet, even if I die, and someone'll set him back on his path. And even if he dies, there'll always be someone to challenge your rule."

"Oh?" Velutio looked sceptical. "And who would be able to stand against us?"

Kiva snarled. "Who could have stood against *Quintus*? But it happened. The world is an ever-changing place Avitus, and you'd do well not to get too bogged down in where you are now. Quintillian taught me that."

"Did he?" sneered Velutio. "Well we'd best make sure he's not used against me again, hadn't we?"

Two more guards finally hauled Quintillian to his feet and pushed him toward the third tree. Kiva watched the young man in consternation as the lad stared at the tree. And that was why he didn't see it coming. The first he knew; the first he realised something had happened, was as the tip of Velutio's sword emerged from Quintillian's chest. The boy's eyes went wide and he coughed, dark blood welling in his mouth and running from the corner down his chin. Kiva stared.

Velutio twisted his wrist and the blade made a ninety degree turn deep in Quintillian's chest, accompanied by surprised gurgles from the last scion of the Imperial family, who looked down in fascination at the foot of cold steel protruding from his sternum. Gingerly, he touched the blade. He looked up at Kiva, his eyes full of confusion.

"Fancy that" he exclaimed as the pupils of his eyes rolled up into his head and he slid forward off the blade to collapse in a heap on the grass.

Kiva growled and tried to move. As he pulled on his arms, he felt a shoulder dislocate and the blood welled fresh at his wrist. He glared at Velutio. At last the anger was there, but too late. He growled.

"I *will* get out of this Avitus, and when I do there is nowhere in the world I won't find you. I'll strip the flesh from your cold bones with my teeth, do you hear me?"

Velutio merely smiled and wiped the bloody sword on the piles of clothing left on the grass. "They're not divine, Caerdin; they never were. You're not cursed and he wasn't a God, don't you see? An Emperor is made, not born and I shall be the next one. At least I won't carry the taint of madness like they did. The line's finally dead and nothing can stand in the way of a new Emperor. You're a relic, Caerdin; a fossil and your time's up."

With a last look, he turned away from the trees and began to stride across the grass toward the palace, leaving crimson footprints on the flagstones he crossed. The sergeant ordered the men to depart and to take the boy's body with them. As the garden gradually emptied of guards, leaving only the standard patrols, Iasus stood alone with Kiva and the hanging body of Julian.

"I am truly sorry it came to this general and I wish the circumstances had been different, but I must do my duty; I'm sure you can see that."

Perhaps Kiva could, and perhaps not, but grief and rage vied for control of his mind and forgiveness was not in him today.

"He'll die!" the general declared. "He'll die hard, and when he does, anyone with him will go too."

Iasus looked up, his hard face looking odd as it registered sympathy. He noted a tear in the general's eye and stood straight, saluting.

"I know you won't appreciate it right now, Caerdin, but I will make sure that Quintillian is taken to the island and buried properly and with honour."

And with a last look at probably the greatest general in the Empire's history hanging like a common criminal on a tree, he turned and marched away to see to the burial of the last Emperor.

* * *

It had been three days since Sathina had first entered the palace. Despite the words of wisdom and the various pointers she'd received from Prince Ashar, she'd not been able to find out anything about the four captives. None of the guards spoke about the prisoners and she'd not heard a single thing even in overheard mutterings. To be honest with herself, she was starting to wonder what she was doing here and whether these prisoners really existed. She'd asked about the Dalertine prison only once, of another servant, and he'd told her to shut up and not ask dangerous questions.

And so she'd gone about the mind-numbingly dull tasks of a serving girl, dealing mostly with the laundry, but with a constant edge of panic, knowing what was at stake if she let on anything about herself. Ashar had given her a good story and it seemed to have passed the test numerous times, a story of a dancer and musician come to the city to get rich, but only getting poorer and having to seek a servant's wage. All very plausible and not a huge leap from the truth of it.

And that was when she'd finally found out. With a basket of laundry in both arms, piled so high she couldn't see where she was going, she'd wandered out into the sun, missing the door she needed in the gateway. Dropping the basket to rub her sore hands and get her bearings, she'd found herself staring directly at a grisly sight: two bodies hanging on trees in the middle of a lawn, crucified. Though she had only the vaguest description of the prisoners, there could have been no doubt that these were they and, making a pretence of rubbing her hands and crouching by the basket, she'd tried to take in every detail of the scene to pass along to the prince. It was then she'd started as one of them had moved. Only very slightly, and just enough to move his head out of the direct sunlight and into the shade of a branch.

A guard had approached her and demanded she move along to wherever she should be. She'd made a girlish light-headed apology and heaved the basket back into the archway, delivering it to the first dark empty room she could find and then making her way to the main courtyard. After three days she knew the routine well. In a little less than an hour the servants would be allowed out of the gates to visit family or to shop at lunch. She'd stepped in through a door and found a small closet to hide in until she heard the bell ring in the tower and servants appeared from doorways around the courtyard and rushed for the gate, making the most of their meagre half hour of freedom. That was when she'd left and made it out into the street, walking fast until she reached a corner just within sight of the gate where she turned and ran as fast as her legs would carry her until she reached the nondescript building that the prince called their 'safe house'.

And now she rushed up the two flights of stairs and hammered on the door three times; twice; three times. The door opened and Jorun grinned at her, making a scratchy noise in his throat. She smiled. The huge barbarian mercenary had taken her under his wing in recent days, looking after her more even than Tythias did. They were certainly an interesting bunch she'd fallen in with. Still, there were more pressing matters. Athas and Tythias sat at a table in one corner of the room playing some kind of board game involving two dice and a selection of pieces that resembled towers and belfries. The rest of the men were absent.

"I've seen them!" she exclaimed.

The board was knocked to one side, pieces falling as it moved. Tythias and Athas were on their feet now.

"Where? What's happening?" The two rushed towards her.

She settled to get her breath. "It's not good. I only saw two and I think one of them was dead."

Tythias and Athas jostled to get in front of her. The one-eyed mercenary won the fight and grasped her shoulders. "Who?"

"I'm not sure. The youngish one with fairly long blond hair's Julian, yes?"

Athas nodded, his heart in his throat. The young mercenary had been the last addition to the unit before Quintillian and had proved to be the perfect Wolf.

"He's dead I think" she said in a low voice. "Crucified on a tree in the palace gardens.

"And?" Tythias probed.

"The other one must be Caerdin. He's alive, but I'm not sure for how much longer. He doesn't look good. They crucified him too. He's been roped and nailed."

Athas shook her. "What about the others?"

"I don't know, but I think perhaps someone died the other day. I thought nothing of it at the time, but some of the guards took a huge wooden crate out of the palace on a cart."

Athas snarled. "Shit! Either Alessus or Quintillian dead, Julian dead and Kiva on the edge." He turned to Jorun. "Go upstairs and get Ashar and the others!"

Sathina shuddered. This was far more important and emotional than she'd ever expected. It had been exciting and intriguing, but she'd never thought to see them hanging on a tree, bleeding the last of their life out. Shaking, she pulled away from Tythias and sank, weeping, to the bench. The scarred mercenary captain sat next to her and took her in his arms.

"There was nothing you could do, and you may have saved the general's life."

As she poured out her anguish, the ageing captain held her close and absorbed her grief while the prince and the others came down and started making feverish plans. Tythias was a soldier and a commander and a good one at that. Upon a time he'd commanded a thousand men in the field, but these others were subtle and knew this business better. He half listened to the plans and arguments going on around him as he held the young girl close until her grief subsided and she sank into a fitful sleep, slouched on the bench in his arms.

* * *

216

Kiva had lost track of time. There had been four sunsets he remembered, but he suspected more. His stomach had stopped growling days ago and begun to waste, eating his own fat to survive a little longer. The pain in his limbs had numbed within the first day and he was hoping for the lord of the underworld to claim him soon, for his shoulders were torn, perhaps beyond repair. He'd taken the coin to cut through the ropes in the hope of rescuing both himself and the boy, but without Quintillian what was the point? All dreams of rebuilding the Empire of Quintus had died with Velutio's blade and he hoped not to live to see the Empire under the command of the scourge of his existence. Perhaps he was dying now? He certainly seemed to be hallucinating, for the tree was moving.

He glanced down. The trees of the gardens and the lawn beneath were so far down now he couldn't understand how he'd changed position without his arms tearing away. The stars instead of being above him were in front as he watched. He smiled weakly. There was the constellation of his birth: the swordsman. What a surprise. This must be it. He'd known his mind was going a day or two ago, and he knew that Velutio had been several times to gloat over him. That sergeant, whatever his name was had been back too. He'd eased things a little he thought. Perhaps the sergeant was a friend, but no. He didn't have friends now.

He smiled as he saw what his hallucinations were bringing him in his last few hours. Perhaps wishful thinking imposing itself on reality. One of Velutio's guards appeared to be standing by a tree but a closer look showed him impaled with a long black arrow driven into the wood, his throat opened and blood gushing down his front, mixing with the red dye of his tunic.

He smiled and passed out.

And here he was again. His hallucinations were getting better all the time. The stars were still there, but in different positions and he had strange floating feeling. In fact, the sound of waves imposed themselves over the eerie silence.

Oh yes. Better and better, for here was a maiden of the Gods leaning over him and mopping his brow. Young and voluptuous and full of beautiful life, waiting to take him home. Perhaps she would seat him in the hall of the Gods for his place at the feast.

Someone's voice from beyond the periphery of his sight asked "how is he?"

"Not good" the divine maiden replied.

With a smile of sheer content, Kiva surrendered himself to this maiden of death and drifted off once more.

Part Four: Loss & Gain

Chapter XIX.

The marble columns wreathed in fire. The purple and gold drapes blazing and falling away into burning heaps on the floor. A chalice of wine on a small table by a couch, boiling in the intense heat. The panicked twittering of the ornamental birds in their golden cages as the room around them was consumed by the inferno. And in the centre of the room, standing in robes of white and purple, a boy. He doesn't look frightened, though the flames lick at his whole world and his face is already grimy with the smoke. What he looks is disappointed, his arm clutching the blade that juts from his chest, soaked with warm blood; gripping the sword that ends his life.

Kiva started awake in a sweat, bleary eyed and wrapped in a blanket of confusion. It was clearly day time, for birds were singing and there was enough bright light to make him squint. Above, a stucco ceiling swam into focus. A glow was coming from the right. He tried to turn his head, but the explosion of painful light and noise in his mind stopped him. Where was he? Clearly he wasn't as dead as he'd expected to be. He sat up.

The next time he awoke he was less sure. His head felt as though miners had been quarrying marble in it. There was light and birdsong. He vaguely remembered something about sudden pain and swimming blackness.

A calm voice said "Don't be a fool."

In urgency, he began to sit upright, but the build up of pressure in his head as he started made him halt mid-movement. Something about pain. He slowly lowered himself back to the oh-so-comfortable bed clothes. Something was wrong with his neck. It felt like someone had mortared it into position. Painfully, but slowly, he levered himself up onto one surprisingly weak elbow so he could look in the direction of the voice. The room came into focus again and Kiva found himself staring into the eyes of Quintus the Golden. His eyes widened in shock for a moment before he realised the wall was crammed with shelved busts of Emperors and great men. His eyes came down lower until he saw the bed; a large comfortable bed yet austere in some indefinable way. Lying in the bed was an old man in nightwear, with a bandage wrapped round his head. Confusion blossomed again in Kiva's mind.

What was this? A museum? A hospital? Both? He squinted at the figure.

"I think you're probably still not well enough to sit up," the figure said amiably. "You fair proved that half an hour ago."

Kiva cleared his throat, suddenly aware of how dry he was and how much his throat hurt. It appeared to be sore, dry and almost blocked. With difficulty, he phrased a question: "Who are you?"

The old man smiled again. "It's been a long time Caerdin, but I find it hard to believe I've changed *that* much."

Kiva frowned, but the usual mixture of muscle contractions was surprisingly painful. It hurt when he frowned? The figure in the other bed was hauntingly familiar. He tried to picture the face a decade or more younger and his eyes widened.

"Sarios?"

The old man nodded. "I'm certain you've aged more than I, Caerdin, so I'm not sure I understand your surprise."

Kiva frowned again and regretted it instantly. "So I'm on Isera?"

Again the nod. Kiva allowed himself to settle back into the soft bedclothes. "That's not good. Velutio's going to be looking for me more than he ever…"

A sudden memory flashed across his eyes, causing him to gasp. A boy watching him in some surprise, a sword jutting from his chest. Kiva's sudden violent curse at the recollection was masked by the creaking of the opening door. A figure wandered into his field of vision; a figure he certainly *didn't* recognise.

"Who're you?" Kiva asked sharply, still reeling from the shock of his memories returning.

"General" the man addressed him calmly, "you need to avoid all such excitement. For my sake as well as yours lie back and remain quiet."

Again Kiva forced himself as far upright as his strength would allow. Only now did he notice the thick bandages around his wrists and the various new scars above and below them.

"I've got to get away." His eyes narrowed. "How long have I been here?"

The man smiled gently. "Almost two weeks. And as for getting away, it's going to be at least another week before you're ready to leave the bed and I wouldn't think you'll be able to walk more than a few yards for the best part of a month after that. You're still wounded and you're very weak."

220

Kiva snorted, but the retort died unspoken in his throat as the memory of the nail smashing into his feet came swimming back into his mind.

"How bad am I?" he questioned, aware that he might not be truly prepared for the answer. The man, obviously a doctor of some sort, smiled reassuringly. "Not as bad as you were. And certainly not as bad as you could have been. Your friends brought two other doctors with them, a man called Mercurias who reminds me pleasingly of myself, and a Pelasian with some ideas that are a little outlandish but they certainly make you think."

He registered the look on Kiva's face and shrugged. "I'm not sure you'd still be here if were just down to me."

"Mercurias made it here? And a Pelasian?"

The doctor leaned down to Kiva's feet and whatever he did there made the veins in his feet and legs run with liquid fire. He stifled a scream.

"A vast improvement" declared the doctor, and then looked up with a smile as he realised he'd been spoken to. "Hmm? Pelasian? Oh yes... Far too many men here now. A big dark skinned man, Mercurias, a man with one eye, a big barbarian with a tattered throat, two men who argue with me all the time and tell me that you just need a drink and a fight, and about a half dozen Pelasians. Oh, and a young woman. It's getting rather difficult to hide them all."

Kiva's eyes gradually widened as he listened. He knew almost every individual from the description. The Wolves, such as they were now, were here on Isera with him. Including himself there would be only five now. And two of the Lion Riders were here? And Prince Ashar's men? And a woman? Who was she? Momentary visions of a handmaiden of the underworld swam into his mind as he remembered water and the creaking of a boat. He'd failed them all. He let his head slump back to the pillow.

The doctor sighed as he stood once more. "Each and every one of them has been in to see you more times than I've allowed them to in your current state. I'll let them come in and see you again tomorrow one at a time. Not today though; today you rest."

Picking up his unopened bag of medicines, the doctor stretched. "I'll be leaving for now. If you get into discomfort, shout out. There's a servant in the other room who can fetch me.

Kiva nodded and a thought crossed his mind. "Doctor, I had a flask..."

The doctor smiled. "Yes, I'm well aware of that. Mare's mead. Quite dangerous when you misuse it, you know? And you do, though from the look of you there's a history there of misuse. You couldn't have taken it anyway while you were out and your Mercurias fellow seemed to think it would be a good time to wean you off it. With two weeks' head start you should be well on the way."

Kiva tried to growl, but it hurt his throat too much. With a scowl, he watched the doctor leave the room and then sighed as the door closed once more.

"It's the end anyway."

"The end?" asked Sarios, leaning on one of his elbows as he looked across at the man he'd shared his chamber with for the last fortnight. "The end of what?"

Kiva gave a hoarse laugh. "The end of everything. You should never have sent Quintillian away from here, and then he wouldn't have found me."

Sarios merely raised an eyebrow questioningly. Kiva made angry noises and settled deeper into his pillow.

"I started to believe, you know? It's been so long since I thought there was any hope for the Empire that it took a long while for me to get my head around it, but I actually started to believe. You'd done a good job with Quintillian; he reminded me so much of Quintus when I first served the man. You remember the young Quintus? The one who set out to make the world civilised?"

Sarios nodded. A curious smile was slowly spreading across his face, not at all in keeping with Kiva's mood or topic of conversation. The general scowled at him, but then sighed and let the scowl that took so much effort to maintain fall away.

"We could maybe have done it too," he continued. "Given enough time, we could have got everyone together; united the few lords still loyal and broken Velutio. It could have been done perhaps, but now it's over."

Sarios' smile was now wide and warm though Kiva failed to see the humour in the situation. "Why over?" the minister questioned.

Kiva blinked. "The boy's dead, Sarios. I saw Velutio run him through right in front of my eyes. I failed him at the end and now the bloodline's gone. He was the last scion and without him there's nothing for anyone to rally behind. Velutio's won and us being on the island's just bringing trouble your way."

"Thinking was never your strong point Kiva. You were always a genius on a battlefield, but in the court or the city you were too

222

blinkered and trusting. You never open to possibilities. Think now why I sent Quintillian out from here. Why did I, Kiva?"

The general sighed again. "Maybe you wanted him to get far away and out of the reach of Velutio. To hide him, yes?"

Sarios grinned. "Don't be idiotic, Caerdin. Your brain's softened. The boy was very important to all of us, but I'm a politician, not his father. Why do you think I would risk him like that?"

Kiva's head whirled. He'd only been conscious for a few minutes and wasn't at all sure he was up to this kind of depth of thought. Sarios had always had that effect on him though; the man could think in spirals where Kiva could only think in straight lines. He mulled for a moment as Sarios watched him, smiling. The smile was starting to annoy him.

"I suppose you're going to tell me you sent him to find me?"

Sarios made a 'so-so' motion with his hand. "Sort of. Certainly Tomas and Enarion were given specific instructions to find you but why, Caerdin? Why?"

Kiva's brows knitted again in concentration but in the end he shrugged, another motion which caused pain throughout much of his upper body.

Sarios sighed. "He was a wild card, Caerdin. Just putting him in the world again would cause change; shake things up. If everything was allowed to run on the way it was, the result would be inevitable: the Empire of Velutio and the deaths of everyone we care about. It may sound harsh to you, but Quintillian was a political tool. If you'd made him Emperor, it would have far exceeded my expectations, but in the end he did exactly what I anticipated. Like a stone dropped into a lake, he sent out ripples throughout the whole world. And even when the stone's sunk, the ripples are still moving. Do you follow me?"

"As far as I care to" Kiva growled. "Like all politicians, you use people. But," he said sharply, pointing a finger at the minister "whatever you hoped to achieve by sacrificing him has failed. Now we're in a worse state than ever. More than half the Wolves are dead. The last Imperial blood is gone. Your 'ripples' are dying away and the stone's still gone."

Sarios grinned again. "Don't sell yourself short, Caerdin. These ripples could become tidal waves. Quintillian brought the Wolves and the Lion Riders together; he flushed a Pelasian ally out of the darkness." His grin slipped as a serious look took its place. "And of course, it's caused a great deal of upset in the city and beyond. There are rumblings of rebellion now even in Serfium after what happened to their priests."

Kiva sighed again. "All immaterial. We don't have an Emperor any more and now there's just more of us trapped and in hiding."

"You're still not thinking, Caerdin" Sarios chided him. "Do you imagine for one minute that no one else could ever take the throne? What do you think Velutio plans to do?"

Kiva shuffled uncomfortably in the bed. "What're you suggesting? That there's other possibilities?"

Sarios clicked his tongue in irritation. "There are endless possibilities, Kiva. There always are. In the past we've had runs of Emperors who selected and adopted their heirs. You can't believe it's been one bloodline from the start? And even if you did want to follow the blood, there are others who carry the same blood; distant relatives of the line. Good grief, you yourself were married into the line and who could inspire an army like the great General Caerdin?"

Another grunt and Kiva rolled over to face away from the minister.

"It's over. And soon us being here's going to draw unwanted attention and Velutio'll burn the entire island clean."

Sarios laughed. "You just don't know how much things have stirred up. Your being here isn't putting us in any more danger than we already were. We're all to die soon and we know it. Velutio's already sentenced us, but the date hasn't been set. It seems that Commander Sabian wasn't ready to execute you or us and he put his own career and his life on the line to send us a warning. That's the kind of ripple I'm talking about, Caerdin. We've been using one of the secret routes out to ferry people off the island for the last fortnight."

Kiva rolled back over, his eyes widening. "You're leaving?"

A nod. "Only a few at a time and always at night, but slowly we're going. We have to be careful. The sergeant on the island's a good sort, but I doubt he'd side with us against his master, so we're shipping out the less well known people first. They're going into hiding in a community I know of. You see, you've not changed anything for us here and as soon as you're well enough, you'll be shipped out too."

Kiva opened his mouth to speak, but was interrupted by a knock at the door. Sarios pulled himself a little further upright and called "enter!"

The door opened and a young man appeared. He was tall, with dark hair and a neat beard. Unlike most of the prisoners on the island who wore soft robes or work clothes, this young man wore travelling leathers and had a sword slung at his side. Kiva blinked in surprise. The garrison allowed the islanders to carry weapons? Strange. The young man glanced once at him with mild interest and approached the end of Sarios' bed.

"Minister, I've had another message from the mainland. It's com..." another glance at Kiva. "...the contact. He says he's going to be going to Serfium, but he wants to speak to Cialo via the signals before he leaves. I haven't answered him yet, 'cos I wasn't sure how good an idea that is."

Sarios nodded. "I wonder what he has planned for the good sergeant? I agree though; I don't think it's a particularly good idea. Ask him about his plans first. Let's try and stop him getting himself into trouble. Darius, I'd perhaps better introduce you to General Caerdin." He looked at Kiva. "This is Darius, one of the promising young men of our island."

Darius made a curt bow, his hand on the pommel of his sword. "General, I've heard and read a great deal about you. Your reputation precedes you."

Kiva struggled a little further up in the bed, ignoring the pain shooting through his limbs. "So you're Darius. Quintillian held you in the highest regard. Perhaps when I'm a little more mobile we should talk?"

Darius bowed again and then stepped back toward the door. "I'll leave you both now. Favio says you're both to be disturbed as little as possible and he already thinks I break the rules too much."

With a final nod at Sarios, he opened the door and went to leave the room. Kiva cleared his throat. "Darius..."

The lad turned and waited. Kiva put on a pained expression. "Your doctor also won't let me have my flask. I don't suppose you fancy breaking the rules a little more?"

Darius smiled a knowing smile. "Hmm. I'll see what I can do, but Mercurias has it now and he won't want you to have it. Leave it with me though." With that he turned and left the room.

Kiva and Sarios exchanged glances.

"He's very sure of himself for such a young one" the general muttered.

Sarios smiled. "And you weren't? I remember you when you first came to the Capital and met Quintus. You were a fresh faced northern lad with the manners of a goat herd, and yet you strolled around the palace as though you were born to it. Darius is one of my pet projects, as was Quintillian. He'll be one to watch in future if we get off this island fast enough."

Kiva nodded. "Who is he? Darius I mean."

Sarios shrugged. "Do you remember the Commander of the Munda camp? Spent quite a lot of time at the palace?"

Kiva nodded. The man had been a passing acquaintance, though his duties often kept him at the training camp. He'd been fairly highly placed. Not as high as Kiva and the other three marshals, but as the man responsible for the army's training regime, he'd been seen around the palace fairly regularly.

"His son," confirmed the minister. "Commander Fulvius was one of the earliest victims of Velutio's proscriptions. His son was somehow saved as he was in the city at the time."

Kiva nodded again. "I can only presume the 'contact' Darius was speaking of was Sabian? He seems a good man. In the old days he'd have made it a long way in the army; maybe as high as me and he's not the sort of person that betrays his position, so why's he doing this? You're the political one."

Sarios shrugged. "I think perhaps Commander Sabian has too high a moral outlook for his current career. He's playing a very dangerous game, I believe. He trusts he can do the right thing by us and still be indispensable to Velutio. He'll have to be extremely careful or he's going to end up taking your place on the cross and to be quite honest, I don't think he's devious enough to pull it off. He's still in service at the moment though. If he's going to Serfium, it'll be as the armoured fist of Velutio to dispel any thought of rebellion."

Kiva growled. "So Velutio moves his army into there again. Strange how history repeats itself. So where are your people going?"

"I don't think I want to tell you yet," Sarios mused. "Let's just say that there are a number of secrets I've carried under three Emperors and beyond that not even they or you knew about."

The minister sighed and locked Kiva with his piercing eyes. "I think our other problem though may require your help."

"Other problem?"

Sarios nodded. "Soon we'll get to the point where absences will be extremely noticeable and then we're in great danger. The sergeant here's a good man, but he'd be forced to deal with us then. We may have to resort to dealing with the garrison first. *That's* what I mean by your help."

Kiva frowned and drew a sharp breath as the pain returned.

"You need to take out the whole garrison as soon as possible. I presume you're not talking about murder?"

"No" confirmed the minister. "I don't want to kill good people unnecessarily."

"I'm sure Quintillian appreciates that" Kiva replied with a touch of acid.

Sarios ignored him. "Perhaps we can drug them and lock them away somewhere?"

Kiva nodded. "That would be my first suggestion."

The two fell silent for a moment, deep in their own thoughts until Sarios leaned back. "I think perhaps this can wait until tomorrow. Your friends will be coming in and we'll need to discuss it with them. You need your rest anyway."

Kiva shook his head and ignored the swimmy feeling it caused. With a great deal of effort and swearing, he swivelled round in the bed and dropped his feet over the edge. For the first time he saw the state they were in and winced. Both feet were a little misshapen and an unpleasant mottled collection or purples, blues, yellows and browns. There were poultices applied to the centre of each foot. For a moment he found himself wondering whether he would ever walk again. Add to the wounds he'd suffered the general weakness and weariness that threatened to overtake him and he almost gave up and slumped back down. It was Sarios' concerned and sympathetic look that spurred him on. He was damned if he was going to lie there and fade while a man not far off twice his age poured sympathy over him.

He did collapse back for a moment, fighting for breath with the sheer effort of hauling his dead weight of a body around. Then finally, his knees reached the edge of the bed and his feet fell with a gentle slapping noise onto the beautiful mosaic floor. He nearly did scream then, tears of sheer agony welling up in his eyes and a shattering mirror of white pain behind his eyes. Gritting his teeth to prevent biting his tongue, he forced himself to stay upright, his feet still on the floor, until he managed to gain control of the pain and force it back down where it came from. He looked up and grinned. "Always was a fast healer."

Sarios shook his head, sympathy and anger vying for control of his face. "Don't be stupid, Caerdin. When you fall over, I'm not going to have the strength to pick you up!"

The grin stayed as Kiva relaxed once more, the pain fading away. Once more he gritted his teeth, set his jaw and heaved against the bed, slowly pushing himself toward the perpendicular. His legs wobbled back and forth, shaking like knotted ropes in a gale as he heaved, sweating profusely and muttering curses under his breath. With a push, he let go and tried to stand. For a fraction of a second he thought things were ok, but then the pain, exhaustion and dizziness came. For just a moment he lost consciousness on his feet, but was brought back to the present with a start as the flaming lava running in his veins set fire to his brain and the explosion of excruciating pain overwhelmed him. He fell like a sack of grain and with no grace, smashing to the floor with such a sound that Sarios heaved himself up to see whether Kiva had broken his neck. Miraculously, not only was he not broken, but had remained conscious, despite his head having hit the floor with no cushioning.

As the general groaned, the door to the room flew open and a man Kiva didn't know entered in a panic. "I'll get the doctor!" he cried and spun on his heel.

Kiva bellowed as best he could, a breathless cry, but enough to stop the servant in his tracks. "No you fucking won't. You'll go out into the grounds and find me two sticks I can use to prop myself up and then you'll come back here."

The servant's face took on a perplexed look and he turned to glance at Sarios. The old man frowned for some time and then nodded. The young man reached out to Kiva and tried to grasp his arm, but Kiva swiped at the hand with his arm and growled. "Go! And on the way back, find me something strong to drink!"

The servant, all aflutter, left the room, still in two minds about what to do. He'd been told to do anything Caerdin asked, but he couldn't imagine the doctor had meant this.

As the door shut, Kiva started pulling himself along the floor with his arms, heaving and sweating with the incredible effort. After a minute, he'd reached the window sill and hauled himself onto his knees to look out. If things were still moving apace and the island was going to rebel and evacuate, he'd be needed. He'd have to take control of it, and he couldn't very well do that from bed.

As Kiva looked out across the island and the sea beyond, not many miles away in the opposite direction, Commander Sabian slammed his fist down on the wall. The top of the golden tower on the headland opposite the palace was the only place he could be alone and untagged during the daylight hours. Fortunately, he'd managed to commandeer the place for the guards, so he had constant access. He growled and lifted the signal lamp back down from the low surrounding wall. What the hell was Darius playing at? He needed to speak to Cialo, but Darius was being deliberately obstructive. Well they'd have to wait and see then, since he couldn't pass on a warning.

He pulled out his spy glass and swept it around to the palace opposite, picking out some of his men as he moved down across the

228

buildings, over the Imperial Gardens and to the cliff, and then down and beyond. He couldn't see the port from here, but somewhere round that corner, four companies of Velutio's personal guard would be standing in formation awaiting his arrival before they boarded the small ship. And standing at the forefront would be his ambitious and deceiving second in command, Captain Flautus.

He smiled. For all he was a soldier, he could be as subtle as the next man and prided himself that he was starting to get quite adept at playing Velutio at his own game. His lordship had agreed readily at Sabian's proposal to remove the regular troops from the island and replace them with the more fanatically loyal of his guard. Indeed, Sabian had been saved a job as Velutio had personally vetted the men to go. The Commander couldn't possibly have done a better job of weeding out those men who preferred his lordship over their own commander. Ever since he'd killed Crosus, he'd been gradually identifying those who didn't maintain the right attitude; those who might harbour grudges or doubts or might even think of betraying him. And in one fell swoop he'd persuaded Velutio to do it for him! And even now those four companies of untrustworthy, dislikeable, greedy assholes were forming up for exile, all the while thinking they were getting preferential treatment. Perfect.

In a few days there would be not a soldier in the city who didn't hold Sabian as his first loyalty, and those he'd sent to the island could be dealt with by the islanders. He knew they were leaving of course; had sent the warning himself. But there was a perfect irony in letting the islanders get away before his Lordship could commit genocide, while landing the blame squarely with those few who could not be trusted. Again he smiled. He would drop the men off at Isera and collect Cialo's companies before returning and heading off to Serfium, but he'd have to talk to Darius and the minister about future plans while he was there.

Chapter XX.

The knock at the door woke Kiva from further fitful dreams that disappeared like drifting fog as he started into consciousness. He glanced around the room. Much better than yesterday. For all the pain he'd suffered dragging himself around the room, his muscles had loosened a little and he could at least move without the irritating stiffness. It was daylight, though what time he couldn't guess. The other bed in the room was empty and neatly made; Sarios had apparently been up for some time.

"What?" he barked at the door.

He pulled himself a little further up in the bed and reached out for the two cane-like sticks that stood next to it. Using them as a lever, he pulled himself up to a seated position and frowned as he reached for the glass of spirits he'd left on the table last night only to find it had gone. Sarios or Favio? One or the other certainly.

He nodded in greeting as Prince Ashar Parishid of Pelasia trotted lightly in, closing the door softly behind him. The prince took a seat on the edge of Sarios' bed and crossed his legs and arms.

"Well I think this is probably the worst state I've ever seen you in."

Kiva snorted. "I'm virtually risen from the fucking dead. I personally don't think I'm too bad considering."

Ashar let out a light chuckle and smiled. Reaching across, he took one of the canes.

"You've been conscious barely a day and already you're trying to walk? My doctor told me you'd not walk for weeks."

"I'm full of surprises," growled Kiva. "Why are you here?"

The prince pulled a mock expression of disappointment. "You almost sound like you don't want me around, Kiva."

"Don't get me wrong," the general replied with a sigh. "I appreciate what you've done; for me and the others, but Quintillian's gone and I can't see why you're sticking around."

"Ha!" Ashar unfolded his body and leaned forward, prodding Kiva gently with the stick. "Sarios said you were feeling sorry for yourself, but I didn't believe him. Where else should I go, Caerdin? Back to my own land, where cowardly murderers rule in my family's place? Off into the wilds to lose myself in blood and self-loathing like you did? No. I'm still on the same journey as before this happened."

"But the bloodline's ended." Kiva grumbled low in his throat. Why did everyone always insist on looking at a bright side that wasn't there?

Ashar shook his head. "The family still goes on though, even if the blood gets more distant. After all you're one of them, Caerdin. I never thought about that until the minister mentioned it, but it makes you twice as useful."

Kiva merely narrowed his eyes and glared at the smiling prince.

"You can be a figurehead too now" laughed Ashar. "You were going to be my blade, but now you can also be the banner. Do you have any idea how many of your countrymen would follow you into battle against the Gods themselves if you asked it? No, no, no. It's far from over yet; you just need to get well very soon."

Kiva shook his head finally. "Don't even think like that." Ashar opened his mouth to speak, but the general rode roughshod over the top of him. "I'm no politician; not an Emperor and I'm not of the Imperial blood. Hell, I'm a deicide and a regicide; I *boiled* the Imperial blood!"

He levered himself over to one side and leaned on the other cane. "Sarios is living in the same fool's paradise as you: that something can be done. Well it can't. Not now; not ever. The next line'll be the Velutio dynasty, or maybe even the Avitus dynasty should he want to revert, but it sure as hell won't be mine."

Again, the prince leaned forward, waving a finger at Kiva and opening his mouth, but once more Kiva drowned him out. "I'm a realist, Ashar. My prime concern now is to help Sarios get these people safely off the island and away from here, as far away as it's possible to go, and then into hiding somewhere they'll never be looked for. After that, I may have a score to settle with our friend the future Emperor, but that's personal. Don't try and convince me of any other grand schemes, ok?"

Ashar held up both his hands defensively. "Ok, I understand. I don't agree, but I understand, and yes the island does need to be evacuated first, but bear in mind that this isn't over for you either. Anyway, I'd best get out of here. Your horde of loud hooligans is on its way like a mobile fish market, regardless of what your doctor recommended and I don't want to intrude. I shall be busy making plans for the evacuation with Sarios."

With a bow Ashar turned and made for the door, just as it burst open and Brendan and Marco poured in like a wave, crashing across the furniture of the chamber. Behind them, Athas came ambling in, grinning like a mischievous child, with Tythias and the others after him. Ashar stood patiently, smiling, until the group were in the room

231

howling like a bunch of unruly baboons, bowed again and then left, closing the door.

The tide of people flowed forward and Brendan and Marco rolled onto Sarios' bed coming finally to a rest as they leaned forward to examine their general.

"Ah, he's fine!" declared Marco with a grin. Brendan leaned forward and with thumb and forefinger pulled back Kiva's right eyelids, gazing into the pupil. "'E looks better than 'e used ter! Bit pale 'n mis'rable, but that's pretty normal!"

Kiva jerked his head back out of the man's reach and growled. "Get off me you big ape. I'm not well."

Brendan and Marco gave him a startled glance and then collapsed against each other in fits of laughter. Athas escorted a young lady to the remaining place on the bed and then he, Mercurias, Tythias and Jorun brought up chairs and a bench from near the window. The general murmur and hubbub in the room washed over Kiva as he sat bemused. He wasn't used to noise and activity at the moment, and the chatter was starting to make his head hurt a little. It took him a moment to realise that the young lady was leaning forward and speaking to him.

"What?" he asked as clearly as he could over the buzz.

"I said how do you feel now?"

Kiva looked perplexed. "Erm. Better than I did, and better than I should do by all accounts." He frowned. The girl was young and pretty and he had the vague feeling he'd seen her before, but couldn't for the life of him figure out why she was here. He smiled uncertainly at her. "Don't take this the wrong way, but who are you?"

Tythias leaned across from the chair he'd just placed next to the bed.

"This is Sathina. She saved your life, you old goat."

Kiva's frown deepened and Tythias smiled, placing his hand on the young lady's arm. "She was the one who got into the palace; the one who told us where you were."

Now the general's brows rose. "You infiltrated the palace when Ashar's men couldn't? I'm impressed. Thank you."

He turned to Athas. "How the hell have you all remained hidden? There's a garrison of Velutio's men here."

"Not so hard," the big man chuckled, "when you have the right friends. Minister Sarios knows all sorts of things about this place that I didn't. I've walked past doors and cupboards in this palace on a daily basis twenty years ago, and never even thought to look closely."

He leaned forward conspiratorially.

"It's quite possible to get from almost any building on the island to any other without passing through a single open space if you know how."

Tythias leaned across to Athas' shoulder and grinned. "Even then it's tough with this load of conspicuous windbags. How do you try and keep Brendan quiet and hidden; or Jorun even?"

Kiva nodded. "Well we're going to have to do something about it soon. Sarios and I both thought of drugging the garrison somehow, but I'm not sure how thorough that'll be."

Mercurias shuffled forward, his chair legs scraping on the floor. "Athas and I've had much the same conversation. I'm damn sure we can come up with something fairly potent considering how bright some of the people here are. Only problem is: what to do about the few that we'll inevitably miss."

Now Tythias grinned, his feral features twisting into a face of morbid satisfaction. "Then we deal with the others the best way we know. Anyway, the Wolves owe Velutio now. Let's even the score a little." He pulled a knife from his belt and started tapping the flat of the blade on his knee.

Athas shook his head. "The islanders like this sergeant Cialo; and his men. The garrison's been good to them, you know? They've been helping them grow food, rebuilding parts of the palace, repairing the water system. Sarios won't want them killed and I can't say I'm fond of the idea either. I saw the sergeant with his men from a window in the Peacock palace and he's old school; like one of us. We have to take them all at mealtime and give any guards that're elsewhere the option to surrender before we kill them."

Mercurias nodded, but Kiva sighed and let his head loll back. "We're all daft. Best of intentions and noble and honourable and all that shit, but as soon as Velutio finds out the islanders have gone and his men were tricked, Cialo and every man under him'll be strung up from the trees of the island. We're not saving their lives, just sending them to a death sentence under Velutio."

The general hubbub died down now as everyone contemplated the truth of what their general said. He was right. There was no forgiveness in Velutio and perhaps it would be better to die by the sword of a soldier than on a tree naked and beaten. The young girl was the one to break the silence.

"General, what are we going to do?"

Kiva blinked and lifted his head back up to look at her. She appeared so young and innocent and he was finding it hard to reconcile her presence among these others. "We're going to get these people off the island and into safety" he stated.

The girl nodded. "I know that, general, but I meant after that… in the long run."

"Not you too?" Kiva groaned. "Why is it everyone I speak to wants to plan for a future. The present's dangerous and complicated enough; let's deal with that first."

The girl leaned forward and stared at him, a very serious look crossing her face. Kiva noted the way Tythias moved with her and tried not to smile. She spoke quietly. "I'm a nobody, general. I'm a serving girl from a small village tavern in the middle of nowhere, but in the last month I've been with people my dad used to talk about in wonder. My dad served in the army 'til he lost an arm you know? Then he left and went into business as an innkeeper. He knew you, general. Oh, you won't have known him; he was just a standard bearer, but he was proud to serve in your army."

Kiva's face took on an equally serious expression. "Your father must have been a good man. Standard bearers were honoured above many of the officers. Important job, that."

Sathina nodded. "He *was* a good man. But that's not my point. You were a general, in command of a quarter of the world's army. Tythias here was a commander of a thousand on his own. I guess Athas, Brendan and Marco were all senior officers; Jorun's the son of a chieftain in the north, and Mercurias was a chief medic. Then there's the Pelasians: their leader's a *prince*. And on top of that I've been trying to help save the last man with Imperial blood by sneaking around dangerous places and going up against the powerfulest lord in the Empire."

She sat back and folded her arms. "And there's me: a serving girl from an inn." Her face had taken on a little colour during her diatribe. "I don't care who you are, you're not going to tell me I've left home, risked my life and helped save yours just so you can all run off with your tail between your legs. No. Not happening!"

Kiva blinked as she leaned forward once more and shook her finger in front of his nose. "The Emperor may be dead, but there's something else we can do and you bloody well think of it. Everyone says you're real clever, so show me!"

Tythias leaned forward and whispered something in her ear and she sat back quietly, though still glaring intently into Kiva's face. He was starting to feel extremely uncomfortable beneath that gaze. He turned to face his second in command, trying to ignore the eyes burning into his temple.

"Athas, we need to discuss this, but when there are fewer people around. I'm finding it kind of hard to think straight with everyone in here at once."

The burly dark man nodded and stood. "Everyone out. You can all come back later, but now the general needs his rest and I need to talk to him in private."

With a great deal of grumbling and mumbling, like schoolchildren being punished, the rest stood and headed for the door. Brendan stopped as the rest were leaving and leaned down toward the general.

"Darius sent yer this sir." He handed over a plain flask of bronze. As Kiva frowned curiously, the big shaven-headed man grinned. "Said 'e couldn't get yer flask, but 'is own doctor 'ad some anyway. Don't tell Mercurias I gave y'it. He'd put laxatives in me dinner for months."

With a last grin, he headed for the door, only to see Tythias coming back the other way. He and Athas stood to one side as the one-eyed captain appeared in the door.

"There's a ship full of troops coming in. Should be here in about half an hour."

Kiva almost leapt out of bed, but remembered as he swung his legs out and slowed down when the horrendous pain came flooding back. He stopped, wincing for a moment and then reached for the sticks, looking up at Tythias.

"Who are they?"

Tythias shrugged. "It was Darius who saw 'em."

Kiva grunted. "Get more information; I need to know who they are. And get everyone hidden away somewhere safe."

As Tythias nodded and he and Brendan made to leave, the tall figure of Darius appeared in the doorway. "Minister Sarios wants me out of the way" he declared as he entered and crossed the room to where the chairs had been gathered.

Kiva whistled to Tythias and made a closing motion as the other captain left the room. The scarred mercenary shut the door tight, disappearing as Athas, his face full of concern came over to the general to help him move with his sticks. Just in time the burly sergeant gripped Kiva's elbow as the general put all his weight onto the sticks and tottered dangerously. Without a moment's thought, Darius rushed over and took the other elbow.

235

Kiva looked sidelong at the boy. He was maybe in his early twenties; not really a boy at all, but Kiva was used to grizzled old veterans and that perhaps coloured his perceptions at times. The young man was almost a foot taller than Kiva, who was no midget himself. He cleared his throat. "Darius, who's on the ship?"

The three of them moved slowly and painfully toward the window that looked down over the Ibis courtyard. Darius shrugged. "I couldn't see him, but I'll give you good odds it's Commander Sabian. It may be Velutio as well. The men on the deck were wearing white, and they had black cloaks and black and white crests."

Kiva nodded sourly. "Velutio's personal guard. Not proper soldiers, these ones, Darius. They're thugs; overpaid, overdressed and over-loyal thugs. Not good if Velutio's bringing them here. Isn't Sabian supposed to be in command of them now?"

Darius nodded. "Oh yes. I saw him skewer their old commander personally. I can't imagine he takes any crap from them now."

They reached the window sill and Kiva leaned on it, his legs still shaking with the effort of standing. The general looked down into the courtyard. "What's Sabian up to?" he mused. "He walked out on Velutio when the man had us crucified, then he warned Sarios of his lord's plans. Then he wants to speak to his sergeant in secret by signal lamp and now he's coming to the island with Velutio's personal guard. I can't for the life of me figure out what his fucking game is."

Darius smiled. "Sabian's a good man, but he works for the wrong type. He's trying to keep all us 'innocents' safe while he guides his master to the throne in the least harmful way possible."

"Then Sarios was right," the general remarked. "He *is* playing a dangerous game. Maybe Velutio's told him to bolster the garrison here."

Kiva regarded Darius with another long, appraising glance. The lad was precocious, there was no doubt about that. He'd told Sarios that the boy was sure of himself, but perhaps it went further than that. It'd taken Kiva years working up through the ranks before he'd had either the insight or the confidence to voice it that this young man had now. Others would never achieve it in a lifetime of service. Maybe the boy had a right to be sure of himself; he certainly seemed to be yards ahead of most people in his thinking and planning. The general smiled at Darius.

"You admire Sabian?" Not really a question.

"Of course," Darius replied. "He's not an awful lot older than me, but he's very like you and all your men: kind of old-fashioned." He

236

laughed. "Not meant in an insulting way; he's got the old values, I mean. I like that and I think you do too, don't you?"

Again the lad's insight. "As a matter of fact he's got traditional values in spades. Yes I like him, but I won't let that get in the way if the time comes I have to deal with him. You seem to be very aware of what's going on around you. You're tactical and clever," he smiled, "and you wear a sword. Not what I expected from the island at all. When we found Quintillian, he looked like a downtrodden servant and wasn't very confident."

Darius nodded. "Quintillian was always a thinker. I'm more of a doer, if you know what I mean. He knew his histories, his poets and ethics and all that crap. I only ever studied political history, strategy and the sword. I know, for instance, every campaign you've ever written about and every one that's been written about you and you only seem to have ever made one mistake."

Kiva's eyebrow rose again. "Oh?"

The young man nodded. "At the battle of Regina, you knew full well the enemy had heavily armoured cavalry that could break your infantry, and yet you let them take your men without warning. You could've deployed your men better to resist their charge and then you wouldn't have lost your infantry."

Kiva grinned. A subject he knew well at last. "Ah, but why'd I do it then?"

"I don't know. That's what I mean."

"Because," Kiva explained, "I *needed* him to deploy his cavalry there. It was bait. Why do you think the infantry casualties were low? Because they knew what was going to happen. They broke and ran the moment the cavalry charged, so the losses were minimal. And because the cavalry were *there*, they didn't have time to return to their colour party and protect their general. We had archers on the hill to the west that showered them for a good two minutes before our best men took the hill." He smiled. "And their general's head."

Darius frowned. "I read about that battle in both Peoro and Rastus, and neither of them mentioned the enemy general dying. They claim your victory was due to your superior efficiency and panic in the enemy ranks."

"Why else did you think they panicked though?" the general asked. "The loss of an absolute commander can be more critical than any number of men. The tribes in the northeast pledge to die for their leaders and would walk into the mouth of hell for them. That means that when their leader dies, they go to pieces instantly. Our military relied

237

on a structure of ranks. If the general died, the only people who would notice would be the next highest ranks. They'd take over you see?"

Darius nodded. "I'd still not have sacrificed the men."

"Then you'd have lost the battle" interjected Athas. "He's actually made plenty of mistakes, though no real Empire-threatening ones. Regina wasn't one though."

"Thanks," Kiva added dryly.

The three went quiet again, gazing out of the window, wishing they could see through the walls of the palace buildings on the other side of the Ibis Courtyard and across the sea beyond. Kiva glanced at Darius again and gestured to the blade at his side.

"You know how to use that then?"

Darius nodded. "I'd kind of like someone new to spar with, but we can't afford to be out in the open, so I just keep practicing myself."

"Nice sword" commented the general. "Looks a lot like mine did, until it got taken away. Northern design."

Darius nodded and smiled. "I used to use a straight bladed standard Imperial design, but Commander Sabian made me try this to vary my training. In actual fact, now that I'm getting used to it, it does seem to feel comfortable."

The three were still watching out of the high window above the courtyard and discussing the tools and tactics of war half an hour later when the first man entered through the Gorgon Gate. Commander Sabian strode purposefully into the courtyard, in full armour with his red cloak billowing behind him and his helmet beneath his arm. Kiva strained to see the man's face, but it wasn't easy at this distance. Velutio's personal guard then entered, four abreast and in three columns. There must have been a hundred and fifty of them all told, extremely impressive in their black and white with javelins shouldered and keeping perfect time. Not so impressive in Kiva's head: they were show; all show and no fighting spirit, he could tell from here. No Velutio though, which was a pleasant surprise.

Two of the normal island guards came stomping down the stairs from the gate house, entered the courtyard and came to attention with a salute. Sabian returned the gesture and then trotted out a couple of orders to them, not loud enough for the watchers at the high window to hear, and Kiva grumbled.

"I'd give a lot to be able to hear what he's saying from here."

The other two nodded, but Darius smiled. "Don't worry. If the commander's alone here, I'll get to see him shortly."

Down below, the two men left through the arch into the Great Courtyard, just as sergeant Cialo and two of his veterans entered from the rooms far below Kiva's very window. Again there was a round of saluting and Sabian and Cialo discussed something unheard above before another order was barked and a man stepped out of the file of guards. Until then he'd been indistinguishable from the rest, but now they noticed the harness of medals on his chest and the solid black crest on his helm. An officer of some sort, then. He and Cialo talked for a moment and then the sergeant led him off through the archway and the entire guard trooped after them, leaving Sabian alone in the courtyard.

Kiva watched the man remove his gauntlet and lean down to the fountain to dip his hand and wipe his brow and face. Then he straightened, turned and looked directly up at their window. Athas pulled the other two back instinctively and with a whimper Kiva crumpled to the floor. They helped the injured general back to his feet, keeping well out of the way of the window until they reached his bed where he gratefully collapsed once more.

Darius sighed. "If you don't need me, I ought to go see what I can find out."

The other two nodded and watched as the tall lad left the room. Athas smiled at Kiva. "That boy's got a lot of strength." He frowned, unsure as to the wisdom of bringing up the subject, but shrugged and did so anyway. "Better than Quintillian was, you know? He's what the other lad might have been like with another year among us. A natural I'd say."

Kiva snorted but left it at that.

Rounding the corner to the top of the flight of stairs, Darius almost barged into Sabian coming the other way and the Commander rocked back and forth over the open staircase for a precarious moment before regaining his balance. He gripped the corner and caught his breath, glaring at the young man who'd nearly toppled him.

"Darius, do your elders permit you to barrel around the island with no sense of decorum?"

The young man winced but then allowed himself to relax as he saw the smile creeping over Sabian's face. He returned the gesture.

"I was trying to find minister Sarios to tell him you were here."

Sabian nodded. "I was just on my way to his rooms."

"He's not there," Darius blurted out, hoping it didn't sound too defensive. Sabian had caught him off guard and he tried to force the most natural smile he could, gesturing past the commander to the stairs. "Shall we go find him?"

Sabian narrowed his eyes. "Actually, I wanted to speak to you as well, Darius. You half scared the life out of me just then. Let's use the minister's study to wait for him. I could do with a sit down."

Darius fought with himself, trying to find a good, plain excuse to not do exactly that, but drew a blank and merely nodded uncomfortably. This could be perilous.

The two turned and walked back along the corridor to Sarios' door. Since it was already open, Sabian strode in. Darius followed the commander, his eyes going straight to the connecting door into the bedroom. The door was ajar by quite some way. Trying to be as nonchalant as possible despite his heart beating out a military tattoo, Darius crossed to the minister's drinks cabinet and poured two glasses of wine, taking advantage of the positioning to peer through the door. Sarios' bed sat in full view, fully made. There was no sign of the two rebel officers or the other bed. Damn, these men must think fast; they must've shifted everything out of view the moment he'd left. He sighed and willed his heart to slow a little. Surely Sabian must be able to hear it from where he sat near the window. Forcing the smile back up, Darius delivered the wine to the table.

Kiva sat as still as he could, though he wasn't used to being out of bed and mobile for such an enforced long period, and his muscles were starting to give. Athas had a huge meaty hand on one shoulder and was keeping the general as steady as possible. They couldn't see Sabian of course, hidden as they were round the corner and behind the door, but they could hear everything. Darius sounded nervous; if he wasn't careful he'd give the game away. They continued to listen as the young man gradually recovered his normal confidence.

"Why the guard, commander? We've not done anything you didn't advise us to do."

A smile crossed Kiva's face unbidden. The lad did have a way of coming to the point. No preamble. It possibly took Sabian by as much surprise, given the brief pause before his reply.

"You'll never make a politician, Darius. No, I'm not here to chastise anyone this time. In fact, I'm about to make things a lot easier for you. In the next few weeks Velutio, along with myself and the army, will be moving out and away from the city, dealing with a number of the other lords. I think you need to carry out the bulk of your evacuation in about three weeks' time, and be entirely gone within a month. As long as his lordship and I are away east, you'll only have to deal with the island garrison."

The commander went silent again and the two eavesdroppers in the next room fretted silently, unable to identify what was going on without enough sound. Finally, there was the clink of crystal on a bronze tray and Sabian spoke again.

"That's why I brought this guard. I'm taking Cialo and his companies away with me to do battle. Every man I leave here tomorrow, the captain included, is a selfish, treacherous, greedy or hateful bastard, or any combination of these. They were all Crosus' men through and through and the longer they stay around me the more chance there is of me having an 'accident' if you get my drift."

There was a light chuckle, though Kiva couldn't identify who had been the source. Certainly the next voice was Darius'.

"So," the young man asked light-heartedly, "you want us to kill your enemies for you and in return we get freedom and don't have to kill our mutual friends. That about right?"

Again, Sabian's voice: "frankly I don't much care whether they live or die, but it might be in your best interest to keep as many of them alive as possible. You never know what the future holds and as soon as his lordship finds out that they've let you escape, their careers are over anyway. And possibly their lives too. You see it's best for all of us."

In the next room, Kiva couldn't help but nod. And now he had a considerably shorter timescale for getting well, he'd best make more of an effort.

"Commander," Darius commented, "what do you intend to do once we're gone? I mean, there's no way Velutio's going to let us go without a fight."

Kiva could almost sense the commander shaking his head. "I've set the ball rolling. There's momentum now and if my lord wants to sit on the Raven Throne, he can't take his eyes off the goal or change his plan. This is the only way it can be done. But one day, when he's ruling the land, I'll come for you and you alone, Darius. Whether it means death or glory for you, you'll not be able to hide from him, but by going to him you might be able to make him relent about the others."

There was the scraping of a wooden chair being pushed back and Sabian spoke again. "Anyway, this is not a pleasant conversation and there's much to do. I'd best go and find Sarios. I need to speak to him, but you might want to go and find Cialo. He'll probably be in the barrack rooms in the Peacock Palace, but he'll want to say goodbye, I've no doubt."

241

There was the sound of footsteps leaving the room and as they echoed in the stairwell, Athas let out a sigh of relief and Kiva sagged in the chair.

"Busy little conspirator, isn't he?" remarked Athas.

Chapter XXI.

Sabian found minister Sarios in the Ibis Courtyard as he left the Palace. The elderly man was looking sprightlier than he'd expected and greeted him with a warm smile. "Commander, it's good to see you. Shall we adjourn to the dining hall and talk?"

Sabian shrugged. "If you're not tired, I'd prefer to walk; particularly somewhere out of the way."

The minister nodded and gestured towards the arch. "Let us amble then. I'll show you what good work your sergeant has done on the baths." With a smile he strode beside the commander through the arch and out into the Great Courtyard. A troop of twelve guards in black and white marched past with drill-hall precision, turning their heads in unison and saluting the commander. Sabian grudgingly raised his hand and nodded at them.

He waited until they were out of earshot and then grumbled. "They may look good, but they're just greedy bastards who wouldn't last five minutes in the field. Crosus didn't pick proper fighting men for the guard, cos there's no way they'd have played along with him. Give me ten of my men instead of fifty of them any day."

Sarios regarded him curiously. "I did mean to ask about the guard, commander. Why they're here, I mean."

"Later" replied Sabian. "I've spoken at length about it to Darius, but I want to speak to everyone over dinner tonight. Everyone that you trust, that is. Cialo included."

The minister shrugged. "I can only assume that what you're doing has our interests at heart commander. You've never been anything less than honourable in that respect. Why do you need to speak to me if it's not about them?"

Sabian glanced over his shoulder to see how far away the guard were, but they'd disappeared through the arch while the two of them were heading toward the doorway that would take them out away from the palaces and into the quieter areas. With another quick scan to make sure they were truly alone, Sabian cleared his throat.

"I don't want officially to know about him" he said out of the blue. "I don't want to know why he's here or what his plans are."

Sarios raised one eyebrow. There was no point in dissembling, but two could play the mystery game. "I'd be interested to find out how you knew?"

Without taking his eyes off the bright doorway in front that would lead them outside, Sabian shrugged. "Where else would he go?

And his rescuers too. They had to be here and frankly, I had a feeling Darius and I were not alone while we talked a few minutes ago in your study. All I can say is: get him off this island as soon as you can. If his presence is discovered and reported, it'll mean the end of my career and the death of every soul on this island."

"You won't take him then?" the minister probed. "I thought you might, good intentions notwithstanding."

Sabian shook his head. "He's done nothing wrong so far. He's not broken any law, not attacked anyone that I deal with. In fact, I can't see why so much effort has been bent toward him so far. Velutio is frightened of him, though; what he represents and possibly for all his blustering of the man himself. I refused to kill him before now for merely being a reminder of a different time. That's not his fault. In fact I rather like him, but I can't help him. I'll turn a blind eye tonight and I'll be gone tomorrow, but if any one of these new guard find him and manage to tell anyone, it'll all be over. So get him off the island."

Sarios narrowed his eyes. "You're a strategist, Commander. Is it wise for you to do this? You can't be sure that some day he won't appear as your enemy, and you could avoid all that now."

Sabian laughed. "And you test me? See how far my sense of justice stretches? Well, I won't execute an innocent man. If he means some time to meet me on a field of battle, then that I'll do. I might even relish the opportunity to pit my skills against his. He is, after all, one of the great tactical minds of the last few centuries. No" he said finally, "I won't betray him now, but his very presence puts us all in danger, so deal with it. Velutio will be the next Emperor and I can't conceive of a way anyone can stop that. I realise that there was some notion of opposition with Quintillian out there, but that's over and rightly so. It never stood a chance anyway and I'd hate to have had to kill the Wolves. If you're all sensible, you'll find somewhere safe and go there. Somewhere like the northern border where Caerdin came from or maybe across the sea in Pelasia. Anywhere that keeps you all well out of Velutio's reach forever more. He's going to be too busy dealing with his opposing lords in the next few months to deal with any of you, I'll see to that."

Sarios smiled as they passed the old Imperial shines. "You're a good man, Commander. Twenty years ago, you'd perhaps have been one of the four with Caerdin and your master. We will, of course, get away as soon as we can and he'll go with us, but I cannot guarantee what the future holds. I am in charge solely of my own destiny."

Sabian laughed. "I think you do yourself an injustice there, minister. There is one other thing I need to discuss, however. We need to speak about Darius."

"We do?" The minister raised an eyebrow. "And why is that?"

"He's important. To you. To me. Most of all to my Lord."

Sarios stopped walking a moment and the commander turned to face him. "Velutio plans for Darius to follow him."

The minister smiled knowingly. "I know. We've been training both he and Quintillian since they were babes, and we all knew what for. I won't let Velutio take him though. He won't be taught the ways of government by that man."

Sabian shook his head sadly. "I don't think you have much choice. Darius is going to have to follow him. I personally think he's is the only logical choice, but I'll come and find him once everything's safe and calmed down. If he comes with me then his future's secure and I can probably persuade Velutio that the rest of you pose no threat."

He gestured down the slope and the two started walking again.

"There is something I want to know though. Darius doesn't know he's Caerdin's son and Caerdin thinks his wife and child died twenty years ago. Right now, given they're both here, why haven't you told them?"

Sarios gave him an appraising glance. "I wasn't aware that you yourself knew. The only people who did before you were myself and Velutio. I won't ask how you found out, but I do suggest that you forget about it completely."

"Why?" Sabian was insistent.

Sarios sighed. "Because it would cause them both a great deal of pain. Can we not leave it at that?"

Sabian shook his head. "I don't think so. Given that I've risked my neck now for both of them and I already know the what, you have to tell me the why."

Another sigh. Sarios dropped his eyes to the floor. "Have you not wondered why Darius didn't die in the flames and how he came to be in Velutio's hands?"

Sabian nodded. "Of course I have. Nothing short of miraculous, I'd say."

"Nothing short of tragedy I rather think," replied the minister. "He survived because he wasn't in the villa that day; indeed he wasn't in Serfium at all. Nor was his mother. The two bodies he found in the villa I fancy must have been two of the villa's servants. No, it certainly wasn't them. You see, I saw Livilla after the fire."

245

Sabian's eyes widened gradually as he listened. "Then they were here?"

"No." The minister's voice had fallen to a husky, sad whisper. "They were in Velutio; in a place that's no longer there. Twenty years ago there was a palace on the headland opposite the Imperial one. The golden tower used for shipping warnings is the only part that still stands. That palace belonged to the Marshall of the Central Provinces, you see..."

His voice tailed off into silence. The tale was clearly causing the minister pain to relate, but he needn't say any more. Sabian's jaw dropped as the connection fired.

"She was with Velutio!"

Sarios nodded sadly. "Avitus as he was known then. They had been lovers for some time. Not long enough for Darius to be his, mind, but some months. She'd been left on her own with a young babe, you see, while Caerdin charged around the world unwillingly committing atrocities for the Emperor. The more Quintus' madness began to manifest, the colder and bleaker Caerdin became. She couldn't cope with him the way he was and I didn't like him much myself towards the end." He sighed. "So I can understand why she did what she did, but I can't forgive it."

"So what happened to Livilla?" Sabian enquired.

"She put a knife through her own throat the day after Caerdin fought Avitus. She was buried on the island here, in an unmarked grave near to her family."

He turned to face Sabian. "You see now why this has to stay a secret. We've brought Darius up to think he was the son of a fairly well-to-do commander. Fulvius has no living relatives and Velutio commandeered the estate, so there's no way to trace the truth. Unless one of us lets it slip. Bear in mind that the truth would not only destroy Caerdin, but may irreparably damage Darius. For both their sakes' we have to keep the whole thing very secret."

Sabian whistled. "Hell yes. It answers quite a few questions, though. I couldn't help but wonder why his lordship was so determined to destroy all of you and any trace of the Imperial blood, but still wanted to adopt Darius. He must have actually cared for her, you know? I've never seen Velutio care for anything. It's logic, whether good or bad, that decides his path, not emotion or values. Gods, I've got to get Darius to him after it's all over. The lad deserves to inherit it all."

The minister stopped as they reached the baths and raised his voice, pointing his finger at the commander. "*Never*! Caerdin and I may have had our disagreements, but he was a true servant of the Empire, loyal above all others, and it would be the worst dishonour I could do him to allow that to happen. If Darius ever inherits the throne, it will be in his own way and through his own merits. Not because of that adulterous coward."

Sabian stood for a moment in silence. The minister's face had taken on a high colour as they'd talked and for the first time in all his visits throughout the years, Sabian'd heard the man shout. It seemed wrong. The minister was the calmest, most stoic and moderate man the commander had ever met. He stood for a moment breathing as the minister glared at him and then turned and walked into the bath house. There was too much to absorb; too much importance here to dismiss it immediately. He'd have to think on it later. Gods damn Isera. Every time he came to the island, life became just a little bit more complicated. With an uncomfortable sigh, he entered the baths.

Brendan had never been the quietest or subtlest of the Wolves. He knew his strengths and his weaknesses and had never been the sort to scout, take point or be a runner. Front line in a fight was fine. And he'd much rather anyone else had been where he was at this time. Marco would have been able to do this so much easier, but there'd been no time to find him. He'd been at one of the ground floor rear windows of the palace when he'd seen the Captain that had arrived on the ship come out of the palace door and duck into the shadows. In a corner that was well hidden from the world in general, but clearly visible from that particular window, the captain had removed his helmet and cloak. He'd donned one of the long robes the elder scribes of the island wore before leaving the shadows again, looking to all intents and purposes like any other islander. With absolutely no time to think, Brendan had stepped out of the doorway and run as quietly as possible to the next tree. As quickly as he dared and not as quietly as he'd like, he moved from vantage point to vantage point, following the captain. Finally, as they'd rounded the ruined walls of the Golden House, he saw what the man was up to. The commander, Sabian, was walking and talking with minister Sarios. He'd no real love for Sabian. However much the others might laud him, to Brendan he was as yet an unknown quantity, still a servant of the enemy; but he did know Sarios for a good man and the two of them in private conversation would be nothing harmful to Darius or the Wolves. So by extension a man secretly following them had to be up to no good.

He'd seen the two men disappear into the doorway of the extramural bath house just as the disguised captain reached the bole of a particularly large tree. He himself skidded to an all-too-noisy halt behind a low bush, watching the captain through the upper tendrils. A moment passed as the captain waited for his quarry to move deeper inside the edifice and then he moved very quietly, but surprisingly fast to the entrance of the baths, taking up a stance by the doorway and leaning close enough to the door to hear the echoed conversation within. The man slowly pushed back the hood from the cloak to facilitate his spying and all his attention was riveted to the bath house.

Brendan smiled a smile of pure malice as he slowly moved to the huge tree the captain had last frequented, hoping his prey wouldn't turn and notice the somewhat noisy pursuer. He paused at the huge trunk and pondered, suddenly well aware that he'd left both his sword and dagger back in his quarters. Hell, he'd only been out to answer a call of nature, otherwise he'd be safely hidden away and blissfully unaware of the events outside the walls. Grumbling quietly to himself about his lack of blades, he looked around desperately until his eyes lit on a large branch lying half buried beneath a wild, creeping bush. Crouching, he reached out and slowly teased the branch from beneath the fronds of the plant. Every time the bush shook or the branch caught on something, Brendan winced and snapped his head back to check on the captain, but each time the man was more intent on what was going on inside and his attention couldn't be easily diverted.

Finally the bulky mercenary had the branch, which seemed to have been stripped down of its twigs and leaves almost as though designed for the very purpose, and wielded it as a club. He hefted it and spun it a couple of times to test the reach and the weight before grinning. With one more look at the captain, he checked out the lie of the land between the two of them. There was precious little cover. That hadn't bothered the captain as *his* prey had been inside the baths, but the man himself was in the open. There were a few low bushes in a line that would cover part of his approach if he was quiet enough, but he would have to run the last half in the wide open space. Well there was precious little he could do about it now. He'd sort of committed himself to a course of action when he'd first left the doorway in the palace and he couldn't go back now.

Keeping as low as he dared without overbalancing, he ducked from the tree to the first of the small bushes. For a moment he considered halting and moving slowly to the next one, but his momentum was too good. Before he'd decided what he actually wanted

248

to do about it, he'd run the length of the row of bushes and burst out into the open. Still the captain hadn't turned. As he ran, Brendan raised the branch to shoulder height, gripping the narrowest end as tightly as he could. At the last moment the captain turned, perhaps out of some sixth sense or perhaps Brendan was making more noise than he thought. In any case, there was nothing else for it now. As he covered the last six yards he let out a roar of anger and defiance and, pulling the branch back behind him, swung it with all his might.

It is often in anticipation that the veteran shows his skill over a green recruit. The captain was of rank and considered himself a good officer. He'd been involved in a few small engagements; enough to have achieved the level he had, but had fought as an officer, not on the front line of a unit. He smiled as he turned, watching the large, shaven-headed man closing on him, branch raised and coming for a swing at head height. In response and perfectly timed, the captain dropped to one knee, reaching into his tunic to withdraw his dagger. At the last moment however, the angle of Brendan's branch changed and the heavy chunk of wood came forward and down at forty five degrees. The captain wasn't even paying attention, struggling with his knife as he was, when the branch connected with the top of his skull. There was an unpleasant cracking sound and a spray of blood across the grass.

To the captain's credit, despite the obvious agony and confusion he was suffering, he staggered back upright, his head rolling and a short blade clutched shakily in his hand. Brendan exhaled gently. The man was slowly shaking his head, coming out of the daze. The bulky mercenary pulled back his club once more and took another swing. This time he didn't attempt to adjust the swing and just let it go at head height, allowing the widest arc he could. The end of the branch slammed into the captain's temple and the crunch this time sounded distinctly final. The captain's eyes rolled up into their sockets and the dagger fell from the suddenly loose fingers. Perhaps in confusion and pain, or perhaps already dead, the captain staggered and twisted twice before collapsing like an old, crumbling column. Brendan watched the legs kick once and then leaned down and pressed his fingers against the man's neck. Nothing.

With a sigh, he stood again and wondered what to do, but never got the chance to decide as Minister Sarios and Commander Sabian both appeared in the doorway of the baths. The commander had his sword out in a threatening manner. He stared at Brendan and then at the body on the floor.

"What in the name of seven hells is going on here?"

Brendan coughed nervously. "I'm Borus the fisherman..." he began a little uncertainly.

"Absolute shit" replied the commander, sheathing his sword. "You're one of the Wolves. I don't know which one, but you're one of them. What are you doing smashing the brains out of my second in command?"

There was a thoughtful look on Sarios' face as Brendan looked helplessly between the two. A thought suddenly occurred to him.

"Sabian" he addressed the commander. "You don't seem right bothered? Why's that, eh?" Since the commander made no reply, the mercenary grinned. "Think I jus' saved y'a job, eh? Yer do know 'e was spyin' on yer, dontcha?"

Sabian sighed and turned to face away. For a moment Brendan considered taking his branch to the back of the commander's head, but decided against it. Sabian stood for a moment and then turned back with another, deeper sigh.

"All Cialo's hard work." He crouched and picked up one of the captain's arms. Dragging the body toward the baths he shook his head. "What a waste" he added as he removed the islander's robe from the body and sheathed the captain's knife once more.

Brendan watched, bemused, as the commander dropped the body of his captain into the passageway just inside the door and then re-emerged, rubbing his hands in distaste. He walked towards Brendan and held out his hand expectantly. The mercenary just stared blankly at him.

"The club?" suggested Sabian.

Still steeped in confusion, Brendan passed the branch over to the commander, not entirely sure why he was trusting this man. Sabian nodded slightly and then turned and walked over toward the bath house. Raising the branch to shoulder height and drawing it back in a wide arc, he swung it with great force, emitting a grunt of effort. The branch connected with several newly placed replacement blocks just below the keystone. The mortar here was new and solid, but that binding the surrounding stones was old and crumbled and the arch emitted a warning groan. Brendan grinned as he realised what the commander was doing.

He stepped forward smiling and held out his hand. "Y'may be clever, but a job like this'n needs brute force."

The commander frowned for a moment and then returned the branch to Brendan. The mercenary dropped the point of the branch to the floor and spat in his palms, rubbing his hands together. Picking up the club once more, he pulled it back and swung it with all his might.

250

The arch stones gave way instantly under the severe blow and the outer few yards of the entrance corridor collapsed in a crash and a cloud of dust. Brendan leapt back out of the tunnel as stones bounced among the falling masonry, almost bowling over the commander in his haste to get away. The three stood in silence for several minutes watching as the cloud of dust slowly dissipated, leaving a scene of absolute chaos. The only sign of the captain was an arm projecting out from beneath the rubble.

Brendan grinned at Sabian. "See. Brute force an' ignorance!"

The commander nodded with a gentle sigh. "Let's move fast. There'll be people here soon to investigate the noise."

The three of them walked quickly away from the bath house toward the grassy slope away to the west between the walls and the sea. Here the trees and scrub were more tightly packed and a few trails created by the islanders in hunting for game or searching for plants were the only means of access. Sarios led them along one such track which ended abruptly at a cliff, the palace wall rising some thirty feet behind them and a drop of forty more to the sea in front. Brendan grinned and located a mound of turf to sit on. He watched Sabian and Sarios find seats of their own and then stretched his legs with a satisfied groan.

"Think you've just dropped yerself in the shit, Commander" he noted.

Sabian frowned. Sometimes the mercenary's colloquial accent made him a trifle hard to follow, but this time his meaning was clear enough. "I rather think that was you," the commander replied, "but I'll sort it out. None of these men support me anyway and the loss of captain Flautus doesn't wound me too closely. I just wish you'd waited until I wasn't here." He folded his arms and regarded the shaven-headed mercenary. "Thank you anyway though. I suppose we're better off than if he'd gone screaming back with what he'd heard. Did *you* hear any of our conversation?"

"Nah" Brendan replied taking off a boot and shaking gravel and muck from it. "I's far too far away fer that. Still I'd like t'know why yer bothering so much about these people an' why y'didn't just drop me in it t'get out of this?"

Sabian nodded. "You think me imprudent for allowing your presence to go undetected. You think perhaps I should report it to my Lord in return for wealth and privilege?"

Brendan shrugged and leaned back smiling. "Why not?"

251

Sabian stared at the mercenary. Why did he, a senior officer in the most powerful army of the modern world and an upholder of the law, feel the need to justify his actions to an outlaw mercenary?

Across the island, Darius found Kiva sitting at the desk. Were it not for the bandages it would be hard to tell that that the general was wounded at all. Certainly his demeanour was all business.

"What is it?"

Darius strode over to the desk, his sheathed sword swinging at his side.

"I've been listening closely to one of the new sergeants" he said, beginning to unbuckle his sword belt. "They're not a friendly lot. They're going to settle in tonight and sort their barracks out, but tomorrow everything's going to change."

"In what way" the general enquired, placing his stylus back on the desk and looking up at the tall youth.

Darius placed his sword and belt on the desk and stepped back. "They want to do a complete contraband check on the whole island. Anything they think prisoners shouldn't have they're going to confiscate."

"So you'll need to hide a lot of stuff" the general nodded to himself.

Darius leaned over the desk, his face close to Kiva's. "I think you missed the point. A complete check of the whole island will turn up more than they bargained for" he said pointedly, gesturing at the general.

"Hmmm." Kiva tapped his lip for a moment. "We're going to have to do something soon then. They won't start anything until Sabian and his other men are already on their way back to the city. I think we need to move before they do and as soon as Sabian's left, whatever the commander's timings are."

Darius nodded. "Shall I ask everyone to come here for a meeting?"

Kiva shook his head. "Too dangerous. Get everyone down to the orchard near the graveyard as soon as it gets dark. That's a long way away from the guard quarters in the Peacock Palace. Tell everyone to wear robes and move as unobtrusively as possible. Get all the off-landers and Sarios. Sabian too if you can get to him."

The young man nodded again.

"We're leaving tomorrow aren't we?"

Kiva tested his weight on his stick. "There's no other choice."

Chapter XXII.

Darius' heart sat heavy in his chest as he watched the boat bucking in the foam, moving slowly away from the dock and back toward Velutio. Sabian stood at the stern rail in his full regalia, impressive and powerful, with the men of his veteran units standing behind him in formation on the deck. Sergeant Cialo stood to one side, a hand on the rail and close to his commander; his face was bleak and unhappy. He'd become quite close to a number of the folk on the island and had as good as made a home there in the short time of his assignment. He was not happy to be leaving, and had confided as much to Darius during their last conversation not long after dawn this morning. He didn't trust Velutio's guard and, although he'd been informed of the plans for the island, was still sceptical about the decisions his commander had made.

With a quick glance over his shoulder, Darius could see Velutio's guard lined up in their ranks of black and white, with a frowning sergeant standing to one side. He knew what was coming. The sergeant was only waiting for Sabian to be out of earshot before he launched into everyone. The lad turned again to face the departing boat. If Sabian was taking the army out on campaign for months and everything was about to come to a head here on the island, it was very possibly the last time Darius would ever see either him or the grizzled Cialo and the degree to which that made him unhappy was a touch disturbing. He'd never really had family, at least for his thinking life, but the commander, the sergeant and their men had become as close to him in the last few weeks as anyone on the island had ever been. He sighed as the boat gradually moved further away until the commander was a red smudge in the general brown and grey of the boat. Only a moment later, a voice behind them all called out in a rasping, deep tone.

"I am Sergeant Caris of the army of Velutio and from this moment on I am taking command of the island of Isera. I intend to enforce the standard rules of prison control, along with a number of other strictures that will apply due to the nature of the prison and its occupants. There will be no more of this open control and free access that was permitted under 'sergeant' Cialo."

With a crack, the sergeant brought down the cane he was holding against the metal greave on his leg, then lifted it and pointed at the group near the dock.

"There will be a complete search of the island as soon as my men have organised the watches and duties. Any contraband or illegal objects found will be confiscated and locked away until the next boat from the city, when they will be taken from the island. After that there will be random searches carried out on a daily basis by different patrols each day. Anyone found with contraband today with be given a number of lashes proportionate to the offence. As of tomorrow, if any search turns up any contraband at all, I will consider the severing of a hand in the Pelasian style. The same sentence will apply for theft or malicious damage."

The man stopped for a moment and cleared his gravelly throat. Darius couldn't help noting the nasty glint in the man's eye and the smug but hungry faces of the guardsmen behind him.

"Furthermore, there will be a roll call every morning, with today's at lunchtime due to the lateness of the hour now. Anyone missing from the call will be punished. At the first such meeting, each prisoner will detail his duties to be noted down. Once these are dealt with, all prisoners will be confined to the places where they eat, sleep and work. Anyone found where they are not supposed to be will be punished. The walls of the palace are your absolute boundary. Anyone found outside them will be...?"

"Punished!" chorused the guards behind him. A vicious grin had now split the sergeant's face.

"The guard will be you wardens and your superiors and will not be working to the benefit of the prisoners. As such you will put aside a proportion of all food and drink that is grown or created on the island for your wardens. Other rules will be applied as they become necessary, but for now you need to relay all of this to any other prisoners who are not here and prepare for the first complete search and roll call."

A low growl issued from the sergeant's throat as he straightened again. "One last thing: I am unconvinced as yet that my captain's unfortunate demise was an accident. I understand that the bath house has been in a bad way for some time and that work had been done on it recently, but my suspicions are still there. I will be having my engineers investigate the building and my medic examine the body. After that we will be interviewing a number of you about the circumstances surrounding the 'accident'. If there *is* anything to find out, be sure that I will find it out."

"That's it" he said, folding the can beneath his armpit, "go about your business."

The islanders looked at each other, sharing a great deal of unhappiness and ill-feeling until Minister Sarios cleared his throat. "Very well... back to the palace everyone."

255

The group shuffled off dejectedly toward the Gorgon Gate, with Darius and the minister at the rear. The young man looked across at the elder and sighed heavily.

"What are we going to do now?"

The minister raised an eyebrow. "What do you mean?"

With a quick glance over his shoulder to check the guard were distant, the lad spoke in a low voice. "There must be almost twenty people missing by now. What's going to happen when they do the lunchtime roll call? How are we going to move anyone to the departure point when we're restricted to certain places? And what if they search too early and catch everything and everyone out?"

Sarios smiled knowingly.

"You must have faith, Darius. How well do you know me? Or Caerdin? Or Sabian?"

The lad shrugged, his face blank. "Fairly well I'd say."

"Then you know that all three of us are the sort of men who plan things in advance. Don't worry. Sabian gave the sergeant the list of prisoners. There may be one or two unaccounted for, but between us we cut the missing people from the list last night. We left a couple because it would look suspicious if everyone turned up the first time. As for a search turning up anything, it won't produce any people unexpected. The Wolves and their allies are already in a hidden place and as soon as the guard leave us alone to set up their watch system and guard posts, we'll take advantage of their busyness to move them the rest of the way to the north shore. Then if they do search the island after that, they'll find nothing."

Darius grinned and the minister drew breath to continue.

"Also, as for the finding of contraband, almost everything we want to save was shipped out of the buildings during the night to the olive-grower's shed by the north shore. We've had to leave the occasional suspicious item, of course, or again it would look too suspicious. We need to give them something to pull us up on; to give them something to do. Don't worry. Everything will go according to plan. We're very thorough men you know?"

The minister chuckled and Darius continued to smile as they passed beneath the Gorgon Gate and into the Ibis Courtyard. Again, Darius was struck by the strangeness of it all. He'd spent his entire life on this one small island and, if the minister was right and today went as planned, this would be the last time he would ever walk through the gate. Odd after all this time.

Everything was changing around him, but he had a great deal of confidence in the people who planned all this and though the outside world was an unknown quantity for him, still he was confident that with the minister, Caerdin and the others everything would be for the best. Casting his mind back over the meeting last night, he was still astounded at the way these people thought. Darius had always known he was a fast thinker and had always considered himself the only person on the island who could keep up with the way the minister's mind worked. And yet last night there had been a crowd of people with that kind of complex, insightful mind. He'd always assumed that the minister was in a class of his own, but Caerdin, the Pelasian Prince, the grumbling medic from the Wolves and others had all talked each other in circles to the point where Darius had given up trying to put his ideas across and just sat back and watched the whirl and spiral of conversation and planning.

The only drawback of the whole meeting had been the mutual presence of Sabian and Caerdin. Though the two spoke of each other in nothing but respectful tones it was quite clear at the meeting that neither felt comfortable in the presence of the other and the reasons were obvious. They tried to avoid eye contact and rarely spoke to each other except when there was no choice, and yet both came up with ideas that were bandied around among the group and agreed to all the plans in the end. When the conspirators had all split up and headed back to their various places, it was equally interesting to note the parting glance the two officers shared; a look that combined respect and intrigue with discomfort and uncertainty.

Darius was brought rudely back to the present as the minister's restraining hand arrested his movement. Looking up, he realised that they had already passed into the Great Courtyard and most of the group had disappeared by now. Scanning quickly around to identify the reason for Sarios' grip of restraint, he noticed two guardsmen marching purposefully across the courtyard toward a young girl. He recognised the girl of course, the daughter of one of the drama tutors, perhaps six years old and innocent as they come. She was holding a small wooden toy that had been crudely carved by one of the island's artisans and smiling broadly at the two men bearing down on her. Darius had a dreadful feeling of foreboding and made to step forward, though the minister's grip on his shoulder tightened in an instant, holding him in place. Sarios shook his head barely perceptibly.

As Darius watched in anger, the men reached the girl and the shorter of the two reached down and wrenched the toy from her hand.

257

The lad's blood boiled as he watched the man snap the toy into two broken shards and drop it to the floor.

"What are you doing out here, girl?" demanded the other guard, brusquely.

The girl stared at him, her eyes brimming, but her jaw clamped firmly shut.

"You should be with your parents wherever they are. If we catch you out here again, you'll get a beating. You hear me?"

The girl's mouth stayed shut as she looked up at the other man, down at her broken toy, and then stamped as hard as she could on the guard's foot. Rather than the heavy marching boots, the man was wearing dress shoes of soft leather and he let out a grunt of pain as the small boot crunched down on his toes. The guard reached down and grasped her wrist, hauling her up into the air by it with the audible click of a dislocating shoulder and slung her like a rag doll over his back.

Again Darius started forward and again the minister's grip tightened. He glanced up at the old man, but as he did so the grip was released and Sarios strode out across the courtyard.

"Put my granddaughter down you evil brute!" he barked. Darius was surprised at the vicious quality of his voice and the power which such an old and frail man mustered as he marched forward. The guards both turned in surprise and one said something to the other that went unheard due to the screaming and wailing emanating from the young girl. The other lowered the girl to the floor again and turned to face the approaching minister.

"This is yours?" he asked, his jaw set and teeth gritted. As the minister drew up to his full height in front of the guard he nodded. The man growled. "Then you'd do well to keep her where she belongs. We're not going to stand for that kind of thing. Give her a good beating and be grateful we're not doing the same for you."

As Sarios glowered at them and reached out to take the distraught girl's elbow, the two guards marched off toward the Ibis Courtyard, muttering to each other.

Darius wandered over to where the minister was crouched with the girl and talking to her. "That was very brave of you, but don't do it again. Now run along and find doctor Favio. Your shoulder will need dealing with."

The girl sniffed and smiled weakly at the island's leader before nodding and tottering off toward the nearest door, holding her arm. Darius sighed.

"Today is not going to be an easy day, minister."

The old man nodded sadly and led them across the Great Courtyard and through a side door into the Peacock Palace. The place was generally considered off-limits now to the islanders, being the place the guard had chosen for their quarters. Following on the heels of the departing veterans, they had selected rooms solely on the top two floors. Down in the servants' level things remained untouched and would do until the full search was made. Moreover, Darius thought, as they turned a corner and unlocked a door, it was the perfect place at the moment to hide anything, where the guards lived and the islanders were not allowed.

The door opened with only a faint creak and the two of them stepped back as Athas stepped forward into the light with his blade poised. As he recognised them, he smiled and sheathed the weapon.

"We thought you weren't coming. It's been hours."

Sarios nodded. "The commander's only just left and the guard felt the need to exercise their cruelty muscle a couple of times before we were left alone." He cleared his throat and stepped back out of the way. "And now we have to get moving. They'll be searching the island before lunchtime and I'm sure they'll be very thorough."

Athas nodded and stepped out into the corridor. Behind him, Brendan and Marco helped general Caerdin out of the cramped dark corridor, followed by the rest of the rebels. The minister smiled and walked back to the corner of the corridor. "Follow me; quietly and quickly."

With Athas and the rebels behind, Darius followed the minister through a number of corridors that he half recognised from childhood exploration of the palaces' more obscure regions. Part way along, as they descended into areas where the light wells no longer shone, the minister stopped and collected four small terracotta oil lamps from a shelf, lighting one and giving the others to Athas. Finally they arrived in an old chapel that had serviced the slave community that once worked in the kitchens and washrooms of the building. The place had remained largely untouched for decades and cobwebs and dust filled the place, giving it an ancient, undisturbed feel. Images of the divine triad decked a small stone altar at the far end and the two statues of the temple guardians flanked the entrance. In the centre of the room were a number of low wooden benches, some of which were rotten beyond help and all covered with years of grime. Along the walls on either side stood tall wooden screens bearing images of divine tales, most of which were cracked, peeled and faded beyond recognition.

It is to one such screen that Sarios turned. With a gesture to Athas, he stepped to one side of it and began to heave the heavy oak screen away from the wall. The burly black warrior stepped up to the other side and easily edged the thing away from the stonework. Twice the wooden edifice almost fell over or broke where the woodworm had been at work, but with half a minute's work, the heavy item stood two feet out from the wall. Behind, a door stood, dusty and rusted and very much hidden. Reaching into a pocket, the minister withdrew a small ring of keys and selected one.

The door creaked open and an eye-watering smell of musty air and ammonia washed out into the chapel. With a nod toward the minister, Athas removed a small oil lamp from his pack and lit it. The flickering light joined the minister's in illuminating the room before he turned and held the light in the entrance to the passageway. The flame of the lamp took on a sickly yellow-green colour and gave the passage an eerie aspect.

"You're staying here?" the big man enquired.

The minister nodded. "With Darius' help I'll get the screen back and cover the tracks. You know where you're going, yes?"

"To the end and turn right" the sergeant repeated from memory, counting off on his fingers. "Follow the main sewer tunnel downhill all the way except where there's a small collecting tank, where we take a left-hand fork slightly uphill and then back down. When we reach the small round room that's a dead end, look for iron rungs in the wall around five feet up. Climb them and move the wooden cover and we'll be out near the shore."

"And then?"

Brendan leaned over from where he supported Kiva and grinned. "I'll take 'em from there ter where we sat yesterday. We'll meet yer there."

The minister nodded. "Once things are in place and we're ready to make a move, I'll send Darius here to find you. You have the rest planned?"

This time Kiva hauled himself with a grunt and a great deal of pain from Brendan's shoulder and growled. "I've planned it all for them. Who goes where and when. Just wish I could be involved, but I'm not even any use with a bow. Guess I'll just be sitting by the shore waiting for everyone."

Marco patted the general on the back gently. "You need to rest sir. You're going to need to be on fighting form soon enough."

Caerdin nodded impatiently and sighed as Athas took a last deep breath of good, clean air and stepped into the passageway. Darius and the minister watched nervously as Athas lit the other two lamps and handed them out and then disappeared down the tunnel. Behind him, Brendan and Marco helped Kiva into the reeking passage, followed by Prince Ashar and his six men and finally Tythias, his arm around the young lady Sathina, tied a scarf around her lower face and entered with Jorun bringing up the rear. As the group gradually faded from sight, only the echoes of their footsteps coming back up to the chapel, Darius frowned.

"There don't seem to be as many as I remember."

The minister smiled. "We do have the two doctors still in the palace, masquerading as two of the missing islanders, remember."

"Yes," Darius nodded, "I know, but I'm sure there were more Pelasians."

"Prince Ashar assured me he would deal with his men, so I assume they are secured away somewhere. Whatever the case, we've done what we can now. Help me get this screen back, then we must fan the dust around so that it settles again."

The sun burned down from on high in the Great Courtyard. The entire population of the island stood in ordered rows, lined up for inspection by the uncaring guards who surrounded the entire square. There were forty or so guards here, the rest preparing their quarters or in position on the walls or various vantage points.

"Cristus?" yelled out a guard and, as a hand shot up among the crowd, he ticked the name dutifully of the list.

"Savic?"

Another hand raised and another name ticked off. With a squaring of his shoulders, the guard slapped the list down on the table beside him and the sergeant leaned over to examine it.

"Four!" he growled and then, turning to the gathered islanders, he raised his voice.

"Four prisoners unaccounted for. That's not good enough."

He strode forward with two of the guard at his shoulders and pointed at a random man in the front row. The guards dragged him out of the line into the open space and then dropped him to the floor. He was not a young man but far from feeble, a farmer with some muscle. He floundered on the floor for only a moment before he made to stand. The guard kicked him heavily in the gut and he fell back to the grass with a groan. The sergeant leaned over him.

"Where are these four prisoners?" he asked quietly.

The farmer shook his head. "I don't know."

Straightening, the sergeant nodded once at the two guards, who proceeded to pulverise the poor man with repeated kicks to the head and torso. After a solid minute they stopped. Darius strained from his position in the fourth row to see, but the man was still breathing, though unconscious. He was battered beyond recognition and Darius found his hate for the sergeant growing ever stronger, aware that this 'lesson' was having the same effect on everyone else. The sergeant was trying to make them fear the guard, but his actions were merely fostering hate and desire for vengeance.

The two guardsmen stepped away from their prone victim and the sergeant moved forward again.

"Where are the missing four?"

Silence greeted him and he glowered at the crowd.

"Very well, I will assume that these four islanders are hiding of their own accord. They will present themselves at the roll-call in the morning and will be duly punished. If they do *not* present themselves tomorrow I, personally, will break all their knees to make sure they cannot hide again. You would do well to pass this on to them when you see them and to remember it yourselves."

He stepped back behind the table and cleared his throat.

"Very well, one by one approach the table from your lines and give your details for duties to the guard. Anyone under the age of ten need not approach; nor should anyone over the age of sixty. Those of you who fall into these categories will be restricted to the Ibis Courtyard, the Great Courtyard and the various buildings directly surrounding them. In due course, a perimeter will be set up around the set areas to prevent straying, but I'll have to rely on everyone's good sense in the meantime."

As the lines filed slowly past the table, with the old and the young being directed to one side under the watchful eyes of the guard, Darius sighed. It was a damned good job they *were* going tonight. If he'd had to go through another day of this, either he or the sergeant would be dead. Perhaps the brute was trying to find fault wherever he could because he'd failed to find the quantity of contraband that he'd expected. If he'd seen the contents of the olive grower's shed, he would have had apoplexy. For a moment a smile crept across Darius' face, but he quickly forced it back down. To be seen smiling at a time like this would be to attract unwanted attention. Ahead of him in the queue he watched Mercurias, the Wolves' medic giving a false name and his career as cook. The guard didn't even blink at him and the grizzled soldier went on in the line to stand where he was told. Five minutes later, as he himself was closing on the desk, Darius watched the Pelasian doctor, whose name escaped him, giving another false name and the title of kitchen skivvy. Again they barely noticed the unusually dark man. A prisoner who worked in the lowly places was all but invisible to these people but then that was exactly what they'd wanted. Finally Darius himself stepped up. He'd no job but a short conversation with both Sarios and Athas last night had left him classified as a smith. Athas had told him a few of the most basic principals in case he was quizzed but, watching the way the guards were dealing with people, he doubted they would care enough to enquire. Sure enough, as his name was ticked off once more, and 'smith' written beside it, he was shuffled off to join the others. He couldn't help feeling this was all too easy.

"The secret," the Pelasian doctor murmured, "is to get the proportions exactly correct. Too little and we merely spice their meal. Too much and they will all be dead within two hours."

Mercurias, busy taking the kernels out of a large basket of peaches, looked up speculatively at minister Sarios, standing at the other side of the table. "I presume you still want us to merely drug them?"

Sarios nodded. "I do not like poison on principle, but if it can be used correctly to merely incapacitate, then we must do it."

Favio, the third doctor in the room, leaned over from his place with a heavy-headed mallet where he was crushing the kernels into rubble. "Minister, there are any number of fascinating drugs we could use that would work with a great deal more control than cyanide, but we don't have an awful lot of time and there are not many sources on the island. Cyanide is the only really feasible option. After all, there are orchards all over the island and so many peaches in storage we could probably poison the entire population of the city if we so wished."

He scooped up the latest pile of peach rubble and, dropping it in a bowl, passed it to the Pelasian, who Darius had since discovered was named Ahmesh. Ahmesh dropped the contents into a large bowl of strong shrimp and onion broth the cooks had been making for an hour, and stirred it thoroughly.

"I would say another ten kernels and ten more minutes of warming through and then we can strain the pieces out along with the remains of the onions." He looked up at the minister. "I *am* hoping we've judged this correctly, minister, but even in my deepest, darkest

263

days of creating cyanide compounds for my Prince, I have never tried to create a cyanide-based sleeping draught for over a hundred men. The quantities to be used are simply too unpredictable. *No-one* has ever tried such a thing, you understand."

The minister once more looked sceptical and unhappy, but Darius leaned across from his position near the door and said quietly "if the quantities are wrong we can pay for it in the next life, minister. These men don't deserve your sympathy or care and you know it."

Sarios glanced back at his young friend. Since the attack on the girl this morning, Darius had become gradually bleaker and darker throughout the day and right at this moment, the minister had never seen him display more of a similarity to his father. Darius, for all his upbringing here, was a Caerdin through and through and the way he'd just spoken had clinched it. The young man had never spoken to Sarios like that. Never on a level like that. The minister began to wonder if involving Darius in today's events would perhaps irreparably damage the young man's soul.

"Just do your best gentlemen. When will it be ready?"

Favio looked across at the head cook, who nodded.

"Twenty minutes should be enough. Dinner will be ready right on time and should be nice and spicy."

The minister turned again to Darius. "You'd best go and get the Wolves into position now."

The young man nodded and turned to pull on the door handle just as it opened and he was almost crushed up against the wall by the heavy oak of the door. A guardsman in full kit with his helm under his arm burst in onto the raised platform around the edge of the kitchens. He glared down at the various people working and recognised the minister.

"You! You're not busy and I'm just going on duty so I won't get dinner. Make me something quick!"

The minister looked up at the guard in confusion and then his eyes widened as Darius pushed hard and sharp against the door. The heavy oak swung back on its hinge and this time slammed hard into the angry guardsman's shoulder, hurling him from the raised platform and down onto a table covered in condiments. The guard floundered around in shock but before he could pull himself together, Darius was on him, jumping from the higher level and landing on top of the guard with his knees. There was an audible crunch as at least one rib broke and Darius rolled off with the momentum and onto the floor before springing lightly back to his feet.

The guard groaned in pain but was tougher than Darius had given him credit for. He hauled himself off the table and reached down, twitching at the pain in his ribs, to draw his sword from the sheath. A low growl escaped from the young man's throat as he reached across to another table and withdrew a serrated knife from a block of wood.

"You can't treat people like this you piece of shit!" he snapped as he stepped forward. He was vaguely aware of cooks rushing to either help or hinder him and the minister shouting at him to stop but, ignoring all the other commotion, he reached out and grasped the guard's wrist, jamming the blade back into its scabbard. The guard's eyes widened as the tip of the serrated knife brushed his broken ribs. He was a guard, not a combat veteran and here was a young boy with exceptional strength threatening his life. He fought his incredulity and tried to free his hand and sword.

"You people are like parasites" Darius continued, firmly holding the sword down. "You just take and don't care. Sabian was right about you. Not one of you is fit to clean out his piss pot!"

The guardsman struggled again and opened his mouth to speak but, as he did, Darius drove the blade deep between his ribs and into his organs. The man was dead before the second blow. By the fifth and sixth he flopped around against the table, fountaining blood from the many wounds as Darius took out his hatred of the guards on one unlucky man. He was still carving the man when Mercurias and Favio pulled him off and the knife dropped.

The grizzled medic looked at the minister as he picked up the viscera-covered knife and Favio supported the now-glazed Darius. "Better tend to dinner. It looks like we've begun."

Chapter XXIII.

Darius stopped at the entrance to the small clearing, his hands dropping to his knees as he leaned over and fought for breath. The group of rebels among the tangled roots gathered up their weapons and Kiva stepped unsteadily forward, his face weighed down with concern. The young man looked exhausted but that was to be expected; he'd run from the palace most of the way across the island, ducking in and out of shadows wherever he passed close to a patrol route or guard post. What the general hadn't been expecting was the blood. Darius' arms were stained to the elbows with almost dry blood, giving the impression that he wore red gloves or gauntlets. Equally, there were stains all over his chest and face. Clearly something unexpected had already occurred.

"What the hell happened to you?"

Catching his breath, the young man straightened. "I evened the odds by one. They're already serving dinner. Time you all got into position, yes?"

Kiva stared at him again for a long moment and then nodded gently. "They all know where they're going. Are you staying with me or going back to help the minister?"

Darius laughed. "No. I'm going to find that sergeant and cut him into pieces you could slide under a door."

Kiva looked long and hard at the lad, tempted to order him to stand down or at least to argue with him, but there was a touch of hysteria about that laugh and nothing the general said right now would change his mind.

"Ok" Kiva agreed. "Your sword's in the pile over by that big rock. You'll need it."

As the lad ran off toward the makeshift armoury, the general hobbled over to Athas. The burly sergeant patted his sword belt in satisfaction and looked across at his commander.

"Yes sir?"

"Keep an eye on that boy. He's got murder in his eyes and I don't think he much cares about anything else right now. Tythias can do your part and his together; he can handle it. You go with Darius and find this sergeant he hates so much, ok?"

Athas nodded and, with a quick glance over to the pile where the lad was untangling his sword belt, squared his shoulders. "Won't their sergeant be in the dining hall with the rest?"

Kiva shook his head slightly. "I doubt it. He seems like a bit of a megalomaniac. If I had to suggest a place to look, it would be the old

266

Imperial apartment on the top floor of the Peacock Palace. It's luxurious and recently renovated and I would imagine he's revelling in the power of command right now."

Athas nodded and turned to watch Darius wandering back towards him with a curved, northern sword slung at his side. Everyone else was now armed and ready and the group came to a halt before the general. The only figure that strayed from the small unit was Sathina who gave Tythias one quick hug and then trotted around the edge to join the general. She and Kiva would be the only two to remain by the shore tonight, though one of the Pelasians had given her a small hand-held crossbow and three bolts as a last defence in case things went wrong and they needed it. Kiva smiled at the gathering.

"You all know where you're going. Now go and be lucky."

As the group filed out of the clearing and started to jog quietly across the turf, Kiva caught Tythias by the elbow as he moved. "Change of plan: Athas is looking after Darius, so you get to cover everything on the western side from the Water Gate to the Gorgon Gate. If you get to the Gorgon Gate and Jorun and Brendan haven't got there yet, you'll have to start picking anyone off from the high place until the others arrive, ok?"

Tythias frowned. "I thought we were giving them the chance to surrender?"

"They outnumber us at least eight or nine to one at the moment. I'd rather they died meaninglessly than we risked everything. Understand?"

With a simple nod, Tythias passed the general and disappeared off into the night. Sathina looked down at the small crossbow in her hand and then up at Kiva. "Will they be alright?"

Caerdin shrugged lightly and groaned; the motion still hurt. "If it all goes as planned, we'll all be fine. If not, then your guess is as good as mine. A lot of this relies on the doctors brewing something up that'll even the odds. If they can take out all the guard that are off-duty, we'll be in a much better position."

They both turned to look up toward the walls and the Water Gate, where the last of several quiet, dark figures flitted across the moon-dappled landscape.

Tythias watched from behind the tree as the guard on the tower of the Water Gate finished urinating over the battlements and disappeared from sight once more. With a quick glance over to the other side of the gate, he smiled. A bush at roughly the same distance from

267

the other flanking tower did very little to conceal the bulky shapes of Brendan and Jorun. Tythias knew full well why Caerdin had split the men as he had. The Pelasians and Marco would be able to move quietly among the buildings of the island, picking off individual guards without being detected. Athas, Brendan, Jorun and Tythias himself were not genetically designed for sneaking. They'd been split into two pairs and sent to the Water Gate. When the first signal came they were to take the gate, subduing the guards any way they could, then they would head off in different directions around the perimeter of the palaces, clearing the walls as they went and meeting up again at the Gorgon Gate, where they would have the best vantage position on the island.

Again he grinned. If it weren't so important, he'd have laughed. Although it'd be inaudible up on the gate in the night breeze and with their crackling brazier, the low susurration of Jorun and Brendan arguing drifted across the grass to where Tythias stood. They were like children at times.

For a few moments more he watched them and then turned his attention to the trees behind them, down towards the water's edge. There was something eerie about the island tonight. A stiff but warm breeze blew, making the torches on the walls gutter where they burned, and causing whispers among the trees and shrubs that filled the night with imagined conversation. He watched.

And then only a minute or so later, there was a single flash from the top of one of the trees. It could easily have been mistaken for the twinkle of a star or possibly even a distant night fisherman's boat from the walls, but Tythias knew it for a signal. That would be his little Sathina with her lantern, high in a tree under the watchful eye of his ally and long friend general Caerdin. He smiled. Along time ago he'd served as a Prefect under Marshal Covis and had been on temporary assignment under Caerdin several times. It'd been said that when Avitus became old and moved into politics, Tythias was one of the names that would be considered as the next Marshal, but the Empire plunged into chaos too soon and that time never came. And here he was now, Kiva and he both Mercenary captains with more than two decades passed since they served together, but it was astounding how naturally it came trusting to the man's leadership and taking orders from him. With a sigh of genuine satisfaction, he glanced over at the other two crouching in the bushes. They were so busy arguing they hadn't seen the signal. With a grin Tythias picked up a small pebble and took aim.

The stone bounced off Brendan's shoulder and he spun around to see Tythias behind a tree gesturing wildly back towards the sea and then up at the gate. With a nod, he crouched lower and whispered to Jorun and a second later, the two broke cover and ran for the gatehouse. Tythias ducked out from the tree and ran with them.

"Keep your mind on your work you two!"

The three of them disappeared under the arch and Tythias pointed to Jorun and at a small door that led to the gate's small guard room. It may be unoccupied but there was light shining out from under the door and enemies should not be left behind you. Jorun nodded and stepped to one side of the door, drawing a heavy mace from his belt. Tythias and Brendan didn't stop to sightsee and the only evidence of Jorun's activities was a brief distant crunching noise as they moved quietly up the steps to the next level.

The first floor of the gatehouse had a long table and a number of chairs, but they were rotten and ancient and largely unusable. The dust remained undisturbed except around the periphery, so no one used this level and probably the next one except to move between the ground and the wall walk.

Sure enough the third level was dusty, deserted and entirely unfurnished. The two rebels spared the room only a cursory glance as they passed through, up the final flight of stairs and out onto the roof of the gatehouse. The two huge drum towers of the Water Gate were connected by a central walkway, with stairs down from each tower onto the wall itself. Tythias had watched the roof for several minutes while waiting for the signal and had counted only three men. Three unprepared men.

The scarred mercenary captain was first out of the doorway, his straight sword with the serrated section of blade close to the hilt held forward and ready. There were in fact four men on the gate, one of whom had remained seated and hidden from the ground. Despite Caerdin's order, he came to a halt several feet from where the four stood and sat around a brazier warming their hands. Moments later, Brendan came scraping to a halt beside him, his own sword out and paired with a long dagger in the other hand.

"One chance... that's all" the captain of the Lion Riders announced clearly, if quietly. "Surrender and no one has to die."

It was a hopeless gesture as far as Brendan was concerned and, as the men rose, their hands going to their weapons, the shaven-headed mercenary leapt forward. The seated man, struggling to his feet with his sword half-drawn was the first casualty. Brendan's knife plunged through the back of the chair, pinning the stunned man to the wood. Letting the knife go, he spun round, his sword flashing as the second man finally freed his weapon. The two blades met with the ring of metal and a few sparks. Beside him, Tythias had leapt for the other two. Brendan fought like a maniac, his blade hammering across and down at the guardsman. The man was good and despite his surprise he was holding his own. Stepping back, the bald mercenary grinned and made a beckoning gesture. Behind the man he saw Tythias' sword rammed deep into another guardsman's chest and even he winced at the noise as the captain withdrew the blade and the serrated section sawed through bone on its way out.

The guard, growling, leapt forward at Brendan, his blade flickering. The mercenary grinned all the more as he turned the dancing blade easily aside each blow.

"We're fightin', not pissin' about!"

The guard came on again and, as his blade flicked again toward Brendan's shoulder, he ducked to one side and brought his foot down very heavily on the guardsman's knee. There was an eye-watering crunch and the man collapsed to the floor whimpering. He opened his mouth to scream and the burly mercenary brought the pommel of his sword down on the top of the man's skull with another unpleasant crack. The body went limp.

Brendan looked up to see that the fourth man had surrendered and Tythias had given him cord with which the man was already tying his own legs tightly. The burly mercenary grinned as the captain glanced over at him.

"Is that one dead?" Tythias asked.

Brendan shrugged. "Dunno. Hang on."

With a grunt, he lifted the body, the lower leg dangling at unnatural angles and, with a step backward, tipped him over the parapet.

"I'd say yes, at a guess."

Tythias grinned and turned as Jorun burst through the doorway at the top.

"Ack!, ah-ah-ah."

Tythias nodded sympathetically and pointed at the man busy tying his own legs together. "Make sure this little prick is very securely tied and gagged and then you and Brendan get going. I'll see you at the Gorgon Gate."

Jorun nodded and Tythias made for the stairs onto the wall. At the last moment, he looked back at Brendan. "And don't try to make him fly. He surrendered."

The burly mercenary gave him an exceedingly innocent grin and then trotted over to join Jorun. Tythias turned once more and jogged down to the wall. "Gods help the Empire with those two running amok together!"

Prince Ashar moved through the shadow of the Arch of the Four Seasons without a sound. He dropped back against the wall and scanned the Ibis Courtyard. Empty. Lifting his hands to his face he called out with the sound of an owl and was answered from all around with the sounds of night-time wildlife. Six. Six men in the courtyard. Ashar was proud of his men and wondered how many guardsmen had met an unfortunate end before they'd all made it here. He waited again for a moment and watched as the door to the Raven Palace opened and a number of the islanders exited with Sarios, Mercurias and his own doctor among them. The Prince moved quietly out of the shadow and made three barely perceptible movements with his hand as he trotted lightly across the stone. Figures melted out of the shadows all around the courtyard. Two came towards the door the islanders had just left, converging with their Prince. The others unhooked already prepared grapple lines from various places around the decorative stonework and began to climb. Ashar and his two assistants dropped back against the wall as Sarios led the islanders past. Neither the minister nor any of his fellows made any sign they'd noticed the black-clad assassins. Ashar nodded. They were being watched then.

Again, he made a motion with his finger and one of his men ducked around the doorway for a split second. When he stepped back he held up his hand, all fingers spread. With a nod, Ashar ducked round and disappeared into the doorway, the other two entering silently behind him. Five guardsmen stood on the ground floor, sharing a flask of something and leaning on the rail of the great staircase. Two of them collapsed instantly clutching their throats; Ashar had made no such promise about taking prisoners.

Not a sound escaped from their victims as they were systematically and quietly dispatched. The last body had not even hit the floor before they were up the stairs and into doorway of the dining room. The sight that greeted Ashar assured him that the meal had gone down well. Perhaps too well. Not a single figure exhibited a sign of life in the room. It had been a slaughter; a mass poisoning on an unprecedented scale. With merely a shrug, he gestured for one of his men to check the room thoroughly while he and the other continued on along the corridors.

271

Athas worried about the young man in his charge. Darius had said nothing throughout their spasmodic journey across the island, ducking from shadow to shadow. He hadn't been waiting for signals and had been moving at pace like a man possessed. And now they were standing at the bottom of the servants' staircase in the Peacock Palace, listening carefully. There were definitely sounds up there... likely the Sergeant was preparing to dine. The meal had been taken through to the rest of the men first, as the Sergeant had sneered at the broth and demanded something special. Well, looking at the glint in Darius' eyes, he was damn well going to get it.

Athas laid a hand on the boy's shoulder and he didn't flinch.

"Listen to me, lad..." the dark-skinned giant whispered quietly. "You killed your first man tonight and that should take something out of you. You should feel something about it and it worries me that you don't seem to care. Killing coldly is not healthy; look at Kiva. Do you really want to become like him?"

Darius turned to face the sergeant and Athas' fears grew as he saw the look on the boy's face. "This isn't murder; it isn't even killing. This is cleansing. Don't worry about me Athas; I'm quite in control."

Before the sergeant could reply, the lad had started moving lithely up the spiral staircase, curving round to the right as he climbed. Muttering unhappily under his breath, Athas followed close.

Darius slowed as they reach the upper levels. This staircase was a private one for the slaves and servants working in the kitchens below to deliver food directly to the Imperial apartments on the top floor and with any luck the guardsmen didn't know about it. Athas remembered the couple of times he'd actually been admitted to the apartments in the old days. The door was disguised from the inside as part of the wall's decoration. The Emperor Basianus had had the door hidden for aesthetic reasons, but that might work to their advantage now.

The staircase came out onto a narrow landing with shelves of stone built into the wall on either side, beneath which stood old bronze braziers. Here the stone shelves would be kept constantly warm and dishes could be left while the rest of the meal was brought up from below. Then, when the entire meal was ready and stored in the warming corridor, the servants could knock and approach the apartment with a full spread. Darius had stopped and was looking about himself vacantly.

"The wall ahead is a door," whispered Athas. "One good push and it should pivot open if it's still in good repair."

Darius nodded and stepped up to the blank wall with the burly sergeant at his side. There were at least four voices within. Darius put his shoulder against the wall, but the sergeant's hand came down heavily on his shoulder yet again in restraint.

"Shh. Listen."

The voices were not clear, muffled as they were by such a thick and heavy door, but the guard sergeant was recognisable, and several other guards were present.

"...figures moving on the roofs and no answer to our signals from the Water Gate..."

Athas ground his teeth. "Someone's fucked up. We'd best get back down to where we can help."

Darius shook his head as he listened. There was the muted sound of heavy booted footsteps leaving the room. "They've all gone bar two. I'm not leaving yet."

Athas made to pull Darius back by his shoulder, but the lad wrenched away from him and slammed his shoulder into the door. There was a creak and a groan from the aging construction. "Help me!" he demanded.

The big dark mercenary growled in frustration, but bent forward and added his shoulder's weight to the lad's. The door swung ponderously open, but the speed of their entry and the noise it caused had attracted far too much attention. The guard sergeant and his companion were already in the middle of the room and moving on the door with their weapons ready. The leader sneered at them. "So the boy brings me one of the missing islanders, eh? That'll save time; I can punish you now and relax a little tomorrow."

Darius shuffled out of the doorway and danced sideways to cut off the exit to the rest of the apartment as Athas walked slowly and purposefully out into the room and dropped his sword point first to the floor and leaned it against the wall next to the door. The big man growled gently as he examined the sergeant.

"I've been trying to convince myself that you all deserve a chance to surrender, but Darius was right. You *are* a shifty piece of shit. You have no idea what's going on, but you assume that you're in control of it. You're not."

The other guard made a lunge for Athas, his blade held out in a very artistic fashion, as though he were engaged in a sport or display. The big sergeant pivoted, kicking the man's wrist hard and the blade skittered away across the floor. He smiled as he stepped in toward the man.

273

"I'm not an islander, you pointless ass."

The guardsman put his fists up to ward off the blow of the big mercenary, but Athas knocked them aside and, reaching out to grasp the man's head, wrenched it around with a crunch, so that the entire head was reversed and the suddenly sightless eyes stared out above the man's spine. Ignoring the body as it fell to the floor next to him, the big man's smile grew wider.

"So, would you like to surrender?"

The guard sergeant's eyes widened as the big mercenary drew himself up before him and the young man with the hateful eyes stepped slowly but inexorably towards him from the other doorway.

"I submit to your charge," the man said, reversing his sword and pointing the hilt to Athas. The big man grinned.

"Ah well, you see I accept your surrender, but I don't think Darius does, so I can't really help you. If I were you I'd turn that blade around, cos I don't think he much cares whether you're armed or not."

As Athas leaned back and folded his arms, the sergeant hurriedly flipped his sword over and gripped the hilt tight, just as Darius was on him. From the start, Athas had been aware that the lad had a good physique and handled his blade like a professional, but had been sceptical about his actual swordsmanship. After all, how good could someone be with only ministers and farmers to train him? Athas' own sword was in reach and in a fraction of a second he could grip it, lift it and land a blow on the guard officer, but as he watched Darius come in for the first strike, he relaxed and settled back against the wall.

The young man stepped in and swung his own blade wide. The blow was slow; ponderous, and the sergeant easily raised his own sword to block it, smiling. However, Darius was lithe and prepared and the manoeuvre had been designed to elicit that very reaction. As the sergeant's blade struck his own, Darius was already spinning back on his heel in the opposite direction. The connection of the two blades had knocked his back and he allowed his arms to join the momentum and carry it back the other way, picking up speed as he pivoted. To his credit, the sergeant saw it coming and managed to struggle his sword back in the way of the unexpected attack, but the effect this time was much different. The blow slammed his own blade into his side flat-first and jolted his arm badly, so that he shook and his arm hung limply for a moment, forcing him to maintain his grip with difficulty. Darius stepped back.

"You're not leaving this room."

274

With another step, the young man dipped to the left and brought the sword up in a jab. The sergeant struggled with his shaken and bruised arm and, gripping the hilt in both hands, desperately tried to turn the attack aside again. This time he prevented the more crippling blow but was too slow to stop it connecting altogether. The point of Darius's sword ripped up through the sergeant's side just below his ribs and the man grunted in pain. Once more the young man stepped back.

"Come on. You're supposed to be a soldier and an officer. Make me work a bit!"

He stood for a moment watching the anger building in the sergeant's eyes. With a smile, he stepped forward a little. "Would you like me to make it easier for you?"

The sergeant's blow came suddenly. So suddenly in fact that Athas couldn't believe the boy was prepared and, sure enough the blow did take Darius a little by surprise. The straight Imperial blade snapped out to one side and although the young man's curved sword dropped to meet it, the sharp edge bounced along his blade to the hilt and scraped across his knuckles as he turned.

Once more Athas reached out to where his sword stood propped against the wall, but again he stayed his hand. Though the blow had caught and blood flowed across the lad's hand, he maintained a tight grip on his sword and once more used the momentum caused by the sergeant's swing to pivot on his heel and, dropping almost to a crouch, he swung the blade three hundred and sixty degrees and felt the edge bite deep into flesh. In fact the sergeant, sure of victory in that moment, had pulled his sword back for a second blow just as Darius' blade smashed into his leg just above the kneecap, shattering the femur and almost completely severing the leg.

The sergeant collapsed with a cry, his sword dropping from useless fingers.

"This is for Sandro," Darius growled, "the poor bastard you had almost kicked to death in the courtyard."

He stepped across the widening pool of blood and kicked the sergeant's sword away from him before turning back to the thrashing figure. With a vicious grin he put all of his might into a hefty kick delivered to the man's wounded leg. The sergeant screamed as the leg flopped around, threatening once more to detach. Urged on by the scream, Darius delivered another kick, this time to the face, shutting him up amid the sounds of breaking teeth.

He drew his leg back for another kick but was thwarted as Athas knocked him roughly aside and brought his own large blade down heavily, severing the sergeant's head and shattering the marble tile beneath. Darius turned on him, sword down by his side, but his face contorted with anger. Few men around had the height to meet Athas eye to eye, but the young man was one such. The big mercenary merely glared back at him.

"What will you do now, Darius? Fight me?"

Darius backed away and reached down to wipe his sword on the sergeant's tunic.

"He deserved so much more than that."

Athas nodded. "Perhaps, but if you give him that, you make yourself what he was. A soldier does not torture. Only a murderer does that."

Wiping his own blade and watching the cavalcade of emotions parading across the young man's face, he turned towards the window. With a couple of steps he sheathed his sword and looked out and down from the apartment.

"Sabian told us there were a hundred and fifty men. We've probably taken out twenty or so around the perimeter. If Mercurias and the other doctors are on form we should have taken out about sixty or seventy in the dining hall. Problem is: we don't know how many more there are and, depending on how well the Pelasians have done in the buildings, there could be anything up to sixty out there that we've missed and one of the guards is out there trying to form them up into some sort of defence. We have to make sure everyone's out of here and moving towards the shore."

Darius continued to glare at the big man for some time and then finally gave a nod of agreement. "The minister will already have everyone out of the main palace. The Great Courtyard's the meeting place for anyone who hasn't got out yet and he'll be waiting for us escort them once the palace is clear."

Athas nodded as he started to move toward the main stairwell. "Problem is: we haven't cleared it. Come on…"

Athas and Darius, swords gleaming in the moonlight, burst out of the Hall of the Swans and into the Great Courtyard. There were a group of around twenty islanders standing in the middle and Brendan and Tythias, both with their swords held in a defensive position, circled them protectively. It took only moments for Athas to notice the danger. There were half a dozen guardsmen blocking the gateway that led toward the shore and a considerable force coming through the arch from

276

the Ibis courtyard. Brendan turned as he heard them running from the doorway.

"'bout time sarge. Got ourselves some serious shit 'ere!"

Athas nodded. The group of guards from the gateway to the Ibis Courtyard had increased in numbers and were moving slowly and cautiously forward. The ones between them and the shore were still only half a dozen but could hold the gate well. Trying to get the civilians through there with only four swordsmen while they had two dozen chasing them down from behind could be a slaughter. Athas considered for a moment herding everyone back into the Hall of the Swans but there just wasn't time.

"Brendan and Tythias, get out front and take that gate. Darius and I'll hold the rest off at the back!" As the two mercenaries made their way to the front of the crowd and the entire group started moving, there was a cry and the guards from the Ibis Courtyard started to run.

"Get them out!" yelled Athas, pushing Darius away and stepping out alone to face the oncoming force. Turning his attention to the rush of men, he failed to notice that Darius had not moved and that others were joining him. Ashar and half a dozen Pelasians fell in beside the sergeant and the young islander, protecting the retreating civilians and bracing themselves against the attack that hit moments later with a sound of crashing metal that rang across the courtyard. Athas smiled at his companions and turned all his attention to the fight, sure of the Pelasians' skill and unaware that Darius remained close by, fighting like a lion.

Blow upon blow rained down on both sides, and Athas twice felt steel bite into his arms, though never deep enough to stop him. Beside him a black-clad Pelasian collapsed under a hail of blows. The guards were not particularly good warriors but odds of at least three or four to one were still favouring them. Suddenly, Athas noticed they had reached the arch and were being slowly pushed into a defensive semicircle. Desperation gripped him as the other Pelasian to his left disappeared underfoot and he found himself fighting three men and protecting the flank of the retreating civilians.

Another blow landed on his hip, mostly turned away by the armour, but jarring him badly and leaving a hefty bruise... and then suddenly they were through. The islanders were running for the shore and Tythias and Brendan rejoined the rearguard. Marco and Mercurias had appeared from somewhere to help and all four were covered with blood. Brendan displayed signs of several blows that had connected, including a new vivid cut on his chin but it was Tythias, his eyes gleaming and swinging his sword like a man possessed, that Athas saw first. His left arm had gone just below the elbow and though the stump dripped gobs of blood as he moved, his other arm swung his frightening blade as though he were practicing against a wooden stake.

"Athas, you big daft sod," he laughed as his blood trickled down onto the big sergeant's boot, "how'd you end up here?"

Athas grinned as he fought back with a renewed vigour. "You know the Wolves. Wherever there's a fight, you'll find us somewhere in the middle!"

The numbers in front were beginning to thin out, but beyond they could see another wave forming in the courtyard as more guardsmen who'd escaped the action gathered to put down the insurrection. Marco shouted a warning to Athas and leapt across to deal with a guardsman that appeared from a doorway in the gate but, as he swept his sword up, a lucky blow from one of the other guards caught him in the armpit as he moved, the blade sliding in deep. With a gasp Marco collapsed, dropping his sword. Brendan caught him as he fell and hurled him over his shoulder like a sack of grain.

Prince Ashar pushed away the man he was fighting and drove his blade into his chest as he glanced around him. "We've got to run Athas; get to the boats. We're losing too many men here."

Much as the burly sergeant hated to admit it, the cost in casualties was increasing as they fought. Already half a dozen Pelasians lay dead, Marco was either dead or unconscious, Tythias fighting with one arm and no sign of Jorun at all. Athas ducked back, sheathing his sword, and reached out for the huge beam that had once barred the ornamental gates. It was not one of the powerful oak beams that held the main gate house closed, but was sturdy enough even after years of neglect.

"Run!"

As the others leapt back, disengaging from the enemy and fled toward the shore, Athas swung the huge bar, slamming it into the guardsmen and knocking them back into a heap. Dropping the timber he ran, glancing briefly over his shoulder at the guard units that had now joined and were trying to get past the carnage at the gate.

Ahead, the others ran with Brendan at the rear, carrying the limp body of Marco. Tonight had already carried far too high a toll and it was far from over yet.

Chapter XXIV.

Sathina shimmied down the bole of the tree with the ease and balance of youth and dropped lightly to the floor next to Kiva.

"There's a whole load of people coming, general. Some are nearly here, but there's others up by the buildings and I think they're being chased by the guards."

Kiva grunted. "Ok. Come on."

Without a word, the young lady collected her small hand crossbow and went to support the wounded general where he hobbled out of the clearing. She was impressed at the speed with which he seemed to be recovering from the most horrendous wounds. Indeed, he seemed to be groaning a lot less too. Though he was slow moving along the path out of the trees, he used only one stick, reaching out with the other arm to lean on branches as he moved. She followed him faithfully along the track and then down to a slight dip.

Here, though few knew it, was a timber cover hidden among the undergrowth that Sathina crouched above and hauled on. The wooden trap door creaked and groaned and fell back onto the turf and scrub with a crunch. Beneath, dank and slippery stone steps climbed down into the earth for around twenty feet where, by faint moonlight, a hidden jetty was visible, stocked with supplies. Three wooden boats bumped into each other repeatedly with the waves.

She looked back up at the general. "What now?"

Kiva peered across the dark landscape. There was the sound of distant fighting, and figures were moving through the trees. "Now you get down those steps and untie one of the boats. I'll take that crossbow for a moment."

Without question Sathina handed him the small, portable weapon and started down the steps, pausing before she disappeared.

"Can you see Tythias?"

Kiva raised an eyebrow as he turned to look down, cocking the weapon. "Not yet, but that's guards screaming, not our men. He'll be here soon enough."

With a smile, the girl disappeared down the stairs just as the first group of islanders burst into the clearing through the sparse trees and undergrowth. A young man with a shock of unruly red hair came to a halt, motioning the others to stop as he saw the crossbow aimed toward them. As soon as Kiva was sure they were all islanders and he was in no danger, he lowered the bow and leaned heavily against a tree stump.

"General Caerdin," the young man said breathlessly. "What's next sir?"

Kiva pointed at the barely visible hole. "Get the people down there, load the boats and be ready to sail."

As the young redhead made to move past him the general held out his hand. "Is there anyone here who feels confident in handling a sword?"

Among the crowd a few hands were raised, somewhat hesitantly.

"We could do with a little help keeping the guard entertained while the first boats get underway. Behind that bush," he announced, gesturing, "is a small pile of weapons. Anyone who feels they can help, grab a sword and stand to. Any sailors or fishermen, head down there and get the boats primed."

The majority of the group stepped down into the passageway, as five men made for the armoury and prepared themselves. They stood firmly beside the general, the young man with red hair coughing nervously.

"How many boats are there down there? There are a lot of people, you know?"

Kiva nodded. "Three boats. Big ones though. These are old troop transports. They can take maybe twenty-five or even thirty each fully laden."

"But there must be well over a hundred of us leaving. How are we going to get everyone out?"

"Actually, there's one hundred and thirty two if we lost no-one tonight. These boats are just for the first group," the general replied, shifting his weight uncomfortably. Then we've got to deal with the guard for good before we move to the second site.

An older man on the other side of the clearing frowned. "Even so, with only twenty-five people in those boats, they'll ride very low in the water. We'll catch on the reefs!"

With a grin, Kiva turned to face him. "Then we're about to find out just how good a sailor we all are, aren't we."

They stood in silence for a moment and watched as the next group of figures closed in through the sparse trees. Sarios was out front, moving with a speed that truly belied his age. Somewhere not far behind came the ring of steel on steel and angry shouting that could only be Brendan and Athas. Kiva smiled.

"Get ready!"

The minister burst into the clearing.

"How many are here already?" he asked breathlessly.

Kiva shrugged and winced again. "Around sixty or seventy I'd say. Send any women and children down to join them."

Sarios began directing islanders, some of whom entered the tunnel and some took up arms and came to join the defenders while the rest were sent into the undergrowth behind to wait until the area was clear and safe. The people were still moving, some stepping into the tunnel, as Brendan burst into the open, his sword covered in viscera and the still shape of Marco over his shoulder. He ran straight over to the nearest islanders and dropped Marco into their arms.

"E's still breathing sir" he gabbled to the general, as he hefted his blade and stepped into line with the rag-tag unit of rebels and prisoners.

Kiva nodded and raised the bow as the battle crossed the thicket and entered the clearing. Athas was swinging his sword with tired arms, but a determined look on his face; next to him, Darius was bleeding from the forehead and paused regularly, his sword flailing defensively, to wipe the red veil from his eyes. Tythias, leaving a trail of blood from his severed arm, fought like a wildcat on the periphery, with Mercurias, Ashar and two other Pelasians, all of them together struggling to hold back the guards, who'd been whittled down to a ratio of perhaps two or three to one.

"At 'em lads!" bellowed Kiva as he unleashed the first bolt from the small crossbow. Remarkably, perhaps, given his general lack or skill and current unsteadiness, the bolt dug into the shoulder of a guard. The man gasped in surprise but never managed to curse, as Ashar Parishid, exiled Prince of Pelasia, jammed a sword into his gut as he staggered.

Nervously, the armed islanders moved into the fight, coming around the sides to join Ashar and Tythias, where they fought to prevent the defenders being outflanked. Three were cut down as they joined the fight, and one of their assailants, grinning with glee at his victory was taken in the chest by Kiva's next shot.

Reloading, the general watched as the odds continued to lower as his own men, the three surviving Wolves, and their allies did what they were best at. Watching, he fired one more shot, which narrowly missed its target, thrumming off into the darkness harmlessly, and dropped the weapon to his side.

"Stop!" he bellowed at the top of his voice.

The effect was strange and instant. The fight petered out with a last ringing blow and both groups, roughly evenly matched, stood tensely watching each other, their weapons raised. Kiva cleared his throat again.

"The fight's over! More than a hundred of your men have fallen to around twenty of ours tonight. Do you really want to join them?"

Silence reigned as the guards eyed their enemy suspiciously, interspersed with sidelong glances to their own friends. Kiva frowned.

"There's no reason to die now. You've fought as hard as you could and there's no disrespect. But we *are* leaving now, whether you live to see it or not. If you drop your weapons, no harm will befall you at our hands, you have the word of an Imperial Marshal."

Again the sidelong glances said more than a thousand words as the silence built to a deafening roar, broken finally by the dull thud of a sword hitting turf. As if they'd been waiting for a signal, the guardsmen threw down their weapons and there was no mistaking the look of relief that crossed most of the assembled faces. Kiva sighed gratefully.

"My men will escort you to the kitchens where you will be temporarily imprisoned. I have no doubt that your master will be back to collect you soon enough, and you may even manage to break out of the place before dawn, but not before we are long gone. There's plenty of space and seating and a lot of food, so you won't starve."

He made a gesture to Athas, who prodded one of the guards gently with the tip of his sword. "Come on boys."

Kiva cleared his throat again as the unarmed men were herded back toward the palace by the unit. "I'd avoid the shrimp broth, though!"

Someone behind him laughed.

The moon had already been high in its arc when Athas and the rest had rejoined Kiva and the islanders and they'd all made their way to the second hidden jetty. It had taken only a few moments for them to locate the disguised doorway and to make their way down to the dock. Two more boats of almost equal size to the first wave had awaited them and Kiva had heaved a great sigh of relief as the last islander climbed aboard and they set sail.

The sea was fairly gentle despite the reefs lurking below the surface all around and Kiva sat at the prow of one of the two boats, keeping a careful eye on the swirling waters and the occasional eddies of foam that betrayed the more prominent dangers. Before the boats were more than a hundred yards from the entrance to the dock, travelling around the shore, the other three vessels carrying the rest of the islanders came splashing gently along in the pale moonlight to meet up with them. Kiva leaned forward further forward, peering into the moon-dappled darkness.

"Minister?"

Sarios returned the call from the lead boat of the other flotilla. "Caerdin. What now?"

Kiva frowned. "You or I to lead the boats? I can't imagine anyone else knows the routes like we do."

The minister laughed lightly. "After twenty years of having your head battered with swords I think I'd rather trust my own memory, general. I'll take the lead."

With a nod, Kiva sat back heavily against the boat's side and looked around him as the five-boat flotilla manoeuvred into a tight group at the minister's instruction. Brendan sat at the other end of the boat, his features twisted with a look of concern and the still form of Marco propped against him. Mercurias and the Pelasian medic together were prodding at his side with worried glances. Kiva tried to see more of what they were doing above the gathered heads of the refugees and clicked his tongue in annoyance.

"How is he?"

Mercurias snorted. "Well, he's not good. If we get him somewhere stable and quiet soon, he'll probably make it, but I'm not convinced he'll ever be a soldier again. He's lost a lung at least and he'll probably wheeze and slow down for the rest of his life."

The Pelasian medic nodded his agreement as he peeled more clothing aside from the wound. Kiva sighed and sack back once more. Another casualty to add to the long list. For two decades the Wolves had taken only minor losses but in the last few weeks they'd come down from twelve to five and one of those would never fight again. Some days the future looked hopeless. Strange really how he used to be comfortable with bleakness and gloom; had lived with it for so long, but in these last months thanks to Quintillian and the islanders, he'd begun to care again. Shame really. When you had no hope, there was nothing to lose, but now the loss of even a civilian prisoner was weighing heavily on his mind. He looked up to see Mercurias watching him.

"*You're* moving well," the medic said accusingly. "You should be in a lot of pain at the moment. Who's given you mare's mead now?"

Kiva shook his head. "Forget about it. Maybe I'm just a quick healer."

"Pah!" Mercurias turned back to Marco's side.

Kiva turned to look at the next boat, bobbing along behind and slightly to one side. Tythias sat aboard gazing at a different boat, smiling, as doctor Favio tended to his severed arm with as much patience as an army medic. A smile crept across the general's face once more; the Lion Riders had a good captain in Tythias. The man had suffered some impressive wounding on the island, matching anything he'd had in the past, losing an arm and yet he'd never looked happier that he did right now, covered in scars and still dripping blood. Kiva didn't need to turn around to see what it was the one-eyed captain was smiling at; or rather, whom. All in all, though tonight had seen its share of loss, given the odds and the conditions they'd been more successful then they had any right to be, and Kiva had no real complaints. He did wish they'd been able to take the bodies of Jorun, felled by a guardsman's javelin, and the dozen Pelasians and islanders that had never made it to the shore, but the boats were loaded down enough as it is.

Somewhere in one of the other boats, a man started to sing an old folk song about a sailor lost at sea. With a relieved smile, the general relaxed back as he listened.

The journey through the reefs was long and treacherous; more treacherous than Kiva remembered. The sun's rays were already tentatively brushing the horizon as the lead boat ran up on to the gravel beach with a crunch. Slowly the occupants stepped out, stretching their cramped legs and loosening their muscles. For many of the islanders this would be the first time they'd ever set foot on the mainland and there were grins and expressions of wonder abounding.

Kiva smiled as he watched a young girl with her arm in a sling crying with worry at this whole new world. Her father crouched and put his arms round her, a wide grin on his own face. The islanders were collectively overwhelmed, but Kiva's attention was drawn back to the present as his own boat grounded with a crunch that jarred him. As the occupants filed out, one of them stopped to help the wobbly general over the side. With some effort he reached the gravel and leaned heavily on his companion as his legs struggled to support him.

Other boats grounded now and the crowd on the beach grew at a rate of knots. Kiva, with the aid of the helpful islander, struggled across to the rocks that stood proud of the beach and hauled himself up onto them with surprising ease. The flask of mare's mead was diminishing rapidly, but thanks to its numbing and soothing effects he was able to ignore and overcome the pain and discomfort his wounds caused. Minister Sarios clambered up onto the rocks beside him and the two stood silently until the crowd gradually fell silent and faced them in a huge semi-circle.

"Ok everyone. Listen carefully. We're currently trapped on this beach. Somewhere on the other side of these low hills is the entire army of Velutio marching toward Serfium. We cannot go inland, and north along the coast will take us straight to Serfium, which we must avoid at all costs. South from here will take us to the city, and I'm sure none of us want to go there. So, make the best you can of this place for now. No one goes far enough away to be out of sight. If you do that, you could find yourself in most unpleasant circumstances."

Kiva smiled. "By this time the guards will almost certainly have escaped the kitchens on the island, but Commander Sabian assured us that it'll be at least a week before the next ship to the island and, no matter where they check, the guards will find that we've scuppered every other boat on the island and brought every signal lantern with us. While it is possible they'll find a way to draw attention to the island it will take time, particularly with Velutio and the army away campaigning, so we have some time to play with."

The general nodded at the minister and Sarios stepped forward to speak.

"Now that we are clear of the reefs, we will rest and then move again at dusk. There are sails stowed away among the gear and we have a number of competent sailors. Once the light starts to fail, we will set off by boat once more, looking for all the world like a small group of night fishermen. It will be too dark for our numbers to be too visible and we are unlikely to attract any unwanted attention. We will sail for however long it takes, I'm afraid, so be prepared for a long journey in some discomfort. The route will take us around the island of Isera once more, this time outside the reefs, to a point south of Monte Bero and the city of Velutio. There, the general and his men will procure transport for us and we will begin the journey into the mountains to a hidden location where we will be safe from our enemies."

He smiled as he continued. "It will be a long and difficult journey by sea and then by mountain path, but remember while your legs are cramped on board and your feet ache with walking, that every step takes you further from your enemies and that we will be safe and sound at the end of the road."

Kiva nodded thoughtfully and announced "time to do as you please, so long as you stay within sight of this rock. I would suggest someone starts organising breakfast."

With that, he turned to the minister and gestured to the rear of the rocky outcrop. Sarios helped the general hobble over to the other side, away from the dispersing crowd.

I know this hidden place of yours is secret, but I'm afraid you're going to have to share it with me now. I need to know what transport we'll need and, if you clarify where we're headed, I might be able to make something of it in future planning."

Sarios raised an eyebrow. "I thought you said we had enough trouble with the present and that we didn't have the luxury of planning for a future?"

The general growled quietly. "To be quite honest, I was never entirely convinced we'd get everyone off the island. Now we've no choice. If we do nothing, Velutio'll take it all and in the end he'll come looking for us. We need to move ourselves and try to stop him from gaining any more power. Times change, now just tell me where we're going."

The minister leaned back against a rocky protrusion. "Hadrus, Caerdin. We're going to Hadrus."

Kiva frowned. "Hadrus was destroyed by an earthquake. I remember all the fuss and the refugees."

"True... all true, but it was also rebuilt on Quintus' orders for the imprisonment of people he didn't want found. Funny, really, isn't it?" We've escaped from a prison made from the Emperor's refuge and we're seeking refuge at the Emperor's secret prison!"

Sarios laughed and the general couldn't help but smile at the irony.

"Ok, minister. Tend to your people and get them organised. I'm going to speak to Ashar... and Darius, of course."

Sarios smiled again, knowingly. "Of course..."

As the minister wandered over toward the chefs who were unloading a case of foodstuff from one of the boats, Kiva scanned the beach and spotted the Pelasian Prince in conversation with his doctor. Hobbling slowly along the rock and climbing down the lowest part with the aid of a helpful islander, he tottered unsteadily across the uneven surface of the beach until he reached the two swarthy black-clad men.

"Ashar, I need to speak to you. Alone" he added, glancing at the doctor. The man nodded and walked away across the beach, leaving his master alone with the general.

"Kiva? You're walking better all the time. I wish I could say it was my doctor's doing, but I know you better than that. What can I do for you?"

"You tried to convince me not long ago to go to war against Velutio. Quintillian's gone, but you said it didn't matter. I'd be your banner."

Ashar nodded seriously.

"Well," the general continued, "I'm still not Emperor material and never will be, but we all know someone who could be. Will you add your banner to the cause for a different Emperor?"

Ashar smiled; slowly at first, but then breaking into a broad grin.

"You know you'll have to create some spurious link to the Imperial line for him if you want people to follow him?"

Kiva nodded. "It's been done before on many occasions. I'm sure Sarios can find some convincing evidence."

"Very well," the Prince nodded. "You put him on the pedestal and I'll help you carry it. I need to find the rest of my men then."

"Hadrus," whispered the general. "That's where we'll be."

Ashar laughed. "The Emperor's prison? That's priceless."

"Some day you'll have to tell me how you find out about things like that. But, yes. We'll be at Hadrus. I'll start pulling everything together, but I'm afraid I need another favour from you."

The Prince raised an eyebrow and the general patted him on the shoulder. "I need you and your Pelasians to track down a number of people and send them to me."

Ashar nodded. "Other captains, I presume? The ones you were sending for before the disaster at Serfium?"

"Yes. Filus and Sithis should both come without question if you can find them. They should both be somewhere south east of Burdium." The general pulled a scrap of paper from his tunic and thrust it into Ashar's hand. "This is a list of other captains that should be open to persuasion and a few Lords who'll likely want to help. It's not much, but it's a start. We need to pull a few units together before we can start building any kind of army."

The Prince nodded. "I'll see what I can do. I'll be at Hadrus inside a month. Stay safe until then and try not to end up in Velutio's hands again."

Kiva smiled. "I take it you'll be ok heading inland from here. You can get around without drawing attention, I know."

Ashar grinned and scanned the beach. "I'll take my men, but you take my doctor. You've over a hundred people here and you may need a lot of medical attention by the time you get to Hadrus. Go safe my friend and stay lucky."

287

Kiva clasped hands for a moment with the Prince, wincing briefly at the pressure it put on his damaged wrist and then watched as the lithe, black figure jogged along the shore to the small knot of Pelasians and started to make preparations.

The general sighed for a moment as a nagging worry caught him. The last time they made this sort of plan it had cost them Quintillian and almost been the end of the Wolves. Was it tempting fate for a cursed man to try a second time? He scanned the beach for Darius and spotted the young man collecting stones from the ground and hurling them out into the sea, trying to hit a small outcrop that jutted amidst foam from the water.

Slowly, the general picked his way down to where the lad stood, far enough away from the crowd to allow a little privacy. Most of the islanders were concerned with unpacking goods and arranging food, and paid little attention to the two figures further along the beach.

"Darius."

The general reached out and plucked a stone from the young man's armful and, taking aim, hurled it towards the rock. It fell woefully short and slightly off target. Darius laughed.

"I think it's going to be a while yet before you've the strength for that, general."

"Shows how much you know," replied the older man. "Even at my best I'd be lucky just to hit the water. That's why I favour swords, not bows."

The young man smiled, took one last throw, and then dropped the rest of his collection back to the ground. "What's on your mind, sir?"

Kiva swallowed. This was difficult ground. How to say what he needed to say without warning the lad off.

"Let's see just how clever you are, Darius. Tell me why you and Quintillian were taught the things you were on the island when all the other youngsters have been taught trades."

Darius shrugged. "They had something else in mind for the two of us. Perhaps they were trying to make us useful enough that Velutio wouldn't kill us."

Kiva frowned. Not a bad angle, and one he hadn't considered, but still not the right one.

"You were both being groomed for the throne. Quintillian and you both. You may think that Sarios is a kind man, but he's not. Don't argue" he added forcefully as anger rose in Darius' face. "The minister is a politician and nothing he does is without purpose. Sarios would use

288

either of you to rebuild what was lost at whatever cost. He uses me and the Pelasian Prince and any others he needs the same way."

A frown crossed the young man's face. "And yet you go along with it because you agree with his goal? His aspirations? I can see that, yes. But Quintillian had a claim to the throne; the best claim you could have. I'm not even remotely connected... and I'm not a politician. I think you're wrong. I think Quintillian was being groomed for the throne, but I was being trained to be what you were for his uncle."

Again the insight the young man displayed made Kiva blink. Another thing he'd never considered, and a observation that was very persuasive. For a moment he found himself wondering whether Darius was right and the minister had been dissembling again. He shook his head; either way it made no difference now.

"That's a possibility I suppose, but it makes no difference. You have the brain, the charisma, the learning and the guts to lead a nation. What do *you* think?"

Darius stood for a long moment with his chin resting in his hand. "I realise that you want me to leap up with glee and say that I'm the man for the job, but it's not that simple. I need to think about this."

Kiva laughed. "And I said you were clever! If you were the sort to leap at the chance, we wouldn't even be having this conversation. I don't expect you to want to do it, or even to agree with it. I want you to think long and hard about it and come grudgingly to the same conclusion as we have: that you are the only person who *can* do it."

Darius' frown deepened. "I have no claim."

"Claims can be manufactured; just watch how fast Sarios finds a link."

"Yes, I'd bet he can at that."

The two stood for quite some time, staring out at the waves with the smell of frying fish drifting along the beach. Kiva studied the young man for a while and finally squared his shoulders.

"I'll leave you alone to think."

Darius shook his head. "Wait. Don't take this as a yes, but would you like to tell me what you have in mind?"

The most momentous occasions are often heralded by peace and quiet. The waves crashed on the rocks and seagulls crowded over the breakfast site as two men stood alone on the rocks and decided the fate of the world.

289

Part Five: Change & Rebirth

Chapter XXV.

Kiva Caerdin, General of the rebel army, strode purposefully across the square. The changes the sojourn at Hadrus had wrung in him were extensive and those who remembered the sullen, old Kiva of the Grey Company marvelled anew every time they saw him. In the two and half months since their boats had landed on the coast south of Velutio, he'd recovered from his wounds at astonishing speed. Though still far from his old form, he was moving well and even found at sword practice at least once a day. Mercurias had washed his hands of the general's state of health, declaring him a lost cause and putting his speedy recovery purely down to an increased and dangerous addiction to the mare's mead that had been part of his life for decades. Whatever the cause, the effect was impressive.

Moreover, gone were the whiskers and the long hair, replaced with a short and severe cut of iron grey hair after the old style. Though he still wore his comfortable and familiar armour, it was now worn over a green tunic and breeches that matched those worn by every other figure in Hadrus that bore arms. He wore the traditional ribbon of service, knotted around his ribs, denoting his rank and status and the grey cloak had gone, replaced by a wolf-pelt shoulder cloak. The banners that fluttered above his headquarters, once the chief warden's quarters, bore the Imperial raven and crown, supported by a wolf and a lion.

And the lions, or Lion Riders, were now as much a part of the army as the Wolves, even outnumbering them considerably. Kiva smiled as he strode past hastily erected workshops where smiths and armourers hammered and rang, pumped bellows and dropped hot steel into buckets of water. Beyond them, an old building of unknown origin had been converted into more workshops for the weavers who worked like devils to churn out green uniforms, cloaks, flags and horse blankets. The whole place was alive with industry and activity and, while Kiva was the driving force now behind it all, much of the credit had to go to Minister Sarios, whose considerable skills in administration and organisation had turned a stream of refugees into a fully working town.

Reaching the other side of the square, just inside the heavily protected and defended gatehouse, he grinned as he reached out and clasped arms with the commander of the Lion Riders. Their captain now went by his old title of Prefect and held the position of Kiva's second in command. Due to the disparity in strength between the two units that had become the backbone of the rebel army, Tythias had suggested months ago that his best men be taken into the sadly depleted Wolves, but Kiva had refused blindly. The Lion Riders, he'd said, were as important as the Wolves and had an equal stake in what they'd planned, hence the flag denoting both units supporting the raven.

Tythias returned the grin as he looked his general up and down appraisingly.

"Kiva? You look ten years younger! I've only been gone a month."

The general shook his head. "A month and a half, Tythias. It was time to start thinking like a soldier again and, I'm afraid, you really ought to go see the barber yourself while you're back. No use wearing the Imperial green if we still look like vagrants, eh?"

Tythias made a grumbling noise deep in his throat, but his smile stayed firmly riveted on his face. "I suppose you're right. Sathina keeps making veiled threats anyway."

With a laugh, the general caught his second in command by the shoulder and, turning, walked with him toward the headquarters building. Behind them, the party of twenty Lion Riders slipped gratefully from their saddles and went about the business of stabling their horses. Kiva stretched as he walked. "Darius is looking forward to seeing you again, on a purely personal level of course, but like the rest of us, he's anxious for news too."

"I've plenty of that, but I must find Sathina first and bring her with me."

Kiva smiled. "She's in there already. Our scouts saw you a couple of hours ago down in the valley, so she's had plenty of time to get ready."

A moment later they were across the open space and entering the heavy stone building adorned with flags. Two men wearing chain mail over green tunics snapped to attention on either side of the door, their spears bearing the raven flag. Caerdin gave them a nod as the two entered.

Inside would've seemed chaos to anyone else, but this was a chaos that had been organised by Sarios and every person moving in the building had a purpose and a destination. No goods, personnel or space was wasted in Hadrus. The crowd of clerks moved around like a human sea, parting respectfully as they reached the General and the Prefect. A looming figure appeared from the flow and slapped his hands heavily down on Tythias' shoulders.

"Tythias, you old goat. You made it then?"

The bulky figure of Athas presented a cataract around which the stream of life flowed. Tythias grinned at him. "A few minor scrapes... nothing else."

Kiva ushered them both through a door on the left and into a large room with a huge wooden table in the centre, upon which were spread maps, diagrams, lists and books. The mercenaries who'd escaped from Isera with the prisoners had since become the command party of the army at Hadrus and Mercurias and Brendan stood in their full paraphernalia with wolf-pelt cloaks and bearing the insignia of captains. Waiting for the new arrival alongside them was Sathina in a new, stunning blue dress and behind her stood Marco, still pale and thin, but alive and smiling. And of course Darius. If the change in Kiva had been gradual during the time they'd been in Hadrus, the change in the young prisoner from Isera had been almost instant. Even en route, before they'd reached their haven, Athas had been at work with the island's blacksmiths every time the column had stopped for the night. The result had been armour of the old Imperial style, with a decorative breastplate etched with images of heroic deeds and mythical figures, greaves and vambraces of embossed bronze and protective edged leather straps on the shoulders and thighs. He looked every inch the living embodiment of the ancient glorious statues of victorious Emperors and, despite his new status, he wore the pelt shoulder cloak of the Wolves to honour those men who'd given their lives for his. There had been no physical change in the young man. He'd not changed his hair or shaved off his beard and yet, despite this he seemed every inch the Emperor to the men at Hadrus. He had only to walk out into the square and people would fall to their knees – a trait, as Darius had confided in the general, that was beginning to annoy him. Strangely there had been no need for ceremony; Kiva had discussed it with Sarios and on the second morning of the journey they had gathered everyone together and announced their intention to defy Velutio and put a new Emperor on the throne. Darius had stepped forward with them, dressed in his old hunting leathers and the islanders and mercenaries had uniformly bowed without comment. Perhaps Sarios had primed them, but more likely their faith and trust in their leaders left them in no doubt that this was the right course. There would certainly be no love lost for Velutio. Every man present had either fought him or been imprisoned by him.

And there he stood, the Emperor in waiting with his commanders. Kiva smiled once more at the sight as he walked around the table and took his place beside his new lord.

Without the prompting he'd needed from Kiva only a month before, Darius leaned forward and placed his hands firmly on the edge of the table as he addressed Tythias.

"What news, Prefect?"

The one armed, one eyed ex mercenary, though every bit the proper soldier, was in company with whom he was tremendously close and grinned widely at the Emperor to be.

"Kiva's been teaching you to be far too formal, highness."

Darius smiled. "Got to practice, Tythias. I keep forgetting when I'm outside. One of the weavers saw me beheading weeds with a stick yesterday and the general here grilled me for hours over it."

Ignoring the scowl that crossed Caerdin's face, Tythias leaned back against the wall.

"There's good news and there's bad news, gentlemen. On the good side, I found Filus and Sithis and their units. They were already heading back toward Velutio; apparently things are getting a little hairy out west. Alongside the other units we were looking for, we hooked up with a couple of the lords who still favour you, so there should be six or seven thousand men arriving in the next few days, and about three hundred of them are veteran units we know well. The rest are just guards and men at arms for the lords, but they're at least partially trained, if not tested. Some of them are cavalry and we've got a couple of units of archers." He sighed. "Other Lords we saw were non-committal though. They're no great lovers of Velutio, but they're not about to stand up against him while our army remains up here, hidden in the mountains. I think a show of arms down on the plains would bring a number of other lords flocking to the banner, but I can't say I blame them for wanting to protect their land where they are now."

Kiva nodded thoughtfully. "And the bad news?"

"The bad news," Tythias replied, drawing a deep breath, "is that Velutio's heard about you now. He knows Caerdin and the Wolves are supporting what he calls a 'pretender-Emperor' and he's offering a rather large reward for news of the army's location. A number of the lords that might have swung our way are remaining resolutely his. He's threatening people you see?"

Kiva growled. "That man is nothing but bad news."

"Worse than that to some" Tythias said sadly. "We'd been to see Lord Palio and he was busy marshalling his men to march to Hadrus when Velutio turned up on his doorstep. He crucified every fifth man and, when Palio wouldn't give him our location, had him quartered and then burned in his own courtyard. We were there at the time. That Sabian may be Velutio's but damn I wish he was working for us. We'd left them involved in a battle out to the west when we went to Palio, but still they almost beat us there. How he managed that I'll never know."

"Sabian crucified and burned people?" Darius' voice quavered. "I can't believe that."

Tythias shook his head sadly. "He didn't give the orders, but he didn't walk away from it either. He's Velutio's chief officer and he's deep in his job now. Just be grateful he's out west and not over here."

The table fell silent for a moment until Kiva cleared his throat. "Well, if we get seven thousand in a few days, we've got just less than two here already. We've got a small unit at Munda watching the place and every now and then a unit looking for us appears there. With those odd stragglers we should number around ten thousand in a few weeks when we're ready to start moving. It's not too bad, but it could be better. Velutio's got twice that without calling up all his various allies, so I reckon he can count on outnumbering us around three to one at least. The only thing we've got going for us is the fact that all our people are fighting for a cause, while theirs are fighting because they have to. I need more information on the makeup of their forces and their plans before I can come up with any kind of coherent strategy."

He leaned forward and focused on Tythias. "Are any of the allies coming to join us the sort we can send in amongst them to spy for us?"

Tythias shook his head. "We avoided anyone of dubious loyalty and all the various independents are waiting to see what happens. I'm afraid you'll have to wait on Prince Ashar and his men for any more info. It's a bit of a bastard. We've watched his army in several engagements, but we've always had to stay a bit out of the way. The moment we're noticed, we're screwed."

Kiva nodded and turned to Darius. "I think we need to make a point. I need to be here to oversee things with Sarios and, to be honest, being in the saddle at the moment is incredibly uncomfortable to me. I think, though, that we need you and a colour party to go out and visit a few of these fence-sitters. Next time the Prefect rides out, you need to take Athas and Brendan and a hundred of the best men and go with them."

Darius blinked and Tythias started making opposing motions with his hands, but Kiva leaned further forward and pointed. "You're going to *have* to go out again. Have a day or two's respite; in fact, wait until your recruits get here, but then you need to head out again. Just to the lowlands; to the lords nearby who could be swayed with the right moves. With the Emperor and an honour guard and captains of the Wolves with you, you might be able to almost double our force. I really can't pass up that chance."

He turned to Sathina. "I'm sorry, and I know you've been looking forward to seeing Tythias again, but this is too important and at least he's not going to be heading into disputed areas this time."

Sathina nodded placidly. "General, I'm as much a part of this now as any of your men. I'd be stupid to let my personal feelings get in the way."

The general and the innkeeper's girl watched each other for the moment and then both nodded, but Tythias leaned across the table from his side, a wide grin splitting his face.

"I've a better idea. A military Emperor is what these people need, but what they *want* is pomp and grandeur. If Darius comes out with us, he needs to *be* an Emperor. He needs a retinue. Let Sarios and Sathina pick out a court to go with him. It'll make the lords feel more important if an entire Imperial court visits and they can be part of it. Sathina can go with me."

He turned his smile on the pretty girl. "That is, if you can cope with living in pampered luxury for a week or two…"

Kiva snorted. "Ok. I don't disagree. Once you two have got your lovey reunion over, go and see Sarios and sort it out. You leave the day after the new recruits arrive." He turned to Darius and grinned. "Sorry to lumber you with the lovebirds for a fortnight, but I daresay you can talk to Brendan and Athas and ignore these two."

Darius returned the smile and straightened. "That everything then? I…"

His sentence remained unfinished, as a breathless and dusty figure arrived in the doorway and saluted unsteadily.

"Sir… Highness, there's a small unit just coming up the hill t'ward the gate! No one we're expecting, sir."

Kiva slammed his fist on the table. "No-one knows where we are expect the people we're expecting. Tythias, you must have been followed."

Tythias bridled. "We were well clear of any of Velutio's army or allies. If someone followed us they must have been near here anyway or very well hidden."

The Emperor in waiting pushed past his general, grumbling. "If you two are just going to argue, *I'll* go and see who it is."

Darius strode out into the square, across the packed earth and stone, and up to the gate with his command group around him. The sentries on the gate had turned the massive bolt throwers down toward the path leading up the mountainside. The officers climbed the wooden stairs to the top and spread out along the battlements.

"Can you identify them? They've no flag" the young man muttered to his companions.

Kiva, next to him growled unpleasantly. "Oh, I can identify them alright. That's Phythian and his archers."

"Phythian?" the young man stepped back. "The man who gave you to Velutio?"

"The very bastard. Wonder what he's doing here." He gestured to one of the guards manning the huge bolt throwers. "Point that thing at the pompous ass down there and if he so much as blinks, let loose."

The unit of crossbowmen, almost a score strong, reigned in their horses not far from the gate and their commander, his fetching grey silk clothing stained brown with the dust.

"General Caerdin!" he called from the path. "We need to talk."

Kiva laughed derisively. "So talk! This gate's not opening until I know why you're here and make it fast. Convince me not to have you shot here and now."

Phythian laughed mirthlessly and swung sideways in his saddle, crossing his legs. "I've run out of time for Velutio. He's not a good employer and, to be honest, a little impatient and bloodthirsty even for me and my boys. Funny thing is: I've been hearing a lot of rumours recently that General Caerdin had resurfaced with a claimant to the throne. This I really had to see, since I'd last seen the good general being crucified and his claimant to the throne had gone the way of all flesh."

Darius nudged Kiva and the general realised his growling had been growing rather loud. He glared down at Phythian as the man continued.

"You're a very hard man to find, Caerdin. But I'd had my doubts about the Wolves that day in Serfium. I couldn't see your old ally Tythias butchering your men, so I just asked around until I found the Lion Riders and then followed them. You see, I think I'd rather throw in my lot with you and whatever potential Emperor you've got than help Velutio get to a point where he's the only employer there is. What d'you say?"

Kiva growled again in frustration and muttered among the others at the gate top "I don't trust him or like him, but we could really do with some good trained crossbowmen. They're few and far between." He reached into a pocket and removed a small copper coin, tossing it into the air where it tinkled to the floor of the gatehouse. He looked down. "Heads," he declared as he straightened and looked over to the soldier at the siege engine. "Kill him."

Phythian slipped from the saddle smoothly and dropped behind the horse. "He's a good horse. It'd be a shame to pierce him. Besides, Caerdin; I know you hate me, but I can be *very* useful to you. Can you afford to put the good of your new Emperor aside just for the pleasure of doing away with me?"

Kiva grunted and smacked his fist into his palm. "The bastard's right. I can't afford to turn them away." He leaned over the parapet.

"You'd have to swear the old oath to the Emperor, the People and the Gods, and take another oath to me and mine as your commanders if I even consider this."

Whatever Phythian said in reply was lost entirely as Kiva was hauled bodily around by his young Emperor. Darius, a hand on the general's shoulder, shook him. An angry glint flashed in his eyes. "You can't seriously be considering taking this fucking traitor in, general? I won't have him in the army."

Kiva stared back at him. "We can't turn down good trained men. We're not strong enough for that."

"Then take his men if they'll join," Darius growled, "but not him!"

"What about him then? I'd like to put a four foot iron bolt through him, but that's not going to inspire his men to join us. Velutio works on fear, not us. Our force grows and stays together because of loyalty."

Darius nodded. "You're right, but treachery needs to be dealt with too." The young Emperor leaned over the parapet in his full paraphernalia and glared down at the assembled folk below. "Captain Phythian? You're accused of treason, the unlawful confinement of innocent men and the murder of five of the Wolves, loyal servants of the Empire. I can either have you executed right now, or you can try and prove your innocence against your accuser?"

Kiva hauled the young Emperor back from the battlements. "Are you mad? He's not the best swordsman I know, but he's been fighting battles for twenty years or more. We can't afford to lose you over a whim like this!"

Darius grinned. "I'm a good swordsman, general. Believe me when I say I can handle myself and it'll do a lot for morale if I can pull this off."

Kiva shook his head. "Don't be fucking stupid. If you lose, the whole world loses!"

"Then I'd best not lose" the young man replied with a smile. "The challenge is given, so I can't really back out now, can I?"

Without waiting for Kiva's reply, he pulled away from him and leaned over the battlements once more. "Your answer?"

Phythian grinned. "I don't quite see it the same as you, your *highness*." He leaned back in the saddle. "And I'm not really sure that killing an Emperor is a good thing, but I suppose it did Caerdin no harm. I accept your challenge."

On the battlements, Kiva punched the stone wall so hard he drew blood from every knuckle. He growled and grumbled under his breath.

Darius stood straight once more and called out in a clear voice "open the gate and make the arena ready!"

Darius was aware, as the officers left the wall and the gates were swung open, of a malicious silence from the commander of his forces. Glancing sidelong at Kiva, he realised that the general was glaring at him. A month ago he would have made no decisions, particularly as important as this one, but it was the general's fault when all was said and done. Caerdin had been teaching and grooming him to take the position he was now in; they *all* had really, so they could hardly complain when he acted like the man he was expected to be. He *knew* that there were risks. He'd never fought to the death on his own; never fought a live target except during the escape from Isera, but this was something that, while it had risk, could also boost the morale of every man in Hadrus and, if the word got out, would put him that little higher on the Imperial pedestal. Darius was well aware that he was not born to the position, and had never aspired to it, but he'd read the histories; he knew the great Emperors. In earlier, more settled times, the Emperors Titus and Sarinus had both led their armies from the front; had both fought duels and made a name for themselves as personal combatants, and that was one thing that had made them great and popular. Velutio was too powerful to take on by sheer strength of arms; Darius would have to have the people behind him to make it through this. Another glance at the general as they strode across the square spoke volumes. The way Kiva watched him suggested the ageing general was sharing much the same thoughts.

The arena, though makeshift, was a fairly solid affair. The warden of the Imperial prison here had had it constructed for rebellious prisoners to fight each other. This was an Imperial prison, so they would never fight to the death, as the Emperors would occasionally have a change of heart and pardon someone, but there would be blood. Today, in the earth and timber arena, there would be blood again. Hopefully not Imperial blood.

Phythian's men were escorted, not quite as prisoners, to the edge of the arena, where they stood and watched their captain stride through the entrance. He'd left his crossbow and cloak outside and drew a long, narrow blade, flexing it and giving it a few practice swings. Behind him the huge timber gate was slid shut.

The other end of the arena remained open for long minutes as crowds of the men of Hadrus drifted in to the surrounding area, taking their place on the slope and vying for the best view of the sandy ground. Within minutes the expectant hum grew to become deafening as the command unit pushed their way to the front. Athas literally pushed men aside to make room for the general and his companions. Kiva stood watching the arena, his brows knitted together in unhappy concentration. Darius, the showman he was becoming, was waiting for the prime moment to enter.

And that moment came. The hum had died away, leaving a low susurration that permeated the air around the killing ground. Into the almost silence strode Darius, in his full armour with the shoulder pelt hanging from his sword arm side. His bronze breastplate shone in the early autumn sunlight as he stepped quietly to the mark that had been drawn in the sand. Removing his sword from its sheath, he swung the curved, northern blade a few times, stretching his arm muscles as the wooden gate was slid shut behind him.

The whispering died away into silence and Kiva watched intently, his knuckles white and his fingernails biting into the wooden perimeter. Next to him, Athas patted him on the shoulder.

"He's good. He really is."

"I bloody hope so," the general muttered, as the two men in the sandy oval started to walk slowly toward one another.

"He is, and he's got something to prove too. Better he does it here in these conditions than on a battlefield against a dozen."

Kiva grunted, his eyes fixed on the action before him, and shook his head as Darius picked up speed, making a run against his opponent. "Too soon."

The general looked away momentarily as Phythian danced lightly aside. Darius hadn't even swung his blade. Pirouetting gracefully, Darius came to a halt several feet from his opponent. Phythian smiled and flexed his sword once more. He spoke in lowered tones that would not be heard by the watching crowd. "I know you don't think much of me, young Emperor, but remember that it's a hard world out there and you do what you have to do to keep yourself and your unit afloat. It will give me absolutely no pleasure to draw your blood, let along kill you."

Darius grunted. "Contrition or excuses, captain? If you're willing to kill a young man of true Imperial blood, what makes you hesitate over me?"

Phythian stood straight and dropped his sword down to his side, point touching the floor. "I have been very wrong in some of my decisions and I freely admit that, but do not expect me to lay down my life easily just to appeal to your ego."

"My ego?" Darius laughed. "You really don't know me. This I do for the Wolves and for Quintillian, who was a brother to me. And for them," he added, gesturing at the crowd. "My ego has no say in this. Truth be told I've never killed anyone that didn't wish the same of me. Don't judge me by Velutio's standard."

With a smile, Phythian made a quick step forward and thrust his sword out at Darius' chest. It was a deliberately slow attack, designed to give the crowd something to watch. The young Emperor knocked it aside with practised ease.

"You expect me to lay down my cards and invite you into the fold because your conscience gnaws at you? You should have thought of that before you sacrificed people on the altar of Velutio's arrogance."

Phythian's smile widened. "You really do believe in this, don't you? You're actually prepared to face the most powerful man in the world and try to take everything away from him. I expected to find a puppet in the hands of Caerdin. You surprise me."

Darius' face remained flat and expressionless. "This verbal duelling is all very well, but it's not what they came to see. Problem is: now that we've started this, there's no way either of us can let the other walk out of here. You know that, don't you?"

Phythian's reply was lost in the action as he made another lunge, this time for real. The blade came dangerously close to Darius' neck, but he bent almost double, dipping out of the way of the blade and bringing his own sword up in a swing that Phythian barely blocked. The

300

two stepped back once more, aware of the roar and murmur of the crowd.

"Truly," the captain commented. "Shame, though. I think in retrospect I'd have liked to have fought with you. You remind me of Kiva in the old days."

As Darius raised an eyebrow, Phythian flexed his muscles. "I suppose we'd best give the crowd what they want, then?"

The young Emperor nodded as Phythian transferred the sword back to his right hand and took a step to the side. The next attack, when it came, was swifter again than the last and from a very unexpected angle, the blade coming down from a height. Darius twisted once more and brought his own sword up to block it, dropping to one knee and rolling beneath as the blade swept down and across. Even as he came back up, he was moving, the sword flicking out behind him and almost catching the captain in the back as he turned.

Again and again they lunged, ducked and leapt, their swords glinting and flickering in the afternoon light, dancing their deadly waltz in the sand. The crowd around them caught their breath; groaned; cheered, and still the energetic frenzy went on.

And suddenly the crowd moaned in dismay. Phythian, coming out of a spin, had lunged forward unexpectedly, his blade piercing Darius' thigh just above the knee and pushing through until it appeared, covered in life blood, from the back. The disbelief and anguish was palatable. Phythian was smiling, where he stood leaning over the crouched Emperor, his blade dripping onto the sand.

And then, grin still fixed to his face, he toppled gently backwards and, as he did, Darius' sword slowly unsheathed itself from the captain's torso, where it had driven in low in the stomach and penetrated inside vertically, almost to the neck. A wash of blood splashed out as the tip of the blade came free and Phythian, shuddering, fell to the sand.

Darius staggered sideways and slowly pulled the blade from his leg, gritting his teeth. He crouched over the shaking body.

"The Gods take you Captain Phythian" he intoned, but the captain gripped his arm.

"Help me up!"

A frown upon his brow, Darius staggered under the weight of the dying captain and slowly hauled him to his feet. As he came upright, a great gob of dark blood poured from the man's mouth and he coughed to clear his throat of blood. He took a deep unsteady breath, the horrible noises from within suggesting that Darius' blade had sheared one of his lungs, Phythian shouted out across the arena.

"Hail the Emperor!"

As the last syllable fell from his mouth along with deep red, he slumped against Darius' shoulder and slid gently to the sand.

For a long time there was silence as the young man stood, putting the weight on his good leg and looking down at the body of the crossbow captain, a confusing mix of emotions running through him. He was vaguely aware of the roar from the crowd and noted without reaction that the commanders had hauled the gate aside and were running across the arena toward him. He looked up in confusion as he was hauled up by the shoulders and all but carried across the sand. Kiva fell in beside him.

"That was brave, selfless, impressive, and stupid. You did well, but don't ever do anything like that again, do you hear me?"

Darius nodded vaguely, still dazed. He barely felt the pain in his leg, though he knew he would later when the adrenaline had faded. H left the arena in the arms of his friends as the crowd went wild with joy over the personal victory of their Emperor. Now all he had to do was give them a victory on the battlefield.

Athas shook his shoulder gently and he looked up in confusion to see Phythian's men standing in two lines alongside the path, their arms locked in the traditional Imperial salute and their heads bowed respectfully.

All things considered, he might be getting the hang of this Emperor thing after all.

Chapter XXVI.

Victory was rarely a thing to be savoured in the immediate aftermath. Sabian glanced with some distaste at the sight of small parties of soldiers piling the bodies of Lord Pelian's men in heaps, preparing for 'disposal'. The survivors had been marched into one of the barrack buildings at the lord's palace, locked in, and were under the guard of Sergeant Iasus' and his men. Pelian and his commander and family, on the other hand, had been delivered to Lord Velutio after the battle and Sabian could see them all standing on the hill just ahead with a number of men from one of Sabian's better units.

He took a deep breath and then clamped his mouth shut as he strode at speed past the rapidly charring remains of the enemy commander where what was left of him dangled from his chains. Even with his breath held, he couldn't fully avoid the smell and fought the impulse to gag. Ahead, Velutio stood with Pelian and his wife and child just out of range of the foul smoke.

Grumbling unhappily under his breath, Sabian strode up to his lord, glancing at the prisoners. The boy and the woman had not been harmed yet, though Pelian himself had been roughly dealt with and showed signs of some serious beating. Behind them, ominously, two more sets of chains had been hammered into the palace wall, one at the same level as the commander's and the other just over half that height. Velutio turned at the sound of the boots crunching on the gravel and smiled a mirthless smile.

"Commander. Report?"

"Somewhere in the region of eight hundred enemy dead, lord. They're being prepared for disposal in burial pits, though again I would ask that we make time for proper burials." As Velutio shook his head, Sabian went on. "Almost five hundred survived, though a lot of them are wounded. They're all contained in the palace barracks, but their doctor died during the fighting, so the wounded are receiving no help."

"Then they'll die," the lord said flatly. "I'm not sparing them our medics. We have wounded of our own. What's our situation?"

Sabian shrugged. "We lost just under two hundred, with roughly another hundred badly wounded and a couple of hundred minor wounds that can still campaign. I've detailed a small medical support party to escort the badly wounded and the dead back to Velutio and commandeered the necessary horses and wagons from this estate."

Velutio nodded gravely and turned back to his captives.

"You see Pelian? Your loyalty does you credit, but the time is long past for such heroics. Your army is gone, your wounded are receiving no attention, and your commander has been executed for non-compliance. Really, everything is lost for you now except your lovely wife and your son. You don't want me to continue where we left off, surely?"

Pelian slumped. "I keep telling you, I don't *know* where they are. I shouldn't think anyone does. I never made a deal with them, I never pledged my allegiance to him, and I never planned to send him my army."

Velutio sighed and hauled on the rope, pulling the other lord back up to his knees. "I've heard the same story from four other lords. You all claim to be fighting for your independence, and yet everywhere I go I see signs of treachery. My scouts saw Captain Tythias and his Lion Riders at your palace just over a week ago. Perhaps they dropped in for a cup of wine with you? To talk about old times?"

He hauled hard on the rope and Pelian gagged as the noose tightened around his neck. "Now, I will ask you one more time and if I don't receive a satisfactory reply, I will have your son chained and burned. I don't want to have to kill such a young child, but I *will not* be hindered by a small lord with a misplaced sense of duty. *Where* are Caerdin and his rebels?"

One of the three soldiers behind them hauled the boy to his feet.

Sabian growled again and stepped forward. "Lord Pelian… answer him for the Gods' sake. Don't let your son burn. Caerdin knows what he's started. He's not innocent, but your boy is. Be sensible."

Pelian stared at his son and at his wife, tears in his eyes and sagged, deflating.

"Munda. We were meeting at Munda. I don't know if that's where he's based, but that was the meeting place."

Sabian nodded in relief as the smile crossed Velutio's face. The steely-grey lord let go of the rope. "Munda… Makes sense. It's unused these days and Caerdin probably has friends there. An army could certainly be marshalled and trained there." He looked at the prisoners and drew a knife, reaching down toward the noose around Pelian's neck. The captive lord leaned back to allow access to the rope and stared in shock as Velutio drew the blade hard across his neck just below the rope. He tried to speak, but there was just a whistling noise from his open neck and a bloody froth from both there and his mouth. His eyes still staring in amazement, he toppled to one side. Sabian shook his head; he'd known it was coming. Velutio was nothing if not predictable.

The old lord stood once more, ignoring the wailing of lady Pelian where she struggled to free herself from a soldier's grip. Walking slowly over to the boy, Velutio took the rope from the guard and lifted it from the boys' neck. Reaching behind, he cut the other cord binding the lad's hands and all the while the boy stared at him. No tears; no quivering lip, just cold hatred. As the boy's hands came free, Velutio stepped back.

"You're now the lord Pelian. Your father once took an oath to me and he broke it. Remember that, as you're bound by the same oath. You're free to go about your business. As soon as we're ready to move out, your troops will be left as they are and you can tend to your wounded as best you can and bury your dead honourably."

He turned back to Sabian, paying no further attention to the glaring boy and the screaming woman. "Munda."

The commander nodded and squared his shoulders. "I need to talk with you my lord; privately."

Velutio nodded and the two stepped away, leaving the three soldiers with the distraught woman hugging the body of her husband. The young boy continued to stand, motionless, watching Velutio with visible loathing.

As they began to amble slowly down the hillside, Sabian cleared his throat. "I would like to think that I've only ever offered you good advice my lord."

Velutio nodded. "On the whole I agree, Sabian. Maybe I should have followed some of your advice at times when I did not, but we're in a position of power now, so I think everything may have worked out for the best."

Sabian nodded uncertainly. "Perhaps. However, I have several things that I feel you need to hear and I would urge you to seriously consider them."

"Go on."

The commander clasped his hands behind his back as they walked, watching the soldiers gathering their wounded comrades into huddled groups while wagons were brought up. "Firstly, you can't leave the boy alive now. Much as I hate it, you've killed his father and he'll seek revenge now until he's an old man. I saw his eyes. He's not frightened, just angry."

"You may be right. However, in addition to serving as a lesson to any who would break their oath, his continued existence speaks of

305

my mercy and you're always urging me to show that. We'll leave it until this war is over and then see what we shall see; after all, he's only a young boy. What else?"

Sabian nodded. He hadn't expected the lord to follow his advice, but it was his duty to give it. "Secondly, this war is headed for a conclusion of epic proportions. Our campaign here has been surgical, dealing with insurrections and small independents. What's coming, on the other hand, will be a bloodbath that will wreck the Empire. I know we'll win; I have not a doubt about that, but we need to think about what happens afterwards. Our army will be decimated and there won't be a lot of manpower to draw on to replace it. Many of the men on both sides are farmers and craftsmen when they're not on campaign and our economy could be in trouble if so many are lost in one swoop. When you're Emperor and our army is not yet recovered we'll be easy pickings for the barbarian tribes; I can't imagine they'll stand by and let the Empire build back up to be the enemy it was decades ago. We will need stability, manpower and money in order to rebuild after all the damage of the last two decades. All in all, war will put you on the throne, but it may make keeping that throne untenable."

"You're suggesting I step down?" asked Velutio with some surprise.

"No, Lord. Not that. But there are other ways than direct conflict on such a scale. We know where the enemy are, but not their composition. They could even have a force approaching the size of ours now. Why cause that bloodbath if it could be avoided?"

"Go on" said Velutio, one eyebrow raised.

Sabian took a deep breath. "Peace. Publicly declare your intention to adopt Darius and offer him co-rulership. After all, that was your intention in the first place, before Caerdin pitted him against you. Offer amnesty for their army and its leaders. You could bring this whole thing down to a political hand-shake without a single drop of blood."

Velutio laughed. "For a man of war, you seem to do everything you can to avoid it, Sabian."

The commander shrugged. "A real soldier will always avoid the battle if there is another way round. Only psychopaths seek battle for battle's sake, lord."

Velutio shook his head. "I might be willing to adopt Darius now and even pardon the various lords that have fallen in with them, but there is no way this side of the river of Death that I'll let the Wolves, the Lion Riders or any of the Islanders live after this. They've

306

pitted themselves against me, not I against them, and now I'll see it through to the bitter end."

Velutio looked sidelong at his commander, who seemed to be fighting his irritation. "I agree in principle with what you say. I'll have my scribes draft a letter offering Darius exactly what he wants and amnesty to the other lords on the condition that Caerdin, Tythias, Sarios and their supporters give themselves up to me. That is as far as I will compromise."

Sabian nodded. It was a small gesture that would likely fail, but it was better than he'd expected. Velutio was not known for his leniency. "Very well," the commander sighed. "I'll have a small party put together to deliver your terms, lord."

"Sabian," the old lord laughed, "you really try to be the voice of reason in an unreasonable world. Your principles are always of the highest quality and you are a great believer in ethics, itself an unusual characteristic in a military commander, but the Empire is a corrupt and debased place these days, and there's precious little room for idealism. Still," he smiled, "it's refreshing to see at times."

Sabian bowed slightly and saluted before he turned and walked away down the hill toward where sergeant Cialo was issuing instructions to groups of soldiers. As he walked he mulled over choices he'd make for better or for worse. Perhaps he had been unwise to allow the islanders to leave Isera, and particularly to let Caerdin free to wage his own war but when it all came down to it the Empire, once it was back on its feet, would need men like Caerdin and Sarios. Velutio was blinded enough by ancient vendettas that he couldn't see the value of men like that, but Sabian could look past the foundation of a new dynasty to where men of vision and intelligence would be needed. Still, Velutio had pushed hard for the last half year and had dealt with whatever appeared before him with the surety of a man possessed. Sabian had played his part as best he could not to be just a general for his army, but to be advisor, counsellor and conscience. It would be satisfying to think even in a small way how much innocent blood had been spared by his interjection but, since there were limits to his influence and his lordship would not follow his counsel along certain paths, he may well be the cause of the greatest war to shake the Empire in over two centuries. That was a disturbing thought and one that came back to him at night when the shadows lengthened. He'd done everything he could to avoid innocent victims but, in doing so, he'd pitted two great armies against each other. In a way, he'd *created* the rebel force.

Grumbling, he tossed around the decisions he'd made and opportunities he'd missed as he walked, staring at the ground, and almost knocked over a man carrying a wounded soldier.

"Watch where you're going!" A little unjust and harsh, but the way his mood was taking him... He stopped and stared at the man with the wounded soldier.

"Wait..." the sentence went unfinished as Sabian looked down. Though the man was a ragged conscript soldier in the clothes of a peasant spearman, the body he was supporting was clearly a dead man up this close and, as his eyes strayed downwards, the knife the man had pressed against Sabian's liver, just under the edge of his armour, was a well-honed and beautiful blade.

"You have my attention" he said, satisfied that if the wielder had wanted to kill him, he could have done it by now.

The man smiled and Sabian was suddenly aware that the peasant was anything but what he seemed. Indeed, he was a man of lithe and energetic frame, short but elegant and with a dark, weather-beaten face.

"Commander Sabian. Interesting. I've no orders for your death, though I doubt the Emperor would lament it under the circumstances."

Sabian frowned. "If by 'Emperor' you mean young Darius, I would think twice. I doubt he would look favourably on you. You're a Pelasian I guess? One of Prince Ashar's spies or assassins?"

"I would call myself a scout," grinned the small man, "though I am multi-talented. An interesting situation we find ourselves in. What are we to do now? Shall I kill you?"

Sabian relaxed a little and the blade scraped against his cuirass as he sank back. "You have the advantage. You can kill me or leave, but I would urge the latter. We have a message to deliver to general Caerdin and you could deliver it for us."

A smile. His only answer.

"A letter," repeated Sabian, "offering terms for a cessation of hostilities. We know you're at or near Munda and there's no way you can beat us in a land battle. I know it and so does Caerdin."

The small man let the dead body next to him drop to the ground and sheathed his knife. "I trust to your word. My Prince and the Emperor both hold you in high esteem. Give me this letter and I will carry it for you."

Sabian smiled. "Just wait here for a moment. I must speak to my sergeant, then I'll be back to see you and we'll go and visit his lordship."

308

Without taking his eyes off the Pelasian spy, Sabian walked further down the hill to where Cialo stood watching him with interest. The veteran pulled himself to attention and saluted.

"Commander. Nothing much to report sir."

Sabian nodded distractedly. "I wish I could say the same." He looked around to see if they were alone. Two soldiers stood digging a pit out of earshot and the Pelasian watched him from the slope with interest. Unlikely the man would be able to hear anything.

"Cialo, his lordship is sending a letter of terms to the rebels. The man over there," he gestured at the small figure, "is a Pelasian; one of Ashar's, and I'm sending him with a letter back to Munda where Lord Pelian informs us the rebels are based. I'm afraid I've a job for you, sergeant."

Cialo nodded wearily. "I expect so, sir."

"I need a small party of men to accompany this Pelasian. Needless to say, it could be extremely dangerous. If you get taken to Caerdin, you'll be able to confirm that's where their base is and that bodes rather badly for you, but I think their commanders are honourable enough that they won't hurt you." He frowned. "And for all my bluster to his lordship about certainty, I'd give a lot to know exactly what this force consists of. You can find that out for me. Take a half dozen of your most diplomatic men with you... men like Crispin; people who got on well with the islanders, you know."

Cialo nodded. "Yes, commander. I'll get some men and some horses and report to the command post as soon as, sir."

As Cialo hurried off to put together a party of men, Sabian sighed and gazed around the battlefield once more. It had been an easy victory, but then they'd outnumbered Pelian by a huge margin. This might not always be this easy.

Julius Pelianus had turned eight years old this summer. In his short life he'd watched three other lords of lands hereabouts fall to mercenary forces or retributive strikes by their enemies, but it had always remained a distant thing; a 'something that happens to other people' affair. And then this afternoon, he'd seen his father's throat cut by the man whom he had apparently served. Anger coursed anew through his veins as he thought of his mother where he'd left her, heaped over the body of his father, crying in anguish. He'd not cried. There was grief, of course, but something stronger, hard and heavy as a rock had settled in his chest and he couldn't have shed a tear now if he'd tried. He'd waited until the soldiers had been ordered back into formation and marched off over the crest of the hill in search of fresh slaughter and then with only a single, wordless glance at his family, had walked purposefully back into the courtyard of the palace.

The bodies of his father's army hadn't been buried. They hadn't even been cleared away very thoroughly, resting instead in heaps where Velutio's soldiers had gathered them. Pausing at the gate to the palace, he examined one such pile of lifeless corpses. The less tasteful members of Velutio's army had done a good job of looting their enemies as they heaped them up. Most of the jewellery was missing, along with fingers where the knuckle had been too tight for them to slip off the rings. Some of the better armour and weapons had gone too, but a lot had been left. He reached down without flinching into the pile and laid his hand on the slimy hilt of a sword. Dragging it out, still covered in blood, he had trouble lifting it higher than his knee. Another delve and he managed to locate the man's sword belt and spent a moment unbuckling it and feeding it out. Finally he was able to sheathe the sword and discovered that, so long as the belt was tight and high and not slouching around his hips, the sword swung freely as he moved without dragging on the floor.

Armed, he made his way to the barrack block. There were four such buildings attached to the curtain walls surrounding the palace, each home to a hundred and fifty men with the rest garrisoned in the main building or outlying fortlets. These huge, long, low stone buildings were divided into fifteen large rooms, each with bunk beds sleeping ten men, leading off a single long corridor with a heavy external door at each end. Velutio's men had left, but had made sure that life would be as uncomfortable and short as possible for their beaten enemy. All the wooden shutters over the windows had been closed and nailed shut with heavy planks of wood and the two doors had been sealed in a similar fashion. Despite the lord's assurance that the guards would not be harmed, the devils had gathered a large pile of wood and cloth and a few bodies against one of the doors and set fire to it. Though it had been less than fifteen minutes since the men could have done this, the smoke and the stench were terrible and inside the building the oxygen would fast be running out. Presumably the men would shut themselves in their rooms, but the boy was willing to bet the bastards had removed the internal doors. In fact it looked suspiciously like those doors had been broken up and used to seal the building.

Julius ran to another pile of bodies and located a heavy fighting knife. Snatching it, he ran back across to the second door and jammed the blade behind the nailed wooden bar. Heaving with all his might he thought he heard the bar creak, but there was no visible movement and now a slight kink in the blade. Desperately now, he ran to the nearest shuttered window and tried the same. The blade snapped sharply and he fell back to the ground.

Looking around the courtyard, his eyes fell upon two of the farm horses tied up near the other gate and an idea struck him. These horses were not good specimens; flea-bitten and old and no use to the victorious army, they had been left behind. Trying hard to ignore the third horse that had been used for target practice, Julius untied the reins and then, gripping both in one hand, geed up the horses, leading them across the cobbles. At the barracks once more, he spent a long moment feeding the leather reins through the heavy iron handle of the door. Tying them off as tightly as he could, he stepped back and slapped the horses' rumps as hard as he could. The reins became taught and strained and the timber creaking at the tremendous stress it had been placed under but steadfastly refused to give. Determined, Julius urged the horses on desperately and became aware of another noise. Someone inside must have realised what was going on. There were tremendous heavy thuds as something heavy was slammed into the inside of the heavy oak door. With renewed vigour, Julius slapped the horses once more and then added what little weight he had to the rope, hauling for all he was worth.

When the door gave, it opened with a crash, splinters and chunks of wood bouncing across the cobbles. The horses hurtled across the courtyard and disappeared from the boy's field of vision as he sprawled, winded, on the floor. Thick, dark smoke billowed out of the door and panicky, choking men spewed out into the open air, collapsing to the ground and retching. Julius sat up and watched, slightly dazed from a chunk of wood that had struck a glancing blow to his head.

Gradually the men who'd been crammed in, enduring inhuman conditions inside for almost an hour and life-threatening smoke for a quarter of that time, spilled out into the courtyard, catching their breath and then moving to make room for the others pushing away behind them. Somewhere among the flood of choking men, a sergeant that the boy recognised looked up from his choking and gagging and noticed him.

"Julian? Thank the gods."

The boy's face didn't look grateful. In fact, from the first glance the sergeant knew that something terrible had happened.

"What is it? Where have they gone?"

311

Julian rubbed his sore head and stood slowly and carefully. The sergeant noted with surprise and some trepidation the sword slung at the young lad's side. He was about to enquire again when the boy yelled out "Quiet!"

It was not a strong voice. Barely audible even above the coughing and choking sounds, still it caught the attention of enough of the men that their coughing became lower; muted, they turned to see from where the small but highly emotional voice had come. Julius stretched and then, turning, climbed up onto a broken barrel behind him.

"I said quiet!"

Men five times his age fell silent and stared at the young man. The sergeant leaned forward, his arms on his knees. "We're listening, young master."

The boy gripped the hilt of his sword with white knuckles. "Your lord, my father, is dead; killed by Lord Velutio. That makes *me* the lord of this estate now and I need you."

By now all other sound had died away and everyone faced the young lord, though still sharing surprised glances.

"I heard my father tell the murderer before he died that there are some rebels who are defying him at a place called Munda. Someone called Caerdin. I don't know who he is, but if he's an enemy of Velutio, that makes him my friend. I'm leaving here. Today. And I'm going to find this Munda and this Caerdin. I want to pledge my family's support to him and that means you men."

A low muttering rippled through the crowd and the boy raised his voice a little again.

"I know you've just fought a hard battle, and if you want to go back to your homes and protect your lands you can. How could I stop you? But I'm going to find these rebels and I'm asking any of you who still have the strength to come with me."

One of the soldiers leaned back and waved an arm.

"'Ow're you going to find 'em, Julian? I've a vague idea where Munda is, but I doubt there's anyone 'ere who knows 'ow to get there, 'specially when we'd got to avoid Velutio and all 'is allies."

Julian frowned. "I don't know, but we'll find out. I'm going to get justice for my father no matter what it takes."

An uncomfortable silence settled on the courtyard as soldiers glanced at each other and then back at the young lord on his half-barrel.

A voice somewhere among the crowd cut through the silence; a slightly croaky sound, but strong. "I know where Munda is. I can take you there and by fairly safe routes."

Julian strained to see through the drifting smoke, still wisping around the courtyard. An old man sat clutching one knee. He had long grey hair or would have, had he not suffered some dreadful disfiguring wound many years ago. The left side of his head was devoid of hair, marked with scars and furrows that continued down his face and cheek as far as his neck. He wore the uniform of Pelian's army, but the boy couldn't remember ever seeing him before. Still, he'd never spent much time with his father's troops, so it was no surprise that even this frightening specimen of a man was unknown to him.

"I can guarantee your safety and acceptance" the man continued. "I know general Caerdin of old. I served with him a long time ago."

The man grinned, an unpleasant sight, given the dreadful facial wounds he'd suffered, and took a deep swig from a darkened metal flask emblazoned with a wolf's head.

Chapter XXVII.

Kiva stood, leaning on the fence with his elbows, watching the training. Sithis, the captain of the 'Swords' had named his unit well. Twenty and more years ago the man had been a captain in Kiva's army and, when Caerdin had disappeared and the army had fallen apart following Velutio's rise to power and the collapse of Imperial order Sithis, like many other officers, had taken a unit and gone his separate way. Sithis, however, unlike the others, had not taken his own unit per se, but had carefully selected a number of men he especially had his eye on. Consequently, the 'Swords' had been born of some of the best swordsmen the Imperial army had to offer. And it showed in their training methods, even in just the four days since Sithis and his unit had arrived. Some of the lowliest men who'd turned up at Munda had been indentured farmers whose livelihoods had been swept away from under them by Velutio's reprisals against unsupportive lords or just his pure acquisition of lands. And some of these peasants who'd never wielded anything more dangerous than a hoe in their lives had a glint of steel in their eye and swiped and parried as well as the career soldiers. Sithis' regime was tough and lasted almost as long as the light each day.

All in all the training was going well. They'd made last minute plans before Tythias and Darius and their party had left on the political mission to gather support. Sithis, Marco and Mercurias had stated that the more time they got to train the army, the better chance they would stand when they finally brought someone to battle, but equally, Sarios and Kiva had pointed out that every day their army got better, Velutio's army and power grew. In the end, a route was agreed that would take the Emperor's entourage in a circuit through seven of the more local lords in the space of two weeks, returning to Hadrus then. One more week would be allowed for any lords who joined them to reach the meeting point at Munda, and then the army would march, hopefully picking up further allies as they travelled.

There were approaching ten thousand men stationed at Hadrus now and, with the exception of certain mercenary units that maintained their independence due to the specific tasks they'd been allocated, the entire force had been organised along traditional Imperial lines. There had been some grumbling among lords who thought they were far too clever commanders to have been allocated lesser positions, such as quartermaster or officer of only a hundred men, but on the whole most people had been placed in positions for which they were suited. The private forces of the various lords had been broken up and dispersed

314

alongside some of the lesser mercenary units and prior loyalties had been abandoned; Kiva had made that clear in his first speech to the army. Every new recruit, no matter what his background, was made to take the oath once more, to Darius, to the people and to the Empire. A second oath had been elicited from every man, pledging individual allegiance to their own officer and the commanders of the army.

It was with tremendous satisfaction that Kiva noted how speedily the engineers had been put together and how little outside organisation and training was required. Engineers were always like that though, and the entire corps had been formed of men with prior engineering experience or interest. They knew their jobs and enjoyed them and the entire force had been constructing, testing and reworking different machines from the moment they'd first formed. Now, in what was once the massive exercise yard of the prison, bolt throwers, catapults, siege engines and strange constructions that Kiva couldn't easily identify lined the walls and he could see even now a half dozen engineers crawling over one of them with tools and sheets of schematics.

The cavalry was nominally under the command and guidance of Tythias, though due to his continued absence, one of his men had remained in Hadrus to train and organise them. Kiva had never been a great believer in the value of cavalry on the battlefield, though Tythias had argued vociferously for their inclusion at a command level. Given his own way, Kiva would use them only as scouts and light, mounted skirmishers, but Tythias had badgered Athas until the big sergeant had ordered his armourers to begin work on chain armour for the steeds. The Lion Riders intended to make serious use of heavy cavalry after the fashion of the eastern peoples.

As Kiva stood watching, a small unit of newly-recruited horsemen in full uniform came riding into the cavalry training area, a large space of lawn that had been previously unused just inside the walls. Dressed in shirts of chain mail that hung down to their knees, they each carried an oval shield and a short spear, with a long sword hanging by the belt loop from the saddle. They clutched the reins and hauled on them as they reached their training officer, a Lion Rider named Peris, who shook his head in irritation.

"Firstly, forget everything you've ever been taught about horses. You're all either trained to ride for fun or sport or you've been trained for battle by an idiot."

There was a grumbling among the horsemen.

"Shut the fuck up. When I talk, you listen and you pay attention. Every one of you needs to lean forward and remove the reins, bit, bridle; the whole frigging lot from all your horses."

Three of the men did so immediately while the others stared at each other. One brave young man thrust a hand in the air.

"This is not a fucking classroom, lad. What?"

"Sir," the young man asked, "why are we getting rid of our reins?"

Peris growled. "You've all been given proper military saddles. I intend to show you how to use them. The saddles are different from the ones you're used to. The four horns at the corners are keeping you wedged in your seat, as I presume you've noticed. You'll also have noticed there's no stirrups. I'm going to teach you how to control your steed with just your knees. Your feet will be free to kick the horse gently or any footman bloody hard. Your hands'll be free to wield both sword, spear and shield liberally without having to fight for control with the horse too."

As he spoke, others began to remove their reins. "As far as your weapons are concerned, you'll bear your shield on your left arm, whether you're left *or* right handed. You'll go into any combat with the spear. Don't throw the fucking thing; that's a waste. When you first ride in, jam it under your arm and lock it as best you can and aim for the torso of the man in front of you. If you're lucky you'll impale the bastard and the spear'll break. If you're *really* lucky, you'll do that and the spear won't break. Best you can realistically hope to get from it's three goes; they don't last that long. You'll then draw your sword and go to work."

The last of the men was now removing his bridle and they sat holding the leather straps aimlessly. The training officer grumbled in his throat.

"You can make use of *them* too. Use your sword and cut a two-foot length of leather from the reins. Then tie it *real* tight around the hilt of your sword, just by the guard. Loop it a couple of times and hang it back on the saddle horn. When you finish with your spear, if you do this, you'll be able to slip the sword off the horn and go straight to work instead of struggling to remove the belt loop. As you do it, you can wrap the leather around your wrist. When you hit someone hard, your arm'll jar and if you're not careful you'll drop the sword. If it's bound to your wrist it won't leave you defenceless."

Kiva smiled. It reminded him so much of his early days at Vengen. This was what the world lacked these days: order and sense.

316

And that was one of the best reasons for doing what they were doing. He turned, still listening to the commander barking out instructions.

"Your horses will be slower and heavier and more difficult to handle when their barding's complete. Several stone of chainmail will make them less responsive, so you'll need to work with them..."

His voice trailed off as the general walked away from the fence. The whole place was alive with activity. He strolled past the forges and furnace where Athas had homed all the personnel with any skill at smithing. Only three men had known how to manufacture chainmail links and put them together, but with expert supervision, that number had grown quickly and shirts and horse armour were now being churned out daily. Still, faster production was needed. Beyond was the punishment yard. Here, decades ago, prisoners who'd broken the rules had been flogged or beaten or locked in the sweat-box. Now it was lined with dummies and targets along the two ends, with standing positions marked in the middle.

Archers had been trained not en masse, but in highly adaptable and mobile units of forty, with these units being brought together in fives under the command of individual missile commanders. It was at times like this when his thoughts turned to the Wolves they'd lost recently. Thalo would have been the best man to command and train the archers; there was no one better. But he was gone and his killers, the crossbowmen of Captain Phythian had been amalgamated with Filus' Western Legion's archers for the sake of surety of their loyalty. They stood in the centre of the punishment yard, ploughing bolt after bolt into the dummies and targets. The speed and accuracy was truly impressive, though even thinking about it pushed him once more into thoughts of the Wolves that these men had killed. A low growl escaped his throat and he forced himself to remember why they were here. They'd taken new oaths and worked with a trustworthy commander now. And they were an asset.

He was still brooding when a voice behind him said "and do you trust them?"

The general turned to see Sithis standing behind him. The captain of the Swords had been a real ladies' man in the old days, a swashbuckler and a man of some reputation among the court. These days, despite twenty some years passing, he really hadn't changed a great deal. The one visible scar he'd picked up ran lightly along his cheek under his eye and did nothing to mar features that still turned the heads of the women at Hadrus. Kiva was fairly sure the captain hadn't spent a night alone since his arrival and the thought made him smile.

"I'm trying to. It's not really their fault. Our men would do stupid things if we ordered them to. That makes it Phythian's fault, and he's already paid for it."

Sithis walked up next to his commander and leaned heavily on the fence. "You don't actually believe that though, do you? I know my men would do it, because I prefer skill and obedience to the ability to command. My men were all swordsmen in their time. Yours were all commanders themselves and they all think like officers. If you'd ordered the Wolves to kill Tythias and his men, do you really think they would?"

Kiva shrugged. "I suppose not, but then these men here weren't selected for their command ability or ethics, just for their ability with a crossbow. I suppose they deserve a chance. Besides," he added as he turned again, "they took the oaths and I'm as bound by them as they are."

Sithis nodded, a quirky smile on his face. "I got a chance quickly to meet Tythias' young lady before they left. How in the name of every god with sense did a battered wreck like him end up with such a gorgeous little woman as that?"

Kiva laughed. "War makes people do crazy things. That little woman infiltrated Velutio's palace to find us when we were all neck deep in shit. If it weren't for her this wouldn't be happening. She's got the respect of every officer here."

"And the hearts and minds of a few too, I'll bet" replied Sithis with a grin.

"Well what about you? Now you're here I doubt there's a single woman in the camp that's not falling over themselves just to wash your tunics?"

Sithis' grin grew wider. "Can I help it if I'm beautiful?"

The two laughed for a moment and then fell silent, listening to the swipe, twang and thud of crossbow practice. After a while the swordsman cleared his throat, glancing down at the weapon hanging from the general's belt. "What happened to your sword? That's new, isn't it?"

Kiva nodded. "Mine's probably decorating one of Velutio's rooms somewhere. This one's alright, but it's just not the same."

"Can you use it?" Kiva glanced across at his training officer with narrowed eyes. The question was loaded with more than just a light query over his new sword.

"Let's go examine the Emperor's new quarters while we talk," the general commented quietly. Sithis nodded and the two of them

318

began to wander towards the residential area of the camp. Long, low buildings that had been cell blocks had been converted for habitation among the army. Out of deference to their status, those who were commanders, civilians or craftsmen had been given the prison guards' quarters to convert. Darius had, of course been given the best available. The greatest building in Hadrus, the chief warden's quarters, may have been converted into the headquarters, but the villa that had been put aside and hastily converted for their new Emperor was as sumptuous as possible in their somewhat limited circumstances. After Kiva's reorganisation of the forces at their command, he'd set aside two hundred men as an Imperial Guard. They'd all been selected by their commanders as the best and most loyal and had all taken a further oath in private to the Emperor and the general. Their loyalty, while nothing in the world at the moment could be truly sure, was unquestioned, and though a hundred of them had accompanied Darius on his travels, the rest remained here to protect his interests. They answered officially to Darius alone, though the young Emperor had told them to follow any orders given them by any man of the Wolves or the Lion Riders. Two such guards stood either side of the door to the Imperial residence, at attention and heavily armed, wearing the black and green uniform displaying the raven and the crown. They saluted as Kiva and Sithis approached and the general returned a half-hearted gesture.

"We're not here to steal the Emperor's valuables, but we need somewhere private for a short time. Go get yourselves a bite to eat. Be back in an hour to resume your posts."

Without a word, the two men saluted again and then fell out, walking swiftly towards the cookhouse. Sithis smiled. "They're just like the palace guard used to be when Quintus was in charge."

"Yes, and with just as much sense of humour." The general opened the door and wandered inside, holding it open for his junior officer. As Sithis entered, he looked around appraisingly while Kiva shut the door once more. It was clear to anyone who knew Darius that the decoration of this entrance hall was not his work. Probably Athas had most of the say. Banners hung from the side walls displaying Imperial symbols, maps of the Empire plastered the rear wall and everything was painted in bright, rich colours. With a smile, Kiva opened the side door into the study Darius tended to use; the only room Kiva had spent time in. This room was virtually bare of decoration, though cluttered with maps, weapons, lists and books. Copies of Peoro's 'On Warfare' and Rastus' 'Battles of the Late Empire' lay open on a desk. Kiva smiled. *This* was the Darius he knew.

319

Sithis shrugged. "Somehow I'd expected it to be a bit more luxurious."

"We have a soldier Emperor now, Sithis. Darius is not the same as Quintus, Basianus or Corus. They were all born to the purple and never had to really fight for it. Darius had proved himself a number of times before the throne was ever put before him. That's why he's the man we need. That's why I'll put myself through the grinder to put him in control."

The swordsman smiled. "I wasn't putting him down, sir. Just a little surprised that's all. After all, I remember the old days like you."

"Yes, well. This is a new world," Kiva replied, "and don't call me sir when we're alone. I've been fighting alongside you at the same rank on and off for twenty years. Wish you'd been around when all this shit first started hitting us instead of gallivanting off in the west making huge piles of coin."

"Kiva, if I'd know all this was going on, I'd have been back like a shot and you know it. So would Filus, Sorianus, Belto and a whole load of others. At least you had Tythias. Belto heard about it but never managed to reach us at the meeting point. I heard they met Velutio's army head-on and totally by surprise. We've never even found Sorianus. He could be up in the barbarian lands for all we know. Problem is: everything happened too fast. If you'd given us another month before starting all this, every unit worth their salt would have been waiting for you at Munda."

Kiva nodded. "I know. I just can't help thinking about might-have-beens. Entirely off the record, Sithis, I'm positive as hell out there in front of everyone, but I don't really see how we can win this. We've got a sizeable force and they're well trained and in high spirits and all that, but that's only worth so much when you're facing odds of four or five to one or more. And I have a horrible feeling that's the odds we're looking at."

Sithis shrugged and collapsed into one of the chairs around the edge of the room.

"We can only try our best. Our cause is right and the gods should be with us."

"Ha!" Kiva dropped into the chair opposite and drew a flask from his tunic. Taking a heavy swig, he stoppered it and let it drop into his lap. For a moment his jaw set hard and Sithis noticed a slight twitch and then a shudder run through the general. Then Kiva breathed out heavily. "The gods won't give me any help, Sithis. I abandoned them a long time ago, and they damn well abandoned me too."

320

Sithis leaned forward in his chair.

"They never abandoned you, Caerdin. You northerners were always so damned superstitious. Those of us born here is the south believe in the gods as long as it's convenient, but if they ever seem to be turning against us we just refuse to acknowledge their existence. It's all quite convenient really."

Kiva laughed out loud for a moment and then winced. Sithis folded his arms. "You're not a well man, Kiva. I was going to suggest you get some sword practice in so I can see how well you're coming along, but I see the answer without going through all that. How long have you been on the mare's mead now? Two decades? Even the most idiotic doctors'll only prescribe it on a month's course."

"You *know* why I take it and you know I was injured a little recently, so I've justifiably upped my intake a little."

Sithis shook his head. "You've upped your intake dangerously. I've been watching you this morning while you were wandering round keeping an eye on things. Four times in two hours you've hit that and you're not even sipping it; you're swigging it. I know damn well that Mercurias isn't giving you it and that doctor from the island seems to be far too above board for that. I'd be interested to know where you're getting it all."

"Never you mind. And don't even think of telling anyone about this. Without doing this I'd still be hobbling around on sticks and I'd be no use to man nor beast. At least for the next month or so I'm going to have to be fully active and on top of things. Maybe then I can lay off and back down a little."

Sithis shut his eyes and lowered his head. "You keep going like this for a month more and the only thing you're going to be on top of is a pyre!"

Kiva growled. "It *has* to be done. I can't stop now. Darius needs to be the Emperor in front of every man, woman and child in Hadrus and *I* need to be every inch the general. Appearances are half the battle here. And I've still too much of a part to play yet to dodder around on sticks."

Sithis stood and wandered over to where the general sat. Reaching down, he prodded Kiva gently in the side. The general grunted and winced.

"Thought so," grumbled the swordsman. "Don't know what's doing you more harm: that shard in your side or the medication you take. I used to have to punch you there for it to hurt like that. I hardly touched you this time. You've got some of the world's best medics here in Hadrus. Let them have a look at you and maybe try and remove it."

Kiva shook his head. "That'd kill me for sure and even if, by some miracle, I lived through the operation, I'd be completely out of commission throughout this whole thing."

He sat up and glared into Sithis' face.

"Promise me now you'll not breathe a word of this to anyone else in the camp. I think we've got the slimmest chance of coming out of this on top anyway, but if word gets out that I'm dancing around the edge of a grave and trying not to fall in, we'll *really* be in the shit. As I said, appearances are half the game."

Sithis nodded. "Fair enough, but make sure Tythias and Athas know about it. If you get too bad you're going to *have* to take a back seat and let your second in command do more of the work."

He stood and flexed his muscles. "I'm here as an officer and a trainer. I don't make decisions above unit level and I sure as hell don't have the brain for strategy. I don't know whether we can win or not, but if there was ever a man who could come up with a way to do it, that's you. That's why I'm *captain* Sithis and you're *general* Caerdin. Use that brain of yours and find a way to turn it round. That's what you're known for."

Kiva's face remained largely blank and expressionless as Sithis stood and walked over to the table. He looked down a grabbed the first book he saw.

"See this?" the captain said, some strain showing in his voice. "Rastus' battles book? I read this a few years back and half the battles in it are yours. The Emperor's reading about *your* victories, Kiva. The book's open at the Mivor plains debacle. Less than two hundred men against over a thousand? Ridiculous! But what happened? Well, it's a bit embellished here, but I remember that battle. Athas came back from Mivor and got drunk for three days and all he could talk about was your solution. What was it you did again, Kiva?"

"I just repositioned some of my men. Any commander could have done it."

Sithis grinned. "No commander *would* have though. They wouldn't have thought of it. You 'repositioned' enough men between their two lines and caused enough panic and havoc that the enemy started shooting each other. Athas reckoned he and the others got out of the middle as it all really started and they lost just four men. Four! That barbarian psychopath you were up against lost *three hundred* before they even realised they were killing each other and not you. It's clever little ideas like that make the history books."

Kiva nodded. "I suppose so, but I'm older and slower and a lot more tired these days. Still, something'll turn up I expect. And whatever happens I damn well have to try."

Sithis grinned. "You realise, I haven't had a chance to talk to you without being surrounded by your adoring public since I arrived. I've been here four days and not a single minute of social time. And I haven't seen you in, what? Six years I'd reckon. Since that 'incident' at Rilva."

"Incident!" Kiva laughed loud. "That's a mild term. I've not been able to work on the south coast since, and I'll bet you haven't either!"

Sithis howled with laughter and sat back in the Emperor's chair at the table. "That pompous, camp little dick thought he'd hired the greatest unit in the northern hemisphere. I got best part of a year's wages for one week with him, and you matched the amount with his lover, didn't you?"

Kiva wiped a tear of laughter away from his cheek. "Oh hell, yes. Lover, enemy, opponent, 'special friend'... call him what you will. A little lover's tiff and it cost them more than most wars I've been in. And your face when you saw us coming up the hill against his tower; it was a picture. What did you actually say to him when you saw us? I never did find out."

Sithis grinned. "Held the bag of money out and told him to shove it where his 'lover' put things. He told me I'd been hired and I'd taken the money so I'd damn well defend his tower. He was getting awfully red."

"And?" Kiva prompted.

"And I hit him in the face with the bag of coins before we left."

Kiva collapsed in hysterics again. "His 'special friend' wasn't too happy when *we* walked away either. Athas saw you coming out of the postern gate and we just turned and left."

"You didn't even give him the money back?"

"No," replied Kiva with a grin. "We'd walked a long way to get to that tower. I don't know where you disappeared to so fast, but we watched that daft little pretty-boy jumping up and down by the tower's door and ranting at his boyfriend. It was really quite funny. I wouldn't have laughed quite so much but for the fact that Brendan went up to him and gave him a corona for his troubles!"

323

Sithis collapsed in laughter once more. "I don't know how we missed each other in Rilva that night. We must have been in every bar getting drunk and laughing about those idiots and if you kept the money, you must have done much the same."

Kiva grinned. "We just settled in a bar down near the dock and stayed there until we couldn't walk."

Sithis grinned. "I didn't know whether you'd left or not until almost a week later. We were waiting for a ship to Velutio when the two pretty boys rolled in to the bar arm in arm, all made up and happy as anything. They never even noticed us, which is probably a good thing, but they kept going on to the innkeeper about the two captains that had seen through their argument and helped them save their relationship. We had to leave. I didn't know whether to laugh or just throw up."

The swordsman looked around the room. "You don't suppose the Emperor's got any special Imperial drink around here? You've nothing serious on or you wouldn't be wandering around watching people train, and I've done a full morning of instruction and handed them over to one of mine for the afternoon. I think it's *crucial* to the future well-being of the Empire that we get roaring drunk and talk about old times."

Kiva opened his mouth, presumably to object, since he was waving a warning finger, but Sithis laughed. "Oh, no. You don't get to make *all* the decisions, just the big important ones. And when we're both ready to crawl back home in a stupor, I'll find myself a nice warm, comforting companion for the night and I'll do my level best to see you get one too. If there's anything you need, Kiva, it's that!"

Kiva's face twisted as a number of emotions crossed it at the captain's insolent comments. Thoughts fleetingly passed him of Livilla and his son, of the few women he'd had any time for over the past two decades, of Sathina and her obsession with Tythias, and finally of the two camp lovers they'd left arguing through the walls of a tower in Rilva. He looked up into the grinning face of Sithis and couldn't help but laugh.

"Alright you idiot. You're a dangerous man, Sithis of the Swords. You find the drink; I'll get the glasses."

Chapter XXVIII

Darius squinted into the shadows as the party of Imperial courtiers passed out of the bright sunlight and beneath the arch of the massive gatehouse into the palace of Lord Silvas. The palace was a massive and impressive structure, designed a hundred years ago as a strategically placed fortress rather than a grand residence. Silvas would be the third lord they'd visited in five days and Darius, though knowing the stakes he kept the façade up, was getting rather bored of the whole affair. Plus, of course, the rich food and wine the lords plied him with were causing upsets with his system. Guards in red and white stood around the battlements and towers of the encircling wall watching the party with a mix of suspicion and interest. Behind him rattled the small carriage that had been sent to carry the Emperor and his close companions, Needless to say, Darius had steadfastly refused to sit in the carriage, preferring to ride a horse. Sathina leaned forward from the end of the wooden bench and spoke quietly, continuing the conversation they'd been having for more than an hour.

"So why does he need a military commander; I mean, if Avitus was one of the most important generals there was."

Darius nodded. "Don't forget though that to go into high politics in the empire, a man needed a military career, unless he was specially favoured by the Emperor. Velutio was no great general, but he needed to achieve a few victories as a Marshal before he could go for high office. The other three marshals at the time were all career military men, so his appointment didn't really endanger anyone. But he's not got a good record as a commander of men. The only truly successful campaign he led was after the fall of Quintus and the only reason that was successful was because he had one of the other Marshals with him, Caerdin was out of the picture and their enemy was outnumbered two to one."

"So he was never a good general?"

Darius laughed out loud. "Ask Caerdin some time. He'll rant for an hour if you let him. No, Velutio wouldn't be in the position he's in if he didn't have Sabian. The commander's a good man and a clever one. Sarios thinks he's probably even Caerdin's equal, which is a little worrying." He glanced back around himself. "We'll have to continue this later."

Tythias and his men had reined in their horses ahead where the courtyard was filled with officials and guards. Silvas stood stern and straight. He was an exceptionally tall man, thin as a rail, but with a certain power about him. His blond hair was short and severe and he was clean-shaven, dressed immaculately and wearing a coronet in the fashion of eastern Princes. By comparison, Tythias had steadfastly refused to cut his hair, despite the protests of Sathina and Caerdin, but had compromised by braiding it to keep it out of the way. Scarred and one-armed, the captain would present a frightening sight to those who didn't know him. With unexpected grace, the officer slid from his horse and approached the lord.

"Lord Silvas? I am Tythias, commander of the Lion Riders and Prefect in the Imperial army. I have the honour to present to you his Imperial Majesty, Darius the first, first citizen of the Empire, high priest..."

"And so on..." interrupted Silvas, gazing thoughtfully toward Darius. "You can dispense with the excess pomp and grandeur, Prefect. It doesn't impress me and I'll make up my own mind. Dismount and follow me into the great hall. We'll all have a welcome drink and then my major domo will show you to your accommodation for the night."

Without waiting for an answer, Silvas turned on his heel and strode back through the heavy wooden doors into the hall. Tythias turned and raised an eyebrow to Darius, who nodded. The entire party began to dismount, conversing as they gathered their personal belongings before handing reins to the stable lads in the courtyard.

Darius watched the two soldiers guarding the door through which his lordship had entered. They looked well trained and disciplined. Their uniforms were neat and clean and the weapons they wore were certainly not just for show. Factor in the severe style of this fortress and the curt attitude of the lord himself and Darius couldn't shake the feeling that they needed this man. He seemed to be a lord after the old fashion, disciplined and independent. Unfortunately, though he'd as yet remained free of Velutio's control, he'd also declined the invitation to join them at Munda. Darius hoped that was due to the need to protect his land rather than a lack of support for their cause on his part, but that hope was starting to waver after the lord's greeting. He placed his hand on the hilt of his sword and strode forward to Tythias, who was scanning the walls. With a weary smile, Darius squared his shoulders. "So, prefect, what d'you..."

He got no further as a look of horror crossed Tythias' face and he dived, knocking the wind from the young Emperor and crushing him to the ground. Darius looked up in amazement as the prefect fell heavily on top of him, an arrow protruding from his shoulder.

The men of Darius' personal guard leapt into action, drawing their weapons and some running to protect their master, others taking up positions to defend against Silvas' guards. Across the courtyard, Brendan and Athas were already running. The archer who'd released the arrow had realised instantly that he'd failed and, dropping the bow, climbed the stairs on which he'd stood, reaching the wall walk and looking about himself urgently. Athas and Brendan glanced at each other and nodded, the large, dark sergeant running for the gatehouse to seal off the man's exit while Brendan made for the stairs as fast as he could. The bald Wolf's immediate fears that there may be some larger conspiracy at work were allayed quickly as he saw the archer run along the wall and try to get past one of his fellow guards. The other man stood firm and gave the archer a hefty push, knocking him from the walk and back onto the stairs ahead of Brendan.

The archer struggled to his feet, drawing a sword desperately. Brendan, his anger rising, reached out and grasped the archer's sword hand, holding the blade away and squeezing the flesh until he heard several cracking sounds. The archer howled, unable to let go of the sword with his opponent's fist closed painfully around his own. Brendan was aware of people shouting things but paid no attention. He smiled at the archer, whose face was twisted gruesomely and butted the man full in the face, accompanied once again by the cracking of bones. The archer fell back onto the steps, dangling from Brendan by one broken hand and the burly Wolf let go in disgust, the sword clattering away and falling to the paving stones below. The archer clutched his broken face with his good hand, sobbing. Brendan glanced around and saw the man's bow. Reaching out for it, he unhooked the bowstring from first one end and then the other with an easy flex of his powerful muscles and leaned down over the wounded assassin. Winding each end of the bowstring around his hands, he looped the heavy duty catgut around the panicking man's neck and pulled it tight. The archer's good hand pulled away from the bloody, broken face and clawed at the tight cord around his neck. Athas' voice sounded from a few feet behind Brendan. "Captain, let go of the cord. We need to know who he's working for."

Brendan growled. "He's working for Velutio."

Down in the courtyard Tythias, struggling with some difficulty due to his one arm, hauled himself off the Emperor and staggered back against the wall. Darius pulled himself up, his face full of concern, but the grizzled prefect grinned. "I have *got* to stop getting fucking

327

wounded..." he realised who was standing before him and smiled weakly, "...highness."

As Sathina rushed to help Tythias break the arrow shaft off, the scarred officer placed his hand on her shoulder. "Sorry, lass. Didn't mean to curse."

Sathina laughed. "Good grief, Tythias. I didn't fall for you 'cause of your poetic tongue."

Leaving the two to deal with Tythias' wound, Darius spun round to take in the situation. His fear that the entire greeting in the courtyard may have been a deliberate ambush was put aside as he saw lord Silvas appear once more from the doorway, a look of concern on his face. To one side, on the wall stairs, he could see an interesting tableau: Brendan was kneeling over a man, presumably the attempted murderer, throttling him with some sort of cord. Athas was behind him speaking quietly. His head fuzzy, Darius looked back again at Silvas then at Brendan again.

Taking a deep breath, he called out "Captain, let some slack in that rope."

Assuming, even hoping, that Brendan had both heard and obeyed, he turned to the master of the palace. "Lord Silvas? This is one of your men. It's not for mine to punish him."

Silvas nodded gravely. "Agreed, but he ceased to be one of my men the moment he shot at a guest in my house. Deal with him as you see fit."

Darius turned back to his men and gave them an exaggerated nod. Athas growled and said under his breath "Brendan, question him."

Brendan glared into the broken face of the archer.

"Talk to me. If'n you give me enough I'll give yer a quick death."

The man stared at Brendan in horror. Athas leaned down over his junior officer's shoulder. "Tell us everything and he'll give you the sword. Otherwise I'll leave you to him and he might take days."

The man coughed, blood flowing through his shattered teeth. "He'd have paid me well and the whole thing'd be over. I don't want to die!"

Brendan looked up at Athas. "Velutio again, but only coz this little weasel's a greedy little cowardly bastard."

Athas nodded and, turning, walked down the stairs to join the Imperial party below. As he left, Brendan smiled at the archer in front of him.

"Damn, can't reach me sword." With a slight shrug, he slowly tightened the cord. The archer gasped, unable to speak and resumed his clawing at the garrotte, his broken hand flopping feebly around with the effort. "Ack, agh…"

"I know," smiled Brendan. "I'm a bit of a liar, y'see?"

Oblivious to the final throws of the man on the walls, Darius, accompanied by his courtiers and the members of his now very alert and unhappy personal guard made their way through into the great hall on the heels of Lord Silvas himself.

The room continued the military theme of the palace itself. Big and impressive, the hall was of stone rather than marble or brick, with buttresses on the interior as well as the exterior on which oil lamps burned, augmenting the small amount of light the windows admitted. Flags in red and white and military regalia decorated the room and the flagstones had been laid cunningly to provide a map of the Silvas lands. This lord was proud of his heritage and Darius dredged his formidable knowledge of political history. He had vague recollections of the name. The family had been local governors for generations; a most unusual situation, since governorship was usually granted on a five-yearly basis by the Imperial court. One of the earlier Silvas members had presumably so impressed the Emperor of the time that the family had been granted the position in perpetuity; no small honour.

Silvas himself stood to one side of his huge chair behind a table at the far end of the room. Again, Darius was struck by how many nuances of Imperial etiquette he had picked up from his classes under Sarios and the other tutors without even realising it at the time. To have taken a seat would have been to deny the validity of Darius' claim. The fact that the lord hadn't knelt showed nothing. He'd as yet taken no oath, but neither did he dispute any claim. He was vaguely aware of Athas and a few others coming in behind him. He glanced over his shoulder at Tythias, standing stern and unmoving, despite the arrow jutting from his shoulder and Sathina behind him fussing and muttering.

"Prefect, have the men fall out to wherever they're allocated. I don't imagine we're in any further danger."

Tythias nodded and began issuing orders to the various lesser officers with them. One of Silvas' servants showed the guard officers outside and to their lodgings, while a half dozen of them formed and remained with their Emperor. Darius paid no attention to the organisation going on, fixing his gaze on Silvas.

"Your lordship, before we begin anything, do you have a doctor that could look at my prefect's wound? I regret we have no medic in our party."

Silvas nodded. "I've already sent for him. Please; there are plenty of seats and tables. Everyone should make themselves comfortable and you and your closest should join me here."

Darius made a few small motions and walked steadily across the hall to the table where a half dozen seats had been arranged. Alongside him, Athas, Tythias and Sathina strode ahead.

"You've met the army's executive officer, Prefect Tythias. May I also introduce Athas, a captain and a member of the Wolves and Sathina, lady of the Imperial court and one of my advisors."

Silvas blinked. "You have a woman as an advisor? A bit of a frivolity, no?"

Sathina bridled and Tythias clamped his hand on her shoulder. Darius smiled. "This is no ordinary woman, Silvas. She's infiltrated a court and saved the life of General Caerdin. I value her highly as do my senior commanders."

Silvas smiled, unsure of whether to laugh or not. As the last of a series of emotions passed across his face, he turned to her and bowed. "Then I'm pleased to know you, Lady Sathina. Such beauty and reckless bravery rarely fit together." He gestured to the seats at the table and, with a nod, Darius took the central one opposite the lord. As the others seated themselves, Silvas being the last, Brendan arrived in the doorway, exchanged very quick words with one of Darius' guard and then strode up to the table.

"Ah, captain, take a seat", the Emperor said.

Brendan smiled as he sat at one side, his forehead smeared in blood. "Sorry I'm late, highness. Bit of a barny m'afraid."

Darius nodded. "Yes, I noticed. I hope it's dealt with." He turned his attention to lord Silvas, who was still watching his guests with a curious and appraising smile. "Where do we begin then? You're an anomaly, Silvas… one of very few powerful lords who've remained independent."

Silvas leaned forward, his elbows on the table and cradling his hands. "I'm well aware that a time is coming when I must put aside my independence and choose a side. I'm not very happy about it, but I'm also aware enough to realise I have no other choice. Lord Velutio has been consolidating a claim to the throne for at least a decade. He may not be of Imperial blood but he knows how to control and he's been very much unstoppable. He ripped the independence out of most of my

330

neighbours either by fear or be the sword and I'm not sure whether it's because of my strength, my reputation or merely inconvenience that he's left me alone thus far. And he'll come for me very soon. He's finished dealing with the western lords, according to my last report and is already on the move back to the city. Once he reaches the central provinces I shall be high on his list and my time will be up. I have absolutely no intention of taking my army to Munda to join with you and leaving my lands to be ravaged by brigands and then by Velutio, but also if the lord should arrive here with his army, rest assured I will take my oath to him there and then to save the lives of my soldiers and prevent the destruction of my territory. I find it very hard to believe that you could persuade me otherwise, I'm afraid."

He leaned back in his chair. "Though you're welcome to try."

Darius cleared his throat. "I came here, Silvas, to appeal to your sense of duty and tradition. I may have been mistaken in that. From everything I've seen so far, you are in no need of any more sense of duty or tradition than you already have. Your army is loyal and strong and you have the support of your men. You seem to be basing your decisions on the good of your men and your lands, which is as noble a thing as I could ask."

He stood and stepped away from his chair.

"When was this flagstone floor put in, could I ask?"

Silvas shrugged. "Almost a hundred years ago. Why?"

"This floor shows your domain as it is today. That means that at least four generations of your family have controlled these lands. Unusual, I'd say. What did your ancestor do to receive that kind of honour from the Emperor?"

Another shrug. "Marcus Pilatus Silvas was a Marshal of the army and a close friend of the Emperor. He saved the Emperor's life during a riot at the games in Velutio. These are our lands in perpetuity by Imperial decree and we look after them."

"Can you imagine Velutio giving out such an honour?"

Silvas shuffled in his seat. "This rhetoric's tiring. No; to answer your question, I can't see Velutio doing such a thing. And before you say it, I've also given thought to the likelihood that he would not allow hereditary titles. All I can do is try to convince him to leave me my lands and if he will not, at least I will have saved them from destruction at his hands."

Darius nodded. "Frankly, lord Silvas, I think you give more credit to Velutio than he deserves. I don't know how much dealing you've had with him in the past, but I would assume not much by the

331

fact that you remain independent. Velutio is cruel and vindictive and not trustworthy. I have personally seen him crucify and beat men to death for doing nothing other than protecting their family. He has burned entire estates and trampled lands merely to remove an inconvenience. You claim to have thought in advance about these things, but I think you are, in fact, being short-sighted. You have no conception of what you are letting yourself in for if you accept Velutio as the power of the land. I don't think I'm here to convince you to join us. I think you should convince us to *let* you come to Munda."

Silvas blinked. His voice was low and angry. "No one has spoken to me like that in my entire life. I ought to have you flogged for it. I do not have to answer to someone with a spurious claim to the throne with the backing of an army led by a regicide. Careful of the ground on which you walk, young man."

Darius nodded. "Small threats should be beneath you, lord Silvas. You are not the man I expected." He glanced across at Tythias. "Gather the men. We're leaving Silvas to his fate."

Turning on his heel, he strode toward his honour guard by the doorway. For a long moment, Athas and Silvas glared at each other across the table and then the rest of the Imperial entourage stood and made their way across the hall.

Silvas clenched and unclenched his fists rhythmically, his teeth grinding until he stood sharply. "Stay your ground young Emperor. I offered you my hospitality and I still do."

Darius stopped at the door and turned. "You have something further to say, lord Silvas?"

Silvas growled as he strode across the hall toward them. "You're a strong willed young man and quite brave; very brave in fact. You may be a good choice for the throne and you'd certainly be a better choice than Velutio, even though I can't conceive of any way in which you can win this. The fact remains that I still haven't made my decision and that despite your apparent unconcern, I know that you need us as much as we may need you. I still will not march my men to Munda and leave my lands unprotected and I also that you are equally unwilling to bring your army here. And so we're at something of an impasse. However, I respect that you truly believe that you are doing the right thing by me and I have the serious nagging feeling that you may be right. We cannot compromise, but I will give you my word on this: If Velutio arrives at my door demanding fealty, I will give it and will not renege. I believe that an oath should not be broken. However, if your army marches and arrives in my lands before Velutio sets his sights on me, I will willingly take your oath and my men will fight for you. More than that I cannot say. Do not think me short-sighted or a coward. I must look after my people and if you aim to be Emperor, you must understand that."

Slowly, Darius nodded. "I apologise for any perceived slight on your honour, lord Silvas. I never intended to imply cowardice. Very well, our army will move out soon and I very much believe you will see us march before Velutio."

Ushering them back toward the seats, Silvas smiled weakly. "I hope so, young Emperor. I very much hope so."

"Do you think he'll really join us?" Darius asked, tipping more rich red wine from the jug into his goblet. "I felt he would have liked to have pledged to us today had we been ready to march."

Athas nodded. "He meant what he said. Silvas is very old-fashioned and believes in the sanctity of the Imperial oath. He'll join us if we can give him a show of strength before Velutio threatens his lands."

Tythias nodded, tearing off a piece of lamb and waving it to emphasise his words. "That's what I've been coming across for months: people who want change and are hopeful that we'll succeed, but unwilling to commit at the time. They won't leave their lands. If we'd rallied our army down here on the plains, we'd have seen a lot more lords join us."

He chewed on the fresh lamb as Brendan leaned forward, slamming his empty mug back to the table. "Problem is, if we'd gathered here, Velutio'd 'ave been on us in a week. We've only stayed safe coz 'e didn't know where we was."

Tythias winced as he turned to reach for his mug. The bandages across his shoulder showed only a small trace of blood, despite the obvious discomfort he felt. Silvas' doctor had been thorough and efficient.

"Nevertheless," the scarred prefect added. "We need these people. Lord Cirpi was nice and easy to convince and I'd say he'll be as loyal as the day is long, but he's got less than four hundred men and they're not even particularly good soldiers. I can't see them making that much difference. Lord Sala said he'd take the oath but that he'll only march his men with ours when we pass his lands. Now *he's* got over a thousand good men, but I'm not entirely convinced he'll do what he says."

Darius reached out, waving his finger at Tythias, but before he could say anything there was a knock at the door of the suite that had been set aside for Darius.

"Come in" the young Emperor called out.

The heavy wooden door swung open and one of Silvas' guards stepped in, sweating and out of breath. "Sorry to interrupt your lordships, but some men have turned up asking for a sergeant Athas and my lord told me to find you."

The group looked around at each other in surprise. "Must be from Caerdin," grunted Tythias. "No-one else knows we're here."

Gathering their cloaks and weapons, Darius, Tythias, Brendan, Athas and Sathina made for the door. "Take us to this man."

The guard led them through the corridors and stairwells of the palace and finally down to the great hall, into which they stepped through a side door. Silvas sat in his chair behind the table looking tired. He nodded at them as they entered and gestured to a small group of dusty and travel-worn men that stood in the centre of the room. As the Imperial party approached, Darius started to make out more details in the low light of the sparse oil lamps in the hall. There were five of them. They were all dressed in heavy and stained travelling leathers with weapons slung at their sides, but one was little more than a boy, perhaps nine years old and the man beside him was old and quite tall, favouring one leg, presumably due to some ancient would. His hair covered only half his head, hanging long and grey down his back, while the other half was a network of scars that ran down his face and around his ear, disappearing at the neck into his tunic. A fearful sight, the wounds made the man appear to wear a sardonic grin even when he frowned, as he did now.

Athas stepped out in front.

"Someone asked for me? I'd be intrigued to know how you knew of me."

The old man looked down at the young boy, who nodded.

"We were passing through the village here on the way to Munda," he said, "when I heard tell of a big black man wearing a Wolf pelt that'd come through this afternoon. That's not a common sight and it had to be worth the detour to make sure."

Athas frowned as he stepped closer. "You were on your way to Munda? Just the five of you?"

The boy stepped forward toward Athas. "There are five hundred and twenty seven of us in total, though the rest of my men stayed in the village. We seek general Caerdin and the new Emperor."

Darius now brushed past Athas and looked down at the boy, only ten years or so his junior. "I am the Emperor you seek, but who are you?"

The boy straightened as best he could. His voice was filled with pride and something else that Darius recognised: loss and hatred. "I am Lord Julius Pelianus. My friends call me Julian and I'm hoping that you're my friends."

Darius laughed. "I think you could say that. Welcome, Lord Pelianus. How come such a young Lord is marching his men to Munda?"

Julian glowered. "There would have been almost three times as many of us, but Velutio has just been through my lands like a plague of locusts, culling anything that moved and breathed. He cut my father's throat for daring to speak out in favour of you. I have brought his men; my men, to serve you as he would have wished." He fell to one knee before Darius. "I give you my oath, my Emperor, that we are yours. Let me help you gut that murdering bastard."

Darius smiled sadly and placed his hand on the boy's head. "I accept your oath, Julian. Be welcome to our army and our court." He glanced over toward Silvas, who was frowning, deep in thought. To say anything to him now would be to press the obvious.

Athas was still staring at the old man with the scarred head who grinned, though perhaps involuntarily, back at him.

"Do I know you?" the burly dark man queried.

"You damn well should," the man replied, stepping forward. "We got matching tattoos once at Germalla. Kiva didn't stop shouting at us for a week." Now the grin was definitely genuine.

Darius looked across at Athas, his brows knitted. "You know this man?"

A broad grin had spread across Athas' face and he took another hesitant step forward. "Balo?"

The man edged forward again and held out a hand in greeting. His arm was as scarred as his face. "I know I've changed a little, but surely not that much."

Athas knocked the hand aside and stepped close, enclosing the man in a great bear hug. It was only once he'd moved out of the way that Darius saw the look of amazement on Brendan's face also. The shaven-headed captain stood stunned as the big dark-skinned man all but crushed the new arrival. When Athas stepped back and released Balo, the old man was struggling for breath. "Hell, Athas, you've got *stronger*!"

Now Brendan pushed past Athas and gripped the man by the upper arms, staring at him. "But you're dead, Balo! Dead a decade ago. How the hell?"

"Ahem. A reunion?"

They all turned to look at Darius, who was watching them with one raised eyebrow and his arms folded. It was at this point that Balo frowned. He walked toward Darius and reached out. The young Emperor flinched for a moment, but the scarred man just reached up to touch the wolf-pelt hanging at his shoulder. "Your majesty wears the emblem of the Wolves. I'm not sure whether to be impressed or offended."

Brendan laughed. "Impressed, Balo. If yer'd seen 'im fight, yer'd think e'd been one of us fer decades. Come on, though... What *'appened* to you?"

"That's a story for another time, when we meet up with the rest of them. Right now, Lord Pelian and the rest of us have been riding like lunatics for a week to get to you. We need to get our men up to Munda and you need to come back too. Straight away."

"Why?" Darius stared at him.

"Because Velutio's commander has sent a letter of terms to you, which is only a day or so behind us being carried by a Pelasian escorted by a few of Velutio's men, but he's also turned the army and is marching it towards Munda. Time's running out, Emperor. You know his terms will be unacceptable and so does he, so he's manoeuvring his army already. Whatever you were planning to do with your forces, you need to get it ready to march straight away if you want to keep any initiative. A battle's coming and it's coming fast."

Darius looked across at Tythias, who nodded, a sour look crossing his face.

"Very well," the young Emperor growled. "If war's on its way, let's get ready to meet it head on. Prefect... have the men fall out in the courtyard. We ride for the camp tonight."

Tythias nodded and made for the door, leaving the others alone. Darius left the Wolves and Sathina with their reunion and strode across to Silvas, who sat drumming his fingers on the table. The lord looked less than happy.

"I presume I've no need to hammer home anything the young lord said just now?"

Silvas shook his head sadly. "I remember Gaius Pelianus. He was one of the old school. If you're marshalling your army to march now, bring them past here. Velutio must be nearly two weeks away if he's moving an army the size of his from Pelian's estate. Bring your army to my lands and I'll bend my knee before you, young Emperor."

Brendan was still staring at Balo and Athas smiled sadly. "Before we reach the camp, there's something you need to know about the rest of them, Balo."

Chapter XXIX

The gate at Hadrus rattled open as Darius and his extended entourage rode up the dusty path from the foothills. On either side of the Emperor rode the young lord Pelian and Tythias, the Imperial 'courtiers' behind them, surrounded by Darius' guard, with the worn and weary men of Pelian's estate bringing up the rear.

Tythias looked up at the sergeant in charge of the gatehouse as he reined in his horse just inside. "Treble the gate guard and be alert for a party perhaps an hour behind us. They are not to be fired upon or admitted until the Emperor, the general and myself have been summoned." Turning his attention to one of the soldiers gathering in the dusty square to help with the horses, he continued as he dismounted. "Go and find all the senior commanders and staff officers and have them go to the meeting hall in the headquarters building."

As the rest of the party rattled in behind him, he grasped another passing soldier by the shoulder. "These are Lord Pelian's men. Have them quarters assigned and take them to draw uniforms and equipment from the stores."

The men inside the gate burst into life, running the various errands Tythias had assigned as Darius and the others dismounted and strode toward the headquarters building. The young lord Pelian looked around himself in awe. "What is this place and where are we going?" he enquired of Athas as they walked.

"To the headquarters," replied the dark-skinned captain. "We need to gather the whole command group and explain the situation before Velutio's party arrives. This is Hadrus. It used to be a city once; then a prison. Now it's a training camp."

There was a shout as they strode across the open ground as Kiva and Sithis appeared around a corner in full armour.

"What's happened? You're not due back for a week and more!"

Darius spoke without breaking his stride as Kiva and Sithis fell in alongside them. "There's been a change of plan, general. Let's wait until we're all together or we'll just be repeating ourselves." Balo lowered his head, a curious smile playing across his face, and kept his features hidden by his long hair.

As they reached the door to the headquarters building, others appeared from side streets or other structures. Mercurias and Marco were already inside, along with Filus and Sarios. Darius nodded at them as they strode into the large meeting hall and took seats around the edge. As he leaned back and stretched his arms, he performed a quick

338

head count. Clicking his tongue in irritation, he watched the door for a few moments as other officers and lords poured in and made their way to their places. Another quick glance confirmed that everyone was there. He stood.

"I know we weren't expected back for a week yet, but circumstances have changed. I assume Lord Cirpi and his men arrived a day or two ago?" A number of nods and a murmur in the room confirmed the fact. "Very well, we've visited lord Sala and lord Silvas and both have agreed to pledge their armies to our cause, but only when we reach their estates. However," he added, taking a deep breath, "the arrival of lord Pelian and his men at the Silvas estate has forced a change in plans."

He gestured to the young lord and a rumble of greeting, mixed with some surprise at his age, rippled around the room. Darius tried not to smile as he noticed Kiva peering intently at the long-haired man seated next to the young lord, his face hidden in shadow. He had to get the important messages out before any further interruptions.

"A small party of Velutio's men was perhaps an hour behind us in the foothills. They certainly didn't follow us, and were making directly for Hadrus led by a Pelasian, so they know where we are. They carry a letter of terms from Velutio."

Kiva grunted loudly, tearing his eyes away from the mysterious man. "'*Terms!*' I suppose they'll be real favourable too. Perhaps he expects us to surrender before we even begin."

Darius nodded, "Perhaps so, but terms have been sent and they will arrive under a truce, I presume. We'll treat this as a parlay but unless he's offering a surrender, which I find hard to imagine, we're not accepting his terms. You see, our latest intelligence is that Velutio's finished in the west and has turned his army this way. He believes we're at Munda and, while we aren't, it's close enough that a conflict is now inevitable and getting close. If his army is on the march then he has no intention of honouring any terms, even if they *are* favourable. So," he concluded, drawing another deep breath, "what I need to know is how soon we'll be ready to march."

Kiva leaned on the arm of his chair, glancing across at his Emperor.

"We're as close as we're going to get, I suppose. Unless we have a massive influx of recruits, we might as well make preparations." He looked across at Sithis, who took up the thread.

"We've made progress with the training. I'd have liked another month before I'd confidently take them onto the field, but even the

339

lowest man at Hadrus is stronger, better trained and in better spirits than any number of the untrained and conscripted men-at-arms in Velutio's army will be. I'd happily accept odds of two to one given the respective qualities of the men."

Athas rumbled deep in his throat. "It'll take at least a couple of days if not more to have everything loaded and made ready for transport. There's a lot of logistical problems regardless of how quickly the troops can be made ready. You can't forget the train of support staff that's going to have to travel with us." He sighed. "And then there's the siege engines. The engineers will have to start making ready straight away."

"So," Darius said with some satisfaction, "if we say four days for a safe margin, we should be ready to move?"

There was a murmur of assent. Mercurias, deep in thought, was muttering to himself.

"Something up, captain?" the Emperor queried.

The grizzled medic looked up. "No. I've just been working it out. If we can put together some protective cavalry squads we can move the support and engineer units out as they become ready and muster them in the valley below. That way they won't block up the narrow mountain road and when the full army's ready to march we should be able to make it down to the plain in reasonable order." He looked across at Athas and Tythias questioningly.

"I worry about the safety of the wagons and engines if they move before the rest of us," Athas grumbled. "I don't like exposing our supply column to danger. If they should be attacked and destroyed then our campaign's over before it begins."

Tythias shook his head. "Velutio's army's got to still be weeks away. So long as we send strong enough mixed cavalry and infantry units down with them we can feel fairly secure and the sooner we get the heavy carts down onto the plain, the faster we'll move when we get started. I think it's a damn good idea."

Kiva nodded. "Agreed. But I want Sithis and Tythias to put together the best units they can for the duty and you can both head down there with the first group to organise things as they arrive below."

Darius stretched and smiled. "Good. That just about clarifies everything. Anybody have anything to ask?" He waited a few seconds in silence and then clasped his hands. "Now let's go over to the gate and get ready to meet these ambassadors for the enemy. Senior staff only. The rest of you've got things to do."

He stepped down from the raised floor that housed the senior staff's seats and made for the door, others trailing behind him. The Emperor glanced behind him as he left and noticed once again Kiva staring at the long-haired man.

"You!" the general barked, pointing at the enigmatic newcomer. "You're part of Pelian's party, but why d'you hide your face from us?"

The scarred old soldier lifted his head. There was a wide grin on the disfigured face. Kiva stared at him, his eyebrows meeting as he frowned, trying to work out why the face was disturbingly familiar...

"Balo?"

Kiva's head whipped round as Mercurias stopped on his way from the room. The medic's mouth had fallen open as he stared at the man. Kiva turned his head once more and stared at the old man.

"*Balo?*" he echoed. He looked around him and saw Athas and Brendan standing across the room with their arms folded and smiles splitting their faces. Marco reappeared in the doorway and leaned around the jamb. "What did you say?" he demanded, and then his eyes too fell on the scarred man.

"It is!" exclaimed Mercurias as he crossed the room to where the man sat. "It damn well is! May the Gods pluck the eyes from my head." He edged forward for a moment, and then jogged across the room to where the scarred old man finally stood up.

The rest of the Wolves, radiating wonder and disbelief, converged on Balo as he pulled his regimental flask from his tunic and took a swig from it, grinning widely.

"At least *Mercurias* recognises me!" the old scarred man laughed. "But then he's not used to seeing *ex* patients standing up."

"Balo?" demanded Kiva again. "But you're dead!"

"Not so, captain." He grinned. "I mean, *general* of course. I was for a while though."

Athas and Brendan now joined them. "Maybe now you three are here he'll tell us about it. He refused all the way here."

"To be honest, you'll all have a better recollection of it than me," Balo said.

"Shit," exclaimed Marco breathlessly. "We last saw you at Pelian's estate. Of course."

Kiva nodded. "Yes, but you went off into a building in one of your rages and we saw your head split open."

341

"I got shot. You know how I used to react to things like that. I chased the little bastard archer back into the building, but his mate hit me with something and I went out like a light."

Mercurias nodded. "Not just something... the biggest club I ever saw."

Brendan leaned forward. "When yer went down, yer 'ead were open like a watermelon and I swear yer brains were spillin' out."

Another nod from the medic. "Hell, yes. Your brains were coming out of your head, man. I tried to get to you, but the building started to go."

Balo grinned even wider. I didn't wake up for a long time. You'd been gone from the Pelian estate over a month before I first opened my eyes, apparently. In fact, I don't really remember anything for at least six months and you're right about my head. Pelian's doctor said I was actually stone dead for around a quarter of an hour and I lost about a tenth of my brain, though I personally haven't noticed much difference."

Marco grinned. "That doesn't surprise me."

"Why didn't you look for us when you recovered?" asked Kiva.

"It was well over a year before I was healthy enough to start being active again; almost a year and a half in fact. But even now I'm slow. I'm not the swordsman I was. Not one of the Wolves anymore, see?"

Kiva opened his mouth to argue, but Balo went on. "I used to get the rages when things like that happened to me; when I got wounded or suchlike, and I know I was a bit of a liability even then. That's why I never had a full command in the old days, and I'm comfortable with that but since the wound the mood's been unpredictable. I almost lost my job in Pelian's army coz a guard cheated me at dice and I kicked him within inches of death. I'd be a real liability to you these days. I'm not here for my old commission, Kiva. I just wanted to see you all again and help the lad, coz he wants revenge for his father and can give him it."

"But you've got to join us, Balo!" Marco gripped his arm. "Look at me! I lost a lung. I'm not always breathing too good; I certainly can't take a frontline fight any more. I can't ride very well and I walk slowly, but I still know enough to train and motivate and lead. The general's still got enough confidence in me that I've got command of a unit of sappers."

342

Kiva nodded, though Balo could read it in his features: Marco had been given a low-responsibility and low-danger command out of perhaps sympathy or respect. He smiled.

"I think not. I'll stick around if that's alright, but you really don't want me in command of anyone; I guarantee it."

A soldier appeared in the doorway and coughed politely.

"Yes?" Kiva said tersely.

"The Emperor requests your presence at the gate, sir."

"We're on our way," the general replied.

As the rest of the Wolves made their way from the room, Kiva slowed and grasped Balo gently by the elbow. "I think we could do with a chat as we walk…"

Dropping slightly back and leaving the others to walk on ahead, Kiva eyed his companion. "You really sure you want to stay out of this? We really could do with your experience and you're about my size. I can lend you tunics and armour for the moment if you want until we can get them fitted. You don't have to command a unit if you don't want to, but I could put you on the staff…"

"It's not a matter of staying out of it," Balo replied sadly. "It's just… I know I'm not good enough for that anymore. Hell, I've been on mare's mead for ten years now and some mornings I can't even grip a sword hilt properly." He glanced across at Kiva. "You must understand that; it's got to have been twenty years on it for you."

Kiva grunted but said nothing.

"You're hitting it hard, aren't you? I can tell just by looking at you…. Don't forget I know how it feels. Is it the same old wound; the one with the liver? Getting worse, I presume? I remember the doctor said it would probably get worse as time went on." He tapped Kiva on the arm as they walked. "Or is it this? These wounds aren't very old."

The general nodded. "Both, really. I'd be barely able to walk if it weren't for the mare's mead. To be honest Balo, I'm in more of a state than I can let on to the rest of them. I've got a lot of fairly fresh wounds that are only just healing and my muscles aren't up to a fight. On top of that, the little shitty piece of metal in my side I think is actually working into my *liver* now."

Balo pulled Kiva's other arm across and examined the wrist. "You were crucified? Got to be, from the wounds; and I'll bet I know who by." The ex Wolf drew a deep breath. "I realise Athas and Mercurias will have told you this plenty before, but if you keep taking it like this, you're going to kill yourself, you know? I worry about it myself every day and I'll bet you take a lot more than I do."

343

Kiva shrugged. "Probably. I don't really care too much about me any more, but I've got to keep going until all this is over. Got to see it through. See, I brought the Empire down and I thought that was the end of it, but we found Quintus' nephew in the early summer and... well, everything's come tumbling back down on me. My lack of foresight got the young man killed and, though I'm going to hell anyway, I've got to put it right. It's all my fault and I've got to put it right."

Balo nodded. So the Imperial line's properly gone then? I always assumed it had anyway. So where did this Darius lad turn up from?"

"He was brought up with Quintillian on Isera; taught everything by Sarios and his people. I gather he was the son of the training officer from Munda. It took me a while to realise a new Emperor didn't have to be the same family as the old one. Sarios hammered it into me in the end." As they reached the door leading out to the wide square, he caught sight of Darius handing out instructions to the guard officers. "He'll make a good Emperor though; of that I'm damned sure."

"I suppose," said Balo as they strode out into the sun, "my next question is: how the hell do you plan to actually beat Velutio?"

Kiva shrugged. "Everyone here thinks I'll come up with some miraculous genius plan to turn everything around and, well, I've had ideas; a few plans in their earliest stages, but nothing I'd pin the hopes of an Empire on. They all feel wrong. There's something that I've missed this far though; something that escapes me; something almost in reach, but I can't quite grasp it."

He grinned at Balo. "But I'll bet you're part of it. You can't go, even if you won't join us. I have a feeling I've a part for you to play yet."

Balo nodded. "If you say so, General. You know I won't back out and leave you all in the shit. I just don't want to be in a position of command."

The two of them wandered out, catching up with the others at the gatehouse. Darius was standing around with the other officers and the gates stood wide open. The Emperor smiled as Kiva approached. "Sorry to cut your reunion short, general, but Velutio's group's almost here and I thought we'd best all be present, eh?"

Caerdin nodded soberly. "Indeed. They'll no doubt want to speak to you, but I would suggest that I act as your intermediary to start with. To give them immediate access to the Emperor will look idiotic,

344

and I'm still not sure how far we can trust them, even under a flag of truce."

Darius nodded. "Agreed. I'll stay at the back with my guards and be very imperial until you need me." He smiled. "Or until I need to say anything of course."

They watched for a short while as nine men on horseback toiled slowly and openly up the slope toward the gate, the dust from their hooves creating thin clouds that drifted across the valley as they travelled. Finally they approached the gate. The lead soldier made a quick study of the defences, noting with interest and approval the narrow approach to Hadrus and its strong walls. Guards manned several huge bolt-throwers on the top of the gate, which were aimed directly at the approaching riders, though the gates themselves remained open and surprisingly welcoming.

Kiva took a couple of steps forward, Athas and Tythias at his side.

"State your business" he called.

A smaller man rode out around the side of the lead soldier and dropped the travel-worn and dusty cloak from his head and the scarf from his face. He was clearly Pelasian; one of Ashar's. "General Caerdin... I believe you will know at least some of these men. Sergeant Cialo if no others?"

Kiva nodded. "Cialo. I'm surprised Velutio would send you rather than one of his politicians or spies."

Cialo saluted; a traditional Imperial salute. Sliding from his saddle he motioned his men to follow suit. The Pelasian remained seated as he looked across the others at the general. "If you will excuse me general, my Prince must know of this?"

Without waiting for Kiva's absent wave of a hand and nod of assent, the man wheeled his horse and began to ride as fast as safety would allow down the narrow path. Cialo, with his seven other men at heel stepped slowly forward, their hands staying well clear of the sword hilts at their waists. The sergeant smiled at them. "General Caerdin, it's a pleasure. I can assure you that it was Commander Sabian that chose who delivered the message, not his lordship."

Kiva nodded. "I realise that you're here under a flag of truce and have no real reason to trust me, but the Emperor is here and I must ask you to surrender your weapons for the time being." He clicked his fingers and a number of the guard stepped forward to receive the items.

345

Cialo nodded. "Of course, general. I understand completely. Darius must not be harmed." He turned and made beckoning gestures to his men. "Crispin? Collect the weapons."

As the Imperial party stood waiting, the sergeant turned, drawing his sword from its sheath. The men of Hadrus around them were already fully alert with their weapons trained on the visitors, clustering defensively around the commanders and watching every move the sergeant and his men made. Cialo spun round, whipping out his short-sword and jammed it with a smooth blow into the neck of the soldier behind him just below the chin, who was busy relinquishing his weapon fully sheathed. The man gasped and gurgled in panic and surprise as the sergeant put all his strength behind the weapon and drove it home to the hilt, the tip emerging from the man's spine red and dripping. Behind that and to one side, Crispin received a blade from one of the other soldiers and in a swift move drew the blade and cut across the man's throat, deep and hard before pushing him away.. Kiva watched with surprise as the party of eight dropped to six and the two limp bodies collapsed to the ground with sprays of blood.

"Interesting, sergeant. And why may I ask?"

"These are *not* my men." Cialo said loudly. "I chose my men personally. These two were sent along with us at his Lordship's request. I expect I needn't explain that to you?"

The general raised an eyebrow but said nothing, so Cialo shrugged, wiping his blade on the hem of a fallen soldier's cloak. Standing once more, he reversed his blade and placed it over his other arm, offering the hilt to Kiva. The general merely stood his ground, brow still raised.

"If I must spell it out, general, I offer you my sword and my loyalty, as well as that of my men. These two assassins spoke and boasted far too much after a jug of ale during the nights on the journey. I'm surprised your little Pelasian didn't deal with them. He must have known. But then perhaps he feared reprisal from the rest of us."

Kiva smiled. "I think you underestimate Ashar's men." He pointed behind Cialo and the sergeant turned his head to see the small Pelasian, still on horseback some distance away but with a bow trained on the group and an arrow nocked. "I don't think he had any intention of letting these two get away."

Cialo nodded. "Nevertheless, I surrender my arms and that of my men to you and formally seek sanctuary with you."

Caerdin shook his head, his eyes narrowing.

346

"Not you, Cialo. I can't believe that. You're old school and I can't see you betraying Sabian. This is some sort of a trick."

Cialo shook his head in return. "No trick I assure you. You will find that these terms are dishonourable and unacceptable. My Commander is an honourable man, but his lord is not. I cannot take an oath to put a man on the throne who takes advantage of a truce to send assassins. I have no wish to betray my commander, but the fault must lie with him. He should have walked away from Velutio a long time ago."

Mercurias appeared from one side and leaned close to Kiva. "If you want to be sure whether he's telling the truth or not, give Favio and me half an hour with him. I've got compounds that'll make him sing the truth like he's talking to his mother."

Kiva smiled. "And if that doesn't work, ten minutes with Brendan and a hammer should do it." He turned back to Cialo. "It is not I that can grant mercy here."

Cialo nodded. "Another reason I must abandon my position. I can find no reason in my heart to make war on young Darius." He straightened. "But before any of this, there's something else I must warn you of. I see you all wear an imperial uniform. We saw several men down the valley and I presumed them your scouts and outriders, but they were in no uniform, so I assume they are not friendly. I would strongly urge you to send some scouts down to the narrow part of the pass and investigate."

Kiva narrowed his eyes again and watched Cialo for some time, weighing the odds of a trap. Finally he turned to Athas. "Have a dozen men fall in in the square and send for Phythian's crossbowmen. I'll check this out personally."

As he stepped to one side, Darius walked out ahead of his guards. Soldiers around the gate had now removed the weapons from Cialo's group and had taken them for storage. Darius stepped up to the grizzled sergeant and stared down into the man's eyes.

"It's been a long time Cialo. I have always held you in esteem and would hate to think I couldn't trust you. I will not let Mercurias drug you or Brendan beat the truth out of you. If all of you will willingly take the imperial soldier's oath here, in front of me, my staff and the army, I will place my trust in you and your weapons will be returned."

Cialo grinned. "D'you know, I always had a feeling that you'd turn out something like this young Darius. I'll gladly take your oath, but

347

it'll take some doing to start using a title for you, so you might have to be lenient with me for a while... your imperial majesty!"

Darius smiled back at him and leaned in close to speak in a low voice. "You have no idea how hard it is to remember to be an 'imperial majesty, Cialo."

As the turncoats of Velutio's army stood in the afternoon sun and roared out the traditional soldier's oath, along with the secondary oath Kiva had demanded to him and his command unit, Athas' quartermasters went about the business of finding uniforms and equipment for them.

As the large, dark-skinned sergeant finished bellowing at an unfortunate blacksmith and turned to face the square once more, Kiva approached him, grinning.

"I think another piece of the plan is falling into place. Don't have the uniforms issued just yet. I have plans for Cialo and his unit. I think things are coming together. Just hope it happens in time."

Athas nodded in agreement as he watched Cialo and his men saluting their new Emperor and a score or more of men scrambled to fall in near the gate.

Chapter XXX

In the end, Kiva had capitulated and let Tythias take the unit down the path form the gatehouse. His second in command had refused to let the army's senior commander ride into what could still very well be a trap and Kiva had reluctantly had to agree with the logic.

There were almost a score of crossbowmen and a dozen good soldiers from Sithis' elite unit, as well as Tythias himself, standing on a rock be the side of the trail. At this point the path narrowed before it entered a stretch known as snake canyon. Here the trail was only wide enough for a single cart or three men in safety and the southern side of the path fell away into a steep scree slope that tumbled down to the river far below. Tythias was sure a fall from here would be fatal since, though the fall was sloping rather than vertical, it was long and jagged shards of rock stood proud from the scree in places. A man would be lucky to reach the bottom alive, let alone intact. And of course, the chances of making it back up to the path afterwards were less than good. The other side of the trail was often sheer cliff face, occasionally dropping to low boulders and small fissures that disappeared up from the trail toward the mountains.

The one armed, one eyed prefect pulled from his pocket the spyglass he'd been given by the Pelasian prince and extended it, raising it to his eye and scanning the rocks to the north. Here, one of the wider fissures ran up into the rock. With a cluck of irritation, he compacted the device and sheathed it once more in his pocket.

"Still no sign of life," he said in a low voice to the sword captain alongside him. "I think we need to move up into the mountains now and work our way around the back."

The captain nodded. "As you say sir," he repeated in an equally low voice. They'd been as quiet and unobtrusive as possible during their journey down from the gate, hoping not to disturb the mysterious visitors until they could determine what they were doing.

With a sigh, Tythias dropped down from the rock and the party of soldiers began to pick their slow and difficult way among the boulders and rocks up into the mountains above the trail. It was slow and painful going and the sun was starting to get very low on the horizon. Tythias cursed both Kiva and himself for agreeing to take a group out down the trail this late in the day. It was stupid and dangerous and they should both know better. Still, they were here now and, if necessary, would have to camp among the rocks. At least the army had been trained in the traditional fashion and marched with everything they needed to set up camp strapped to their backs.

He sighed again and made a low whistling noise, a prearranged signal to gather on the prefect and take a rest. He'd not realised how much he missed his left arm until it came to things like climbing among rocks. He took a swig of something sharp Athas had filled his flask with and, wincing, watched the men catching up from behind and crawling back down the slope from ahead. He made a quick head count to check they were all there as he took another pull from his flask and one of Sithis' swordsmen came jogging energetically down the slope and across to where he sat.

"Signs of life just up ahead, sir" the man whispered. "I can hear voices and sounds like there's a work camp up there. I don't think we're in danger of being heard with the noises going on."

Tythias frowned. A work camp? What the hell was going on here? He nodded at the swordsman. "Good work. We'll take a ten minute rest and then we'll all creep up there and take a look."

They sat around in virtual silence, taking the occasional swig from a skin or flask and a bit of the emergency rations they carried. Tythias regarded the men around him. While he had no love for the crossbowmen, they had proved to be very good with their weapon of choice and had shown nothing but loyalty to their new commander. The swordsmen Sithis had trained and selected as the best of the recruits were as good as Tythias could hope. With the two groups he should be able to deal with anything short of a small army.

He leaned back for a moment against the rock and relaxed for a few minutes as best he could before standing once more with a stretch and whistling.

"Time to move on gentlemen. Let's get up to that point." He gestured at the man who'd informed him of the noises. "You take the lead and get us up to where you were. Everyone else stay behind him and as soon as you sight anyone, get down and into cover."

As the swordsman moved off at the front, Tythias and the others came up behind him and began once more the tedious and unpleasant crawling between boulders. Time dragged and the sun dipped lower, now touching the peak opposite. Another fifteen minutes or so and there would be only a difficult half-light. He was still grumbling when he noticed the front men up ahead dropping to the ground among the rocks. Picking up speed, he rushed ahead of the men around him and dropped to the rocks at the top with the lead men. Lifting his head, he peered over the rocks.

There were perhaps thirty or forty people around below them in a large depression separated from the gorge by a rock of immense proportions that must reach most of the way back to the gorge. Many of the men were around small camp fires in the depression and wore a black and silver uniform. The rest appeared to be barbarians in their dishevelled furs and leathers who stood guard around the edge end disappeared around the sides of the rock for minutes at a time before returning.

"What the fuck are they doing?" Tythias grumbled as he reached into his pocket and once more removed his spyglass. The swordsman next to him shuffled back from where he too had been scanning the area.

"They're quarrying, sir."

Tythias blinked. "They're what?"

The two poked their heads above the crest once more and the swordsman started to point. "I worked in the quarries at Carira sir. That's how you quarry; or one of the ways anyway." He gestured to the sides of the gargantuan rock. "You can just see the glow from the fires if you really strain. It'll be easier as it gets darker. They set fires all over the cliff face and heat the rock up for days until it almost glows itself and then douse the rock with huge amounts of cold water. The rock just cracks and falls away. Only real way to quarry hard stones like granite. See?" he gestured to another place. "Loads of barrels of water and they're being hauled up to the top ready to split the rock. They probably won't do that 'til the morning, cos it'll be quite dangerous and they'll have to be able to see what they're doing."

Tythias peered at the swordsman beside him. "You're an absolute mine of information. And can you tell me why they're doing that?"

The swordsman tapped his finger against his lip. "Well you'd think they're trying to block the pass, but there's no way the stone from the sides of this rock is going to come down on the trail. Unless..."

Tythias blinked in surprise and then frowned in annoyance as the soldier plucked the spyglass from his commander's hand and scanned the area closely. The man grinned.

"They *are* going to seal the pass. They're not trying to use this rock to block it, but if they've set their fires where I think they have, they should just get it right to collapse that entire rock against the next one."

"And?" asked Tythias in annoyance, snatching back his spyglass.

"And this rock is granite, I think; or something like. The ones by the gorge are much softer rock. If they bring this big bastard down against the next one, they'll both fall across the trail."

"Shit!" Tythias compacted his spyglass again. That would delay us for weeks and give Velutio the chance to get prime position on the plains and deal with all the other lords before we get there. We've got to stop them destroying that rock."

He turned to the others clustered below and behind him.

"There's quite a few people down there and we need to get rid of them all. This must be the only way out, cos the next fissure upwards isn't for a mile or more down the gorge. I want all you crossbowmen to get to high points and find yourself a good position as quietly and unobtrusively as you can. I'll give you twenty minutes to get in position. Then I'll give a hawk's call. That'll be your signal. You should each mark a man and fire as soon as you hear the signal. Then reload and try to get another shot off. It's quite likely they'll get into cover after the first shot, but by then the rest of us will be making our way down there. Try to take down the men in black and silver first. They're Janus' spearmen and they're good. If you spot a man dressed like them but with a red cloak, take every effort to kill him. Captain Janus gets you fifty corona when we get back as a reward. We'll move round the edge and deal with these barbarian hirelings of Janus'." He looked around the faces of the dozen swordsmen. "We need to take them out and then we'll split into two. Half of you will stay with me and we'll cover this exit so they can't get away while the crossbowmen still pick off any target that presents itself. The rest of you will go with..." He looked down at the man next to him that had explained the quarrying. "What's your name?"

"Velitus, sir."

"The rest of you," Tythias repeated, "will go with sergeant Velitus and dispatch any men you come across at the quarrying site and tear down the fires and dispose of the water safely. I'm not sure how you'll go about that, but I'm sure Velitus can figure it out and that's why he's just been made a sergeant."

He glanced around the assembled men. "Any suggestions or comments?"

The captain of the Swordsmen nodded and tapped his fingers on his sword pommel. "I think we need to get someone up to the top of that rock sir. They can cut the rope they're using to haul the water up and sabotage the barrels so they pour the water back down into the camp rather than the other way."

"Good," accepted Tythias. Pick the best man you have for the job. I'd have liked to send back to Hadrus for more men, but we need to stop this as soon as we can. I can't risk them blocking the gorge."

He smiled as he drew his sword. "At least I'm getting convinced that sergeant Cialo is on the level now. Ok. Move!"

He watched with interest as the crossbowmen started to climb the rocks and scree slopes around them, struggling to find the best vantage point they could. Further across the ridge, the man chosen to deal with the water barrels sheathed his sword and spat on his hands before rubbing them together. Several men patted him on the shoulders as he moved among them and then disappeared out into the dusk, remarkably light on his feet.

Tythias looked across at the captain. "Seems like a good man for the task."

The captain nodded. "He's been in jail at Velutio a couple of times for burglary, but the times they *didn't* catch him, he was starting to become quite a wealthy man."

Tythias laughed quietly. "Thieves, vagabonds, turncoats and mercenaries. Quite an army we've got."

He turned his attention once more to the ex-thief running lightly across the rocks. The man leapt from one to another with fine balance and took a long run across a particular rock, sailing silently through the air above the barbarians that went regularly to check on the fires. Landing with the faintest of thuds, he started to climb very slowly and carefully up the giant rock towards the water cache at the top. Tythias smiled. "Guess we won't need to worry about that problem then."

He watched for a while longer as the swordsman reached the peak of the rock and positioned himself near the barrels of water. With a quick glance behind him he noted that the crossbowmen had all vanished from sight. With a satisfied hum he waited, figuring another ten minutes at most would be needed before the signal could be given. With a sigh he turned and watched the sun slowly sinking behind the mountains opposite. In peaceful circumstances the view would have been soothing and relaxing. In their current position, he worried how much light they'd have when he put out the signal. Would half-light be enough for the crossbowmen? They were good; he knew, but how good?

A long time passed. Probably the ten minutes Tythias was hoping for, but it felt like a week. With a deep breath, Tythias put his fingers in his mouth and issued a call at best reminiscent of a hawk. Holding his breath, he gestured to the men.

353

"At the first shot, we move. You; you; all of you," he added, gesturing at men, "are with me. Time to go."

He waited tensely for a few more minutes until he heard the first cry. With a satisfied glance as he climbed over the rock and ran down with his men he noticed three of the black and silver uniforms punched heavily by crossbow bolts and the men disappear to the floor in blood and screams. His grin was positively wolfish as they took their defensive positions on the rocks, cutting off the escape route for Captain Janus, watching the rest of the swordsmen disappear down toward the narrow defile that served as a passage between the camp and the mining operation. On the rock there was a clatter as the barrel held by the rope clattered down into the camp area and the barrels on the top were smashed open with violent force. Gallons of water cascaded harmlessly from the summit into the camp, ruining hours of work the Spears had undertaken.

He watched with further satisfaction as the Spears and the few barbarian hirelings they'd brought as workers charged for whatever cover they could find. Phythian's crossbowmen did their job with ruthless efficiency. Having spread out almost a third of the way around the depression, their field of fire was impressive and men screamed as they were pinned to rock and to tent frames even in places they believed were safe.

Finally, a number of men had been gathered in a position behind an overhanging rock and their captain was with them. Janus looked around him in some panic and then, with a single wave of his arm, launched his men toward the gap where they could clearly see Tythias and his men waiting.

Tythias grinned. Janus was making straight for him and the man wouldn't make it an inch further. Janus' position and opposition had been responsible for the route the Wolves had taken to Serfium, leading them into danger, captivity and death, and the men killing them as they ran were the men who'd captured the Wolves. There was some small satisfaction in that.

The prefect, with only one eye and one arm and scarred so heavily he would be unrecognisable as the youth that had left Rilva thirty-five years ago, seeking a life and glory in the Imperial army, stood at the ridge and watched Janus running toward him, surrounded by his men and barbarian allies. Twenty five years ago, Janus had served with him at a level rank. Even then he'd been a man Tythias wouldn't have trusted, as many games of dice had attested. His grin widened as he hefted his sword and prepared. Even with only half his

354

faculties, he knew full well how much better he was than Janus. This would be sweet.

And then Janus vanished. Half way through his run, the first crossbow bolt hit him in the shoulder, spinning him round where he stood. The second took him through the leg, causing a fall and, while he floundered on the floor, the third took him through the hip. In unbelievable agony and unable to move, Janus screamed his heart out as he bled onto the dust and gravel. Tythias shrugged. He'd be fifty corona poorer when they got back, but the men had deserved it. He'd make it sixty and split it three ways. With a sigh he prepared himself for the rest of the men running up the hill at the defenders, though a number of them vanished to crossbow fire as they ran. He smiled. And Kiva thought hr had the monopoly on strategy.

Kiva smiled as he looked down at the man on the makeshift stretcher, built out of tent canvas and spears. Janus had looked better. The three crossbow bolts still protruded from him and he was pale, with eyes that rolled wildly. The general looked back up at his second in command.

"You couldn't capture any of the others?"

Tythias grunted. "Frankly, general, it never crossed my mind. Not a single life made it out of that depression after the captain here. Phythian's crossbowmen are just too good and Sithis trains men well. You're not going to tell me you mourn them?"

"No," Kiva replied, "of course not. It's just unlike you to not take prisoners. That's where we've differed for years. No, I don't really care," he added with a sigh. "I wonder what to do with Janus here though. We could interrogate him, but it seems pretty clear-cut to me. He's either working for Velutio with orders to cut off our egress and slow us down, or he's still independent and greedy and thinks if he does it himself, Velutio will cover him with gold. Either way you've stopped him and he's in the shit. Cialo's saved us a lot of trouble, you know? That man's a good man to have, I think. Sabian prized him highly."

Tythias nodded. "So long as this isn't all some convoluted plan to drop us in the shit."

"He's taken the oath and we'll be very wary around him, but don't worry about it. I've plans for Cialo."

He turned to one of the soldiers behind him. "Fetch sergeant Cialo at once."

The man ran off toward the barrack buildings, but Cialo was already out of the door and marching across the square, out of uniform and in his rough clothes for sleeping. The sergeant ignored the mutterings of the soldier and marched past him to where Kiva and his second in command stood over the wounded captain.

"My, my. Captain Janus."

Kiva nodded. "Yes, the infamous captain Janus. And he's here because of your warning, Cialo. As such, I feel, since I'm unsure what to do with him, I'm inclined to ask you your opinion…"

Cialo looked down at him and shrugged. "He's a captain from the old days. That means he's taken the oath. If he took the oath and is fighting against the Emperor's army, he's a traitor. You should probably crucify him for that."

Tythias and Kiva stared at each other.

"On the other hand," Cialo continued, "these being the times they are and him having done nothing other than fight on the wrong side, I'd be tempted to despatch him quickly and by the sword. He's a soldier after all."

Kiva nodded. "Good. We're in agreement." He drew his blade and poised it over the heart of the wounded man, bubbling and gibbering on the stretcher. With a last glance at both Cialo and Tythias, he put all his weight behind the blade and drove it down through the body and the canvas below until it struck the ground below. He stared down at the corpse and watched the last life ebb with a few twitches.

"Cialo… you're a man in the most peculiar position. I wonder how far you are willing to go for the cause of peace and the Emperor?"

The sergeant straightened. "I'm the Emperor's man now and I'll do everything I can. There's no nobler cause than to strive to repair the imperial peace."

Kiva smiled. "I'm glad you see it that way, as I've a rather unpleasant job I need doing and there's no one else I can think of that can do it."

Cialo slumped slightly. "You want me to spy on my former commander?"

"Actually, no." Kiva smiled and placed a hand on Cialo's shoulder. "I don't want you to do anything that brings you into direct conflict with Sabian. However this all goes, he's a man of honour and I think he'll come out of this for the best. What I want you to do is to go back and put the first phase of a plan that's gradually coming together into effect."

Cialo narrowed his eyes. "Go on, sir."

"You, I presume, are of the same opinion as the rest of the commanders; that direct conflict between our two forces with do irreparable damage to the Empire. The only way out is a peaceful solution?"

The sergeant nodded. "Commander Sabian, I know, is of the same opinion, but as long as Velutio is the man at the top, there'll be no peaceful solution."

"I'm not so sure about that," replied the general. "But I need a number of things to fall into place for it to work, and I'm still very vague about how it's going to happen yet. I know that the first step has to be yours. Will you do it?"

"Of course I will, sir," replied Cialo, coming further to attention.

"Very well," Kiva breathed out heavily. "What I need you to do is this: get back into your other uniforms and head back to Velutio's army. You can take the reply to his offer, which is that the Emperor Darius will not share his throne with a treacherous murderer and that the commanders of his army will not submit to his judgement. Feel free to tell him anything you want about the army here; our numbers, makeup of forces, location and so on. He will think it strange if you don't give him plenty of information. Then you can settle back into your place in the army temporarily."

Cialo cocked his head to one side. "And then?"

Kiva smiled. "And then I need you to make your way around the other lords. I need you to identify all the lords in the army. I need to know which ones are staunch Velutio, which ones are borderline rebellious. I need to know which ones are strong and which weak. I particularly need to know which ones are the sort that might consider backing out of the conflict if there was any way to do it without retribution. All in all, I need to know everything you can find out about every lord in the army."

Cialo frowned. "I can do most of that for you now. And here."

"Yes," continued the general, "but that's only the start. Once you find that out I need you to send a messenger you trust to me with the details. Then you and your loyal men need to befriend the smaller lords who would rather go home in peace than fight and you need to start to drive a wedge between them and Velutio. Basically, anyone who's worthwhile you can work on and I'll probably persuade to walk away when my plan comes to fruition. Don't worry about the larger lords that are closer to the borderline. I'll take care of them once I know who they are."

He put his arm around Cialo's shoulders. "I don't want you to have to bring harm to a single person. I just need information and a little

357

persuasion. And when we finally meet as armies, face to face, I'll make sure you're brought into our lines under protection unless you can get to us beforehand. Rest assured, Cialo, that there are a lot of people who have the greatest respect for you, on both sides I believe, including your Emperor. We *are* going to win this and everything will be fine in the end."

Cialo nodded, a little unhappily. "I was rather looking forward to being on the good side and all above board, where my mother, Gods bless her, would have been proud of me."

Tythias smiled. "If the general has a plan and it hinges on you, then we'll all be proud of you, sergeant. I'll have uniforms made up for you while you're gone." He glanced at Kiva and the general nodded. "Captain, I think." Men of substance are few and far between."

Still frowning, Cialo saluted with exaggerated motions and turned toward the barracks. He started to jog as he moved to wake his men.

"Can we trust him?" Tythias asked.

Kiva shrugged. "I think so. If not, then he's not gone back with any information that Velutio won't know soon enough. If he falls foul of Velutio there's little he can tell them that'll wreck our plans. I'm still not sure of the way it's going to pan out yet. The Gods stopped talking to me decades ago, but I'm hoping to hell they start again soon. I need a little divine help, I think."

Darius stood on the balcony of his villa with Athas by his side, gazing past the main gate and down the valley. The night was clear with a sprinkle of stars in the sky but a chill settling in. Summer was clearly over and autumn getting into its stride. The valley was a vague impression of shapes and shadows by moonlight. Within the gate on this side, the first group of wagons, along with a wheeled bolt-thrower and an engineer's cart stood ready to move at dawn. He sighed.

"Do you think it's all going to work?"

Athas smiled next to him. "Kiva thinks the Gods abandoned him. He abandoned them. They've kept an eye on him for decades and they've not stopped yet. He's got luck and ingenuity and that's what you need, highness. Luck and ingenuity."

Darius smiled wanly. "I hope you're right."

Sathina lay in the comforting fold of Tythias' good arm as he stared down at her. The scarred prefect was the archetypical mercenary that looked dishevelled and battered and rough, but had quickly proved to be the most gentle and caring man she'd ever met. She lay for a while wondering if he would marry her. It surprised her that he hadn't already and she'd worried over it for a long time until she pieced it together. Tythias wouldn't marry her before he went to war. To marry her now and leave her a widow in a month... She bit her lip. That thought was creeping in all too often now. Tythias didn't seem to have the best of luck in fights. Oh he'd survived plenty of years and plenty of battles, but his wounds were starting to become severe. If this all went well, he'd have to quit the army if he married her. If it didn't go well, then there was no issue to worry about.

Brendan and Marco sat in one of the rooms of the officers' quarters. Their thoughts were dark and often bleak, but neither would speak of it as they played dice over and over again, drinking unwatered wine as though they'd never try it again.

Many leagues away, Sabian stood in the command tent of Velutio's army. The meeting had finished and the other officers and the independent lords had all gone their separate ways, leaving Sabian standing before the table, opposite his commander.

"You go too far, my Lord."

Velutio looked up with one eyebrow raised. "I wasn't aware you were her to dictate policy to me. You are welcome to advice, but you criticise just a little too much, commander."

Sabian gritted his teeth. "That letter was a genuine offer, albeit an insulting one, under a flag of truce. I would never have allowed Cialo and his men to leave camp if I'd know what you were doing. It's an insult to the honour of the army and to your own honour."

Velutio stood sharply, slamming his hands to the table, palms down. "I will do anything in my power to bring this to a quick end. You are too stiff for your own good. If it takes deaths, assassins, treachery and deceit to win a war and to stop a massacre, I will try it every time. Caerdin's too sharp to fall for any of them anyway, but I must try. And now, this meeting is over. You have talked out of your place for the last time Sabian. You will leave without a word and go about your preparations for tomorrow and the next time you criticise or defy me, you will be stripped of your command and, if I'm particularly peeved, crucified."

He pointed a finger at Sabian. "Now get out of my sight!"

The commander carried out an extravagant salute and turned on his heel to leave the tent and marched out into the night, growling. Nothing was worth this.

Part Six: Imperium

Chapter XXXI.

Darius took a deep breath to steady himself. The army had been down on the plains now for two days and had begun to move slowly and steadily toward the sea and the inevitable clash with the army of Velutio. The Emperor was, despite his lifetime's study of the great campaigns, amazed at the incredibly slow speed at which a full army travelled. The infantry were not as fast as the cavalry, obviously, but the entire army was forced for move at the same speed as the slowest unit among them which turned out to be the siege units and wagon trains that toddled along at the back as though out for a country ramble. The commanders of the army seemed to be taking it all very stoically and Darius tried to be patient, but the fact that Velutio's army was reputed to be moving with a worrying swiftness kept preying on his mind. Tythias had tried to explain that this was because they had foregone siege units and engineers in favour of speed of travel and that they required no wagon train as they had been in foragable lowlands their entire time, rather than in bare and inhospitable mountains like the rebel force. Also, Velutio had allies and vassals everywhere that provided their army with supplies as they moved, whereas all the allies the rebel army had were travelling with them on their route.

He sighed and glanced around himself at the others. They rode quietly, their faces expressionless as the noise of thousands of men and horses blanketed them and the dust rose like the column of smoke from a forest fire.

"How long 'til we reach Silvas' palace?" he enquired of Caerdin, who rode alongside at the head of the column.

"We're almost there now. We've been on his land for an hour now. You'll see the top tower of his palace over the ridge any minute..."

Darius nodded and turned to face their destination again just in time to see three of their mounted outriders come galloping over the hill and rein in urgently in front of the command party. The scout officer saluted and coughed a little in the resulting cloud of dust.

"Your majesty... Silvas... he's under attack."

Kiva reined gestured to one side and the scouts and command party both moved off the road onto the springy loam while the slow procession of military might plodded and trundled past. "Details, man!" demanded the general as soon as they were out of the way.

"Dunno sir. It's not Velutio's army. There's maybe three or four different uniforms down there. They've not got much in the way of cavalry, but there's quite a lot of infantry. They've got tents set up half a mile away, but they're swarming around his walls and there are a couple of siege towers and a battering ram floating around among them."

Tythias rumbled deep in his throat. "Can you identify any of them?"

The scout shook his head. "No, sir, but they're a mix of men wearing black, green and blue."

"That could be just about anyone" the one armed commander grumbled.

One of the scouts saluted and spoke up. "Sir... one of the tents I saw had a flag. It was black with silver trim and had a rearing bull standing on a tower."

"Ah." Kiva smiled. "Lord Tilis shows his colours now. I thought he'd stay damn close to Velutio. He doesn't like to stick his neck out for anything. Velutio must have sent him in command of two other lords to make sure Silvas didn't get to join us. Silly bastard. If he'd just asked instead, Silvas might've joined them willingly, but still; all the better for us."

The general wheeled his horse and looked up at Darius. "Your permission, highness?"

Darius nodded and Kiva grinned, turning back to Tythias. "Get your cavalry marshalled and take them out to the east. I want you to cross the river over by the mill and get in position in the ditches there. If you do it right you can get behind their camp and a few hundred yards from the fight without them even knowing you're there. I doubt they're concerned about their rear lines; they'll be concentrating on the job at hand. When you hear the trumpet signal to advance, take out their camp and form a cordon around them with your light cavalry. What you do with the heavy cavalry's up to you."

Tythias nodded and, grinning, wheeled his own horse before charging off to find his cavalry captains. Kiva turned to face Brendan and Sithis. "We've not got time to bring the whole army into position. Get the two lead regiments and draw them up a few hundred yards away below the crest of the hill. When we move in, Sithis, you'll take the first regiment down into the centre of the fight and aim for their command units. If you can get to them, take out their officers. If they offer surrender, take it. As much of this is public relations as it is war. You know what to do."

"Brendan, old friend," he smiled. "You take the second regiment and make directly for the front entrance. I need you to take out that battering ram and form a perimeter outside the gate to hold the enemy away. If all goes well, once the units are all in the melee, you'll be able to close up like a swinging door and push them back against Sithis' regiment. Tythias' cavalry will be there keeping them hemmed in for you and I suspect he'll have battered their morale with a few cavalry charges by then."

"Athas," he continued, turning to the large dark-skinned man. "You need to get all this lot halted and make sure they don't move forward and get involved in the fight. If there's any way you can get the bolt throwers out to the crest, do so and get Filus' third regiment to give you cover. Can you do that?"

Athas grunted. "It'll be at least ten minutes before we can get the bolt throwers out to the front, even using all the manpower we have. They're at the front of the siege column, but that's behind eight regiments of footmen. Will ten minutes be enough?"

"It'll do," the general replied. "To be honest I thought it'd take a lot longer than that. Tythias won't be in position for at least five more minutes himself, so it should work out nicely. Once you've got them in position, pick your targets carefully."

Athas nodded as Brendan gave his commander a grin that Kiva recognised as a sort of hunger and nodded. "An' what'll you be at, sir?"

Kiva smiled. "I will be taking young lord Pelian and his men, along with a select few units, to deal with those siege towers. Once they're down and the battering ram's out, Silvas is safe. The man's stood up against our enemies for us and we can't let him down now."

There were nods of agreement from around him and Kiva squared his shoulders before reaching down to draw his sword. Darius noted briefly the look of pain that passed across the general's face as he bent to one side and feared for a fraction of a second that the man would fall from the horse. However, Caerdin recovered so fast no one else seemed to have noticed. "Let's move!" the general cried, and the command party went about their business.

As Darius watched the column fragment, he wondered where to place himself. He knew Caerdin would disapprove of his getting involved in the front lines of the battle, but he could hardly be seen to be standing idly by as his army fought. Gritting his teeth, he dismounted and walked over to Sithis, where the swordsman was giving orders to his regiment.

"I'm going to be joining you, Sithis. I know you don't approve, but I'm joining you anyway so don't think of arguing."

"I wouldn't dream of it, highness" the swordsman replied, beaming.

Kiva watched with a frown as the Emperor dismounted and took a position alongside the first regiment with his sword drawn. Well, perhaps the lad was right. Watching their Emperor fighting alongside them in battle would do more for the army's morale than an extra thousand men. Young Pelian rode alongside him, looking eager. The general worried about inexperienced people who eagerly anticipated blood and violence. They were usually either psychopaths or dreamy youths hopelessly lost in a romantic notion that would soon be ripped from them among steel and blood. Gritting his teeth, he turned to the young man. "Lord Pelian. Gather your men and have them assemble just below the ridge to the left of Sithis' regiment."

Pelian nodded once and veered off to the side, bearing down on his own officers. Kiva turned the other way and headed for a small unit of men in full uniform walking out to the grass at one side. The crossbowmen, though they'd been combined at an operational level with Filus' archers, were serving under no specific officer. In fact, Filus' archers tended now to travel with them and their unit had a sort of autonomy that Athas disapproved of mightily. However, since Filus now commanded the third regiment, no commander had been assigned to the archers. This had been a mere oversight until Tythias' skirmish in the rocks below Hadrus, and Filus had continued to command both groups but, since Tythias' report of how well the crossbowmen had handled themselves, Kiva had taken more of an interest in them. Now he considered the archers an independent unit and allowed them their semi-autonomy in return for their ability to work and act as a perfectly-organised and balanced unit. Whatever that prat Phythian had done, he'd trained his men well and they seemed to have no crisis of conscience serving in the army of his executioner. Kiva called out and waved them over.

"Get your entire unit up behind the crest of the hill alongside lord Pelian's men. I'll be up there taking command of the small group. Move out!"

Bearing out his opinion of them, the crossbowmen and their archer comrades immediately fell out with no other order having to be issued and made their way to the target location. Kiva smiled. If only

364

Phythian had thought further than his purse in the first place he could have been leading them now.

He waited until the last unit was on the move and turned his mare to the front of the column. With a slap to her hide he cantered for a moment until he was ahead of the army and then slid gracefully from her back and tied her to a tree. As he wrapped the reins around a branch, he turned away from his men. No need for them to see the signs of exquisite pain that flitted across his face at the sudden jarring of organs. He grumbled and, looking around to see make sure he wasn't being watched, lifted his tunic to examine his side. There was a tiny bulge in the skin as though it were filling with liquid like a waterskin. Damn. It was too early yet. He must have a word with Favio after the fight. Mercurias was too motherly over his unit, but Favio might be persuaded to help rather than hinder. With another wince, he turned and drew his sword.

Walking steadily out from the shade of the tree, he made his way directly toward the gathering troops at the crest. With a last mental calculation, he took his place in front of the two groups, alongside the young lord Pelian. Taking his flint and tinder from his belt pouch, he struck a fire among some moss and bracken on an old milestone. "Here's what we're going to do, people. You archers need to keep this fire fed. In a couple of minutes I want you to dip in your oil flasks and prepare to fire burning arrows into the siege towers. I want a concentrated barrage on the tower we can see from here. I want you to make sure the fucker's burning properly before we move on to the next one. Once it's truly on fire and they're having to sort out the crew to put the fires out, we'll move you onto the second tower. You'll then be left with a small defence unit as the rest of us move in to make sure the first tower stays down.

There was a chorus of nods around the general and a couple of the crossbowmen bent to collect twigs and foliage to add to the small fire on the milestone. Kiva watched in trepidation for another minute or so until the entire group settled and units stopped manoeuvring on the road. He gave a wave to the small group of heralds at the front of the column. Seconds later a complex trumpet call blared out and the infantry units began to move over the hill. Around Kiva the archers, their missiles doused in oil, dipped the tip into the flame and watched the arrows and bolts leap to life, wreathed in fire and deadly. Stepping a couple of paces forward, they could see over the crest of the hill and spotted the siege tower jammed up against the powerful walls of Silvas' fortress-like palace. Without waiting for the order, the unit released

365

their bolts and arrows and the various missiles thudded into the siege tower with a crash, followed by a deafening roar as the flames immediately took the dry wood. The men inside filled every floor, with the top group fighting the defenders for a means of egress onto the wall. There was a shout of alarm and burning bodies fell from the upper levels.

"Good! Now step around to the left until you can see the next siege tower, start another fire and do the same." He looked down at the young man. "Lord Pelian: you have to protect these archers at all costs. If the second tower goes and the battering ram's still moving, start them on that. Otherwise they can pick their targets."

The young lord gave a disappointed nod and gathered the twenty or so men that Kiva hadn't waved aside to move along with the archers. Kiva started to jog across the brow of the hill. As the various swordsmen of Pelian's unit fell in behind him, Balo jogged ahead with him.

"Just like old times, eh general?"

Kiva turned to look at his old comrade. "Yes and no." He turned to look at the men as he ran. "Fight as much as you need to to get through them. Don't stop to pose or play; just get through them and keep going for that siege tower. When we get there, we just need to make sure it's out of commission. If you see anyone carrying a bucket of water, make sure he dies. If we all get in there, we need to tip the damn thing over somehow. It's been guided into position with ropes and if they're not burned away we should be able to use those to tip it."

A vague chorus of agreement went up behind him and he paid no further attention to the men with him as he and Balo led almost a hundred men down the hill and charged the rear lines of the attacking force.

At first there was a silence; the silence born of the brain not being able to comprehend the tremendous noise assailing it. As Pelian's men became accustomed to the din around them, sound crept back in, distant at first and then louder and closer until the crash of steel on steel and the screams of the wounded and dying became impossible to ignore. With a fury born of absolute pride and belief, Kiva's unit fell on their enemy. Kiva was aware of men around him hacking, slashing and stabbing, trying to cleave a path through the lines. Their attack was served well by the fact that they hit the enemy from behind and lord Tilis' army was ill-prepared to defend against attacks from that direction. Crushed as they were in their efforts to push forward against the walls of Silvas' palace, the enemy were at a tremendous disadvantage, often failing to turn in time to block the blows crashing down on them. Kiva was familiar with the pure butchery that came with a surprise attack and his men cleaved limbs and severed heads and torsos as they moved like a harvest through the corn of the enemy ranks. Some of Pelian's men who'd obviously not served long in the force and had received little training from Sithis had to pause to vomit copiously among spilled livers and intestines and hacked-off limbs. Kiva ignored them. Such men would become used to the horrors of battle or would soon desert. In that case, the army could well do without them.

Kiva glanced over his shoulder as one of his men went down in a spray of blood, an unnoticed blow from one of the more astute and prepared defenders catching him in the neck. Kiva thrust out with his own blade and neatly skewered the offender, turning back just in time to duck a sweeping blow that threatened to remove his scalp and it was then he realised what a mistake he'd made getting personally involved in the fight. A sudden pain hit him so hard he doubled over further. Balo noticed the general bent double beside him and ignoring his own opponent, blocked the blow of the man attacking Kiva before delivering a second, sweeping blow that cut from shoulder to shoulder, carving a deep line across the man's chest.

Balo bellowed at the men. "Make for the tower and tip it!" before reaching out and gripping Kiva by the upper arm. The general straightened slowly, wiping his mouth, but not before Balo had noticed the smear of blood. The general had coughed up dark blood and was trying to hide it. "Kiva, you bloody fool!"

Caerdin pushed his old ally away and wiped his mouth further, removing as much as he could of the blood, though more welled into his mouth. He stood as straight as he could and gripped Balo's shoulder for support. "Lead them. You know how to do it and I don't give a *shit* whether you think you're right for it or not."

Balo fought a cascade of conflicting emotions and tried to hold Kiva steady. "You need looking after, general!"

"Fuck that!!" Kiva waved his sword loosely and weakly toward the tower. "The men need you. I'll see you afterwards."

Balo took a long, steady glance at his commander and then nodded curtly, if unhappily. Letting go carefully, he watched in grim silence as Kiva once more doubled over and a fresh gobbet of black blood fell from his mouth. Tearing himself away, he turned to the fray and cried "make for the ropes!"

Kiva continued to stand as he was for a while, clutching at the hilt of his sword with white knuckles as the pain roared and seared its way through his abdomen. He coughed once more and a further stream of dark blood poured forth.

"I can't die here," a voice muttered nearby.

"What?" Kiva barked, glancing up as best he could. A man stood in front of him with a vicious gash from his right shoulder down to his hip, his right arm flapping helplessly around. Kiva squinted through the pain. The man wore a green uniform.

"Who's your lord?"

The man staggered slightly and his blood ran down to mingle with Kiva's growing pool on the floor. "I'm Geraldus' man. A sergeant."

There was a moment of silence.

"And I think I know who *you* are."

Kiva sighed. "Then you've got to kill me where we are."

"Don't be ridiculous, general. I've no sword and I can't lift my arm or turn my head. I'm done here." He sighed deeply and winced. "Possibly done for altogether."

Kiva nodded. "I can't be. Too much more to do."

He coughed once more and was surprised and disheartened at the quantity of life's blood that ran from his mouth. "Help me get back to our line and you'll be treated."

The wounded sergeant grinned painfully, his eyes showing a deep sadness. "How can I pass up an offer like that?"

The two men limped and stumbled their way across the bodies and limbs, slipping in puddles of blood and viscera, slowly making their way back toward the column of the rebel army. A deafening twang and a rumbling and whistling noise announced the arrival of Athas' war machines into the fray. Their stumbling continued and then suddenly there were arms around them, helping them up the hill. The concerned face of Athas appeared and said something that Kiva entirely missed.

"Athas!" he demanded breathlessly. "Shut up and stop fussing. Have us taken to Favio and don't let word of this reach Mercurias or I'll nail your testicles to that machine."

Athas frowned at his commander and then nodded at the men supporting them.

Kiva must have blacked out somewhere along the column, for he stopped hurting for a while.

The marble columns wreathed in fire. The purple and gold drapes blazing and falling away into burning heaps on the floor. A chalice of wine on a small table by a couch, boiling in the intense heat. The panicked twittering of the ornamental birds in their golden cages as the room around them was consumed by the inferno. And in the centre of the room, standing in robes of white and purple, a man. He doesn't look frightened, though the flames lick at his whole world and his face is already grimy with the smoke. What he looks is desperate, his arm extended toward the sealed and barred door separating him from a future and a life. Dark pools of blood surround the man and he takes a step toward the door, slipping and slithering in the blood until he collapses on the floor and is brought face to face with the knife that's been drive hilt-deep into his side.

Kiva woke with a small cry and looked around him in panic. He was in his command tent and there were braziers flickering within and by the entrance. It was night and he was alone. They must have won the fight for the men had taken the time to erect the command tent before laying him carefully inside. Ideas had hammered at his consciousness as he awoke. Something to do with the old dream. That one thing; the one plan that so tantalisingly hung an inch away from his reach was there. Given a minute he might remember it. He focused slowly on the world around him and finally saw the items on the table next to his shoulder. There was a loaf of bread and some butter, some fruit and a bottle with a scruffily-written label on. He picked up the bottle, wincing at the pain and squinted at it. In Favio's writing it said "drink this – at this point it can't hurt." Suspiciously, he pulled the stopper and sniffed. Mare's mead and very strongly mixed by the smell. He smiled a weak smile and took a deep swig just as the curtains at the entrance were pushed aside and Tythias strode in.

"Thought I heard you shout."

Kiva nodded slowly. "I take it everything went well?"

"Pretty good. Very few losses considering. I see despite his protests, Balo ended up leading your unit. What happened to you then? Favio wouldn't tell us."

The doctor, arriving at that moment behind him, aimed a meaningful look at Kiva as he replied: "he took a glancing blow to the ribs that might have done him some serious damage. He's lucky to be here."

Tythias glanced over his shoulder suspiciously at the doctor and then shrugged. "Fair enough. I take my own fair share of stupid wounds. Well now you're awake I'd better report. Lord Tilis was taken

369

prisoner, lord Geraldus was found about an hour ago impaled on a cavalry spear and there's no sign of lord Herro. We presume he's long gone with his bodyguard. The siege engines were all taken out and we've a total of around five hundred prisoners. Don't know what you want to do with them, but Brendan's convinced we can't spare the manpower to guard them if we take them with us."

Kiva nodded. "He's absolutely right. Tell him to have their weapons and armour taken away from them and then let them go. They're only farmers and servants pressed into service for their lords."

Tythias pulled up a seat and collapsed next to the bed as Favio bustled around, holding Kiva's wrist and counting under his breath.

"Silvas is a happy man" the one armed Prefect continued. "He's done nothing but sing your praises and Darius' since he joined us. His men are quartered with everyone else now, but he's retaining control of them. I've assigned them the title 'Ninth Regiment' and left him in control. Seemed the best way to deal with it. They're pretty well trained and organised anyway."

Another nod from Kiva who, though listening, was watching Favio's ministrations suspiciously. "And?"

"And everyone wants to come in and see you, but the first in line is sergeant Cialo who arrived in camp about an hour or two ago. I think you can safely say he's not going back. He spat on his Velutio uniform and then burned it, along with the rest of his unit's. Oh, and he's brought a few more this time. There were twenty three of them when they turned up tonight."

A smile suddenly flashed across Kiva's lips. That was it. The missing piece. He pulled himself a little further upright in the bed and his eyes rolled as the pain lanced through his middle. Favio grumbled. "What's the fucking use in me mending you if you go and do it all again. Lie still."

Kiva looked urgently across at Tythias. "Look, don't take this the wrong way, but I need to speak to Favio for a minute and then I need to see a couple of people. Send Cialo in five minutes, then Balo in ten and tell the most senior crossbowman to find me first thing in the morning. After I've seen the other two, I'll put in a general appearance."

Tythias nodded unhappily and stood, stretching. "Ok. I'll see you in a while, you mad old bastard."

As the second in command left, Kiva reached up and gripped Favio's wrist. "You told them I'd been knifed?"

"Seemed the best way," the doctor agreed. "Believable and realistic. I assumed you didn't want anyone knowing the truth or you'd have gone to see Mercurias."

"And what is the truth?" the general pushed.

"You'll be dead next time you do anything like that. You may even die tonight anyway. I think it's settled in place again, but now you've got some actual liver damage. Any serious exercise and you'll be bringing up blood again. If it's serious enough, you might open it up properly and then you'll just bleed to death where you stand. You're looking quite pale right now and I don't know if you could stand another session of what happened today."

"So," Kiva pressed further, "how long can you keep me going? I reckon I need a week or two."

Favio shook his head. "You're a strong man, general, but even you can't make it that long. If you lie very still you might make it past a month, but if you walk and ride you'll be dead in days I reckon. It'll only take the one wrong move that jars that little shard on your liver and you'll be gone in minutes. What happened today was just a scratch. Put a hole in your liver and this'll seem like a little headache."

Kiva growled. "I need at least a week."

Favio nodded. "Well you'd best start praying then."

Without looking any longer at the general, Favio turned and strode from the tent. Kiva growled gently. He'd survived a duel to the death, twenty years of war and a crucifixion. He damn well wasn't going to lie down and accept this when there was still something to be done. And as for prayers..."

He ignored the sharp pains and pulled himself upright in bed, checking to make sure he didn't leak once he'd done so.

He sat for a few minutes mulling things over. The plan was finally falling together and there were just a few things left to work out, but he had to make it until the armies met or it was all for nothing. He continued to turn aspects of it over in his mind until sergeant Cialo, now wearing the uniform of a rebel captain, strode in and saluted.

"General Caerdin."

"Cialo," the general smiled. "Sit down man. I need to discuss a couple of things."

The veteran nodded and took the seat by the bed, leaning forward.

"I assume you want my report sir?" As the general nodded, he went on, unravelling a piece of parchment he'd drawn from his pocket and placing it in the general's hands. "As complete a list of the lords in

371

Velutio's army as I could manage. There's probably names missing, but nearly all of it's there."

Kiva nodded once more.

"And there are a number of lords among them who're verging on walking out anyway. We've done our best to sow disaffection among them but, to be honest, commander Sabian's doing that for us and far better than we ever could. There's been some kind of rift between him and Velutio and I can't for the life of me think why Sabian's still serving him. I heard that they had two hundred and eight deserters in one night just before I left."

"Good," the general replied. "I hear you've brought more men with you. I'm going to have a very special job for you all when we meet Velutio in a week or so."

Cialo frowned. "Not another spy job, sir? We can't really…"

Kiva shook his head and interrupted. "This is more important. I can't tell you about it yet, but it'll keep you off the battlefield and out of the action, and it's absolutely crucial if we want to bring this to a satisfactory end."

Cialo continued to frown, but nodded. "If that's the case, I'm your man sir."

Kiva nodded with a smile. "I'll talk to you further in a day or two. In the meantime, I hear Balo outside and I need to speak to him."

Cialo stood and saluted before turning and walking out of the tent. Kiva watched him go with some satisfaction. There had to be something said for their cause if it drew the men of morals and values away from the enemy side. He was still smiling curiously when Balo entered.

"That's a funny smile Kiva. What's so amusing?"

"Oh, nothing" the general smiled. "It still hits me every now and then that we're doing something great, positive and worthwhile. I spent so long being worthless that it feels odd. And it's all the doing of a young blond lad who changed everything. Or maybe just me."

"Did you bring me here to listen to you being soppy and feeling sorry for yourself, Kiva or for something else?"

The general looked up sharply, but Balo appeared to be grinning, insofar as he appeared to be permanently grinning anyway.

"Balo, I'm dying. Pretty quickly according to Favio."

Balo nodded. "I've as much as told you so myself. It's shit, but it'll come to all of us in the end, and I don't think I'll be all that far behind you."

"I need you to do something for me."

Ten minutes later, Balo left the command tent, his finger pressed against his lip in thought. 'Let's hope the Gods are with us' he muttered to himself as he made his way back down to the camp proper.

Chapter XXXII.

Favio growled up at the general. "You're an idiot, Caerdin. You'll be dead before the sun sets."

Kiva smiled in return from the back of his horse as he settled deeper into the saddle with a small grunt of discomfort. The ridiculous harness that Balo and Favio'd come up with to prevent too much damage coming to him as a result of the horse's motion was heavy and cumbersome and resulted in more than a little pressure in the lower back. Balo leaned over from his own horse and helped the general wrench one side of the contraption back into a more comfortable position. Behind them the newly-commissioned Captain Cialo of the Ninth sat uncomfortably astride a horse of his own. None of the three wore uniform, though Balo hadn't yet touched one anyway. The three men were in rough travelling leathers, with their swords buckled at their sides and a full day's rations attached to their saddle. A fourth horse was brought forward and the reins handed to the doctor.

"Favio, I don't care what you need to do. Keep me going. If I die before I'm ready, I'll be haunting the shit out of you from now until the end of time."

A gentle voice called from the tent flap behind the doctor as Minister Sarios stepped into the open air. "Favio, whatever Kiva needs to do is more important than anything else right now. Do as he says. Keep him alive, even if you have to poison him to do it."

The general nodded in recognition to the old minister and watched with barely concealed amusement as Favio slowly and clumsily mounted the horse.

"I'm not good with horses," the man grumbled. "Never had to ride much on an island you could walk across in five or ten minutes."

Kiva turned away from the amusing scene and looked down at the aging minister. "Sarios. Keep an eye on Darius for me. This is all going to come to a head in a few days and he needs to stay controlled and Imperial. He doesn't have to command; Tythias can do that; but he damn well needs to look in control. If he continues to *be* the Emperor, the army will do anything he asks." Turning back to Favio once the man was finally in the saddle, he smiled. "Come on. We've got to get gone as soon as possible."

The four riders, with varying degrees of skill, began to walk their horses down the gentle slope and toward the gate of the temporary camp where the army had bedded down late last night. The actual fortifications were not of the traditional ditch, mound and palisade variety. With an army of fourteen or fifteen thousand combatants and all their varied support, the camp was massive and would have taken a day or more to build. Instead, a 'hedge' of giant caltrops had been placed around the camp, formed from the sharpened stakes carried by each soldier and also among the supply wagons. Soldiers patrolled at very regular intervals and each gate was under the control of a guard of ten men. The gatekeepers glanced up to see their commanding officer approaching, along with three peripheral members of the staff and hurriedly pulled the gate open. Kiva reined in his horse.

"I thought you were all given orders to challenge anyone passing in or out of the camp, sergeant!"

The sergeant, ruddy faced and out of breath saluted.

"Sir. Yes, sir. But you're the general sir, travelling with a captain and one of the Imperial court, sir."

Kiva growled. "No fucking excuse. When you receive orders, you follow them, sergeant. They're orders, not suggestions." He turned to the man who stood next to him. "You, soldier. You've just made sergeant. Take control of the gate duty and send this man to Prefect Tythias for disciplining."

Next to Kiva, Favio grumbled. "You *can't* be thinking of having him punished for that!"

"Can't I, doctor? The man's not going to be hurt, but I doubt he'll make sergeant again and Tythias will want a few choice words with him."

He looked down at the dumbstruck sergeant. "Go!"

The former sergeant handed his helmet with the insignia crest over to the man the general had indicated and, turning, marched speedily away up the hill toward the command centre. Kiva nodded and looked down at the new sergeant.

"I trust you'll remember to follow your orders?"

The man swallowed noisily and then saluted before gesturing to his men. The unit fell in, blocking the gateway with their spears.

"Password?" he demanded of the four riders.

"Stadium," announced the general and waited for the men to unblock the gate.

"Pass, friend" the sergeant called with another salute. Kiva nodded and began to walk his horse once more, passing out of the camp. Favio was still muttering under his breath and his brows met in the centre as he pondered on the military mentality. With a quick glance at the doctor, Kiva looked across at Cialo.

"You were a sergeant until very recently, Cialo. What would *you* have done with him?"

Cialo shrugged. "Frankly, I'd have had him beaten by his comrades for putting them and the camp in danger. That's what we used to do in the old days."

Favio glanced up briefly and then resumed his grumbling. Kiva nodded. "I agree. I'd have done that in the old days and, all being well, it'll be like that again. Discipline, Favio, is of utmost importance in the army. Without it, you can't rely on the man next to you. Everyone has to be totally trustworthy and reliable or none of it works. Things are a little different right now, but that's because we're only a few days away from a battle that surpasses anything any of us have ever seen. A little leeway is required right now unless we want to risk the same kind of dissatisfaction and desertion as Velutio's seeing."

Favio grunted. "And why check people *leaving* the camp anyway?"

Kiva smiled. "We've had spies in *their* camp and you can be sure they've done the same. If everyone's challenged going in or out, we've more chance of controlling things."

"Huh." Favio returned his gaze to the floor.

Balo glanced back over his shoulder and, noting the increasing distance between them and the gate, cleared his throat.

"Now that we're out of there, Kiva, would you kindly explain where we're going? I saw Tythias' face this morning and he didn't look happy. Why've we got rations for a full day and why aren't you two in uniform?"

Kiva smiled and Balo rolled his eyes. The general was still worryingly pale and winced almost every time he moved. Despite what he'd heard of Favio's good reputation round the camp, he didn't imagine that even the Gods could keep Caerdin upright for many more days. The general gestured to the two behind to join them and the four quickly pulled into a line, riding alongside each other over the grassy slopes and down toward the distant sea.

"I need to scout out the land ahead of us. I'm looking for specific things in a site for battle and I think I know where it needs to be, but I want to be absolutely sure and you and Cialo both need to know it in advance. Favio, I'm afraid that you've become my personal physician for the next few days or, in fact, for the rest of my life; whichever comes soonest."

More grumbling ensued from the doctor while Cialo and Balo exchanged worried glances. Balo cleared his throat.

376

"Everyone will be wondering what you're up to Kiva, spending all your time with Cialo, Favio and me. You're their general. You should be with the commanders."

"I will be after today," Caerdin replied. "But I need to set certain things in motion first, or it'll just come down to numbers and bloodshed."

They rode for some time in silence before the turncoat captain began a marching song from the old days that soon brought on all four voices.

Darius sat in the command tent in his tunic and breeches, rubbing his shoulders where the cuirass had chafed during the previous day's travel. He eyed the armour with distaste and took another bite of the bread, cheese and olive oil that had been delivered for breakfast. In the main room of his tent, his chair formed part of a circle and several of the others were currently occupied. Sarios looked somewhat out of place surrounded by Tythias, Athas, Mercurias, Brendan, Marco and the rest of the commanders. They sat patiently, eating their own bread and cheese and waiting for their Emperor to speak his mind.

"I want to discuss the command of the army with you all."

There was a gentle murmur in the room, but not of surprise, considering the company.

"General Caerdin is more than just a great commander, he's a figurehead to whom people have flocked. Our army would be half the size it is without his name." Darius swallowed. It hurt him to talk like this. "But we have to consider the possibility that he will not be in a position to command by the time the lines of battle are drawn."

Now the murmur grew louder and angrier, but Mercurias waved his hand. "Shut up. He's right, you goat-brained idiots."

Darius nodded at the medic. "I hate to have to consider this, but we'd be failing the men if we didn't at least think about it. I know that we've some very capable commanders in our midst here. I know that Tythias and Sithis, among others, are qualified and experienced in leading an army in the field. I expect that, as second in command, you all agree with Caerdin's decision that Tythias would take command in the event of his absence, much as he has now." He turned to the one-armed Prefect.

"The only question is: do you think you can beat Sabian, Prefect? I know that Caerdin worries about that himself and he's one of the most celebrated generals in Imperial history. Without Caerdin's brain and presence, can we hope to outmanoeuvre Sabian on a battlefield?"

Brendan leaned forward. "Kiva ain't dead yet, yer majesty. 'E'll surprise y'all yet, an' I'm sure e's got a plan as twisted as a God's dick."

Darius nodded. "Everyone believes that and he probably does. He's certainly been planning something for some time now, but no one knows what it is. He's playing everything so close to his chest that no one has an inkling. Whatever he's planning involves Cialo. Ever since the man's joined us, Caerdin's had him running missions and now he's taken Balo, Favio and Cialo to scout out the battlefield he wants. I know he's up to something with Cialo, and Favio's obviously there for medical support, but I've no idea why he's involving Balo, since the man plainly stated he wanted nothing to do with command."

The young Emperor shifted uncomfortably.

"The problem is that the general's health is failing rapidly. I don't know how many of you have seen the signs?"

There was another murmur around the room, this time registering some surprise. Mercurias leaned forward again. "The general's old wound is getting much worse. I can only assume we're reaching a critical stage since he won't let me near him. I know that his dosage of mare's mead has at least tripled over the last week and his body can't stand much more of that. Kiva's trying to push himself along to do things rather than lie back and extend his life expectancy, and that's probably doing him more harm than the wound itself, but he's a surprisingly robust man and I'd not be surprised if he managed to keep active a lot longer than Favio expects."

He sighed and leaned back.

"But I think the general will not outlast this campaign. The army must *not* hear about this under any circumstances. I'm sure you can all understand why."

"So…" Darius straightened again. "Tythias. As soon as Caerdin gets back you need to find out what his plan is. We need to know in case he doesn't live to see it through. In the meantime, we need to think about any necessary reorganisation. I would like Sithis to take the position of third in command so that there's still two senior officers should anything happen suddenly to the general."

There were nods of agreement among the long and unhappy faces in the room. Brendan stood and straightened himself. "Mercurias is right though. Kiva's strong. 'E'll surprise us all yet." Turning, he

378

saluted the Emperor. "Is that all, highness? I got a regiment ter get mobilised."

Darius nodded and the officers began to stand and dissipate. The world here was a vastly different place to the confines of Isera where he'd had to make no decisions affecting other folk. Now he was forced to plan the fate of thousands; maybe millions. In the past weeks, Kiva had been with him constantly, suggesting and nudging him in the right directions, making sure he did what was best and right without having to handle the crucial decisions himself. In the last week, though, the general had begun to pull away from that, spending more and more time alone; admittedly often because of convalescence. Caerdin seemed to spend all his time now with Cialo and Balo, even eschewing his own unit, and his lack of counsel was a loss that Darius felt deeply.

As the commanders in the room stood and made their way bowing and saluting to the door, Athas stepped toward Darius. Waiting until the last of the others had left, he pulled a seat closer to the Emperor's and collapsed heavily into it.

"You worry a great deal about losing Kiva, don't you?"

Darius nodded. "Of course. He's the linchpin that holds the army together and our strategist..."

"I'm not talking about that, Darius, and you know it. Sarios spent his entire life on the island preparing you for this, but he was never close to you, was he? I know how close Sabian was to you. I suspect he even felt like family; an uncle or some such?"

Darius looked down at the floor and nodded slowly.

"And now he's gone from you," the big black captain went on. "He's the enemy and that's hard enough for you to deal with. And then you got to know Kiva and he's taken much the same role with you: protector, advisor, even father-figure perhaps. And now you know you're going to lose him. It's *going* to be hard on you; you're still a young man, Darius. It's cutting *me* up deep inside knowing in a few weeks he'll be gone from us. I've known him almost all my life and I've never been as close to anyone. He's been a brother to me since we met on the battlefield at the Galtic Narrows and the rest of the Wolves feel much the same. Mercurias deals with it by being angry at him for what he sees as shortening his own life for the sake of the campaign. Brendan's in denial; he thinks Kiva will live forever. Marco's all but stopped speaking to people and I notice he's started drinking quite heavily. And I'm bottling it all up, because someone has to keep control. That, I suspect is why he's spending so much time with Balo, Cialo and Favio. He can't be with us at the moment, because it's distracting. He needs to concentrate on what he's doing and those three are less interested parties; outsiders if you prefer."

Darius lifted his head and Athas was not surprised to see the tears in his eyes.

"I'm just not prepared for all this," the young man said, his voice thick with emotion. "Battles and campaigns I was expecting, but there's too much more than that; too much personal trouble. I always thought Sabian would somehow help us; I couldn't believe he'd bring an army against us for that man. If he leads his force against us; against me... It feels like my family are betraying me or deserting me. Sabian's going to fight me; Kiva's going to leave me. Gods alone know how many of the rest of us are going to die in the next week. Even if we win this, who's going to be left? I might be alone."

Athas nodded. "It's a distinct possibility. But you've got to plan for every eventuality. You'll always have a good civilian support even if all of your commanders die. Sarios, Favio, Sathina and all the elders of the island will be able to help you after this is over. I have to admit *I'm* surprised Sabian is still with them, but he's a man of his word. He took an oath to Velutio and he'd rather die than betray that oath. His loyalty may be misplaced, but that's the kind of honour the world's sadly short of. If we lose, he'll have been proved right. If we win, it won't be him we've beaten; it'll be his master. Either way, he'll fight honourably and fairly and you can't ask more of him than that. I'd certainly rather he was in command of the enemy than someone with *no* morals."

The Emperor shuddered as the tears fell. "I just don't know if I can do it Athas. This last quarter of an hour actually hurt. I spent three hours steeling myself to have to say the things I did, and I think Brendan's angry with me now too."

Athas shook his head. "As I said, Brendan's in denial. He'll not blame you. We need to get the army moving and you need to dry your face and stand up straight. You're the Emperor, remember, not just Darius of Isera now."

The young man gave him a weak smile as they stood slowly and walked slowly toward the exit. Darius wiped his face on his sleeve and held his head high. Outside, the camp was a blur of activity, as regiments packed up or moved into position. Athas' engineers and supply wagons were already on the move, having set off under armed escort as soon as the sun had risen. The rest would catch up within the hour and they'd be safe from trouble with Tythias' scout units constantly monitoring the surrounding area and reporting any sign of a

380

life. Tythias and Athas had made the decision to remove some of the safeguards from the slow-moving units in order to speed up the general movement rate of the entire army.

Darius and the burly, dark-skinned man strode across the grass in front of the command tent and were about to go their separate ways when one of the gate guards came running, out of breath, up the hill to the officers. He stumbled to a halt and saluted clumsily.

"Your majesty? Sir? There's a man at the gate... whole load of men with him... doesn't know the password but demands to be let in... Says he's the Prince of Pelasia, sir."

Darius turned to Athas, a grin slowly spreading across his face. The first good news he'd heard in days. He sighed as some of the tension fell from his shoulders and nodded at the soldier. "Go and find Prefect Tythias and tell him to join us at the gate. Then come back down, but don't run. You'll do yourself an injury; look at yourself man... you've gone purple!"

Athas laughed and patted Darius on the shoulder as they strode slowly down the hill toward the west gate. Already the first and second regiment were moving down the hill toward the gate with their full packs. Men ran everywhere organising and busy, though each and every one stopped in mid-run to salute their Emperor. Darius stopped one of them.

"What are you doing now?"

"Sir! I've gotta go fetch the standards for the third regiments, sir,"

Darius smiled. "Ok, but go via the command area and tell my guard to pack up and get my gear loaded on the wagons. And have one of them bring my armour and horse down to the west gate."

"Yessir!" the man saluted again and then jogged off up the hill.

At the gate, Ashar stood with his arms folded watching them approach. Behind him the entire Pelasian unit sat ahorse, watching with interest. Ashar grinned as Athas and Darius approached the blockade.

"Quite an army you've got here now, young Emperor."

Darius returned the smile. "Ashar. Your intelligence must be slipping if you don't know our watchwords."

"Ha." Ashar leaned over the barrier. "'Stadium', yes? And yesterday was 'fish sauce', the day before was 'provincial'. Need I go on?"

"Then why wait at the gate?" Athas enquired.

Ashar smiled. "I'm not actually part of your army. It would be impolite of me to enter a foreign nation's military capital under false

381

authority. Plus, I owe it to the Emperor here to treat him with the respect I would hope he would treat me."

Darius returned the smile. "When this is over, Ashar, and we've rebuilt the Empire, this army will be travelling with you to put you back on your own throne. Rest assured the terms between our two countries will be good as ever they were if not better. In the meantime..." He leaned round the prince to address the Pelasian riders. "Go ahead and get yourself a bite to eat. The mess hasn't been packed up yet and the cook should still be able to find you something. Have an hour's rest, because by then the last of the army will be ready to move out."

He turned back to Ashar. "Sorry to speak to your men over you, but we're a little pressed for time."

The prince nodded. "Agreed. I saw Caerdin and a few other men riding out a few hours ago. We passed them down on the Tosco valley trail. I presume that's where you're planning to meet Velutio?"

Athas nodded. "Kiva hasn't confirmed it yet, but that's where we're making for. He's gone ahead to check out the ground."

"Yes. It would be somewhat amusing. And a good spot so long as you get there first. How large is your army now?"

Darius squared his shoulders. "Just under fifteen thousand, split into nine regiments and other cavalry and missile units under independent command. Then there's engineers and their weapons and the supply train."

Ashar nodded. "It's starting to get a lot more even. I couldn't get an exact count, but if you'd met Velutio's army a week ago, they'd have walked across you without stopping to see what they'd trodden on. Now I shouldn't think it's even two to one anymore. There've been whole units of deserters we've come across in the last week."

Darius smiled. Perhaps whatever plan Caerdin was working on was already having an effect...

Late in the afternoon Kiva rode slightly ahead of the group, down a narrow track and round the side of a hill to see a wide valley open up like a saddle. The sun was setting slowly ahead of them in the low point of the valley in the direction of Serfium and Velutio, as well as the direction that would soon see Velutio's army on the march to meet them.

Reining in his horse, Kiva turned around as best he could in the contraption that held him rigid in place and surveyed the valley. Just like he remembered from all those years ago. There's been less cavalry involved then, but he'd had the high ground and they'd held the saddle against their enemy. He looked back at the others. Balo was frowning.

"Problem, Balo?"

The scarred man shrugged. "Twenty years since, but Velutio's got a long memory. D'you really think he'll meet you here again in the same circumstances?"

"I think it's kind of poetic really. I brought Avitus to battle here in support of an Emperor and beat him. Now it's a different Emperor, but the generals are the same, so why not the place. I think Avitus or Velutio or whatever the hell he wants to call himself these days will meet me here. In fact, I think he'll be eager to. See, he doesn't like to be beaten and he holds grudges. He'll want revenge for the last time and he'll want to do it right; to do it here. The important question is which one of us will get the best positioning and that depends who gets here first. The best thing we've got going for us is that I doubt Sabian will be happy with this place. Velutio'll have to order him to fight here and that might help drive the wedge between them a little further."

He looked around again, smiling with reminiscence. "This is definitely it. This is where it'll happen. We need to get Tythias and the others moving faster. I want the high ground here and the sun in their eyes early in the morning."

Balo nodded. "It's nice ground, I agree, but why are *we* here *now*?"

"You need to remind yourself the lie of the land and where the lines will be drawn. I know you were there, but it's been a quarter of a century and we need to be prepared."

He stopped and glanced around the low hills surrounding them and the spurs of land on either side that jutted out like horns. Balo's gaze followed the general's. At some places on the hills the land had been terraced for farming and fields of vines and groves of olive trees surrounded picturesque white villas. Some of the buildings here were fairly grand affairs being, as they were, the centre of large estates belonging to wealthy landowners. He squinted. His initial observation in the slowly fading light had been misleading. These villas, including the two expensive ones in prime position on the spurs of land, were empty and had stood empty for some time. Though there was no sign of damage or neglect from this distance, the lack of sound or movement was disconcerting and saddening, and no smoke rose from the buildings. No animals barked or lowed and no peasants or slaves moved around the tangled fields. War had loomed and struck here several times before this and the villas' owners were gone or dead some time since.

Quiet reigned in the valley, disturbed only by the whistling of a gentle breeze and the rummaging of some animal in the undergrowth nearby.

Cialo coughed. "I've no idea why we're all here general, but if there's something you need to tell me, I guess now is the time?"

Kiva nodded. "Yes. This is it. I figure we've got two days; three at the most before both us and Velutio are here. We ride back to camp tonight after we've had a little rest and a little sightseeing and I think we'll be there around dawn to join the column. Balo, you know what you need to do here. Keep your eyes peeled and take in absolutely everything you can. You'll need it. Favio, you stay with Balo for the time being." He turned to the man who'd served Velutio for two decades until his conscience would let him no more. "Cialo, I said I had a job for you, and I do. Come with me and I'll explain."

Chapter XXXIII.

Sabian gripped and ungripped both fists rhythmically as he strode from the command tent. The sound of his teeth grinding together drowned out the sounds of camp being broken after the night. He swept his gaze back and forth around the camp. Since the disappearance of Cialo, he'd no one to talk to on a personal level. His position was becoming untenable in this place. Velutio was making command decisions and then forcing him to deal with them and the various lesser lords in the army were bypassing him and taking their gripes directly to the old lord. He might as well not be here other than the fact that Velutio still claimed he valued Sabian's battlefield expertise. True enough that he'd taken Velutio's army through months of warfare and their army had suffered only minor losses and no defeats, but morale was at an all time low now. They'd lost more men in two weeks of desertions than they'd lost in months of battle. So far no individual lord had tried to pull out, but Sabian had a feeling such a state wasn't all that far away. Perhaps he should've been more decisive in those days on Isera. If he'd taken up with Caerdin then, none of this might have happened. Equally, if he'd not let the islanders and the Wolves leave, the same applied. It was his fault directly that this was happening and, having given his oath to Velutio and supported his stand against Darius as a rival claimant. The most irritating thing was that less than a half dozen people the world over knew that Darius actually had a direct claim to the throne rather than some spurious one that Sarios had invented. Velutio, on the other hand, had no claim. In all truth, he was supporting a usurper, but it was too late to do anything about it. All he could do was bring the army to the Tosco valley as Velutio had ordered and try to beat the rebels there and claim the high ground. All he could do was try his best to win the battle before their entire army deserted.

And yet...

He strode down the hill from the headquarters and kept his eye on the troops folding tent canvas and gathering their equipment; perimeter guards relinquishing the night's passwords and heading back to their units. In the last few days the camp guard were much more concerned about people crossing the boundary from the inside than the outside. Was Sabian the only one who thought of that as a sign?

Perhaps he should just give up and walk away. There would be no dishonour in that. Not desertion, of course, but resigning his commission. He could turn round and stride back into Velutio's tent and leave his sword and uniform there. Walk away.

No. Not now.

He continued to march down the hill, anger still flooding through him. Velutio was being unusually sentimental wanting to re-fight an old battle with Caerdin and he could see why, but Caerdin had almost certainly engineered it to happen this way. Sabian knew he was a good strategist and a damn good commander, but could he hope to beat Caerdin on level terms and especially on ground Caerdin knew and had the advantage on?

Damn... damn... damn!

He spotted Lord Dio standing outside his tent in full armour, slugging back watered wine from a goblet. Dio was a man who in the right circumstances would have been a friend and probably a staunch imperialist. He'd served Quintus as a governor in the last days of the Empire and had been a friend to Caerdin. Steeling himself, he changed tack and made for Dio's tent.

The elderly lord placed his goblet on the small table next to him and wiped his mouth on the back of his hand. He turned and smiled at the approaching man.

"Commander. To what do I owe this pleasure?"

Sabian regarded Dio. The old man had long, grey hair tied back neatly after the fashion of the northern barbarians from whence his family had come many generations back. He was clean shaven with startling blue eyes and a tall, thin frame. He certainly didn't look as old as Sabian knew him to be.

"Lord Dio. Are you in a rush? I'm in need of some conversation..."

The elderly lord nodded. "As a matter of fact I was just going to do the rounds and check on the men. They like to know I take an interest. Care to join me?"

"Actually," Sabian replied, "I'd prefer to talk in private if I can tear you away. Your troops don't really need to see you anyway. They must love you; they're one of very few units who haven't suffered desertions yet."

Dio nodded soberly. "Very well."

He turned and, picking up his goblet and helmet, walked back into his tent. Sabian consciously stopped grinding his teeth and strode in after the man. Inside, the tent was organised much as a military command tent, rather than a lord's personal habitation. Four chairs sat around a table full of charts and maps and lists and the insignia of Dio's forces hung from the rear. A small bed and a travel chest were the only concessions here to comfortable living.

Sabian stopped in the entrance and glanced around to make sure Dio's guard were not attending too closely. Fortunately the old lord was respected enough that the guard felt safe to keep a perimeter some distance away. Just in case, he closed the flaps of the tent and tied them shut anyway.

When he turned round, Dio was watching him quizzically. "If I didn't know you better commander, you have the look of a man about to desert."

"Funny you should say that…"

Sabian walked across and sat heavily in one of the chairs. "Do you mind?" he enquired, gesturing to the jug of wine on the table.

"Be my guest. Pour me another while you're at it."

Sabian did so, a half smile as far as he could push his face.

"I'm not deserting, Dio. Don't worry about that. As much as I can't see you deserting either. We're both men of honour and we don't betray our oaths."

A simple nod.

"But some things; most things even, about this campaign disturb and annoy me and I'm on the verge of resigning my commission."

Dio nodded again. "It's no secret you're not happy. Most of the army talk about it. You'd be surprised at just how popular a subject you are right now. No." He picked up his goblet again and took a sip. "I'm not planning to desert either, but should you or I go, I think a lot of this alliance would fall apart. I would like to think, anyway."

Sabian gritted his teeth again and took another swig.

"Problem is: Velutio wants us to fight a battle that I think is wrong in the very last place I would choose to do it with an army that, by the time we get there, may be outnumbered."

Dio smiled. "Your conscience playing you up, Sabian? You're not old enough to remember the Empire when it was a power. Maybe the battle will be fought in their favour, but the Gods will be with us and we can't fail. The Gods know our cause to be right, so you've got one thing wrong there."

"Why's that?" muttered Sabian, staring into his goblet.

"Because Avitus was the second most powerful man in the Empire after Quintus. Caerdin was the most important military man, but Avitus was also a governor and destined for office at the Emperor's side. He's got a claim and precedence. This Darius was just the son of some courtier or officer or some such. We're in the right and the Gods know when you're in the right."

387

"You're a pious man, then?"

"Of course." Dio took another sip. "I wouldn't say the Gods ruled my life, but I certainly try to respect their wishes whenever I can and not fly in the face of their rules."

Sabian smiled. "And what if I told you that you were wrong, Dio. What would you think then? If the Gods had deserted us?"

Dio narrowed his eyes. "What is it you know, Sabian?"

"I know who the 'Emperor' Darius really is. And having spent some time with him, I'm of the horrible opinion that he might be just the man the world needs."

"What do you mean who he 'really is'?" the old lord leaned forward in his chair.

Sabian shrugged. "I'm sworn to silence. I'm straining to keep that vow, because it's suddenly more important than I could ever have thought when I made it."

Dio growled. "Sabian... if this is as important as you seem to be suggesting, the Gods will be your judges, not whoever you made a vow to. Speak!"

The commander sighed and leaned back in his chair. "If I do tell you, you cannot make it public. I may take you and even others into my confidence, but I'm not about to announce this for a whole variety of reasons."

He shuffled in his seat and took another swig of wine before refilling his cup.

"He's the Caerdin child."

He watched the startling serious of expressions crossing Dio's face with some satisfaction. He'd been holding that particular secret in so long he couldn't believe how freeing it felt opening up to someone.

"He's Caerdin's son and that makes him Livilla's son too, and a member of Quintus' Imperial household by blood." He smiled weakly at the elderly lord. "*Now* tell me who's got the true claim."

Dio sat for a long moment and whistled through his teeth. "I think I can see why Velutio's keeping this under wraps. But the enemy don't know either, do they, or we'd have heard it by now."

"Very astute," agreed Sabian. For a number of reasons there are only a couple of people in Caerdin's camp who know and they can't reveal it either. That's a personal matter and not something to be lightly undertaken. It's not for Velutio I'm keeping this quiet, but for Darius and Caerdin. Even the general and the boy are unaware and it has to stay that way."

Dio stared at him. "You've perhaps too much honour to do your job properly, Sabian."

The commander laughed out loud. "You have no idea how sick I'm getting of hearing that. But you're a man from the same mould, Dio. Hell, you supported Caerdin against Avitus after the Emperor's fall from grace, I seem to remember."

"True." Dio sat cradling the goblet between his hands and staring at the floor. "I'm in a quandary now, commander. You know that, because you put me there and I can't help thinking you did that on purpose. You won't desert, but your conscience is pushing me to do it for you. I should, by rights, turn and walk away with my men."

Sabian nodded. "But then by rights, so should I. If you went with your men, I wonder how many of the other lords would follow you?"

"You've given me a lot to ponder commander. I am, of course, taking your words at face value despite their importance, but I have the feeling you're telling me the truth. I think I'll come with you to the Tosco valley before I make my decision. I think I'd like to see this Caerdin child first."

Sabian nodded. "I hope the Gods grant you a reasonable path and that it's the right one, for I can't help but think I'm on the wrong one and heading for hell."

As Sabian and Dio sat within the lord's tent, deep in discussion, a figure moved among the men of Lord Vassario's army a few hundred yards away. He was of average height and average build in a red tunic bearing Vassario's emblem of a tree and a sword, with a military scarf pulled up around his throat. A common soldier carrying a sack was a figure to be ignored and no one paid any attention whatsoever as the extremely average man threaded his way between other soldiers carrying gear.

Certainly no one examined him closely enough to spot his swarthy, Pelasian skin under the dirt covering that was so common of soldiers in autumn campaigns. He struggled with the sack of grain on his shoulder and found his way to a tent. It was only a small tent by the standards seen elsewhere on the camp; certainly not the size of the lords' command tents and considerably smaller than the eight-man tents the troops shared. A medium-sized affair, it nevertheless had the unit's insignia on a standard thrust into the turf outside. The Pelasian looked around quickly and disappeared inside.

Terrico was once of lord Vassario's three captains and probably the least popular. A martinet, he had a reputation for cruelty and it was possibly only that reputation that had prevented more desertions from the army, or so Terrico would like to think. A stocky man with a thick black beard, he turned in the midst of shaving his upper lip, a silver mirror in one hand and a sharp razor in the other. He glared at the intruder.

"What in the name of Bellas' arse are you doing in here?" he demanded.

The dirty soldier dropped the sack at the doorway and saluted hurriedly.

"Sir, I've a message from the quartermaster. He says it's urgent."

The captain scraped another patch of foamy hair from his lip and then nodded, examining his face in the mirror. The soldier walked across the tent, reaching into his tunic and producing a rolled parchment. He bowed his head and held the parchment out of the captain, who replaced the mirror and blade on the trunk by his side and grasped the parchment, unfurling it as he did so. His surprise at being confronted with a blank sheet was as nothing compared to his surprise when the dirty, unimportant soldier reached past him with lightning speed and drew the razor back and up, drawing it in one smooth move across the captain's windpipe.

There was a rush of expelled air and blood frothed from the man's neck as he arched backwards, his eyes wide with surprise. He never even got the chance to scream. Dropping the parchment, he clutched at his neck, but nothing he could do would help now. He floundered around for a moment, trying to get past his attacker and to the tent flap, but the soldier was always in the way wherever he moved. With a sigh he finally slumped to the floor, the whistling noise dying as he did so.

The Pelasian pulled a stylus from his tunic, dipped it in the captain's blood and began to scribble on the parchment. Finishing his note with a flourish, he laid the parchment flat on the captain's chest and pinned it there with the shaving knife. With a last ironic salute, he stepped away from the figure and collected his sack of grain. Plodding to the rear of the tent, he crouched and glanced under the leather side. Empty. With a grin he pushed the sack underneath and crawled after it, disappearing from the scene an ordinary soldier with a job to do.

It would be almost an hour later that a soldier, sent to find out why captain Terrico was late, would stumble into the tent and across the

390

body of the captain lying in a pool of congealed blood and a note pinned to his chest. Five minutes later the note was in the hands of Lord Vassario, but not until after it had been seen by more than a dozen men. The parchment had simply said: 'Darius Imperator. Thus die all tyrants.'

By the time the army reached their next night's camp, Vassario's army had lost almost four hundred men to desertion and the lord found himself in the command tent explaining the losses in a panicky voice to an angry Velutio.

And the word of the note had not stopped with Vassario's men.

At the same time as Vassario was being berated by his master, the army of the Emperor Darius made camp in a deep valley of vineyards and farms, stretched out over some distance due to the slope of the terrain. Darius made his way into his command tent, which was still being set up. Soldiers of his personal guard carried chairs and tables and other furnishings in from one of the wagons as the Emperor sighed and gratefully unfastened the buckles that held his cuirass together. He lifted off the front and tossed it carelessly on the bed that had just been dropped to one side, before taking the rear plate and treating it much the same way. With a long stretch, he rubbed his sore shoulders and collapsed heavily into a chair.

Caerdin entered a moment later with Tythias and Balo. The general continued to look paler and weaker by the day and every time he set eyes on the man, he felt fresh waves of worry and sadness. Trying not to show it, he smiled and gestured to the other seats.

"I thought with all the extra time we'd made up and the travelling until dark had fallen, we were going to be at your chosen place by tonight."

Kiva nodded. "We probably could have been with a couple of extra hours, but it's no longer urgent. Tythias' scouts report that Sabian's army is still at least a day away and are camping down each night. We're maybe two hours away. Under these circumstances, I'd rather we arrived early in the morning and the men could get a good idea of the terrain. Plus it'll be a lot more comfortable drawing up our defences in the daylight. We'll have all day to set up before Velutio arrives and we can have the entire army fortifying our position in rotated groups while the others rest and eat. Our force will be nicely rested and fully fortified by the time the enemy get there. All in all, I'm happy with the progress."

391

"Good." Darius smiled, reaching out for the jug of refreshments one of the soldiers had delivered. "I think we're just about ready then, or as ready as we'll ever be, anyway. Now what we need to do is discuss what's going to happen on the day itself."

Kiva relaxed. "Firstly we're going to be in our absolute finest. Full ceremonial gear for all senior officers and all of your guard. That means no plain cuirasses. Embossed breastplates are a must. Full military cloaks, crests, standard bearers with all the banners and cavalry masks."

"Cavalry masks?"

"They were worn in the old days by cavalry officers on parade and sometimes on the battlefield. Burnished steel face masks that attach to the helmets. Apart from the 'scaring the hell out of the enemy' effect they were originally designed for, it's no secret now that I'm not a well man. I don't want Velutio or Sabian, or even our men to see how death himself is leaning over my shoulder these days."

Darius thought long and hard about this. He wasn't sure how comfortable that would be, but there was a lot of sense in what the general said and he'd seen pictures in some of the old texts of the cavalry in their expressionless masks. They certainly would make a startling impression.

"Very well. And what next?"

Tythias leaned forward then.

"Next is the parlay. You and Kiva and I, along with any staff officers who don't have direct command of a unit, ride along our front ranks a few times to get the men's blood up and some cheering going. Banging of swords on shields and so on; you know the sort of thing. Then we all ride out to the middle of the battlefield and meet with Sabian and Velutio and whoever else they bring with them. We demand their surrender. They laugh and demand ours. We laugh and then we all go our separate ways. After that, it's down to whatever strategy Kiva's got lined up for us."

Darius nodded. "And that is?"

Kiva smiled. "While we're at the parlay, I've got something planned. Cialo and his men will be absent for that time running a very important little errand for me. If all goes well, we'll all know what to do within minutes of the parlay ending. I'm not revealing the details yet. The more people that know about it, the less chance there is of it succeeding. If it works, we can all heave a sigh of relief."

Darius grumbled.

392

"That's all very well, Kiva, but what happens if it fails, or if you're too ill to come out to the parlay. *We* have to know what's going on in case *we* have to deal with it."

Caerdin grinned weakly. "Let an old man have some surprises left. I've made it all this way and I can assure you, I've absolutely no intention of being out of the way until I've seen it through one way or the other. You'll just have to trust me on that."

Minister Sarios yawned and flicked open his eyes, rubbing at the gritty sleep that threatened to hold them shut. He turned his head this way and that in the bafflement one suffers after being suddenly awoken from a deep sleep. The hammering on the wooden tent frame came again. He clicked his tongue irritably and climbed laboriously out of his cot. Groaning, he shuffled towards the door, scratching at his side.

"Who's *that* at this time of night?"

He unhooked the toggle and pulled back the leather tent flap to see Sathina standing silhouetted by the campfires that burned around the valley where tense soldiers tried to relax. Sarios blinked.

"Miss Sathina? What on earth are you doing up at this time. Only drunken soldiers are by now."

Sathina smiled. "We've a favour to ask of you, minister."

"We?" queried Sarios, and then noticed the shadowy and bulky shape standing to one side where the light of the campfires didn't illuminate him. "Ah... that 'we'. I see." He sighed. "Well, you'd better come in."

Leaving them to their own devices, the minister turned back to his tent and, reaching down to the small table in the centre, lit the oil lamp which slowly pushed back the shadows in the circular room. Three chairs sat close to the table and Sarios gestured to them as he slowly sat back on the side of his makeshift bed with a groan.

Tythias entered behind Sathina as the young lady made her way across to the seats.

"Sorry about the lateness, Sarios." He grinned mischievously. "Did you know you wear virtually the same thing in bed as you wear in public?"

The smile fell from his face as Sathina elbowed him sharply in the ribs and the two took the seats.

"There's a jug of water on the table and some apple juice on the cabinet at the back. If you would like to rummage inside, you may even find some plum brandy I brought from Isera."

393

Again that smile crossed Tythias' face until he caught sight of the expression on the girl's face. "Erm... water will be fine. Thank you minister."

Sarios nodded and stretched out his legs. "Let me guess. You would like to be married and you're both so excited that you couldn't wait until the morning to talk to me. Am I correct?"

Sathina nodded as Tythias smiled and said "am I that transparent?"

"I'm afraid the two of you are no secret," the minister replied with a gentle smile. "I've been wondering for some time when you would decide this."

"So you'll do it?" Sathina smiled.

"Yes *and* no," the minister replied seriously. Ignoring the sudden looks of distress on the visitors' faces, Sarios sighed. "I'd be pleased and honoured to marry you two, but your timing is wrong, I'm afraid. I have no doubt that you're very committed to one another, but tomorrow or the next day the prefect here goes into battle and could very well die. I'm sorry to put such dark thoughts into your minds at this point, but you need to be aware of that."

Tythias nodded. "It's true and we're both well aware of that, but it doesn't change our minds." Next to him Sathina nodded purposefully.

"I expect not," replied the minister. "But I will not marry you on principal until after the battle is over. Once there is no danger, I would be pleased to do it, but I will not make a wife for a day when she could be a widow the next. It is not right."

Tythias rumbled as he leaned forward.

"That's a very reasonable and noble thing, Sarios, but unfortunately not enough. There are a dozen or more people spread among the units of this camp that could legally marry us, but we don't want them to. We want you to."

Sarios was opening his mouth to reply, shaking his head, as Sathina leaned forward.

"It has to be now, minister. I was hoping to break this in better circumstances, but I'm carrying Tythias' child and I won't let it be born without a legal father."

Sarios stopped before he began and looked from Sathina to Tythias, who was staring at her, his mouth open and eyes wide. The minister smiled.

"I think that perhaps that puts an entirely different light on the matter. I do think you ought to have told the father before the priest, though." He gave a light chuckle as he watched Tythias' jaw flapping aimlessly. "I think we'll arrange for something tomorrow afternoon if that fits in with your plans. I would suggest something tasteful and quiet with only a few friends rather than the entire army watching if I were you."

Tythias tore his eyes away from Sathina and stared instead at the minister.

"She..." his voice tailed off as he returned his gaze to the woman by his side.

Sathina patted him on the arm. "I wasn't going to tell you until after the battle. Didn't want you to have something like that on your mind when you need to be concentrating on the job. Still, now I suppose you'll have all the more reason to make sure you come back alive."

Tythias continued to stare and the minister cleared his throat, standing slowly.

"This is obviously going to take you some time, my dear. I might as well stretch my legs for a few minutes now that I'm up. If you get sense out of him, just leave my tent unfastened and I'll be back in a while."

Smiling at them, he reached down to the cabinet and, moving a couple of containers out of the way, retrieved a bottle of his plum brandy. He poured a large measure into two exquisite glasses and placed them on the table before turning and walking out of his tent, carrying the rest of the bottle. He smiled beatifically. Even in the midst of tension and horror, hope and life had a way of springing up and reminding you that they were there. It had been pleasing to note that nothing, from the death of comrades or the prospect of earth-shattering war to the loss of an arm even fazed the prefect, but Sathina could floor him with only a few words.

His smile broadened as he walked slowly toward Sithis' tent further along the valley. The swordsman would still be up and would surely welcome plum brandy and a little conversation.

Chapter XXXIV.

There were cheers and congratulations of course. Tythias and Sathina made an interesting couple to watch. She wore a beautiful azure blue dress, augmented with gold embroidery and jewellery and he wore his full uniform, weapons and all. Kiva laughed outrageously as the minister came to wrap the cloth and intertwine the couple's arms only to find that they were an arm short and had to turn the prefect to face away from her so that they could be bound together in the traditional fashion. Darius gave his imperial blessing in a curiously embarrassed fashion, and Mercurias wished them a future of good health. All in all it was a short wedding in close company and full of good humour and there was a celebration planned immediately afterwards outside the command tent. In fact, Kiva and Darius had already informed the senior officers of each unit in the valley and amphorae of wine had been delivered to each quartermaster with orders for one drink only to be distributed to every man in the army.

Tythias and Sathina made their way arm in arm out of the tent and into the open of the Tosco valley, where the army of the Emperor Darius spread out from one spur of land to the other and half a mile deep. They had arrived four hours ago and the camp was already well fortified, ditches lined with sharpened stakes and small areas of strategically-placed palisades. Kiva had heaved a heavy sigh of relief once they had arrived and could manoeuvre into position on the high ground, having beaten Velutio to the site.

Soldiers cheered as the happy couple made their way a hundred yards or so to where a large open air table and benches had been set up. Wine and spirits stood in jugs on the table along with the very best supplies the quartermaster chief could come up with, especially since Athas had stood at his shoulder making grumbling sounds all through his planning. Behind the two of them came Sarios and then the Emperor with the rest of the staff and the members of the Wolves.

The party was approaching the table when a young soldier, out of breath, ran directly into the path of the bride and groom and stopped, rocking slightly and looking tremendously embarrassed.

"Sorry to interrupt, sir. My captain sent me to warn you that Velutio's army has just been sighted at the bottom of the valley. They'll be here in about an hour, sir."

He glanced at the bride and blushed.

"Real sorry sir and congratulations from all the Fifth!"

Tythias smiled at the soldier. "Go back and get your wine soldier, or you'll miss it. Velutio won't do anything today. By the time they line up the light'll be starting to fail, so he won't make a move until morning."

The soldier saluted, still glowing furiously, and turned to head back to his unit. Tythias smiled weakly at his new wife. "You realise we're going to have to break our wedding celebration in the middle."

Sathina nodded. Her smile was riveted to her face as though she were afraid it might fall away. "I knew you were a soldier, Tythias; if I'd wanted safe, I'd have married a grocer. Just be careful."

Tythias nodded as Kiva approached them. The general gave a sad little smile. "We can spare an hour for the meal before we do anything." He winked at the girl. "And he won't be needed overnight, you know…"

Sathina smiled. "I know, but I'm entitled to worry, general."

"Of course you are, but there's nothing on earth's been made by man can get rid of your husband. He's been wounded by every type of weapon I could name and probably most of the animals and he's still here."

For a moment Sathina's smile faltered and then she looked back up at the general. "He'll be fine. Now let's celebrate."

"Indeed." Sarios walked past them and intoned a prayer to various gods before they began. The staff waited patiently for a few minutes until he fell silent and then made their way to the various seats around the heavy wooden table.

The meal began with toasts and jokes and then bread was broken and wine drunk as every man and the few women at the celebration tried their hardest to have a good time, despite the foreboding feeling triggered by the nearby sounds of an army making ready for brutal war.

It was perhaps an hour from sunset when Tythias finally stood and turned his glass upside down. "No more for me now until I return. I don't think infantry support is necessary, general. This is just a teaser, so I'll take the cavalry."

He leaned down and kissed his wife for a long moment before standing straight once more. "I'll be back before you know it."

Sathina watched as Tythias gave a slight bow to his friends and peers and then turned from the table and strode away toward the stables. Three of the celebratory party, all ex-members of Tythias' company, stood and adjusted their tunics before following their commander.

397

Despite the Lion Riders having been split up into more useful roles, many of the cavalry officers originated from the that unit.

She sighed and swallowed hard, forcing the tears welling in her eyes to stay there.

"I wish he'd stop saying things like that. Tempting the fates is never good."

Athas, two seats down the table, reached across where Tythias had been sitting and squeezed her wrist. "It's alright, Sathina. Kiva here's the only one the Gods have got it in for."

It wasn't exactly a joke, but it certainly turned their thoughts away from Tythias' immediate danger.

Down at the stables, Tythias prepared his horse as his commanders donned their armour and weapons. The prefect's plans had been well known by the cavalry since before they'd arrived in the valley and officers were already present in the makeshift stable, while their units were formed and waiting by the front line.

As he and the other commanders finally mounted up in the dusky light with a deep blue-grey sky showing through the cracks between the wooden walls, he smiled at them and hefted his sword.

"Let's get out there. I want to be out ahead of our front line and see what we've got. Then I'll know how best to hit them."

There were murmurs of assent from the other officers and the six riders made their way out of the hastily constructed officer's stable and past the corral that held most of the remaining steeds, down toward the front line at a steady walk. Five units of cavalry milled around close to one of the stockades guarding a crossing of the ditch, waiting for their commanders. Three were light, skirmishing cavalry of the style the Imperial army had traditionally used for harassing the flanks of the enemy, but the other two were equipped after the fashion of the more civilised of the eastern horse tribes; their horses were armoured with chain mail and the riders wore a suit of chain interspersed with steel plates that promised good protection but also extreme weight. They held spears and shields, with their swords attached to the horns of their saddles. All in all, they were the heaviest cavalry Tythias had ever seen fielded within the empire. *He'd* made the decision to train heavy horse units, but had passed the responsibility itself down to Peris, the best horseman of the Lion Riders, who even now was approaching them and eyeing them critically.

"You!" the officer called out. "Straighten up in that saddle and hold your shield like you might want to use if you daft bastard."

Tythias smiled. "Officers to me!" he called loudly as he walked his horse across the ditch crossing. Behind him the five unit commanders followed him into the no man's land, watching the distant lines of the enemy. Peris pulled alongside as they walked their horses and addressed his commander in a low voice.

"You *do* realise, sir, that you can just tell us where to go and what to do. You don't actually need to come along. You're a senior commander and we're not daft."

Tythias raised an eyebrow and Peris sighed.

"You've a wife back there, sir and you've been married less than two hours. Don't you think you should be *with* her?"

The prefect smiled. "I will be shortly, but I'm not passing up the opportunity to find out what we're up against." He squinted into the distance. "I see they're still not properly set up. We know what their army comprised a few days ago, but they may have picked up others now. They've passed the lands of several of his allies now. I want to have a look at the rear ranks that are still arriving."

With a smile, he turned to Peris. "Here's a chance to test the mettle of the heavy cavalry. Peris and Crucio, take your two units to the right hand side of the valley. I want you to make your way right to the slope at the other side and then make a charge against the end of their line. Hit 'em really hard. I want you to frighten the shit out of them and draw all attention there. Once you've finished your charge, rally and pull back across the field. As soon as you're a good distance away, turn and do it again. You know what to you're doing."

Peris nodded. "I doubt we'll get three charges in before they're prepared and the shock'll have gone."

"That's fine," Tythias nodded. "Try for three if you can. Just keep them busy and give them something to think about. Meantime, the rest of us are heading up over this hill on the left hand side and we're going to go round and hit them from the back. I want to see the support that's coming up now and harass them a little."

Peris squared his shoulders and peered across to the enemy's left flank. I'll give it ten minutes once we're over there before we charge. We don't want to go too early or our attack'll be over before you even reach position."

The prefect nodded and, turning his horse, led the light cavalry along the line behind the front ranks of men, heading for a farm house low on the slopes of the valley side where they could enter an orchard and cross the brow of the hill relatively unobtrusively. Peris watched him go and then nodded to his fellow officer.

399

"Well, Crucio. Time we went too, eh?."

Tythias frowned. From their vantage point on the lowest slope of the hill among sparse fruit trees, he could see everything that was happening at the rear of the enemy force. Something was wrong here. They must have already fielded half as many men again as Darius' army, and yet there were still long columns of troops coming in. More than that, there were huge wagons bearing catapults and bolt throwers being escorted by strange unidentifiable low-grade infantry. Where had all these extra men and machines come from?

He grunted and strained to see back across the field. The heavy cavalry were in position and waiting. Any minute now they'd charge and Tythias would be able to move his skirmishers down past the other flank without drawing all their men back from the front. He turned his gaze back to the columns coming up from the west and that was when the banner finally appeared among riders behind the siege machines. The column seemed to be a full army in itself, with a cavalry unit at the front, already past their position and taking their place among Velutio's lines. Behind them an infantry unit in black were getting into position, followed by the cart bearing their massive weapons, surrounded by light infantry. Behind them in turn came units of musicians and standard bearers light with burning torches or lanterns on short poles. And there, behind the musicians came the black banners bearing a Golden crown and two rearing horses flying over a covered black wagon draped with gold and black curtains. The banner of a Pelasian lord, the Satrap of Siszthad. He must be the usurper that had taken Prince Ashar's family's heads. And now the bastard was marching with Velutio. Surrounding the wagon were a number of over-dressed but under protected glittery guards. More courtiers followed the wagon in their own palanquins and chairs, beyond which the Pelasian infantry swarmed.

Tythias glanced back over his shoulder and spotted the two heavy cavalry units of Crucio and Peris hurtling across the field toward Velutio's army. This was it; time to go.

"Ok." He called out to his men. "We've got one small chance to do something *really* useful here, boys. Some of those units are carrying torches and lanterns against the dark. We need to take them out and use those torches on the war machines. I don't care how you do it, but burn as many of those bastards to the ground as you can. They won't have enough water with them while they march to put them out. Stay in groups and don't get too split up. We're going to be short on time here."

He turned again to face the siege engines. "Go, lads, go!"

The skirmishing units charged wildly, disregarding any ideal of formation other than staying in small groups, through the loosely planted orchard and down onto the flat turf. Shouts of alarm went up from some of the footmen who were now clearly of Pelasian origin. The bastard Satrap had brought the war machines with him. The loose formation of footmen tried to pull themselves into an ordered line, but they had not been expecting an attack from the rear and were truly unprepared for the ferocity of Tythias' cavalry. Spears lunged and stabbed as three hundred horsemen rushed a thin line of defenders. After a couple of thrusts with their spears, swords were drawn and the cavalry went to work on the simple butchery of their disorganised enemy. Tythias wheeled his horse in the midst of the chaos.

"Stop fucking around and get those torches!"

As his men made for the flickering lights, Tythias looked around. The only units within the column bearing torches were musicians, flag and standard bearers and senior men in gaudy golden silk costumes. That made their targets easier to identify. The prefect grinned and watched five of his men dispatch the last defenders in front of a huge catapult. He waved to one. "Get this thing burned. You four... come with me."

Turning, now flanked by four of his men, Tythias rode along the column, past a small unit of drummers who were being brutalised for the sake of the lanterns their unit carried, and toward the flags he'd seen. From this viewpoint, the road down the valley was visible and the rear ranks of the Pelasian contingent were arriving; perhaps two thousand heavy infantry in all. "We'd best get out of here before they reach us," he called.

The three charged toward the large, black wagon surrounded by guards in black and gold with some variety of feathery headdress. Grinning, Tythias leaned in his saddle. "You four keep them busy. I'm going to have a look inside that thing."

Trusting his men to do their job, Tythias looked around for other men nearby and, spotting a group of riders pouring lit oil onto a bolt thrower, called "over here!" He rode for the black wagon and reined in, his sword ready. A guard with a gold-burnished breastplate leaped down from the rear of the wagon, bearing a curved knife and attempting to unhorse the prefect. Bracing himself, Tythias swung his sword up in a wide arc. The blade caught the falling man on the hip and sliced diagonally up across his abdomen. The body crashed into him and the man, still alive though barely so, drove in the knife he held as he fell. Tythias grunted in pain as the blade dug deep into his thigh. The

401

body fell past him then to the floor, bleeding out its life, while the dying guard clung on to the hilt, dragged alongside Tythias' horse. The prefect scowled and wrenched the knife from his leg, watching the Pelasian crash to the ground and thrash painfully. Reaching up, he ripped the silky black curtains aside.

The Satrap of Siszthad was a corpulent man with an oily complexion and small, dark, piggy eyes. His scalp was shaved barring the topknot and his clothing was as ostentatious as Tythias could ever imagine. Gold and silver silk adorned with jewels and peacock feathers threatened to make the prefect laugh out loud. He leaned into the doorway.

"You can either come with me, or I can skewer you and take you anyway. The choice is yours."

The Satrap stared at him and then screamed "Guards!" in a surprisingly falsetto voice.

"Ok. Have it your way."

Tythias stuck his sword, point first, in the wooden side of the wagon and, reaching inside, delivered a powerful punch to the portly man's face. There was a distinct crunch as the Satrap's nose broke beneath the blow and, in a spray of blood, the man blacked out. The prefect looked around urgently. Men were rushing up from behind and, ahead, wooden carts on fire had brought the column to a halt. The defenders were rallying properly now and in minutes the light cavalry would be in serious trouble. Only one of the four men that had come with him was still in his saddle, desperately fighting off two guards at the front of the vehicle, though other riders, having finished their work, were bearing down on the Satrap's wagon.

"To me!" the prefect cried, aware that the cavalry were fragmenting into small melees and would soon be too dispersed to deal with an orderly retreat.

Reaching out, Tythias grasped the saddle of one of the fallen riders and guided the horse clumsily closer to the wagon. Reaching inside and grunting with the sheer effort, he hauled the corpulent unconscious body of the Pelasian usurper out of his seat and to the door of the vehicle. Several more horsemen appeared as if from nowhere and help him heave the ruler's figure out and onto the horse. With a last glance around him, Tythias called "Fall back! Back to our lines!"

Slapping the over-burdened horse on the rump, he launched back along the lowest level of the slope toward their front lines. Members of the three cavalry units pulled back in alongside him as they rode. There were fewer survivors than he'd hoped to see. The action had at the very least halved their numbers, but the damage they'd caused Velutio was incomparable. The loss of his Pelasian ally, his siege engines and a number of dead infantry, compared with the thinning of the Imperial cavalry? Tythias smiled across and down at the slumbering heap laid uncomfortably across a four-horned saddle.

"Is Ashar ever going to be pleased to see you, fat man."

He rode, aware of the growing numbers of horsemen surrounding him and the unconscious body of the Pelasian Satrap. Glancing over his shoulder, he could see that the Pelasian cavalry contingent was mobilised and was already chasing them back toward their lines.

"Shit!" The Prefect was well aware how far they had to go and how little chance they had to reach their army before their enemy overtook them, fresh and speedy as they were.

"Move!" he cried to the men around him.

Reining his horse in, he turned to face their innumerable pursuers, both annoyed and gratified to note the number of riders who had also brought their steeds to a halt and turned to join their commander in defending the rear of the departing cavalry and their prize.

He'd made light of it to Sathina and it was a shame to disappoint her, but he was damned if he was going to disappoint his Emperor. The thought of Sathina in her beautiful azure dress going alone tonight into their tent filled him with an inordinate sense of loss and, more than that, with an insurmountable rage. If these Pelasian bastards were going to take him away from his wife, he was damn well going to make them suffer for doing it.

At least a dozen other horsemen had lined up with him.

"When we get back to the lines," he cried with a mad grin, "you're all on a charge!"

The Pelasians, all light cavalry, but numbering in their hundreds just in the first wave, thundered towards Tythias and his scant defence. They may not be able to hold them for long, but maybe just enough to afford safety and a chance of survival to the rest.

He sighed as he hefted his sword and swung it a couple of times before drawing it back and ready for the first blow, his reigns tied around the saddle horn and guiding the horse with his knees.

"I'm sorry," he said to the open air and braced himself for the collision.

And as he watched the Pelasians thunder towards him, was aware of the miracle the Gods had granted him. His eyes were locked

403

on his attackers and he wasn't even aware of Crucio's heavy cavalry charging past him in the other direction, neatly bypassing the Prefect and his few defenders, until they were already past. The ground shook under the hooves of the heaviest cavalry the Imperial world had ever seen as Crucio's men hit the Pelasians like a tenderising mallet. The enemy advance was smashed and fragmented, with terrified Pelasians trying desperately to turn their mounts and head back to the safety of their own lines while their compatriots were literally thrown from their mounts or battered by the spears and shields of the heavy steel machine and obliterated. The Pelasian advance had met the Imperial wall.

Tythias stared for a long moment until his agape mouth slowly formed into a mad grin.

"You took your time sir!" A voice called from behind, as captain Peris drew his mare to a halt and leaned across in the saddle.

Tythias turned the mad grin on his subordinate.

"Where the hell did *you* come from?"

Peris smiled and proffered a waterskin of something that smelled like ammonia.

"We managed three charges in all and got back to our lines and there was still no sign of the rest of you, so we though we'd best come and look. Your wife would tear me to shreds if we left you for dead, you know that, don't you sir?"

Tythias laughed and took the skin, drinking deeply and coughing.

"I honestly thought I was a dead man."

"Nah…" Peris took the skin back and took a swig himself. "Didn't you hear the general? Nothing on earth's been made that can get rid of you!"

Tythias laughed a relieved laugh and, watching the chaos and carnage in front of him for a moment more, sheathed his sword and turned his horse back to the Imperial lines.

The night was deep and thick and an eerie mist had risen from the ground to fill the valley. The tents of Sabian's army were hard to discern and only from one of the valley sides could the tips of them all be seen, scattered around the camp fires that burned away the worst of the miasma. In the old days, the summer was the campaigning season and war was done with before now. Sabian grunted unhappily. If only war had been done with before now. He really had precious little wish to fight young Darius. He relished the opportunity of pitting his wits against Caerdin, but not really for the glory of the man who would take

404

the crown, and certainly not after having been forced to give the best ground and positioning to the man and to fight him on his own terms. He gritted his teeth once more. Many years ago his mother had berated him for that habit and he'd long since grown out of it, but he seemed to be doing it more and more these days. The loss of the siege engines was a blow, but nothing he wasn't prepared to handle. They were decoration as far as he was concerned anyway. The bulk of this fight would be on foot and with blades and that is where destiny would be decided. The loss of that despicable and thoroughly dislikeable Pelasian Satrap was more of a blow. While he hated the ostentatious idiot with a passion otherwise reserved for his superior, the Pelasians had withdrawn to the rear of the field and were no longer prepared to face Darius' army. He stared back through the mist to where they were quartered, having pulled out of the front line, but not entirely abandoned the cause. Where they stood now was anyone's guess and despite Velutio's assuredness that they would remain where they were, Sabian was less sure.

Currently, after yet another blazing row with his lordship that had brought his close to either resigning or being dismissed, he was on his way to find a likeminded friend to have a drink with. He knew his position was safe now. Velutio couldn't possibly dismiss his general on the eve of the most important battle he would ever fight, but Sabian could still walk away...

Ahead of him, Lord Dio's flag fluttered above his tent. He'd really expected Dio to have been gone by now, but the old lord maintained his stand. He would see this new Emperor before he made up his mind.

A man brushed past him in the mist and made a slightly surprised sound. Sabian would normally have berated such an act, but the man was one of the Pelasian contingent and was unlikely to care what the commander had to say to him. The small Pelasian disappeared into the mist without even an apology. Such was the respect now in this army. Sabian grunted. He really had to talk to Dio. He seemed to be the only man in this entire army who still made any kind of sense.

Shahar Siliyad, right hand man of Ashar Parishid, true Prince and ruler of Pelasia smiled as he ambled down the hill. Sabian had been so obsessed with his various distresses he hadn't even thought to question a Pelasian walking deep into the camps of the rest of the army. He could have laughed out loud, but tonight's mission was far too important for that.

405

Making his way around the muddy turf lanes between banks of tents, he made for a specific camp fire. As the banner, a boar's head above two lightning bolts, swum into view in the thick grey mist, he smiled more and removed general Caerdin's list from his tunic. Running down the list of names with his stylus, he found the first one that had not been crossed off and made a mark next to it.

With a deep breath, he straightened himself and strode into the lit area of the campfire where Lord Irio's men caroused as men will anywhere the night before a battle. Two men in blue tunics bearing the boar's head stood and drew their swords.

"We've no dealings with Pelasian betrayers here," one of them spat.

"That's as maybe," Shahar replied without letting his smile falter for a moment. "However, I bear a vital message for you lord and must see him now. You may search me for weapons if you wish and escort me to him. I assure you, you will not find any. "He laughed quietly. "Which is not to say that they aren't there..."

The guardsmen muttered to each other for a moment and then one ran off toward a large tent at one end while the other stood glaring at the intruder in the misty darkness. No words were exchanged for several minutes as Shahar stood pleasantly whistling a lullaby tune from his childhood. Moments later, the other guards reappeared and nodded.

With no deference to the fact that in his home city, the small Pelasian would have outranked their lord, the two soldiers marched Shahar across the open ground and to the tent of their master. One entered, bowing and stood to one side, while the other ushered the Pelasian in at sword point. Shahar narrowed his eyes in the low light. Lord Irio was a barrel-chested man with a bushy moustache and thinning hair. He sat in his armour at a table, reading. Shahar was delighted to note, as he cast his professional eye around the room, that the text the man was reading was an ancient Pelasian lovers' manual that was long outdated back home. He tried hard not to laugh and, instead, grinned at the barrel-chested lord.

"Lord Irio. I am most delighted to make your acquaintance. I realise that you have no reason to trust me, but I have important words and would speak to you alone. Rest assured that if death was my intention, you would probably be dead and I would not have announced my presence to your men."

Irio waved the small man's words aside and grunted to his two soldiers. "Get out. I think I can handle this midget."

As the guards left, Shahar wandered over to the table and smiled again. "I would recommend page thirty seven personally."

Irio's face flashed with annoyance. "What's your business?"

"It has come to our attention that you are not altogether content with this battle." Irio made to speak, but Shahar continued blithely. "Please do not disgrace yourself with denial. I'm sure you've heard how accurate Pelasian intelligence can be."

He took a seat opposite the lord whose colour was slowly rising.

"You see, I know that you are the lord of a fairly large estate and that in this battle you will be committing and losing many men that will make next year's harvest tough for you. I know that you hope for grander office, but you know that Velutio has favourites above you and you will get nothing from this fight but loss. I know that you are not considered a nice or fair man, but still, my current master, the Emperor Darius, would like to offer you an alternative."

Irio narrowed his eyes as he looked across the table. "Go on..."

Shahar smiled again as he reached for Irio's glass of wine and took a sip with a look of distaste. "There is a way to end this without battle; without the war. The armies can go peacefully about their own business. This is an offer being made only to some few lords, so this is for your ears only. If you wish to end this peacefully and preserve your lands, visit the villa on the western hill just before dawn tomorrow. General Caerdin sends his personal oath that you will be unmolested and there will be no soldiers waiting for you."

Irio watched him, doubtful and Shahar smiled. "Or don't. It's your choice."

Chapter XXXV.

Darius fumed at the leather strap on his breastplate. For some reason this morning he was having trouble with the simplest of things. In all honesty, he was struggling with a level of nervousness for which he was ill prepared, though to those around him he blamed lack of sleep. Finally feeding the leather strap through the buckle, he sighed and tightened the fastener.

"I swear that battles should be held later in the day; perhaps at a civilised noon-ish."

Kiva grinned. "Need to start early, or we'd be fighting during the dark hours and that's a nasty job. Want some help?"

Kiva himself had already been completely suited up barring his weapons and helmet when Darius had first arrived at his tent, followed by two of his guard carrying his own armour. He didn't know why, but he felt the need to share this time with Kiva and, though there was still over an hour til dawn, he'd been awake and fretting early. Tythias seemed to be calm as a glassy sea on the other hand. Darius had passed him on the way; seen him making jokes with his cavalry commanders while his wife did her best to make him look presentable.

Balo, sitting in the corner of the tent with a bowl of grapes and a glass of goat's milk, smiled. "I don't really miss the old days that much you know. There's not a lot that's good comes out of a battle, but a good bowl of fruit is a joy." The old mercenary still steadfastly refused to join the command party or even to don a uniform and sat in his travelling leathers.

Darius regarded him coldly. "I don't understand how a man of your background can refuse to help us, Balo."

"My Emperor, when you're as old and as injured and..." he laughed wildly, "mentally unstable as I am, *then* you'll understand." The man sighed. "I'll be here giving you moral support. Hell, if the lines get pushed this far back, I might even take up a sword, but don't expect me to go out all shiny and glorious and charge their lines. I'm not that person anymore."

Kiva nodded. "I won't ask you to. Everything that happens here today has to be by choice. That's what all this about."

Darius shrugged. "I suppose you're right. What do we do next then? You're the one with the plan to organise."

An enigmatic grin. "Don't worry about that. The plan's already well underway. You may have noticed Cialo and his men aren't around. Their tents were packed up at nightfall last night. Now all that remains is for us to go as soon as it's light and parlay with Velutio. Time will tell whether this has worked or not and you'll soon notice if it has."

Buckling the last strap of his breastplate, Darius stretched and reached down for his helmet and the coldly beautiful silvered faceplate.

"Well I need to see Sarios before we set off. He wanted to speak to me before we went out there."

Kiva nodded. "He'll have some good advice to impart no doubt. I'll be out in a short while myself. Need to find Tythias and discuss a couple of things about his cavalry first."

With a last look at the general of his army, the young Emperor turned and made his way out of the tent and the lamp light and into the dark valley spotted with campfires. The fires of the enemy glittered like myriad fallen stars further down the valley and from this distance Darius was sure there were at least twice as many twinkling lights there. With a sigh, he set off to find Sarios.

Twenty yards down the hill, Ashar stood with several of his Pelasians, deep in muttered conversation. Darius stopped close by.

"Highness," he greeted the handsome, olive-skinned Prince. Ashar smiled. "Majesty," he replied lightly. "It seems that the Pelasian contingent of Velutio's army is less than enthusiastic about this morning. I gather they are gathered around their camp fires as though this were some kind of family outing without donning their armour. If they still have any motivation to face us, I think my new banner may change their minds."

He gestured over his shoulder and Darius looked up, his eyes widening before he hurriedly looked away again. The Satrap of Siszthad, corpulent and bloated and, though in pain, still clearly alive, hung stretched with ropes on a frame of sturdy wood held aloft by four Pelasians. He had been opened up expertly from neck to groin and side to side by Ashar's medic and his innards were displayed to the world while being tightly held in place with thin catgut. He would, of course, bleed to death slowly, but the doctor had also given him something that had considerably slowed his heart and numbed the pain to prevent death coming too quickly from blood loss or from sheer overwhelming pain. It was astounding how the man had managed to keep him open like that without the blood flowing freely, merely trickling in places. The Satrap would still be alive and groaning as the Pelasians carried him across the field. Darius fought the bile rising in his throat and tried to smile.

"Ashar, you are truly a frightening man."

The Prince laughed. "Nothing more than this usurping fat egomaniac deserves and little more than he did to my uncle. I owe

409

Tythias a great deal for this. I came to support you in order to regain my own title and here I find that we both fight for the same thing in the same battle. If we lose today, we both die. If we win, we two become the two most powerful monarchs in the world. There's nothing like a little incentive, is the?"

He laughed again. "Anyway, I've got to organise my unit. I'll see you out in front of the line as soon as it's light, eh?"

He turned back to his subordinate and Darius continued on toward Sarios' tent. The old man sat at a desk just inside the entrance, squinting at papers in the low lamp light. He looked up and smiled as Darius approached, helmet and face mask held under his arm.

"Every time I see you, you look more an Emperor, young Darius. Indeed, you bear a striking resemblance to Corus these days. He was Quintus' grandfather, you know? The first in the dynasty and the only dark-haired one. *He* was a soldier Emperor who brought the country out of years of civil war when I was a young man and created a solid line of rulers. It is very important that you know what you want, young Darius."

Darius shrugged. "I want the world to be peaceful and happy and safe."

"That's a very admirable goal, though a little fanciful I might suggest. The world will never be entirely peaceful, universally happy or particularly safe. If you can strike a happy medium in all three you will have done as well as anyone could hope. I have a feeling that today will end well, but not without its tragedies, and when it's over, you need to make sure that you start looking at the future. There must be continuation of the line, but dynasty may not be the way. Corus' dynasty produced great men, but they came with a price. Madness ran in the blood, and was the eventual cause of their downfall. You will have to decide in your time whether it is more prudent to pass the power on to your own children one day or whether to select a capable man for the job. Either way, remember that your toil does not end today. It only starts here, but most of your work lies in the days and years ahead."

Darius nodded solemnly. "I was expecting some kind of advice for today, really."

"Today?" Sarios smiled. "Today is Caerdin's day. You just need to make sure you survive so that you can face tomorrow. Tomorrow is *your* day."

The first rays of the sun came late and rose above the hills behind Darius' army, shining down the valley and striking the tips of

410

the army's tents and standards. Kiva came trotting gently out of the stables on his steed bedecked in Imperial livery, his armour gleaming and his curved northern sword slung at his side. The helmet with its green crest of horsehair and tail hanging down the back was augmented by the steely impassionate cavalry mask and the wolf pelt hung with pride from the shoulder. It escaped the majority of viewers, but as Darius and Tythias sat ahorse in front of the men, they could clearly see the pain and discomfort riding was causing the man. And yet, the general had done exactly what he said he must. He'd survived until the end, whether it be for good or for ill.

Caerdin rode between the men, eliciting a cheer, and out in front to the others. He pulled up alongside the Emperor and gave a slight bow, as much as his seated position and full armour allowed. Darius returned the gesture. "Are we ready to go, general?" he asked, his voice hollow and metallic through the mask.

"Not yet, highness," the equally hollow reply came. "First we show our strength to the men. We get them cheering and screaming for enemy blood. It'll scare the hell out of Velutio's army."

Darius nodded as Kiva wheeled his horse and started to trot along the front line of men. Darius and Tythias goaded their horses to catch up with the general and the three began to pick up speed, cantering now along the line.

"For the Emperor!" cried the general, the call being taken up instantly by the footmen as they passed.

"For the Emperor!" Tythias joined in the cry as they rode and the call spread throughout the army. Reaching the end of the line, where the grassy slope led up toward the deserted farms and villas, the three horsemen made a wide turn and then galloped off in the other direction, racing once more along the front line with their cry. The noise filled the valley and echoed off the hills at the sides as the sun fell full onto the army. In the centre of the lines, Sithis began to bang the flat of his blade rhythmically on the bronze rim of his shield and the first regiment picked up the rhythm with their own swords. Within a minute all nine regiments, the entire width of the valley were hammering out a steady beat that threatened to bring down the mountains, drowning out all other noise, including the thundering hooves of the three commanders where they rode, summoning up the blood and stiffening the sinews of their men.

Reaching the far end of the valley, the three turned once more and charged back to the centre, where a number of flag and standard bearers on horseback had assembled. Beside them, Ashar Parishid, prince of Pelasia sat on his chestnut mare, four footmen behind him bearing the grisly banner of Ashar's erstwhile enemy. As the three reined in at the centre of the line, Caerdin clutched his side and had to steady himself. Between heaving breaths, he addressed his Emperor in that deep and echoey metallic voice.

"When we reach them, let me handle it first. Sabian will speak as the commander of their army, and I should speak as commander of ours. It's not the place for you or Velutio to air your disagreements and you shouldn't be the first to break the rule. Velutio won't be able to resist saying something and then you can speak your mind once he's broken it."

Turning sharply, Caerdin stared at the Pelasian Prince. "You've a right to be here Ashar, but keep that corpse of yours well away from the Imperial banners. Not the sort of impression we're trying to give out. You're a foreign dignitary and should be separate from all this." Ashar nodded.

"I shall ride alongside you, rather than with you. I have my own affairs to settle here."

Darius nodded. It wasn't done for the nobility to get too intimately involved in the gritty details of the battle. Their job was to look important and noble and to inspire the men, though Darius knew that even if Velutio was too dignified to take a part, he himself would refuse to take a seat at the back. He was a warrior Emperor and needed to take his place on the field. Still, first thing's first: the two commanders should parlay and try to persuade each other that there was an alternative.

Setting his jaw, he turned and walked his horse slowly across the field toward the enemy lines, with Caerdin at his left shoulder and Tythias at his right. Behind them, among the flags and standards, a musician began to blow a horn, calling for parlay. Off a little to the left, with them and yet separate, rode Ashar with the bloated breathing corpse of the Satrap floating along in the air behind him, silhouetted against the morning sun.

Minutes passed as they rode out to where they judged the centre of the field to be. In all the accounts Darius had ever read, the two parlay groups had ridden out simultaneously to meet, though no one had explained how they knew when to do this. Presumably it was a 'first-light' thing. The riders pulled up their horses and sat staring at the lines of Velutio's army. Darius turned and looked quizzically at his general. Kiva wouldn't be able to see his expression, of course, but the general seemed to know what he was thinking.

"They're a little tardy, aren't they," intoned Caerdin with no surprise in his voice.

Darius nodded. "Why so reluctant?"

"Ha!" Caerdin squared his shoulders. "I think they're probably starting to get a little panicky by now. An army falls apart a lot easier than it's put together in the first place, and a lot quicker. Things are moving along quite nicely then."

Darius glared at the general from behind his silvery face. Why couldn't Caerdin have shared his plans with at least the command party so they knew what to expect and what was going on. Even now, when whatever it was that Kiva had done was already taking effect, still the man revealed nothing. He must have words after the battle with his general. He swallowed as he once more saw Caerdin rock gently in the saddle before righting himself. That was, of course, assuming the man survived to see then end of the day.

The three sat in silence for some time with the flags and standards fluttering behind them. The musician bleated out the call for parley every minute or so. With a little discussion, a consensus was reached and the command party moved closer to the enemy lines; not close enough to put them in danger, but certainly close enough for they and their enemies to clearly view each other.

Time passed.

Still, as the only sounds remained those of the horses impatiently stamping their hooves and the hollow sounds of breathing behind steel face plates, nothing stirred.

Finally, after almost fifteen minutes of watching the enemy lines, Tythias leaned forward. "I was about to suggest we went back to have lunch, but I've just seen their command unit moving back there. The others squinted among the shining metal of the enemy ranks and there, sure enough, were several horsemen and standards moving through the crowd toward the front. Darius almost laughed out loud as they appeared between the front ranks. Sabian and Velutio rode together with their flags and standards, but the most senior Pelasian representative broke from their lines some distance away. The fractures in the enemy command were all too obvious now.

Darius watched in interest as the Pelasian made his way directly towards Ashar. Even Sabian, as they approached, locked his gaze on his southern ally.

The swarthy man in black and gold armour rode confidently across the field and reined in just in front of the Parishid prince. In a single graceful move, he dismounted, sliding from the horse's back to

413

the turf and striding forward. Five or six yards from the prince, he drew his sword and, dropping to one knee, drove it deep into the grass and down until only the hilt and a foot of blade projected. With a single heave, he bent the hilt away to one side and snapped the blade, leaving the rest in the ground. Standing once more, he dropped the hilt to the floor and saluted Ashar.

"I am Captain Sashir of the Satrap's army. I have come to give you my life so that you might spare my men who fight only for their masters."

"Sashir," the prince replied calmly. "I remember you from my uncle's palace. You were one of his captains even then and, if you hold the same rank now, you must have been one of those who betrayed him. The Gods will curse you for what you have done, but your debt is now paid." He growled. "I accept your life. Your men may leave the field and at the end of the day they may give their loyalty once more to the Parishid house."

Sashir turned and bellowed something in his own language and then Darius blinked as he watched the captain pull a small but very sharp knife from his tunic and draw it across his own throat. The man shuddered and the knife fell from his twitching hand as the blood flowed thick from his neck and ran in rivulets down his front. With what sounded like a sigh, he toppled forwards and landed, with a splash of crimson, at Ashar's feet. Ashar looked down at the man, his face impassionate and nodded slowly, as if talking to himself.

The Emperor, on the other hand, looked up, aware of a commotion among the enemy lines where it was clear that the Pelasian units had not even taken their place among the lines. They had remained camped in the rear and had turned on the command of their captain and marched away from the field of battle without ever drawing a blade.

Sabian squared his shoulders where he sat on his white steed.

"Never did trust that Satrap. Altogether too self-important and untrustworthy for my liking." He turned back to face his opposite numbers. "You're looking well Darius; very Imperial, I must say." He nodded in turn to the others. "Tythias. Caerdin. Nice to see you again, though the circumstances could be better. I expect you're about to offer me a good opportunity to turn away and end this without blood. And I expect you think I'm on the verge of being able to accept that, yes?"

Kiva nodded. "Are you having a little problem with motivation in your army this morning, Sabian? Anything wrong? You took rather a long time to come out and meet us."

"Interesting." Sabian smiled. "Some day if we both survive this, you'll have to tell me how you managed to spirit away a dozen of our most important lords before it got light. Almost a quarter of our forces refuse to fight this morning. Their lords left them with instructions not to take any part until they return. And now the Pelasians have left as well. I would think you currently outnumber us by a fair, but not considerable margin. Interesting how these things turn out, isn't it."

Caerdin nodded. "That's only the start, Sabian."

Reaching up, Balo unbuckled the face plate on Kiva's helmet and let the silver mask fall to the grass. He squared his shoulders and smiled his half-frozen smile. "The world is an interesting place, commander Sabian, and always full of surprises."

Lord Irio stamped impatiently round the floor of the villa's main living room. A number of other lords sat around in the somewhat faded comfort and luxury of a country villa. A mosaic of the Imperial raven adorned the floor, while paintings of rural landscapes graced the walls. A bowl of fruit had been thoughtfully provided on the small circular table and a jug of excellent wine sat beside it. A warming log fire had clearly been set some hours earlier and regularly fed and cast an amber glow across the room. In all it was an outstanding comfort compared with the cold of the tents in Velutio's camp. Irio seemed to be the only one bristling with impatience. He glanced out of the window, divided into small pains with lead and across the valley where the two armies faced each other in the deep porphyry and dusky blue of pre-dawn. The sun was almost up and if no one showed here in the next few minutes, he would have to get back to his men before the battle.

"Ah gentlemen." Caerdin entered through the main door of the room that led to the entrance hall, kicking the door to the hallway closed once more with his heel. He was wearing travelling leathers and had a small hand-held crossbow in each hand, with another hanging from his belt and a small quiver of bolts on the other side. Despite the orange glow and the comfortable warmth in the room, Kiva's face was pale and unearthly.

Irio turned from his pacing and strode purposefully toward Caerdin, who calmly raised the bow and shot the lord in the leg.

"I suggest you take a seat, Irio."

The bulky lord with the thinning head of hair staggered back, clutching at the bolt protruding from his thigh and fell into the closest chair.

"Lying bastard!" the man cried. "Your Pelasian said we wouldn't be harmed!"

"Ah, no." Kiva settled gently into the seat by the door. "He said you would be unmolested and no soldiers would be waiting for you. I have no intention of molesting anyone unless you make a move on me, which I consider self defence and, as you can see, I wear no uniform today."

He smiled broadly. "In fact, you'll find that the fifty or so men I have outside are not soldiers either. All of them, drawn from Sabian's army I might add, are in their own clothes and have been given their final service agreement. There are no soldiers here. Indeed I, myself, have left my letter of resignation in my tent for whomsoever finds it."

Now another lord stood; Tito, Kiva seemed to remember.

"Explain yourself, Caerdin."

"Gladly." Kiva settled back into the chair, one crossbow on his knee and another hanging from his belt. He withdrew a number of small bolts from the quiver and placed them on his lap, reloading the third spent bow as he did.

"I used to play towers with Quintus. I expect you remember him. He was your Emperor a couple of decades ago." He smiled benignly. "...and the only way to beat that genius of a man at the game was to set up a trap for half an hour and then bring down as many towers as you could in one fell swoop. Now think of today as a game and yourselves as the towers."

In a rush, others stood and a cacophony of dispute rose in the room as some lords hurled abuse at Kiva, while others argued with each other about what they'd done. Kiva sat in the face of the blast and smiled. He waited until the last voice died away before he spoke.

"Without you, your soldiers will be unsure. They're unlikely to blindly serve a man they don't know except by reputation, like Sabian or Velutio, and I expect people they don't know trying to push them into the front of a fight for a man they don't serve will probably just make them all the more obstinate. Velutio will lose a third of his army before this even begins and my officers know exactly what to do to end this without a single drop of blood being drawn in the valley. Darius will be Emperor by sunset." He shuffled in his seat. "But that, unfortunately, requires that you gentlemen be removed from the equation."

"You want to keep us here until the battle's over?" demanded Irio incredulously.

"Oh, no. I'm afraid you'll all be dead by then."

416

Irio laughed. "There are twelve of us and only one of you. Even with your crossbows, most of us could just walk out of here."

Kiva smiled again, his pale, drawn smile. "I used to be rather bad with a missile weapon, you know, but I've had practice recently; lessons from an expert. The first three or four men who rush me are dead before they get here," he said, pointing two bows at the gathering of lords. "You'll find the place sealed tighter than Velutio's arse anyway. All the windows are locked and the doors are barred. I've had Cialo and his men seal this place completely. We're here until the end, people."

Irio staggered toward him.

"You're a bluffer, Caerdin. You can't keep us away from the battle like this."

"Oh, I can." There was a twang and a crossbow bolt dug deep into Irio's neck, amidst a spray of blood. The barrel-chested lord fell to the floor gurgling and writhing.

"Who's next?" Kiva asked, dropping the spent bow and picking up the third in his offhand. "Anyone feeling brave? No good getting past me anyway. That door behind me's well and truly sealed."

A thin, reedy lord at the back stood sharply.

"Can anyone else smell smoke?"

Kiva grinned. "Yes, it's nice and cosy in here and it's about to get an awful lot hotter."

"They've set fire to the building!" one of the lords cried, triggering pandemonium. Men ran to and fro. Tito, a small, wiry lord with a squint eye, ran to the window through which Irio had recently been looking.

"This is only lead-paned glass!" He picked up the chair the barrel-chested lord Irio had used and smashed it against the window. The glass shattered outwards in a glittering cloud, catching the very first rays of the sun and lead strips buckled and came away. The group of lords rushed towards him and his means of escape, but fell away again in a panic as an arrow flew with deadly accuracy through the window and took Tito in the eye, hurling him back away from the hole, still holding the fragmented remains of the chair. He skidded across the floor, dead before he came to rest against the small table, tipping the jug of wine and the bowl of fruit to the floor.

Kiva laughed. "I told you I had fifty men outside. You can be damn sure they're not going to let you get away. Hell, they've got orders to let nothing escape, even me."

417

"You!" a tall thin lord whose name escaped Kiva bellowed as he made a run at the general. Kiva lazily, almost as if in a daze, raised his hand and released another bolt. All those hours of tuition with Phythian's men had been well worth it. Besides, these things were much easier to use than a bow. The bolt took the man in the solar plexus, shattering his breastbone and punching through into internal organs. He took advantage of the widespread confusion to reload the other bow and rest his hands on the chair arms.

"I can assure you that there really is no way out. Consider this penance for siding with a spineless and self-centred megalomaniac and not supporting the Emperor."

The men in the room ran hither and thither in a panic, opening the other side doors of the room, only to find outer doors heavily locked and barred and any window they came to covered from outside by archers. Some tried to climb out to freedom, only to be struck by whistling shafts of ash before they'd even touched the earth outside. Others ran in a panic looking for other ways out, only to find that when they opened a door, the room behind was already an inferno. Battered by waves of heat and clouds of choking smoke, they ran in blind panic and not one of them paid any further attention to the sentinel by the main door with his two loaded weapons.

Kiva watched them run. In his mind he remembered a room of marble and gold. He remembered the golden-haired Quintus in his purple tunic smiling as he moved a white tower, knowing he'd beaten his favourite marshal. Quintus would laugh in that buoyant way of his and reach out to the wine jar, pouring another drink for both himself and his opponent and stop, mid-way as he realised his error. It was then that Kiva Caerdin, marshal of the northern armies and friend and confidant of the Emperor would trigger his unexpected move and seven of the Emperor's remaining eight towers would vanish in one move.

"You'd be proud of me now, Quintus" he muttered to himself as the flames licked at the panes of glass and the lead of the room's windows. "Twelve towers in one move. That's more than I ever managed in our games."

He smiled as he watched the room explode into a ball or yellow and orange flame, timbers finally giving way under the extreme heat and stressed glass shattering inwards in a million shards reflecting the inferno. He would burn soon enough, but that wouldn't matter now. He reached up with a hand, ignoring the crossbow in it, and wiped at his chin. Dark blood flowed in rivers down it. The pale northerner smiled as his life and spirit flowed from him for the final time; from his mouth and from the wound in his side, where it spilled out into a dark stain on his grey tunic; a tunic of the Grey Company who were no more. Funny that; how now everything looked grey. Even the orange flames as they tore across the rug in the middle of the room. Somewhere there was a scream, but even that seemed grey and faded.

Kiva was dead long minutes before the fire reached his boots and breeches and ran up and across his body, wreathing him in a golden liquid fire.

And with him passed the last of the old world and the lords that had stood in the way of the new. The villa sighed and collapsed in on itself.

Chapter XXXVI.

Velutio urged his horse forward, the colour rising in his face, and pushed Sabian out of the way, almost unhorsing him. "What is the meaning of this? We came to parlay with your general, not some underling or his puppet '*emperor*'."

Balo smiled, regarding the lord of Velutio coldly. "Caerdin is no longer the general of this army. He resigned his commission this morning as I myself was there to witness. He firmly believes there will be no need of a general today but that if there is, Tythias here is amply able and prepared for the role. I also am not a commissioned member of this army and am here only as a spokesman for Caerdin."

Sabian nodded bleakly and pushed his way to the front once more, glaring at his lord. "Caerdin has gone to deal with those other lords in our army that he could rely on to think of themselves before they thought of you, Velutio. He's had something going on for some time now obviously, possibly even for months. We've had deserters all the way around the coast and I thought it was because they believed in Darius or possibly felt oppressed by us, but perhaps it was Caerdin's doing all along."

Balo smiled. "In actual fact commander, we've had nothing to do with your desertions. Caerdin only intended to deal with certain individuals he felt he could trust to rely on greed overcoming their loyalty. Only a dozen lords or so have been dealt with, but that'll cripple a large portion of your army. Your army's *deserting* because they don't believe in your cause. They don't want this man to be their emperor, and I can see why, whereas Darius is a man of Imperial blood with a solid claim to the throne and the Gods are with him."

Sabian nodded again, his fingers pressed against his temples. "He's brought your army crashing down, my lord. He's abducted a dozen of your commanders and their men won't fight for you now. In fact, I doubt we'll ever see those lords themselves again." He pulled himself up straight. "If you insist on going ahead with this, you're walking into disaster."

He turned to Balo. "What terms do you offer?"

"No!" Velutio turned and pushed hard, hurling Sabian from his horse and glaring at Tythias. "There will be *no* terms. I still have the better army and without Caerdin, your own army is nothing but a collection of badly-trained rebels. There will be war here today and I will walk in your blood, all of you. Get back to your lines, 'general' Tythias and prepare your men. I will see you in the battle." Sabian

420

growled and began to rant at his lord, explaining the myriad reasons for withdrawing against a torrent of abuse.

Balo smiled at the argument and leaned close to Darius, motioning the young Emperor to raise his silver mask. As he did so, Balo whispered to him. "Now's your time."

"What?" replied Darius.

"Can't you see? The enemy commanders are arguing. Many of their lords are missing. The Pelasians and the absent lords' troops won't be prepared to fight and the rest of the army's dithering, unsure of what to do. You'll never get another chance like it."

"So what do I do? Caerdin never explained his plan."

"He didn't need to. He's cleared the way for you. This army's in tatters and if you're strong and you take control, they'll take the oath; maybe not all of them, but enough to shatter the rest of his army and make them yours. Kiva set everything up for this one moment, but you need to be strong!"

Darius blinked. Caerdin had done so much with only Balo and Cialo's men? He realised that the world was holding its breath and he was being regarded by more than just the half-dozen men here. A quarter of a mile behind them, the ringing of swords being hammered against shield-edges continued, somewhat muted by the distance. A few hundred yards ahead, Velutio's army stood in lines, some looking fierce, but many confused or worried, watching their commanders in heated debate. The young Emperor smiled. It could all end here and without a blow, but he had to be every bit the Emperor his men expected of him.

He sat as straight as he could in the saddle and faced the enemy lines.

"This is the Empire! The Empire has always been strong and unified until the lords carved it up. Now, there will *be* no more lords!" he bellowed at them. "One army, one Emperor and elected governors of the people. You no longer have to owe allegiance to the men you did yesterday! You are either slaves to your lords or free men of the Empire and if you are free, I expect the Oath of allegiance from you."

A voice from somewhere in the line called out in a nervous voice "Who'll pay us, though. What'll we do? I'm a sergeant now but I can't afford to be a free man!"

Darius smiled. Here all the lessons in political history and rhetoric Sarios had put him through on the island would be of prime use. It was no good being a great rhetorical speaker if you had nothing of substance to say. 'Always have a point; always have an answer' his rhetoric tutor had drummed into him. And from the histories: 'always think of the future before you act for the day.'

"The regional armies must be disbanded," he announced, "but the Imperial army has already been recommissioned. They stand a quarter of a mile up the valley hoping they won't have to fight their countrymen. A civil war does good to no one but the barbarians. You will be able to join the Imperial army for regular work and good pay or to retire in peace with a generous settlement to be agreed by your provincial governor. All you have to do is take the oath! Any man who declares himself for me now will be considered a loyal citizen of the Empire and a valued ally. Any man who stands against me stands against the Empire and will be deemed a traitor."

Some time during this exchange, the enemy commanders had stopped arguing and were paying attention to the young Emperor. Sabian watched Darius high on his horse with something of mixed respect and pride. He turned and glared up at his lord. "It's over, Velutio. Your men won't fight for you anymore. *I* won't fight for you anymore. There's a new Emperor and it's not you. See how your army begins to kneel to your enemy?"

Ignoring the pure malice of the old lord's gaze, he strode round to where Darius sat on his horse. Turning to face his army, the commander removed his helmet and stood straight as a spear shaft.

"On your knees!" he bellowed with a force that made Darius start and look down at the man beside him. "On your knees for your Emperor!" Darius stared at Sabian, a flood of strangely conflicting emotions running through him.

The commander turned back to the young man and bowed his head. "I should have seen it months ago, highness; in fact I did in truth. Had I not been bound by oath, I should have come to you then."

Turning once more to Velutio, he smiled. "I hereby resign my commission in the armies of Avitus, formerly lord of Velutio, and make my peace with my Emperor. Long may he reign."

With a sad note in his voice, he looked back up at Darius and spoke again quietly. "Highness, I beg for nothing. I've led armies against you and committed treason to the throne. I submit myself for your sentencing, be it death or exile."

"I also," called Lord Dio, stepping out from the front lines of the army. "I wasn't sure whether I would fight today or not. Sabian told me a lot about you, young Emperor, but I wasn't sure how accurate he was. Seeing you now I think that, on reflection, he may have been spot on. I have been your enemy, but no more." He plunged his sword point down into the turf and bowed his head to the young man.

Around them, men continued to sink to their knees in small groups, gradually building into a wave. Velutio was staring, wild-eyed, at the men around him. Everything in this last minute was falling apart. Here, where Caerdin had beaten him twenty years ago, the man had done it again without even being here, and this time without a blow being struck. Still, while *his* army was led by a collection of lords and had fallen apart without them, *Darius'* army was reliant on their one symbol. He leaned in his saddle and called over to his flag bearers.

"Kill the boy!"

The small unit carried standards and flags, yet were curiously well armed and armoured for ceremonial soldiers. Clearly drawn from another unit, the tips of bows were visible beneath their cloaks and they had not kneeled to the young horseman. The flags and eagles they bore were hurled to the floor as they lifted short bows from under their crimson cloaks and drew arrows from hidden quivers.

Sabian ran back past his former lord to the unit and, with a great heave, pushed the first man in the line to the floor.

"Belay that order!" he bellowed, drawing his sword. "No one fires a shot or I gut them!"

Behind him, Velutio glared with hatred down at his commander and then back at the archers. "I am still your lord. You will kill that boy now!"

Sabian turned and, with his spare hand, grasped Velutio's shin and pushed upwards, tipping the old lord gracelessly from his horse. He stared down at the old, grey-haired lord floundering around on the floor in a fury and growled.

"I have had enough of your bitter, petty, pointless commands. You're not their lord any more. Look around you, *Avitus*! Your army kneels to their new Emperor, ready to take the oath. No more lords, he said. You don't exist any more. You're not Lord Velutio; you're not even Marshal Avitus. You're just plain old Avitus, lord of nowhere and commander of no one, just like I'm plain old Sabianus, not a man of power or land. You deserve to be nothing now. I've known for a long time that you were treacherous and wicked, but you would bring assassins to a parlay under the guise of *heralds*? If I were still their commander I'd have every man in that unit executed for dishonouring the standards. They threw your flags to the ground as though they were worth nothing and you don't even care. You've less honour than a weasel."

423

Velutio struggled to his feet, keenly aware of the fact that nine tenths of his army knelt to his enemy and the few who remained standing looked decidedly unsure. Sabian glared at them and flung his helmet at the archers standing among a pile of discarded flags and standards.

"Kneel you bastards! Kneel to your Emperor!"

Sabian was aware of the danger only at the last moment as Avitus fell on him, wielding a small knife that had hitherto been secreted in his belt. Before he could turn to face the old man, he felt the blade plunging down between his scarf and breastplate and deep, vertically into the point between his neck and shoulder. With a growl, he reached up and grasped Avitus' left wrist where it held the knife, turning it until the knife slipped back out, sawing through muscle and bone as it exited; until he heard the bones in the old man's wrist cracking and splintering.

He winced at the pain in his severed muscle and, clutching his neck, Sabian turned, his sword still in his damaged arm.

"You have to be the most bitter, twisted, vengeful, spiteful, evil, ungrateful old fuck I have ever met and you've just made your last mistake. You should have listened to me over the past months and taken my advice and maybe now you'd be looking at a governorship, but no... you always had to be right. All the people around you that actually cared about what they did left you long ago. Even sergeant Cialo went over to Caerdin and that should have been the greatest warning of all. He's a man of honour and integrity as I'm sure your new Emperor is now aware. And yet out of some outdated, misguided sense of loyalty, I followed you. Right to the end I followed you. And now you stab *me* in the back?"

He growled as he lowered his arm and let the blood flow free from his wound, soaking his red scarf and running down the inside of his cuirass to pool on the skirt of his tunic. Glaring at Avitus, he changed his sword to his good arm. "I try to get you to make peace, but you sent assassins instead! I try to teach you the honourable ways of command but you use them to hide your treachery. I try to tell you it's over, but you won't have it! There's nothing in you but malice and now you've turned on the one man who's tried to protect you from yourself. No more!"

He stepped forward, forcing Avitus to step back. The old lord fought the pain in his broken wrist, but his face displayed only rage. Drawing his sword, Avitus steadied himself. "I may have lost my army, but I *am* Velutio. I always was and I will not submit to a boy who owes his training, his knowledge and his very life to me! I will *not* kneel! If you want me to, you'll have to kill me and, old though I am, I can assure you I am every bit a match for you."

He swung his sword at the commander in a wide arc and Sabian stepped easily out of the way. "I'm not going to toy with you, Avitus. This is not a duel; this is an execution."

Avitus laughed mirthlessly as he steadied his sword and made another lunge. With barely a move out of place, Sabian stepped in towards him, knocked the sword out of the way and, bringing his knee up and his arm down simultaneously, broke the old man's sword arm at the elbow.

"You..." Avitus gasped, his shattered wrist flopping uselessly by his side and now his splintered elbow matching it. He stood pathetically, watching his sword lying on the ground, hopelessly beyond his reach with his broken arms.

"You're a match for *no one* these days, old man," Sabian grunted. "Without a hidden knife or an archer at your shoulder you're nothing. Caerdin has lived twenty years with a wound you probably gave him by accident, and yet even as a man over fifty years of age, the general is a match with a blade for any man on this field. You've just relied on your reputation and your money to cover your weaknesses as a man."

Avitus growled, glaring with pure hatred.

Sighing, Sabian stepped forward and raised his sword, pulling it back over his shoulder. With a last sad look at his former lord, he swung, the blade sweeping through the air and barely slowing as it met the resistance of Avitus' neck. The iron-grey head toppled and rolled across the grass, a short fountain of blood rising from the severed neck before the whole body collapsed gently forward, folding in on itself. Sabian stood silently for a long time, staring down at the body and then turned.

He looked up at Balo on his horse. "Caerdin met with the other lords before dawn and disposed of them I presume?"

The mercenary looked over his shoulder and the rest of those present followed his gaze to see a white villa on a spur of land overlooking the valley, flames roaring around it and thick roiling black smoke pouring up from the hillside.

"He thinks it's redemption," the scarred man said sadly. "He burned Quintus and thought the Gods cursed him for it, so he's making amends by burning himself now and taking our opposition with him. Destroy and rebuild, see?"

Darius fumbled for the neck clasp on his helmet and let it fall away to the ground. "He's dead?"

"Must be by now," the mercenary replied. "Roof's gone on that place. Nothing inside will have survived. In fact, I can see Cialo's men coming down the hill now, so they must consider the job done."

"The *job*?" demanded Darius incredulously. "He didn't have to…"

"But he did," interrupted Balo, "can't you see? That's the only way he felt he *could* do it. It's the only way he thought the Gods would let it happen. He was dying anyway; you've watched him. You know he didn't have many days left in him, so he chose to end there and make sure he got the job done. This morning he was so bad he worried he'd even get as far as the villa."

Ah thought occurred to Darius and he turned in his saddle. "Tythias?"

But the man wasn't there. The one armed prefect was already half way across the battlefield, making for the burning building. Darius sighed and turned back to Sabian.

"There's been enough killing in these past months. Let Avitus be the last. I've no wish to execute you, Sabian. You're responsible for our freedom and without you, we'd never have been here to face Avitus. You saved the life of everyone on Isera several times over and you've never lifted a finger to harm me or any of mine. You've committed no treason."

Sabian bowed his head gently and uncomfortably, a fresh stream of blood running from his neck.

"Highness, there's something you should know; something you really need to know and I'm one of very few people left in the world that's aware of this…"

Darius sat on his horse with one eyebrow raised, waiting with a curious air. Sabian cleared his throat and, when he spoke, there was a strangely emotional quiver in his voice.

"I came across several documents when I was on Isera; documents that had been secreted away and stored under lock and key. Sarios will be able to confirm this; I expect he has the scrolls with him now. They were genealogies; histories of the Imperial line and its offshoots. Sarios' carefully constructed claim that you're of the Imperial blood isn't far from the truth. I expect he laughed about that as he passed out your supposed fictional claim. The blood of the line *does* run in you, though, Darius. Not directly, but it's still there."

Darius' brows furrowed. "Go on…"

426

"Your mother was the lady Livilla Dolabella, a cousin of Quintus the Golden and a child of the house of Corus. That means that you truly *are* the claimant to the throne, by blood and right..." His voice trailed away and he stared at the ground.

"And?" urged Darius. "There's more, yes?"

"And your father was not Fulvius. Your father was Caerdin. It's been hidden from you both since you were a child." He swallowed hard. He'd promised Sarios a long time ago on the island not to reveal the truth, and some of it should be forever buried, but at some level, Darius needed to know. "You were rescued from the Caerdin villa when it burned, but fell into the hands of Avitus. He had you imprisoned on Isera, knowing who you were, and never told anyone that you'd lived. Your birth name was Quintus, not Darius; Quintus Caerdin, named for the Emperor. The scroll I found must have been put together after your imprisonment, as it has your current name, not your birth name. I'd expect that it was Sarios himself who drew up the genealogies, or at least replaced your name on it so that some day someone would find out. Caerdin's never even suspected anything. His wife and child died twenty some years ago when the villa burned. I only tell you this now because he's gone and you should know."

Darius stared at the commander for a long moment and then cleared his throat. "Commander Sabian? I hereby confer on you the rank of Marshal of the Western Provinces. As such, I want you to deal with this army; *your* army. Any lords still in command of their men are to be invited to the command tent on the other side of the field. There I and my counsellors will see them all individually and we can decide whether or not they deserve to be given public office. I have the suspicion that most of them will, as Caerdin..." he paused for a moment, his eyes glazing for a second before shaking his head and taking control again. "...as Caerdin seems to have dealt with the rest of them. I want the soldiers bringing to the middle of the field and there they can take their oath shortly. After that I'll leave them with you to organise. You'll want to promote some and discharge some no doubt." He smiled a very strange smile.

"Unfortunately, right now, I have more urgent business."

Sabian blinked. He was still standing slightly stunned by his sudden promotion as Balo winked at him and the two men turned and rode off back toward their lines. Prince Ashar rode up and slid from the back of his horse.

"You're a very lucky man, aren't you? Darius has always been rather fond of you, Sabian, and you have a good reputation, but was it really fair to tell him that now?"

"He had a right to know," the commander replied, still watching the retreating riders. "What gets me though is how easily he took it."

Ashar laughed. "He's a Caerdin sure enough. I'd better get back to my men and tell them to stand down, and you've got enough to keep you occupied, Marshal of the western Provinces." He laughed again and, wheeling his horse, rode back off toward the Imperial lines.

Sabian stood and watched him go for a moment before turning back with a curious smile to the lines of kneeling men. His grin widening, he tore his insignia from the sleeve of his tunic and dropped it to the floor.

"Alright! Form into units and prepare to move! If you don't know the Imperial Oath, don't worry. You can just repeat it after me. Anyone of noble rank here should come out front as the Emperor would like to see you personally. Now move!"

The grin on his face widened. "Oh, and somebody get me a medic..."

On the hill, Darius reined in with Balo close behind to find not only Tythias but all of the Wolves and several other commanders of the army watching the white walls collapse into rubble. There was a groan from the stressed beams as another section of wall gave way and fell inwards. Through the flames and smoke. Darius could just see a figure, torched and unidentifiable leaning out through one of the open windows, the charred shaft of an arrow protruding from the burned face. The lords had not met their end stoically apparently and Cialo's men had been forced to contain them. For some reason the young Emperor was assailed by images of the ruined Golden House back on Isera that swam in and out of focus. The charred octagonal room where he used to go for sword practice. More than two decades ago Caerdin had sealed the doors, possibly of that very room and watched as his best friend burned inside. And here another villa on its way to becoming a ruin and he'd done the same again, only this time he'd locked the door from the inside

Mercurias wordlessly uncorked a wolf-embossed flask and took a swig of the neat spirit inside, before flinging the entire thing through a broken window and into the building. There was a brief flare as the liquor burned. "Rest well, you old bastard," the medic sighed.

428

Next to him, Brendan uncorked his flask and did the same, followed by Athas and Marco. Balo slipped from his horse, unstoppered his own wolf flask and took a swig, handing the flask up to Darius. The young man, suddenly acutely aware of the long-term camaraderie of the men around him and the link he himself had to them, took a swig of something that tasted foul and then slung the flask into the dying fire.

"Goodbye father."

The rest of them turned to face Darius. Only Mercurias betrayed no surprise, with merely a knowing smile. Brendan, his eyes wide with astonishment, strode over to the young Emperor. "Whaddya say?"

Mercurias grinned. "Don't you mean 'whaddya say, *your majesty*'?" he laughed.

"When did you find out?" the grizzled medic asked, turning to his Emperor.

"Sabian told me just now, down on the field. And you?"

Mercurias gave a sad smile. "I've known for a while. Pretty much since I met you, I'd say. I'm somewhat surprised no one else ever made the connection. You don't quite look like him, but it's mostly cos of the hair colour and that comes directly from your mother. She was raven black. If anyone looked at you and tried to combine what they saw in Kiva and Livilla, it'd have been pretty obvious."

He laughed. "I'm a doctor. We notice these things."

Brendan whistled through his teeth. "'E's right though. Y'can see it clear as day if'n y'know what yer lookin' fer."

Darius nodded, "I know much the general meant to you all. I'm only really starting to come to terms with what it meant for me and I think I'll have to sort that out later. It may seem a little unfeeling, but I don't have time to deal with all this right now and I don't have time for you to either. I need you back down in the valley. There's a whole army to administer the oath to and deal with down there. Then there are a lot of lords to meet. The lords are going to be abolished entirely, though the deserving should get estates and public offices. I'm going to need so much help with this, I can't even picture how enormous the task is. I've appointed Sabian as one of the new marshals. I want Athas and Tythias to join him if you're amenable, and Sithis when I see him?"

Athas looked across at his young master and smiled in a sad way. "I'd be honoured, though I'm not sure how I'll ever live up to the reputation of the old marshals. No one'll ever match him. You know that? For all his faults, he may have been the best man I've ever known."

Tythias laughed, again with an edge of tragedy to his voice. "Don't be daft, Athas. Kiva was the best of the marshals, but don't forget Avitus was his peer and look at *him*. I think you're exactly what Darius needs in a marshal. Kiva may have been a leader to the Wolves, but you've always been their father. I'd be proud to serve you, highness. Your father was a great man."

Marco looked across at them. A tear had run down his cheek and left a glittering trail in the grime caused by the smoke. "What of everyone else, Darius?"

The Emperor smiled. "In the old days, a man with your record and the wound you took in service to the Empire would be pensioned out and when everything settles down, I intend to revive most of the old traditions. A villa somewhere, or an inn or something, Marco. Time to calm down now there's going to be peace. And you, Brendan, Balo, and all the others down there like Filus and Crucio. The army's going to need Prefects and senior officers. We'll need you all…"

Brendan smiled unhappily. "Don't think my heart's in it anymore, Darius. With no Kiva, I don't really want to be a soldier. Hell, I'd have finished years ago if it weren't for him."

"There's decades ahead of us to sort everything out, Brendan. We're going to have peace, finally. We need to organise things in the valley and then the world will be what we make it. Time to mourn the dead when we're at rest ourselves. For now…"

He turned his steed and looked down the hill and into the valley, where the two armies had met in the middle of the field with no blades and no blood and the world was being made whole again.

"For now? Let's go and build an Empire."

Epilogue

The Emperor Darius the Just struggled out of his bed and winced as his tired feet touched the cold floor. Every day it was getting harder and harder to get up in a morning. These old bones were not as light as they once were and the muscles not as strong. He sat on the edge of the bed, wondering what time it was. There was light outside, so it was clearly after dawn and his eldest son Kiva would be here before long no doubt, with a list of official duties for him. Kiva would never be a soldier; that was clear. He was quiet and gentle like his mother, but an extremely able administrator. The younger one, Quintillian, was the soldier and reminded Darius so much of himself in those old days of imprisonment that he couldn't help but smile. Kiva would be Emperor soon and would do a good job of it in these days of peace, but Quintus would always be there looking after his older brother and there was virtually nothing the two of them couldn't accomplish as long as they were so close.

He sighed, wondering whether to go and find his robes or just stay in his sleeping garments for now. 'Who cares?' he thought to himself and struggled to his feet. With slow and weary steps, he wandered over to the window. The sun must be over the horizon certainly, but most of the garden was in shadow from here. Various people in the past decades had tried to persuade the Emperor that an east-facing window would be better for him, but Darius liked to watch the sun set from his chair by the window and the view from Sarios' old room was just too familiar for him.

A few years ago he'd had a long avenue cut through the western orchard so that the view from his window was unobstructed. For some reason it gave him great comfort to see the graveyard down there where so many friends lay buried. All the former marshals of the Empire lay there now, alongside his father, the great general Caerdin, whose body had been removed from the wrecked villa all that time ago. Marshals Tythias and Athas had both gone less than a decade into the new Emperor's reign, within a month of each other, amidst memorial ceremonies that had taken place across the length and breadth of the Empire. They'd both been popular with both the army and the people. That had been a hard year for Darius; harder than Sithis going six years later, though Sithis went out the way he'd always intended, leading a charge against a small barbarian army that had crossed the northern border. The hardest of all had been Sabian last year. After that autumn morning when Darius had strode out into the grassy courtyard to see the

431

marshal face down on the grass, surrounded by concerned guards and servants, he'd suddenly realised that he was the last person alive who could remember all those men who'd been instrumental in rebuilding a shattered empire. Mercurias had dropped dead from a heart attack while administering a lecture to the palace doctors in the Peacock Palace years ago, Marco had died from his wounds only a year after Kiva, and Balo less than two months later from an overdose of mare's mead, since when its use had been outlawed Empire-wide. Even the younger ones were gone. Cialo had died in a riding accident a decade hence, leaving a huge family that seemed to swarm around Isera every summer when they visited. Sathina had seemed to just waste away after her husband had been taken and one morning just never woke up, discovered in her bed with a sad smile on her face by their eldest. All gone except him.

Still, he chided himself, there was no call for such maudlin thoughts. People went and that was the way of things. Soon he'd be able to see them all again in paradise. The high priests had assured him that his father would have been admitted to paradise for he'd redeemed his actions. Darius had laughed about that and made sure that it was made public knowledge empire-wide that he was their Emperor, but by no means divine. When he died, he would just go where all the ordinary folk went and enjoy their company.

And, of course, for every one of them that had died, there was their legacy. Titus Tythianus was already a prefect in the army, rising rapidly and, being a good friend of both the Imperial heirs, he would likely be a marshal before long. He reminded Darius so much of his father. He'd lost a finger in his sword training even as a boy and already ached when the winter snows came on. The aging Emperor chuckled to himself. Then there was young Sabianus, who was currently engaged in writing a history of the civil wars and took every opportunity he could to bother Darius and make him strain to remember the smallest details.

There were others. He couldn't really remember them all. His memory wasn't what it once was and the court seemed so full of young people rushing around these days. Thank the Gods young Kiva was there to organise him.

Where was Kiva this morning? Surely he should be here by now with his lists of foreign dignitaries waiting for audiences and the appointments with members of the senate seeking his approval of new laws and amendments and so on. Perhaps young Ashar would be here today. He'd been in the city for a month now, so he might drop in again. The current Parishid King was unlike his father, more involved in mercantilism than politics or war, but had stood firmly behind his father's position on the alliance with the empire. Pelasia and the Empire enjoyed a free border these days with no trade restrictions and no taxes. The citizens of both states were commonly seen in the cities of the other.

Darius smiled and looked down the avenue of trees toward the graveyard. Some days, even with the bad sight that had crept up on him since his sixtieth birthday, he fancied he could actually make out his father's gravestone. He'd stopped visiting it a couple of years ago when such long walks had become too much of a strain for his tired frame and he refused to be carried in a litter like a fat old autocrat.

Strange somehow that he'd spent the first twenty years of his life imprisoned on this island and feeling trapped and inhibited by it and after only a year or two in the outside world, he'd longed to be back there. Oh he'd travelled all over the empire in the next four decades, even to visit Brendan and his family in their villa up near Vengen where they owned a considerable vineyard, but he always came back here. Isera was home.

He smiled and leaned his chin on his steepled hands, gazing out across the western side of the island and that was how, less than an hour later, the Emperor Kiva the Golden found his father, the last of the architects of Interregnum.

And, insofar as these things ever really have an end, this is it.

LaVergne, TN USA
28 November 2010
206497LV00003B/20/P